THE JAGGARD CASE

Charles Dickens Investigations
Book Ten

J. C. Briggs

SAPERE
BOOKS

THE JAGGARD CASE

Published by Sapere Books.

24 Trafalgar Road, Ilkley, LS29 8HH,
United Kingdom

saperebooks.com

ISBN: 978-1-80055-789-5

For Tom

'Umbrellas to mend, and chairs to mend, and clocks to mend, are called in our streets daily. Who shall count up the numbers of thousands of children to mend, in and about those streets, whose voice of ignorance cries aloud as the voice of wisdom once did, and is as little regarded; who go to pieces for the want of mending, and die unrepaired? Orphans, either by death of their parents, or by transportation, or being born like brutes, and bred in ignorance of any home… bred in squalor, ignorance and vice…'

Boys to Mend by Charles Dickens
Household Words, 1852

CHARACTERS

Charles Dickens
Catherine, his wife
Katey and Mamie, Dickens's daughters
Superintendent Jones of Bow Street
Elizabeth, his wife
Eleanor and Tom Brim, their adopted children
Posy, their servant
Scrap, errand boy and amateur detective
Sergeant Rogers
Mollie, his wife
Constable Stemp
Constable Feak
Inspector Bold of the Thames River Police
Constable John Gaunt of the Thames River Police
Doctor Woodhall of King's College Hospital
Henry Meteyard, barrister of Lincoln's Inn
Sampson Meteyard, his father, butcher in Limehouse

IN THIS NOVEL:

Dickens's Household:
Georgina, his sister-in-law
Anne Brown, Mrs Dickens's maid
Topping, Dickens's coachman
John Thompson, Dickens's manservant

Members of Dickens's circle in real life:
Mark Lemon, editor of *Punch*
Nelly, his wife

Lally and Betty, his daughters
Thomas Talfourd, judge and poet
Lady Talfourd, his wife
Doctor John Elliotson

The Miller Family:
Alice Miller, mother
Abel Miller, father
Phoebe Miller, in service with the Henchman family
Matthew Miller, her older brother, ran away to sea
Sally Miller, her younger sister
Frankie Miller, her younger brother
The blacksmith, Alice's brother
Mrs Gall, Alice's cousin
Joan Gall, her daughter, servant at The Copenhagen Inn

The Henchman Household:
Mr Julius Henchman, banker
Lily, his wife
Darius, his brother, young man about town
Rose, Mrs Henchman's maid
Mrs Plum, the cook

The Jaggards:
Martin Jaggard, forger and criminal
Mrs Maria Jaggard, his aunt, workhouse matron
Miss Tilda Todd, his aunt, doll maker in Wapping
Sir Titus Jaggard, former judge, a distant relative

The Criminal Element:
Cora Davies, once mistress of Martin Jaggard
Joey Speed, Cora's new man

Mrs Speed, brothelkeeper
Livvie Slack, Jaggard's new mistress
Thoddy Cragg, engraver
Jacko Cragg, his son
Tipper, once in the coining business
Crackbone, landlord of Eel Pie Inn
Mrs Amelia Wand, high-class brothelkeeper
M. Jean Baptiste Tête, Belgian forger
Mademoiselle Hormel, in league with Monsieur Tête and Jaggard

The Police:
Inspector Shackell, G Division, Clerkenwell/King's Cross
Constable Doublett of Bow Street
Inspector Jolley of Bow Street
Inspector Fall, N Division, Islington
Constable Flint, E Division, Holborn
Commissioner Mayne, always keeping his eye on Superintendent Jones

The Witnesses:
Mr Decker, pawnbroker
Mr Crouch, a businessman
Lady Nora Lockhart, a widow
Lieutenant Hoskins Brown, actually Registrar of Merchant Seamen
Lieutenant Barnes, former shipmate of Matthew Miller
Mrs Davies, Cora's mother, in Kent
The Tramping Girl, a waif and stray
Catch, the workhouse master
Shadrack Argent, a goldsmith in Clerkenwell
Polly Stooks, looking for her missing sister

William Herring, menagerie keeper
Mr Bartlett, actually landlord of The Copenhagen
Benjamin Foster, actually landlord of The St. John of Jerusalem tavern
Mr Stagg, landlord of The Ship
Mrs Younger, landlady of The Old Baptist's Head
Ma Cobb, a laundress for Amelia Wand
Alfred, a crossing-sweeper
Patrick Quilp, a drunk
And Slucius Dry, a dweller in the Marsh Lands

1: MISSING

The front door was open, light spilling out onto the steps. Dickens was expected, of course — they'd know what time the Bristol train came in, but John wouldn't leave the door open on a winter's night. He felt a sudden dread. Something amiss? Catherine was expecting another child and was not always well. Bad news? A telegraph message?

Dickens pushed open the door, calling out, 'John?' Three pairs of eyes stared. Catherine, standing a few steps up the stairs, looking concerned, John, his manservant, at the bottom, and Scrap already taking a step towards him, his eyes wide and anxious. Something about the superintendent? Sam Jones was on the trail of a dangerous murderer.

'Mrs Jones — I 'ad ter come, Mr D. — she don't know, but I knows you'll come.'

'What? Where?'

'To Norfolk Street — Posy ain't come back.'

'Where's Mr Jones?'

'Gone to Southampton an' Mr Rogers an' Mr Stemp —'

'Tell me on the way.'

Dickens looked up at Catherine, who asked, 'Can I do anything?' She knew Elizabeth Jones, the superintendent's wife and liked her.

'I'll send word, my dear. I'm sorry, but as Sam's away, I'll have to — John, take my bag. Is all well here?'

Catherine nodded. He'd have to go, of course. He always had to go. She couldn't stop him. 'Yes, go — let me know if there's anything at all that Elizabeth needs.'

She raised her hand in farewell, but the front door closed. That was always the way of it. Someone needed him and he was gone.

Dickens and Scrap were out into Tavistock Square within a minute. It would be quicker to walk than try to find a cab. Dickens's cab from the station had already rolled away.

'Posy?' he asked as they hurried towards Gower Street.

'Went off with that friend, Phib Miller — you knows?'

'Phoebe, I know — where did they go?'

'Up beyond Belle Isle where 'er folks lives — bit of an 'oliday, says Mrs Jones. That was Friday. They was ter — to come back yesterday, but they didn't an' Mrs Jones waited, thinkin' they was jest late. Went to Phib's missis. They wasn't there, but a servant says not to fret. P'raps they'd took an extra day, since the missis an' master was away. No sign this mornin', an' I calls after the shop closed — keep an eye, Mr Jones said, cos 'e ain't there. But Posy an' Phib, they're not back. Dark by now, so I says I'll walk up to King's Cross an' along Maiden Lane ter see if there's any sign, but then I thought, Mr D. oughter — to know —'

'Mrs Jones hasn't been to Bow Street?'

'Not yet — but it ain't like Posy. She'd never let Mrs Jones down.'

No, she wouldn't, Dickens thought. Posy, the Joneses' young servant girl whom he'd found for them — an orphan who'd sold artificial flowers in the streets, and whose hard-faced employer had gone out of business, leaving the girl destitute. Posy, who loved Mrs Jones and worshipped the superintendent, and in whom Elizabeth Jones had absolute faith.

'Two girls, Mr D. — lost in all them fields up there. Anything could 'ave —'

'I know, I know, but they could be lost — just lost. And the children — where are they?'

'Keepin' shop with Mollie Rogers — treat, Mrs Jones told 'em. They could stay overnight. She didn't want 'em to know, 'specially Nell. She's that fond of Posy.'

'That's good. Now, let's see what Mrs Jones can tell us.'

At Norfolk Street, Scrap knocked and there was Elizabeth in the hall, pale and anxious. 'You've been an age. I was so —' She saw Dickens. 'Oh, where did you spring from?'

'Mr D. was out, so I 'ad to wait an' —'

'Yes, on some business.' Dickens didn't want her to know that he had just come by train from Bristol.

'Oh, Scrap, you should have told me.'

'You'd 'ave said not to, but Mr D. can give us advice, an' me an' im can go an' search.'

'In the dark?'

'Perhaps not,' Dickens interrupted, 'but you must tell me everything and we can decide what's best to do.'

They went into the parlour.

'From the beginning,' Dickens said.

Posy's friend Phoebe Miller — known as Phib — had come for her on Friday at lunch time. Sam Jones had provided the money for a cab to King's Cross, from where the two girls would walk along Maiden Lane towards Belle Isle. Elizabeth had given Posy money to treat them for refreshment at Copenhagen House, a well-known inn beyond the village, and then they would walk on to Phoebe Miller's home, a cottage by some fields where her father was labourer to a farmer.

'It was to be a reward, Charles — to stay away for two nights with a friend. She works so hard, and she has had no opportunity for friends, but she wouldn't stay away for longer without —'

'Unless there is a good reason — illness in Phoebe's family, Phoebe ill, Posy not well, and not able to send anyone —'

'I'm sure they would have sent a message. And if Phoebe were sick, then Posy would have come back alone. She'd know I'd be worried.'

'Do you know the address of the cottage?'

'Harper's Farm Lane, beyond The Copenhagen Inn. But where beyond, I have no idea.'

'I've been to The Copenhagen. We can ask there.'

'But in the dark, Charles, you'd never find the cottage.'

'At first light, then. In the meantime, tell me what you know about Phoebe. Have you met her employers?'

'I did call when the holiday was mooted by Phoebe. I wanted to be sure that it was all above board.'

'You had doubts?'

'Not really — well —'

'Something about Phoebe Miller? Something troubles you, I can tell.'

'She is pretty, very lively, and Posy admired her, of course. She was thrilled to have a friend — such a pretty one, too — but Phoebe seemed a little forward, over-familiar with me, and pert with Sam, as if we were not quite what she was used to. The Henchmans are very well-off, but she spoke of them in a rather derogatory way at times — but then that's the way with a lot of servants. I don't want to be unfair — knowing, I'd call her.'

'Scrap?' Dickens turned to him.

'Dunno, really, jest a girl, didn't see much of 'er.'

Now, that was uncharacteristic. Scrap was always spot on with people. "Bad 'un", he'd say, or "don't trust 'im" — or her, as the case may be. Dickens left it. He'd find out more later. He looked at Elizabeth again and asked, 'And the mistress, you spoke to her?'

'Mrs Henchman —' she saw Dickens's lips twitch and smiled — 'I know, and it suits her. She is rather large. Yes, I saw her at Grafton Street. She wasn't very welcoming. She seemed baffled by my concern about a servant. She knows, of course, that I am a policeman's wife — Mr Julius Henchman is in the banking way — and she knows that the father of our adopted children was a shopkeeper.'

Dickens felt his anger rising. He felt instinctively that Mrs Henchman — what a name — was the enemy. 'And your father a clergyman, your uncle the Dean —'

Elizabeth did smile at that. How Dickens's eyes flared at any perceived slight of a friend. 'I forbore to mention it. Tempted, I admit, but Sam needs no excuse, nor do Eleanor and Tom, nor Mr Brim — a gentler, more sensitive man —'

'Than Mr Julius Henchman, I'll bet. What did she say?'

'I don't think she was much interested in the social engagements of a servant, but she confirmed that as she and her husband were going away, it was in order for Phoebe to go to see her parents.'

'Know anything about them?'

'Not really — just that they are poor. The father's just a labourer and the cottage is tied to the farm. There are two younger children. Phoebe never seemed to care much about them. In fact, I didn't get the impression that she cared very much for her home at all, but she did seem keen to take Posy there, and Posy was so excited that I didn't want to seem — well — as if I disapproved. You know how much she needs our approval still.'

'What were the girls wearing?'

Elizabeth Jones could not for the moment answer the question, which pointed to the idea that they really could be missing. Dickens saw the knowledge in Scrap's eyes, too. Scrap had gone missing from home — not that anyone had ever looked for him, or missed him. But he knew only too well what might happen to unprotected girls.

There were always notices in the newspapers giving details of missing persons: *a pallid complexion, dark hair, or fair, five feet one inch … or two, or six feet*, or whatever, *wife of, daughter of, husband, brother, last seen*, etcetera, the statistics telling nothing of the living, breathing, loved, lost one. Too often never found. You glanced at the notice, felt a pang of pity for those deserted, left in limbo, but you didn't think again until you remembered the description of the missing one found destitute, found drowned, found dead.

Dickens thought of the terrifying statistic he had read in the newspaper: two thousand persons missing in London in any one year — and less than half ever found.

And, as if she read his thoughts, Elizabeth's eyes widened in fear. 'Oh, gracious, Charles, I am so afraid — that question makes it seem so real, and talking about Phoebe makes me wonder if she could have led Posy into danger of some kind. There's something headstrong about Phoebe.'

'I know, I know, but first things first. Scrap and I will go to the cottage. If they are not there, then we can ask about if you tell us about their dress.'

'Posy was wearing a brown stuff dress and a brown felt bonnet with — a blue ribbon. She was so pleased with that. I told her it matched her eyes, and I gave her a little blue flower to sew onto the ribbon — she looked so sweet — I couldn't help thinking of her when she first came here — in rags — oh, Scrap, oh, Charles —'

Dickens took her hand. 'And what else?'

Elizabeth felt the warm pressure of his hand and was steadied. She was a policeman's wife. She knew a great deal of what went on in the streets and alleys, the dark courts and corners, the lodging houses — and the brothels. Not the moment for hysterics. 'A warm drab coloured cloak and brown lace-up boots.'

'Phoebe?'

'A bit more elaborate — a black beaver bonnet with red ribbons and a green feather, a green woollen dress — moss green, a dark green cloak and the same brown lace-up boots. Oh, and a fur tippet — all cast-offs, I should think, but rather showy for a labourer's cottage.'

'Unless she wanted to display her finery — it would be understandable. She's young. And maybe to reassure the family that she was prospering.'

'And they have so little occasion to dress up.'

'When will Sam be back?'

'I'm not sure. He and Alf Rogers have gone after the Jaggard man — they had intelligence that he is on board a ship for America. They went to Southampton this morning — I don't want to go to Bow Street. Not yet, anyway. It's too soon. And I can't have them bringing him back — this case —'

'I know it's important, but he might be back in a day or two, and Scrap and I can take ourselves to Harper's Farm Lane first thing. And then we'll see.'

'It is so good of you.'

'Scrap did the right thing.'

Elizabeth looked at Scrap fondly. 'He always does.'

'Mr Jones said I was to look out fer you. He'd 'ave wanted me to get Mr D.'

'I know, I know — it's good of you both.'

'And the cab — it came here for them?'

'Yes, it was Mr Hob — you know, from Wellington Street.'

'I'll find him and check that they did get out at King's Cross — whether he saw them go up Maiden Lane. If they didn't…'

'Then they went somewhere else — oh, Charles, I hope not, but I don't think Posy would have done that, unless Phoebe deceived her in some way. Oh, I don't know what to think.'

She saw him to the front door. Scrap was to stay with her, and Dickens would come early to fetch him. He simply pressed Elizabeth's hand again. No use telling her that all would be well. She was a policeman's wife. If anyone knew into what dangers young girls could fall, she did. He knew and Scrap knew, too. His face looked pinched in the gaslight over the door. He looked older suddenly, older than he should be. Thirteen, and the weight of the world on his narrow shoulders.

Dickens hurried down to Wellington Street. Hob, his favourite cab driver, lived just off Bow Street in a house behind which he kept the horse, Bob, and he'd probably be off duty now. Dickens didn't know what use it was to ask Hob. He could have taken Posy and Phoebe to King's Cross and not had any idea of whether they had gone on to Maiden Lane. It was something to do.

2: ALL AT SEA

The black water churned, thrashing against the side of the steamer which pitched and rolled perilously on the swell, or so it seemed to Superintendent Sam Jones, standing on the deck, gripping the rail. Black and fathomless, and freezing. He was not at home on the sea, a sea all alive with a force that seemed huge and unstoppable. He looked away from the heaving waves and peered into the blackness ahead, hoping that the lights in the distance beyond them were the lights of *The Excellent*. They'd pursued one large vessel for five miles — and that turned out to be a cargo ship on its way to Ireland. Waste of time, but it could have been.

Midnight. And they'd left Gosport at half past eight and the lights ahead were seeming to move always further away, though they'd been assured that they could catch *The Excellent*. In similar circumstances the police had caught up with the ship *Victoria* when they were pursuing Mr and Mrs Manning — another pair of murderers. *The Excellent* was out there somewhere, possibly taking his suspected murderer, Martin Jaggard, to New York with the woman, Cora Davies. *Only possibly*, Sam Jones thought, *only possibly*.

It was the fact that they'd received a tip-off that a Mr and Mrs Davies were travelling to New York on *The Excellent*, out of Southampton, that had prompted this hurried chase after the murderer. Sam Jones had been sceptical — the information had come from a reporter who said he had heard it from someone who knew someone connected with a violent gang of coiners and forgers of whom Jaggard had been the leader, and a ruthless one at that. He was now suspected of the murder of his former employer, Sir William Pell, for whom Jaggard had worked as a valet before setting out on his criminal career.

Sir William Pell was a titled man and a connection of Sir George Grey, the Home Secretary. The murder had made headline news. Mr Mayne, the Police Commissioner, was ambitious and moved in high circles. Mr Mayne wished Superintendent Jones to pursue *The Excellent*. Naturally, Superintendent Jones had bowed his assent.

Sergeant Rogers had been dispatched to the shipping brokers, but the passenger list only showed the names of the steerage passengers. Sergeant Rogers doubted that Martin Jaggard would travel steerage — he and the so-called Mrs Davies would want better than that. Good Lord, travel with the poor and the stinking. A man of substance, was Mr Jaggard — a good deal to be made in coining and forging if you were the top man. But the list of cabin passengers was with the captain — on board the ship, at Southampton. Undaunted, Rogers took himself to the baggage department at the London Docks, where he discovered that luggage had been taken aboard by a woman who styled herself Mrs Davies. The description of the woman was vague — youngish, wearing a black cloak and a black bonnet. She could have been any Mrs Davies.

However, Mr Mayne had issued his instructions. Superintendent Jones had wisely kept his doubts to himself and had set out from Waterloo Station for the three-hour journey to Southampton. *The Excellent* had sailed, of course, and, according to telegraphic communication, had already passed Portsmouth. The next step had been to apply to the admiral, who gave order for *The Comet*, a fast frigate, to give chase.

Captain Hastings of the frigate had expiated on the advantages of the screw propeller as opposed to the paddle steamer in rough seas. And as much as ten knots, he had said enthusiastically. Or twelve miles per hour, he had added, looking at his landlubbing passengers. It seemed that the screw propulsion machinery was lower in the hull — more stability in heavy seas. Sam Jones did not know if the seas he had been looking at were, according to the captain's experience, rightly deemed heavy. Rough, he would have said — terrifyingly rough. He hoped only that *The Comet* would live up to its name and catch *The Excellent* as soon as possible.

He glanced at Sergeant Rogers, who was not keen on the sea, either, and looked a little queasy. Constable Stemp stood in the hurling wind as if his forbears had been admirals of the fleet, relishing the salt spray on his lips, his hand to his brow, peering into the wind. Nelson himself. He ought to have had a telescope to his eye.

It was no use speaking. They'd made their plans. When — when — for the Lord's sake, soon — they caught *The Excellent*, the policemen would go aboard. How that would be accomplished, Sam Jones did not dare to speculate. They would inform the captain of their business. It would be the captain's duty to escort them to the cabin of Mr and Mrs Davies. How far they would have to go to reach *The Excellent* was something else Jones did not wish to dwell on. This heaving sea in the English Channel was quite enough for him. He'd heard enough from Charles Dickens about the mighty storm which had blown up to assault *The Britannia* steamship taking Dickens to America, and about the ship's saloon which Dickens had likened to a gigantic hearse. Hearse, indeed.

He made himself think about Sir William Pell, who had been stabbed to death in his laboratory. He had a reputation as an eccentric scientist, a phrenologist and mesmerist. 'Peculiar man,' Dickens had observed to him when asked. Jones wasn't at all surprised that Dickens knew him. 'Astronomer, mesmerist, alchemist, they say, photographer — interested in anything scientific. Socially, a recluse nowadays, but years back he held consultations in what he called his laboratory. Felt your head and told you your character.'

'You didn't —' Jones had said.

'Not likely. He wanted to, of course, but it was a demonstration. I had no desire to be an experiment. Not heard of him recently, though, except for the murder.'

'I wonder if he did Jaggard's bumps.'

'No organ of benevolence there, I'll bet, and a well-developed murderous bump.'

But Dickens hadn't been able to give much help. He'd gone off to Bath and Bristol for a week with his amateur actors. Besides, Jaggard and his coiners were not the kind of men he could afford to entangle Dickens with. Jaggard was a violent man — he was suspected of killing anyone who trespassed on his patch, and when the police had raided his premises, a policeman had been shot — not killed, thankfully, and Jaggard had vanished. Then, months later had come the murder of Sir William, a particularly gruesome stabbing. Pell's head had almost been severed from the body. The laboratory had looked like a slaughterhouse. For an elderly man, Pell had fought hard for his life.

What had thrown the investigation off course was the finding of the body of another of Sir William's former servants in an alley in Seven Dials. He had on him Sir William's gold propelling pencil and a few gold sovereigns, a couple of which were scattered on the ground nearby and some further way as though someone had run off after the attack, dropping some of the gold as he fled. The man had been sacked by Sir William and it was first thought that he had killed his former master and robbed the safe in the laboratory. The gold in his pockets and that on the ground was only a portion of what had been stolen, and the attacker had got away with a cache of other jewels described by Sir William's valet. It had seemed straightforward enough until, after a few days, a terrified parlour maid had told one of the policemen that a man had come into the mews behind on the night of Sir William's murder.

The parlour maid had been idling there with her sweetheart, a footman from a neighbouring house. The stranger said he was looking for Sir William. She had been given a card with the name of a Doctor Frederick Mansell, a name she knew. The man who proffered the card told her that he had an important message for Sir William. She had gone back into the garden where the laboratory was situated and was instructed to bring the doctor's man. She had not been in service for very long at Pell's house, so she had not recognised Jaggard.

She hadn't at first confessed that she had been out in the alley with her sweetheart — too afraid of being sacked, and she had believed in the doctor's man whom Sir William had consented to see, but the police inspector who questioned the servants again had noticed that she had seemed more scared than the other servants and had threatened her with a night in a prison cell if she did not tell what she obviously knew. Then she had confessed that he had been very charming — and handsome. And, very reluctantly, she admitted that he had given her a florin. Sir William, he had told her, had very private business with Doctor Mansell.

The delay had cost days in the investigation. Time, of course, for the perpetrator to vanish. That the dead footman with Sir

William's sovereigns had been in league with Jaggard was very likely. Jaggard was ruthless enough to use the man in some way then kill him.

But that could never be proved, Jones reflected. Not only was the former footman dead, but he had left no trace. Nothing at all had been found out about him. One of the missing, the disappeared, of whom there were thousands every year in London, gone from the Pell house after his dismissal, to reappear like a minor actor in the tragedy, and vanish again. This time into his pauper's grave.

The lights had remained on in the laboratory late into the night. The house servants, including the parlour maid who had not at first mentioned the visitor, the new footman, Sir William's valet, the cook, and her scullery maid, had retired to bed as they were used to do when Sir William was busy in his laboratory. Sometimes he was there all night. The butler had stayed overnight at his sister's house in Lambeth. It was not until his return in the morning that the murder had been discovered, the safe opened, and Sir William Pell's valuable jewellery and watches had vanished, as well as notes and gold worth two hundred pounds.

Enquiries had shown that the late-night visitor was not anything to do with Doctor Mansell, but the parlour maid's description had elicited an angry exclamation from the butler. 'Jaggard!'

It seemed that Mr Jaggard had called upon Sir William Pell a week before the murder. The butler had been reluctant to admit him, but Sir William Pell, looking at the card the butler offered, had consented to receive the man. He had been in the laboratory with his former employer for some time, but the servants could not say why he had visited, nor had Sir William enlightened them.

But Jaggard was nowhere to be found. Had he taken his passage to America with the stolen valuables?

The question was still on Jones's mind as he looked at the roiling sea and the lights of the fishing vessel they had passed, and the Postal Packet boat they were leaving behind. He could hardly believe that Martin Jaggard would be fool enough to book his passage in the name of his mistress. And, in any case, why would he take a woman with him? Not a wife, just a mistress. A man like Jaggard could get another one of those.

However, Sergeant Rogers had pointed out that Jaggard might think a respectable married couple in a cabin wouldn't raise suspicion and, in any case, he would never believe that someone would have the nerve to give information to someone who gave it to the reporter.

'I mean, sir, whoever it was, was riskin' a deal — unless he really believed Jaggard was on his way to America.'

'True, Rogers, Jaggard might have let that slip, but even if we find him and arrest him for the murder of Sir William, we have to prove he did it.'

'He'll have alibis,' Rogers had said, 'alibis crawling out of all sorts of holes like rats.'

'Even the rats'll swear he was home on the night. We've only the parlour maid's description.'

'You can't mistake Jaggard,' Rogers insisted, 'an' he was seen at the house not so long before the murder. It's him, sir.'

Now Sam Jones thought about Jaggard. It was true, the man was distinctive. Well-dressed, tall and handsome with his dark curly hair. Piercing green eyes. Something of the gentleman about him. High cheekbones and very full red lips. Jones remembered the impudent smile when his constable had been shot — and the loud peal of laughter as Jaggard vanished up the stairs, shoving away the boy who acted as lookout, the crow, they called them. This one's feathers were a bit crumpled as he tumbled down the narrow stairs into Jones's waiting arms. He was taken away, kicking and screaming. Just a lad, and Jaggard cared not a whit for him.

Sam Jones had known that Jaggard would escape out onto the roof to leap across to another roof and vanish into some attic which would lead to yet another house where the equally criminal residents wouldn't give him away. In any case, Jaggard had not shot the constable — too clever for that. They didn't know who had done it. In the general mayhem of their raid on Jaggard's coining premises, the shot had been fired from a doorway. Jones had rushed in only to find a gaggle of women screaming and shoving each other about the hall and Jaggard at the top of the stairs, waving goodbye. Jones had not noticed if Jaggard displayed a particularly murderous bump on his head. He was more concerned about his constable's bleeding shoulder and the wretched guard dogs snarling and barking.

They'd shut down the coining operation and arrested some other odds and ends of Jaggard's cohorts; most of them had vanished into some hole or other. They confiscated the coining equipment from upstairs — coiners liked the light to work in, and, as had been proved by Jaggard's escape, a narrow staircase would hamper the police when they mounted a raid. It gave time to destroy the evidence, but this time they had found the plaster of Paris, the sulphuric and nitric acid, the silver spoons, and items of Britannia metal for melting. Some valuable silver items — stolen, no doubt; there were the galvanic batteries, the copper wires and the lampblack and oil for dirtying the shiny new coins, ready for circulation — two hundred pieces from crowns to sixpences. A very profitable operation, indeed. Jones knew that Jaggard would start up again somewhere else.

Months had passed without a sighting of Jaggard. He could have started up anywhere from Devil's Acre in Westminster to Whitechapel and beyond, as far as Limehouse — anywhere. Inspector Bold of the River Police knew of Jaggard's coining enterprises in Limehouse. Bold had received intelligence of counterfeit American dollars being sold to poor emigrants. Jaggard's name was mentioned, but Jaggard had moved on before Bold had caught him. Same story — the lesser fry had copped it, but the shark had flicked his tail, no doubt smiled his secret smile, and swum away. He probably had — vanished by the river rather than the highway. Or over to that empty wasteland above the East India Docks called The Marshlands where a man could hide out for months, years even.

And of interest to Superintendent Jones was an announcement from Her Majesty's Mint a couple of months ago, which warned about a new process of coining by electroplating brass or copper. A quantity of half-crowns had been found, and very convincing they had been — the milling round the edges of the coins had been perfect. On coins produced from moulds, it was often easy to see that the milling was clumsy. The only thing wrong about the half-crowns had been the ring — the sound was not true. The new process would be an expensive business so somebody with means had set it up, but where? And there were rumours that a Belgian forger had escaped from Paris, where a coining ring had been shut down and most of the perpetrators arrested. They'd used electroplating and forged banknotes were found. It had been a sophisticated operation.

Then Jaggard's name had come up in connection with the murder of Sir William Pell. Jones thought about the contents of Pell's safe — a good deal of valuable jewellery and money. Jaggard, the former valet, would surely have known about it, and if he were involved in a new process of coining, then he would have needed money to set it up. And if he could pin the murder on a disgruntled former employee of Pell's, then he'd believe he was untraceable. Except somebody had blabbed about America.

There was no other suspect. The butler hadn't done it — he really had been at his sister's house. She lived with his invalid wife, both of whom he supported. There didn't seem to be anything untoward about the other servants. But you never knew. Inspector Grove and Constable Feak were onto their backgrounds. The neighbouring footman had admitted that more than flirting had gone on in the mews passage, which accounted for the parlour maid's terror. And he was betrothed to another maid in another household. No wonder he had kept quiet. However, there was nothing to suggest any complicity with Jaggard. Pity, he thought — a neat little household murder with a simple motive, and then he wouldn't have to be gazing queasily at the English Channel's thrashing waters.

'It's a big ship,' Rogers said, 'this could be it.'

He was right. A passenger ship, Jones hoped, *The Excellent.*

3: COPENHAGEN FIELDS

Hob had confirmed that he had taken Posy and Phoebe to King's Cross. He hadn't seen which way they went. Dickens hoped that the girls had not, for some reason, gone into the labyrinth of streets by the railway station, beyond which were the fever hospital and gas works. Not a very salubrious area, and crowded, with a few decent boarding houses, granted, but mostly grimy tenements, and cheap lodging houses — more fever in those than in the hospital. They wouldn't know where to start looking for them.

There were narrow streets on the right-hand side of Maiden Lane, too, but Dickens and Scrap didn't stop until they reached Maiden Lane Bridge over the Regent's canal. The railway line was to their left and then there were fields spreading out towards Agar Town. He could see Randall's tile kilns ahead, and beyond those were Belle Isle and more fields leading to The Copenhagen Inn.

They looked down at the leaden, sluggish water for a few moments. Dickens knew that Scrap, uncharacteristically quiet on their walk, was gathering his thoughts. He gave him a moment or two more before he asked, 'What about Phoebe?'

'Couldn't say in front of Mrs Jones, but I ain't sure about 'er.'

'And your reason?'

'More than one, Mr D. A few things what made me think. She comes to the shop — just passin', she says, an' then she wonders if I can lend her some money — to buy a present fer 'er ma. She an' Posy, she says, don't want to go empty-'anded. An' she don't want to ask Posy cos she'd invited 'er, an' Posy wants ter buy somethin', but she, Phib, don't think it right —'

'A long-winded tale.'

''S'what I thought — an' all the time she's smilin' an' fiddlin' with 'er curls. Five bob, she says, as if it's nothin'. I tells 'er I ain't got that much, and she asks, laughin', wot's in the till? I says that's the shop money an' not mine an' she says, oh, she thought I was in charge — sorry, 'er mistake — just the erran' boy, then? I didn't answer that one, but I knows she's tryin' ter rile me. I wasn't born yesterday, Mr D.'

'No, indeed — you saw quite clearly what she was up to.'

'See, Mrs Jones was right when she said about Phib's thinkin' nothin' about 'er employers. She thinks we're all the same — take what you can get away with. I knows 'er type.'

'Anything else?'

'Seen 'er with a toff — at the 'Enchmans' 'ouse. Very friendly, they was. Laughin' together an' she doin' 'er stuff with the curls. 'E gives 'er somethin' — money, I 'spect. Then she goes down the area steps an' 'e knocks at the front door an' goes in. Don't know if 'e lives there or just visitin'.'

'You'd know him again?'

'Fair hair, bit o' moustache, top hat which 'e tips to 'er as 'e goes up the steps, an' yeller gloves, an' she's smilin' like she knows a secret an' puts whatever it is in 'er pocket.'

'And this friendship with Posy?'

'Didn't believe it. She ain't Posy's type. An' before you ask, too late to say anythin' to Mrs Jones. It was all arranged an' Posy was that excited. 'Ow could I? An' then I thought — up in the country, what 'arm?'

What harm indeed? Dickens thought, not liking the sound of any of this. A sly little piece, Phoebe Miller, but he only said that they should get to the cottage as soon as they could. 'Then we'll know.'

They walked along Maiden Lane, now surrounded by fields. It was a dreary prospect under the flat, grey sky. Dickens felt the sting of sleet in his face and the wind cutting sharp. There was nothing to see except the road ahead, the conical chimneys of the next set of tile kilns by a field where clay and brick earth were dug up for the making of bricks and tiles, and the cluster of houses and buildings which made up Belle Isle. Varnishing factories, fat and tallow melting and gut scraping, match making, bone boiling, knackers' yards, and an abandoned chemical factory constituted the noxious industries of Belle Isle — you could smell them as you passed. It was a relief to get to the fields again. At least the air was breathable if cold.

'Belle Isle. What's it mean?' Scrap asked as they walked on.

'Beautiful island — belle is a French word.'

'Blimey, Mr D., was they jokin'?'

Dickens laughed. 'I've no idea where the name came from, but you're right. Beautiful it is not.'

Twenty more minutes took them to the old inn and its pleasure gardens. It had been there since the seventeenth century — supposedly named for the Danish prince or ambassador who had lived in Copenhagen House during the Great Plague. It wouldn't last much longer, however; tunnelling had begun under the fields for the railway and the inn was to be demolished in a year or two. *Pity*, Dickens thought. It was a popular resort for those who wanted to get out of the city, and, no doubt, to escape the smells of varnish and boiling bones. And it was famous for its political rallies. Only a few weeks ago there had been a gathering in support of Lajos Kossuth, the Hungarian political exile. It was quiet now — too early for demonstrations against oppressive regimes, but there was a solitary lad in an apron sweeping the steps. He could probably direct them to Harper's Farm Lane and the cottage of the labourer called Miller.

And ten minutes further on, down a track behind The Copenhagen and down the hill, they found the lane and the cottage by the end of another lane, which a sign told them led to the farm whose chimneys they could see through the bare branches of the trees.

It was not an easy conversation for any of the participants, not for Dickens and Scrap, who were told that neither Phib nor her friend had come on Friday. Mrs Miller, a woman worn to the colour and texture of used string, with a yellow face underneath a limp brown bonnet as wrinkled as old skin, vacant eyes, and very few teeth, was not surprised, for Phib didn't always come when she said she might. The missus — mean ol' cat — sometimes changed her mind. That's what rich folks did. And then it was not easy for Mrs Miller to understand that the gentleman whose name was Mr Dickens — which meant nothing — was telling her that her Phib and the other girl were missing.

'Ow d'yer mean missin'?'

Dickens patiently explained what was supposed to have happened and what had happened. He did not mention the police, and certainly not Superintendent Jones of Bow Street, only Mrs Jones, Posy's employer. He asked if Mrs Miller had any idea of where her daughter might have gone. She had not. Phib was a good girl. 'Ad this Posy taken her somewheres? Phib wouldn't go missin'. She 'ad a good position, good food an' a decent dress ter wear. She was a good girl.

Dickens was sure that she was and equally sure that Posy was, too, but had Phib mentioned any friends she had made or anyone at the Henchman house who might be a special friend with whom Phib might have gone somewhere?

No, she 'adn't. Phib was a good girl — allus a good girl an' no one could say different, an' them as did say things woz wrong, an' anyways missis didn't approve of followers or such. This Posy — did she 'ave some follower an' taken Phib alonger some place?

It was hopeless and Dickens knew it, but he made a last attempt. 'Is there any friend about here who might know? Or Phoebe's sister, perhaps?'

'Yer can ask our Sally if yer wants. She's out the back. I'll get 'er.'

Our Sally was about twelve. Not as pretty as Phoebe, but then Phoebe was well-fed at the Henchman house and had the means to kit herself out in better clothes than the loose dress and clumsy muddy boots that were Sally's hand-me-downs. Phoebe's hand-me-downs were of better quality than Sally's. No wonder Phoebe had ambitions beyond this two-roomed cottage with its ladder to the loft upstairs where there might be a bedroom, and its few sticks of furniture and general air of poverty and neglect. Sally was uncommunicative and looked at them with a sullen face as if she, too, did not understand the concept of missing. Mrs Miller had blurted it out. Sally merely shook her head when Dickens asked his questions about possible friends.

'Have you any other children?'

'Frankie's outside somewhere,' Mrs Miller answered vaguely. ''E's only eight. No use askin' 'im.'

Dickens promised to let them know if he heard news of Phoebe. He did not offer any remark about being sure they would turn up. He wasn't sure at all. He thought of all those wastes of fields, and, worse, that nest of streets round King's Cross, and he thought of Phoebe and whether she didn't always go home for a reason other than the caprices of missis.

And that word "might" — did that mean that Phoebe Miller had not intended to go home at all? That put a rather different complexion on the matter. And who were them as sometimes said that Phoebe Miller was not a good girl? And why? Scrap knew something about that, but there were others, perhaps.

They were back in the muddy lane, in the middle of which stood a boy with the same blank eyes as Mrs Miller. Frankie, no doubt. He looked as cold as they felt in his ragged trousers and jacket. His feet were bare, and his narrow little face was blue.

He looked up at Scrap and asked, 'Where's Matty?'

'Who's Matty?' Scrap asked, squatting down.

'Don't know where. Matty gone.'

And then he was gone, too, through a hole in the hedge like a small animal back to its burrow.

4: CRIBBED, CABINED AND CONFINED

'It is *The Excellent*,' the captain told Jones and Rogers, who were with him on the bridge where he was training his telescope on the lights ahead. 'I've signalled for her to stop.'

The fast frigate plunged on for another hour or so. At least the lights were getting nearer. *The Excellent* seemed to have stopped. *The Comet* tied up alongside the steamship, and a rope ladder was let down for them to climb aboard. Rogers went first, followed by Sam Jones, who did not look down into the water heaving in the wash of the ship, but he could hear the smack of the waves on the ship's side and feel the pull of the water as well as the sting of spray on his face. Stemp came after. It seemed a long way up and rather nerve-wracking, but strong hands helped them onto the deck. At two o'clock in the morning, there were no passengers taking the air, for which he was thankful. They were quickly escorted to the captain's cabin, where Jones explained who he was looking for and why. The captain showed them the cabin passenger list. They were there, Mr and Mrs C. Davies.

Down they went, through a wilderness of passageways and staircases to hesitate by a firmly shut door from which no sound came. The captain turned the handle and Superintendent Jones and the captain stepped in. On the top bunk — narrow as a coffin, as Dickens had said — a startled head appeared, a woman by the look of the curl papers. The lamplight showed him Cora Davies, not as pretty as she used to be on the stage of The Hoxton Theatre.

'Bloody 'ell —' was all she could manage. *And she a cabin passenger*, thought Jones wryly. She hadn't changed. 'What's the game?'

'Your husband,' he said.

'Ain't my —' She stopped herself. Martin Jaggard was not, of course, her spouse.

Superintendent Jones went to address the person apparently still sleeping in the lower bunk with the blanket over his head, and was not unpleased when, after a sharp poke in the chest, a head shot up and cracked itself on the iron frame of the bunk above. Nasty bump, tomorrow, he wanted to say, but was forestalled when the head looked at him indignantly. Not Martin Jaggard. Nothing like him. Tow-coloured hair, a thin face, and eyes the colour of mud in the lamp light. Certainly not Jaggard's eyes.

'Who the hell are you?'

'Superintendent Jones of Bow Street.'

'Wha'd'yer want? I ain't done nothin'.'

That's what they all said. 'Martin Jaggard. You and Miss Davies will please get dressed. I want to talk to you both. Two minutes. We'll be outside.' He left the door open. They'd know he would hear if they attempted to concoct some story. But apart from a lot of shuffling and grunting, nothing was said. When the movement stopped, he went back in, and Rogers joined him. They had no choice but to stand at the door. The cabin was as narrow as a coffin, too, and the two passengers seemed to fill it. Cora Davies was a beefy woman.

'You are?' Jones asked the man.

'Joey Speed — if it's any o' your business.'

'And Miss Davies, what have you to tell me about Martin Jaggard?'

36

''Ain't seen 'im fer ages. Me an' Mr Speed are goin' to America — an' you can't stop us. We ain't nothin' ter do with Jaggard now.'

'You have heard about Sir William Pell, the man who employed Jaggard as a valet, the man who was murdered, and in connection to that murder Jaggard's name was mentioned.'

''Oo the 'ell did that? No one peaches on Marty. Course I 'eard about it, but it ain't nothin' ter do with us.'

'Then you won't mind my searching your luggage.'

'I bloody do,' Joey Speed answered. 'I'm a respectable man on my way ter better things, and my luggage is my business.'

'And murder's mine. You see, Miss Davies is a known associate of Mr Jaggard — wanted for murder — and I want to know what you're both carrying away to America. Stolen goods are my business, too. Your keys, if you will.'

There were two boxes stowed under the bunks and a portmanteau on the end of the lower bunk. Jones kept his eye on the two passengers while Rogers shifted the boxes and opened the first. Underneath Cora Davies's clothes was a sort of false bottom, which Rogers removed to reveal a few little leather bags in which he discovered some jewels: a gold ring set with an onyx, a gold tie pin set with a diamond, a gold watch, a gold pencil, and some gold sovereigns. They fitted exactly the description given by Sir William Pell's new valet — but only a small portion of what had been stolen. Cora Davies had not been given any of the diamonds that Sir William had kept in his safe. Had Jaggard wanted rid of her for some reason and paid her off?

'Property of Sir William Pell. Murdered. Possibly by Martin Jaggard, your former associate, Miss Davies. Where'd you get 'em?'

Cora Davies was silent. She wouldn't dare, thought Jones, but it was enough to take her back to London and to put her in a cell. And whether she told or not, she'd be safer in custody. Not that he had much sympathy. She was a thief and an accessory in the coining business, accessory to worse, probably. When they'd raided Jaggard's coining den in Seven Dials, he'd been aware of the number of women, some young girls, some appearing to be twelve or thirteen, and younger children, too. Cora hadn't been there — out distributing false coins, no doubt. That's what many of the women did — they were the smashers who delivered coins to customers and who spent coins in the markets, the bakeries, the grocers, the chemists. Respectable housewives out shopping by day, whores at night. And Jaggard making his profits on all his sordid enterprises. And children with little fingers were used to pour the molten metal into the plaster moulds to make the fake coins.

No doubt she'd dream up some story, but she must have known something about the whereabouts of Martin Jaggard. Now as to Joey Speed, who had taken the name of Davies for the voyage — what had he to hide? He looked distinctly uneasy as Rogers tackled the second box, which was similarly contrived and revealed a quantity of twenty-pound notes — a hundred pounds' worth.

'A tidy sum, Mr Speed. Where did you get it?'

'Won it. 'Orses.'

Well, that could be verified. He told them that they would be removed to the waiting navy frigate and be taken back to London to answer further questions about the death of Sir William Pell.

'Possession of stolen goods,' he said as Cora opened her mouth. 'Transportation, I should think — Australia. Not America, of course. There's the murder, see.'

5: FANCY MAN

Dickens and Scrap made their way back to The Copenhagen where Dickens could ask the landlord if he had seen the two girls on Friday afternoon, and Scrap could question the sweeping boy.

Dickens wound his way through the passages and little panelled rooms which made up the old house and found John Bartlett, the landlord, coming down the darkly carved old oak staircase, looking not unlike a King of Denmark, somewhat ghostly in his white apron and white shirt in the gloom of the morning. Dickens knew him as a warm-hearted, sensible man — he'd be sorry to lose his house to the railway. Dickens thought it a shame, too, looking up at the gallery above where minstrels had played, perhaps, for a glittering company.

'Mr Dickens —' John Bartlett knew him — 'what can I do for you at this early hour? Come into the parlour. I've a fire going, and some coffee, if you'd like.'

When the steaming cup was before him and he felt the warmth of the flames about his feet, Dickens told Mr Bartlett the story of Posy and Phoebe Miller, asking if he knew the latter.

'Oh, aye, Abel Miller's girl. 'Tis a blessin' she's out of that cottage. They're a poor lot. Labourer for Harper, the farmer. He's not a bad employer, but Abel's not much of a worker, an' his wife — well, she's a bit weak-minded, I always think, after — ah, well, never mind that. Was Phib here with her friend on Friday? I can't say as I saw her, but I'll ask the girl. Joan!' he roared out.

Joan materialised through a stout oak door, a big-boned girl with hands like hams and a red face, the colour of raw meat, and little shrewd eyes that wouldn't miss much, Dickens thought. He asked if she had seen Phoebe recently.

'Phib Miller — saw 'er Friday, all dressed up — a fur tippet if yer please, an' givin' 'erself airs as if she don't belong ter that stinkin' little cottage an' a mother wot's soft in the —'

'Never mind all that, Joan. The gentleman's here to ask about the other girl.'

'Oh, aye, shy little thing. On their way ter Phib's, so Phib tells me — takin' 'er friend ter see 'er folks — though why yer'd take anyone ter that cottage — they're all —'

'Joan, stick to the point, will you?'

'Did you see them leave?' asked Dickens.

'Nah, saw Phib with 'er fancy man, though, out in the gardens.'

'You didn't know him?'

'Seen 'er with 'im afore — few weeks back — Sunday, it woz. Phib's day off, p'raps.'

'Can you describe him for me?'

'I dunno — toff, I'd say. Well-dressed, anyway. Topper and yeller gloves — noticed that. Tall feller, but I only saw 'im ter a minute or two.'

'I didn't see him, Mr Dickens — could have been anyone. We get a lot of gentlemen, of course — the boxing matches and so on.'

Joan could tell him no more, but Dickens gave her tuppence and when she had gone, Dickens asked Mr Bartlett to send him a note if the man came back, or if he found out his identity. 'I'm worried about the girl, Posy, servant to close friends of mine. They want her back.'

Someone shouted for Mr Bartlett, and he went off, enjoining Dickens to finish his coffee. Scrap came in. Dickens gave him some coffee and as Scrap warmed himself, Dickens told him what he had heard.

'The lad saw the girls walkin' towards the road, but no one with 'em.'

'Did he say in which direction?'

'No. But the toff,' Scrap said, 'wonder if it's the cove I saw Phib with?'

'Could be — Joan said he wore yellow gloves. I'll go to the Henchman house — see if I can find out who that was. In the meantime —'

'Posy's with 'em. I don't like the sound of that, Mr D. — an' that Phib's done it before. Said she was goin' 'ome an' didn't. What we goin' to tell Mrs Jones?'

'All of it, Scrap. Let's get on to Belle Isle. Someone might have seen them.'

They retraced their steps and made their way along the road to Belle Isle; just before the settlement, they came upon a blacksmith's where a couple of horses waited patiently, and they could hear the strike of the hammer on the anvil. No one was attending to the horses, which were tied securely, so they went inside to find the blacksmith working on a shoe and a boy working the wheezing bellows to keep the glowing fire hot. They waited until the smith stopped to plunge the shoe into the water tank, where it hissed angrily. He took it out with his tongs. He looked up then, a man with a sooty face and two dark eyes which seemed to blaze like the red-hot horseshoe.

Dickens explained what they wanted. The smith put down the shoe and the tongs on the anvil and wiped his face with a rag dipped in the water. The cleaner face which emerged looked wary.

'Mrs Miller's my sister — what did she tell you?'

'Only that Phoebe didn't always come when she said she would.'

'True enough — can't blame the girl. It's a miserable hovel. She's better out of it — make somethin' of 'erself, I 'opes.'

'Did you see her at all? She did go to The Copenhagen.'

'Yes, saw 'er pass by with the other girl. Said that's where they was goin'.'

'She didn't say she was going home?'

'I jest assumed. They both had bags.'

'They seemed to have met someone at The Copenhagen. A man.'

The smith's eyes narrowed. 'A man?'

'Only what the servant said — Joan, that is — top hat and yellow gloves. She'd seen him before with Phoebe.'

'Gentleman?'

'Sounds like. You don't know of anyone — a follower she might have had?'

'I don't know any gents that she'd be with — unless the friend —'

'No, no. You didn't see them come back this way?'

'Too busy.'

Dickens thought that the top hat and yellow gloves did not necessarily mean a gentleman. 'No other man Phoebe was involved with?'

'My sister never said, but then she wouldn't. She ain't very — but the girls are missin', you say?'

'We don't know where they are. Here's my card, anyway, should you hear anything.'

The smith put it in the pocket of his leathern apron without looking at it. Dickens hoped it would not end up in the fire. They turned to go as the smith took up his tongs.

'Who's Matty?' asked Scrap.

The smith put down the tongs with a sudden movement. He looked alarmed. The name meant something.

'Who mentioned Matty?'

6: EVIDENCE FOR THE PROSECUTION

Sam Jones had left Cora under the eye of Sergeant Rogers in her cell at Southampton Police Station. Joey Speed was under the stern eye of Constable Stemp. The two prisoners looked distinctly worse for wear. The seas had seemed to Jones even heavier on the way back and the cold even more biting. And neither wind nor waves had done much for Cora's curl papers, which had practically dissolved. She was more furious about that than the arrest. Cora liked to look her best. Joey Speed's sea-legs were turned to water — whether from fear of what awaited at Bow Street or seasickness, Jones couldn't tell. Joey Speed had nothing at all to say for himself. A trip in the open air, handcuffed to a handy rail had certainly rendered them both speechless — for now. Separated, one or the other might tell.

When Jones returned from telegraphing his news to Mr Mayne, Cora was ready to tell him what she knew about the jewels and money, which, she admitted, Martin Jaggard had given her.

"Adn't seen 'im fer ages — after that policeman was shot, we — I mean, Marty an' me, thought we oughter lie low. Dunno where 'e went, but me an' Livvie — Livvie Slack — got lodgin's in Clerkenwell. Livvie's cousin, see, Joey's ma's lodgin's. Joey an' me, well, we got tergether.'

Jones remembered Livvie Slack from the shooting — one of the sweepings from Martin Jaggard's coining house, one of the gaggle of women who had got in their way after the shooting, got in their way so that Jaggard could escape. A witness worth following up. Clerkenwell was interesting. A good deal of coining went on there, and the buying and selling of jewellery. Pawnbroking, too. A veritable manufactory of crime.

'And Livvie's still in Clerkenwell?'

'Dunno — she mighta moved on now that — well, that shootin' business is over, so…'

'Moved on with someone?'

'Yer knows what she did fer a livin', Mr Jones. More men, Livvie had than 'ot dinners. No one partickler.'

'Address of these lodgings?'

'Bridewell Walk, but Mrs Speed ain't got nothin' ter do with Marty — she only lent me an' Livvie a room. An' Livvie wouldn't stay if she found somethin' better.'

Jones noted that Cora was very anxious to protect Livvie, but he left it. 'Well, tell me about Martin.'

'Marty turns up one night —'

'In Clerkenwell at Joey's mother's house?'

'Yes.' So, Martin Jaggard knew where Joey Speed lived. Jones did not comment. 'Wants ter lie low. Goin' inter business with a new — associate —'

'Associate?' Now, there was an interesting word.

''S'wot 'e said — Marty was waitin' fer the word — somethin' new, 'e said, money ter be made.'

'He didn't say in what line?'

'Didn't ask. Marty only stayed a few days, but 'e give me the jewels — said, why not go ter America — make a new start.'

'When was this?'

'Dunno exactly — few weeks, mebbe two.'

About the time of the murder, Jones thought. 'Why didn't you leave straightaway?'

'I've a kiddie. Needed to sort things out with my ma down in Kent — told 'er I'd send fer 'em when we got straight, see. I knew she wouldn't like it. 'Ad a deal o' persuadin' ter do, but she agreed in the end.'

'Who's the father?'

'Marty, o' course — that's why —'

'He gave you the jewels and money.'

'Told me ter take 'im out of it, an' I woulda, Mr Jones, I would. Means a lot ter me, that kiddie. Marty ain't all bad — 'e wanted somethin' better for the kiddie — honest, 'e did. 'E thought me an' Joey'd look after 'im in America. Maybe make somethin' better fer 'im.'

'And you heard about the murder and read the description of the jewels. You knew they were stolen.'

Her eyes flashed at him with something of their old fire. 'Course I did. I knew when I saw 'em. Where else would Marty 'ave got 'em? Didn't know about no murder then. In any case, what's Marty ter do with Pell?'

'He worked for Sir William Pell. He knew him.'

'Years back — honest, Mr Jones, I didn't know where they came from when Marty give 'em me. I didn't think of murder. Business, Marty said.'

She'd want to believe that, Jones knew. She'd have closed her ears to murder and opened her eyes to money and jewels. Just as she believed that Martin Jaggard cared about the child. He might have done, he supposed. Sometimes the most hardened crook wept over a dead child, and he thought of some very fine houses with some very precious sons and daughters — fine houses acquired by fraud and theft — even murder. Nevertheless, he couldn't let her, or Speed, go to America. He needed her. There was the child in Kent, and the mother. Kent — where Jaggard might well be hiding out.

'You've no idea where Martin might be?'

'I swear it, Mr Jones. I was gettin' out. An' Joey don't know, either, before yer asks. At least let 'im go — I know what yer thinks o' me, an' yer right. I knew they was stolen goods, but what else was I ter do? Don't tell me ter make an honest livin', cos there ain't no such thing for the likes of us. But I 'ad a chance in America. Let Joey 'ave it — it'll be the only one 'e ever 'as. Joey ain't bad.'

He left her. Time to find out what Joey Speed knew about Jaggard. Something, no doubt — Jaggard had been to Clerkenwell. Constable Stemp came to meet him.

'The notes, sir, what Speed 'ad — I'm sure they're forgeries. Good 'uns, too. Remember them ten-pound notes back in '48 — fooled a good few people, but the bank said the paper was too dark, an' there was warnings about 'em in the newspapers. It all went quiet then, but Speed's notes don't look right.'

Martin Jaggard and Joey Speed linked by forgery; Livvie Slack, Joey Speed's cousin and a friend of Cora's, in a Clerkenwell lodging house. People coming and going all the time. Maybe that's how the idea got out that Cora was going to America with Martin Jaggard — just gossip. And Livvie and Cora in that coining house. Had Speed been part of that? Very likely, as he had used the name Davies. Wheels within wheels, as Dickens would say. Now, forged notes — that was new for Jaggard. Coiners could set up easily enough, but forging notes required expensive equipment — plates for engraving, a printing press, paper, though that was where the forger had the greatest difficulty. It was impossible to duplicate the Bank of England's bill-paper. Nevertheless, as the 1848 forgeries had shown, a very skilful engraver could print a very good copy which would pass all but the most expert scrutiny, and a cashier's signature was easy enough to imitate. And there were paper mills where banknote paper was manufactured. Someone on the inside? Jaggard had connections, no doubt. Foreign currency forged and smuggled out of England to the continent? It had been done. And Jaggard had acquired a good deal of money. Jewels could be taken out of their settings and sold in Clerkenwell.

Speed denied any knowledge of Martin Jaggard's whereabouts. He had to admit that he knew the man, and that he knew where the jewels and sovereigns came from, but the notes — course 'e didn't know they was forgeries — sold some o' the jewels an' a gold watch ter a man in Clerkenwell — fair an' square —

Fair and square by his twisted logic. A murdered man's valuables sold on. Not that Jones believed in the man Speed had dealt with, but whose name he had conveniently forgotten. Oh, the pub was John's in Clerkenwell — lot o' jewellers about there — Superintendent Jones oughter ask in Clerkenwell — it was 'e, Joey Speed, 'ad bin robbed — nothin' ter do with murder. They 'ad nothin' on 'im —

Speed and Cora could stay in their cells for the time being. Superintendent Jones had business at the docks. Jaggard would not, like Cora, be foolish enough to use his own name, but the dockyard police could be warned. Though Jaggard might look like someone else altogether by now, and other people had green eyes. Needles and haystacks came into Jones's mind, but his report to Commissioner Mayne would need to be thorough.

7: THE DROWNED

'A brother?' Elizabeth Jones asked.

'Matty,' said Scrap, 'the kiddie, all innocent, like, asks me if I knows where 'e is. Mebbe a friend, I thinks, mebbe 'e thinks I'm a friend of Matty's, but I wondered, an' I asked the blacksmith if 'e knew — an' 'e did —'

Dickens took up the tale. 'He was reluctant to tell us anything, but we knew there was something — he looked very alarmed when Scrap said the name. I pressed him, emphasising the missing girls, and I do think he was worried about Phoebe, so he told us all about Matty.'

'Older brother?'

'Oh, yes, Matty is about twenty now, Phoebe is seventeen, and then there's Sally, about twelve, and it's in that gap that the story lies. There were two other sisters, Liza and Susan.'

'Were?'

'Both drowned in 1844. They were found in a pond. The three girls, Phoebe, getting on for tenthen, Liza aged eight, and Susan, aged seven, had gone roaming somewhere — which they often did. I doubt that Mrs Miller is a very attentive mother. She was busy with the baby — Frankie.'

'What asked me about Matty,' Scrap put in.

'Five-year-old Sally had been left behind — we don't know why. Phoebe came back on her own, telling her mother that the other two were still out playing. Those two were very close, it seems, like twins. Mrs Miller didn't think anything of it and sent Phoebe off to Harper's farm to get milk.'

'An' they never come back, the two girls. People searched with the pa, Matty an' Phib an' the blacksmith, an' it was the blacksmith who found 'em — saw a bonnet on the surface. Pond wasn't deep, it bein' summer, an' in 'e goes.'

'What a tragedy.'

'It was worse than that. They were strangled by a shawl with which they'd tied themselves together. The inquest verdict was accident. The idea was that they'd been playing some game, fallen in, and got caught up in a rope which was found tangled in the shawl, an old rope covered in slime, thought to have been tossed into the pond at some time, but —'

'There was talk, o' course — 'ad someone done fer 'em?'

'Quite,' Dickens interrupted, seeing Elizabeth's horrified face, 'and shortly afterwards Matty left home — gone to sea, the story was.'

'Never been seen since.'

'Mrs Miller was never the same, it seems. I must say I thought her rather vague, and Mr Bartlett at The Copenhagen said something about her being weak-minded after — and then he stopped. Joan, his serving girl, said she was soft — in the head, I presume.'

'Poor Phoebe — no wonder she was a bit hard. A tragedy like that would change a girl, no doubt, and what about the father?'

'The farmer kept him on because the pond was on his land, though the blacksmith has no opinion of Mr Miller's labouring skills. He thought they should have pulled themselves together. He was glad to see Phoebe get away from it all. She went into service at the age of thirteen — found a place through the farmer's good offices.'

'What did the blacksmith think about the possibility of the brother having —'

'Said he didn't believe it. He says that Matty was driven away by the gossip, but I couldn't help wondering about that look of alarm when Scrap said the name.'

'There was talk about Phib as well — that they was in it together.'

'Dear Lord, Scrap, what danger is Posy in? Why did they think —'

'There was no evidence. Cruel gossip, the blacksmith said. Phoebe and Matty made a pair just as the girls, Liza and Susan, did. Phoebe stuck to her story that she had left the girls and that she had not seen Matty all afternoon.'

'Where was he?'

'Working on the farm — confirmed by Mr Harper, the farmer, at the inquest. The father and son swore they were working together, clearing out some barn over the fields. That's all Mr Miller was fit for, according to the blacksmith, but a neighbour thought she saw a man in a lane by the pond. Only thought, however, and Mr Miller said it wasn't him. The only possible evidence was the scratches on the elder girl's arms, but they were put down to her struggling to get free of the rope.'

'What can we do now?'

'The servant at The Copenhagen saw them with a gentleman, possibly. I thought I should go to the Henchman house —'

'See, Mrs Jones, I saw Phib talkin' to a gent outside the 'ouse an' we wondered —'

'Only wondered,' Dickens said, thinking to spare Elizabeth the details, but she was too quick, and turned to Scrap.

'Why? What made you wonder? You'd better tell me everything.'

'A toff, I thinks, an' Phib, well, they was pretty friendly an' she was fiddlin' with them curls — you knows 'ow she does — flirtin' with 'im, an', well, when the girl at the pub says Phib was with a gent, I thought of 'im.'

'Mr Henchman has a younger brother who lives with them. Phoebe has spoken of him — I did wonder myself. Handsome, she called him. She seemed to think he had a liking for her. Of course, I thought it was her imagination, but I should have thought more. A single young man and a pretty kitchen maid — and Phoebe so forward.'

'I'll go round there now. See what I can find out.'

'What about Mr Jones?' Scrap asked.

'Jaggard wasn't on the ship. I had a message from Inspector Grove. He should be back tomorrow with Cora Davies and the man she was with. Sam must think they know something.'

'Mr Jones'll know what to do. 'E'll find 'em, an' Mr Dickens'll get evidence from them 'Enchmen.'

Dickens exchanged a smile with Elizabeth. Henchmen, indeed.

8: FLOWERS AND FRUIT

The Henchmen lived in Grafton Street. Not exactly Fitzroy Square, but that's what ambitious folk put on their cards as in: *Grafton Street, Fitzroy Square*, and ambitious people in humbler Norfolk Street were tempted, too. A genteel address was something when you had not very much. The young, aspiring shorthand writer, Charles Dickens, had put Norfolk Street, Fitzroy Square, on his first business card, and had felt himself a swell at seventeen. No matter that the family lodgings were above Mr Dodd's grocery shop. Even his card had smelt of cheese and pickles.

The Dickens family had lived in Fitzroy Street, too. Not that Mr John Dickens had added Fitzroy Square or given any address. Too easy for the creditors to find him. And after Fitzroy Street, a flit to Bentinck Street, or was it Buckingham Street? All the same dreary, cabbage-smelling, smoke-filled, close rooms. He had always wanted air. That's why he loved the sea so much, he supposed.

Very handsome, though, Mr Julius Henchman's residence, a fine, four-storey, Georgian stuccoed house with a smart, black, double front door, gleaming brass doorknocker and pristine blanched steps. Had Phoebe Miller polished that door knocker on Friday before she'd left?

Mrs Henchman might well have been a nobleman's bodyguard — she was large enough. *Stout is a better word*, Dickens thought, as he took in her broad shoulders adorned with red ribbons to match the red of her bright red and yellow tartan dress — the latest fashion — for a girl of eighteen, perhaps. Lily Henchman — a touch overblown by now. She rose to greet him. She seemed to be having trouble breathing — too tightly laced, perhaps — and to be in perpetual motion, her carefully ringleted curls bobbing, ribbons dangling, her head nodding, her bosom heaving where her little hands opened and closed about her lace collar. Somewhat dizzying for the spectator.

'Oh, oh, oh — it is an honour, Mr Dickens. I never dreamed — your card — I could hardly believe —'

'I am a personal friend of Superintendent and Mrs Jones.'

Her eyes bulged at that. Mrs Lily Henchman had standards, or rather Mr Julius Henchman, her liege lord had, he being superior in birth to his wife, daughter of a grocer, albeit a wealthy one — but still a grocer. Mr Henchman was a city man, a banker, whose youthful indiscretion had brought him disappointment, the lily flower's early fluttering prettiness having soon departed. Not that he paid much attention to her, except when he needed money for his pleasures. One daughter. No son. He had interests elsewhere. Home was not the place for dalliance — so he had warned his younger brother who also liked a pretty face, especially a pert one.

Dickens knew what those bulging eyes meant, and he knew what the stoutness and juvenile ribbons and curls meant, too, but he smiled and said, 'Mrs Jones is much concerned about her maid, Posy, as I am sure you are about Phoebe.' He gave her a chance to agree, but she seemed not to have regained her senses, and gazed at him as if he had landed from a distant planet.

'David Copperfield,' she breathed, 'Miss Trotwood, that dreadful Heep — you wrote —'

'Yes, indeed I did. However —' best to be brisk — 'the matter of the two maids.'

'Oh, of course, but why are you — I mean, my kitchen maid — hardly a person you would —'

He assumed his most benevolent air. The woman was not the enemy — just a halfwit, but she must be wooed. 'My dear Mrs Henchman, it was I who placed the child with Mr and Mrs Jones, whom I knew would willingly take in the poor orphan. You see, I found little Posy selling artificial flowers in the street — she had been abandoned by her employer and was selling the last of her stock. After that, the workhouse, I suppose.'

'You are so good, Mr Dickens — so charitable, an example to us all, though we do what we can, of course. I am on the local Linen-Box Committee — clothes for the orphan school — of course, the poor children need whatever we who are so fortunate can give.'

'Indeed, it is very thoughtful of you. So, you see why I feel responsible for Posy. Perhaps you could tell me where they might be.'

'Tea,' she said abstractedly, 'oh, and Mr Dickens, you must sit down. My manners — oh, do — do sit down.'

Tea might very well lubricate the conversation. 'Tea would be most welcome.'

'I'll just —'

While Mrs Henchman bustled away in a whirl of silk, Dickens looked round the room, crowded with little tables and what-nots for the display of trinkets, silver boxes and porcelain figures; a white Carrara marble chimneypiece with an ornate clock, bronze figures, shell flowers, an ornate glass chandelier from which the gaslight fell onto the room through the frosted globes; a brand new 'sociable' — a set of two joined chairs in figured bright red velvet. He'd seen such a one at the Great Exhibition in May. He stood by an upright chair by a table near the fire — he had no wish to share the 'sociable' with Mrs

Henchman. The fire burned brightly in the ornate fitted grate — the latest in style, all brass cherubs and flowers. The Henchmen had money, certainly, if not taste. The room seemed too hot — he needed air.

Mrs Henchman returned to sit in an elaborate velvet easy chair which she filled amply, if dazzlingly, her red and yellow flickering like a Christmas candle against the bright green chair. 'Rose will bring the tea in a moment.'

Dickens was glad to sit down. She might keep still for a while, he hoped. 'Now, do think about Phoebe, won't you — hazard a guess.'

'I don't think I could — I mean, I hardly know Phoebe. She is not my personal maid — she could hardly be that. A kitchen maid, you see —'

'I do see, but you gave her leave to visit her family.'

'Yes, Mr Henchman and I were to go to the country — my daughter, you see — and Cook asked, of course. I said yes, though Phoebe is allowed home once a month — sometimes oftener. Her mother is an ailing woman, I believe, so if Cook can spare her — I don't know how she will manage now. And Mr Henchman is very exacting about too many servants. He doesn't like waste. He might not — and Cook will — oh, and the parlour maid doesn't like because she has to help me, too, and there's Darius, of course — one never knows —'

'Darius?'

'Mr Henchman's younger brother who lives with us.'

Tea came with Rose, the parlour maid who didn't like. *She wouldn't*, thought Dickens. A long nose expressly designed to sniff at any perceived slight. And to poke where it ought not to. Eyes like two sharp pins. A distinctly thorny variety. Very much on her lean dignity and not much respect for her mistress, as could be told from her sighing entrance with the tray — it was all too much for her, it seemed. Now, he wondered, what did Rose think of the errant Phoebe? Sniffed, no doubt. Poked, maybe? And Cook?

The richly laden tray set down with a bang, the tea poured, and cake cut, Rose departed with an air of sniffing martyrdom, and Dickens reluctantly accepted a piece of cake — a large piece, and rather dry. Seed cake was not a favourite, but Mrs Henchman seemed to like it. It was cheap, maybe. Perhaps the exacting Mr Henchman got the choicest dishes.

'Not that Darius could tell you anything about Phoebe — a kitchen maid, you see — neither Mr Henchman nor Darius —'

'No, I am sure not. He and Mr Henchman are busy men, I'm sure — at business. No time for kitchen matters.'

'Mr Henchman is, of course, in the city — he has much pressing business at the bank. He scarcely ever has time for leisure —'

'So, your weekend in the country would be a rare treat.'

'It should have been, yes, but Mr Henchman could only come down on the Saturday for the day — fortunately the train brought him to Epsom by lunch time and that was something, I suppose, though he never seems able to relax — I don't know — he is so often away on business these days.'

'So, you had a gallant brother-in-law to accompany you instead,' Dickens hazarded.

'Dear me, no — oh, no — my daughter's husband is a clergyman, a curate in Epsom — I'm afraid he is rather a serious young man. Darius is so very lively, so very light-hearted. He doesn't find my son-in-law very — well, in any case, Darius has his own life to lead — but Mr Dickens, do excuse my rattling on. It hardly helps with the matter of Phoebe. I don't know how I can help you.'

'Might I speak to Cook?'

'Cook?' The idea seemed to amaze her. 'In the kitchen?'

'If that is where she is. I don't mind at all going down to see her. She might know more about Phoebe, you see, and as I have said, I would like to get some clue as to where the girls might have gone. Just in case Phoebe might have talked about friends to Cook.'

'Friends?' As if the idea of a servant with friends were a phenomenon too much to contemplate.

'Servants, perhaps, in another household. Of course, she may know nothing, but I should like to try — and then I shall not trouble you again. It has been a great pleasure to take tea with you. So, if I might go down to your kitchen?'

'Oh, no, Mr Dickens, I could hardly let a gentleman of your — your distinction — in the kitchen — I mean, Mrs Plum could come up here, or I must accompany you.'

'Not at all, my dear Mrs Henchman —' this was hard work — 'you must finish your tea. Indeed, I could hardly expect a lady of your distinction to bother her head about a little talk with Cook. You know what they say, "a thorough lady is one who has not entered her kitchen for seven years."'

That fell flat. 'As many as seven — dear me, I'm sure I have been down there — oh, dear. Lady Nora — oh, dear —'

'Lady Nora?'

'Lady Nora Lockhart, my neighbour, just round the corner in the square — a dear, sweet lady and so fond of Darius — he is often — her kitchen — no, not in her kitchen, of course — I never thought —'

'Just a saying, dear lady —' now he sounded like the curate — 'no, no, do not trouble yourself. Your parlour maid can show me the way.'

Dickens stood up and made for the door. Mrs Henchman followed. Dickens had to let her go first, though he was itching to thrust her out of the way — Cook would not speak freely if her mistress were hovering. However, sniffing Rose was just coming upstairs with a letter, which she handed to her mistress.

'Oh, my daughter — news — a baby coming, Mr Dickens.'

'Delightful — do stay and read it. Perhaps Rose would —'

'Rose, my dear —' stroking the petals, avoiding the thorns — 'Mr Dickens would like to speak to Cook — if you wouldn't mind showing him the way to the kitchen —'

'Goodbye, Mrs Henchman, a great pleasure to meet you. Let us hope we meet again in less trying circumstances,' Dickens said, then wished he hadn't.

'Oh, yes, certainly — Mr Henchman would so like — Darius is a great reader, of course. A dinner — yes. Perhaps, Mrs Dickens —'

'Perhaps, perhaps,' he offered vaguely before darting down the stairs after the disappearing Rose.

Mrs Plum, red and shining, and ripe as, was taking her tea at the pine table. The kitchen was neat and clean, and there was a smell of roasting meat and of newly baked bread. Dickens introduced himself, was offered more tea, and declined just as Rose, all over prickles, barged in with the tray from upstairs.

'That cake,' Mrs Plum said, 'made of sawdust, I'll warrant. Not mine, Mr Dickens. I see you didn't eat much. Try a nice, hot fruit scone — soft as a pillow. Made this morning — unlike that cake. That Phib — she'll never make a cook.'

'No, indeed, Mrs Plum, thank you. However, it was Phoebe I wanted to speak to you about.'

Rose answered, 'She's a madam an' no mistake. I'm not surprised she hasn't come back. I told that Mrs Jones, that policeman's wife, that Phib would take an extra day if she

could — the mistress bein' away. Give her an inch, that one —
'

'So, you did, Miss Rose, but I am acting for Mrs Jones now. I am most concerned about Phoebe's friend, Posy. I placed her with Superintendent Jones and Mrs Jones, my dear friends. I want to know if either of you has any ideas about what might have become of them. Mrs Plum first, please.'

Rose knew who he was. His stern gaze cowed her into sitting down, her pinpoint eyes lowered, and her mouth grew sulky. He'd get to her in his own time, but he was interested in her obvious dislike of Phoebe Miller.

Mrs Plum began, 'Rose is right, sir. Phib is a bit too fond of her own way — thinks she's above bein' a kitchen maid, or any maid at all, I'm thinkin'. Unreliable — never where she should be, but I don't know where she'd go — 'cept home, an' your girl — a nice little thing, sweet as jam. I couldn't tell why Phib took up with her, but opposites attract, they say.'

'She never mentioned any other friend — any follower, perhaps?'

Rose sniffed at that. Dickens turned to her. 'If you know something, Rose, then you'd better tell me.'

'Not a follower, as such, sir, but I've seen her gigglin' an' whisperin' with Mr Darius.'

'He's a nice young man, Mr Dickens, friendly an' that — I am fond of him. I know he wouldn't mean —'

'She would,' Rose said, 'she'd think she was good enough — she's a little fool.'

'Well, don't let Mr Henchman hear you sayin' anythin' about Mr Darius, Rose. It won't do any good. See, Mr Dickens, Mr Henchman's very fond of his brother. He won't want him gettin' into any trouble.'

'Then Mr Darius ought to behave himself. He shouldn't encourage her.' Sniff.

Dickens had heard enough to make him think about Mr Darius Henchman, but he turned the conversation back to Phoebe's absence. 'Rose, you said you were not surprised at Phoebe's stealing an extra day. She was expected back on Monday when the family came back. Mrs Plum — you were not surprised?'

'No, sir,' Mrs Plum said, 'but I thought p'raps they'd come Monday evening. Phib knew Mrs Henchman would be back. Mr Darius didn't go with them. Mr Henchman didn't go down until Saturday morning — he was here on Friday for a late supper — very late it was, and he askin' where Mr Darius could be.'

'At one of his clubs, I daresay,' Rose put in, 'stays out all night, sometimes. Mr Henchman don't like that.'

'Oh, dear, he does sound like a fellow who enjoys himself — but then, ah, youth —' Dickens sighed, suddenly seventy years old and past it — 'and did he come home on Friday night?' he added — just an indulgent old buffer, envious of a youthful scapegrace.

'If he did, then he must 'ave come in with the milk. He wasn't back before Mr Henchman went to bed, and he wasn't out of his bed until Mr Henchman left for the train.'

'A long night, perhaps —' still smiling jovially at Mrs Plum — 'and Phoebe's own family, Mrs Plum, I believe her mother is not a well woman.' No need to say that he had been to Harper's Farm Lane.

'So Phib says — always ailin', but then there was a tragedy. Two daughters drowned. And, in fairness, Phib feels it. Cried a deal when she told me all about it —' another sniff and not the tearful kind — 'I know you don't like her, Rose, an' I lose

61

patience at times, but that's a thing we can't understand, an' Phib does go home as often as she can. That's why I asked the mistress — Phib said her mother was bad.'

'And there are other children?'

'Sister Sally, about twelve, I think, and there's a boy.'

'An older brother?'

'No, sir, just a little 'un — 'bout eight, Phib says, an' they've not much money. Phib gives what she can — she's a bit pert, I'll grant, but not bad-hearted, I'm sure.'

Another sniff indicating how much Rose doubted all this, but she didn't elaborate.

They couldn't tell him about any other friends, and, no, they hadn't heard the name Matty. It was time to go, and give some thought to Mr Henchman and his whereabouts last Friday — and to Mr Darius Henchman, of whom the various ladies were so fond. Except for thorny Rose, of course.

Dickens walked into Fitzroy Square — quiet in the early evening. Dusk falling, the gas lamps coming on; somewhere in the distance, the sound of a barrel organ starting up, faltering plaintively, essaying a few louder notes, then giving up. Someone moved him on? He pictured a lonely Italian man making his weary way to another street, or, perhaps with a boy, a little son to take the money. Wrenched from their roots to find themselves in heartless London, under its louring skies, shivering in its bitter east winds.

He thought of Posy — where had she been taken? Wrenched from the life she loved. He thought of Joan at The Copenhagen asking why Phoebe would want to take anyone to that stinking cottage. It was a very reasonable question. And the answer was surely that Phoebe had not intended to take Posy there. Phoebe Miller and her gentleman companion had taken Posy somewhere else. But why? Well, there were answers to that question — and most of them terrifying.

It was time he went to his office in Wellington Street. There was a meeting later with his sub-editor, Harry Wills. They were to look over the articles for the Christmas number of *Household Words*. Contributors had been asked to write about what Christmas meant to different people at different times. He thought of the words he'd written already before he had known about Posy: *Lost friend, lost child, lost parent, sister, brother, husband, wife, we will not so discard you.* They wouldn't.

Home. That's what Christmas meant to Sam Jones, home with Elizabeth and Eleanor and Tom Brim, their adopted children, and Scrap, of course, and Posy, who had never known what Christmas meant, or even what home meant until she had found one at Norfolk Street. Lost child found — and lost again.

He thought of Sam, longing for him to return and share his wisdom and his resources. And dreading, too. Elizabeth having to tell him, and Sam knowing, as he did, all the things that might have happened. All the missing, who were never heard of again. But it was his job to do what he could. At least, he could go to Sam tomorrow with some information about the Henchman brothers.

The lights were coming on in the houses. He thought of Lady Nora Lockhart, so fond of Darius Henchman. Dickens knew the name, but he had not met her. Who did he know in these marble halls who might be neighbour enough?

'Mr Dickens,' a voice said, 'how very good to see you.'

9: THE PAWNBROKER

'You are a long way from home, Mr Decker.'

John Decker, silversmith, jeweller, dealer in nautical and mathematical instruments — and pawnbroker, was a long way from his premises by St. Anne's Church in Limehouse, or from his shop in Poplar, or that in Clerkenwell. A substantial man of business, Mr Decker. Dickens knew the shop by the church. He had passed it many times on his way down Church Lane where his godfather, Christopher Huffam, had lived, though in that time, John Decker's father had owned the business. The Deckers had known the Huffams, Christopher Huffam being in the marine trade as a rigger for the navy and a ship's chandler. And, by a coincidence as fateful as the conjunction of the invisible stars above, Dickens had been to Mr Decker's shop only last week — researching a piece for *Household Words*, a piece on pawnbroking, and Mr Decker had proved an astute businessman, and a fair one to his borrowers — as his father had been. Dickens had no idea if his own father had pawned anything at Decker's shop in those old times, but he wouldn't have been surprised. He remembered only too well the various pawnbrokers' shops he had visited as a boy — pawning the household goods until there was nothing left but two bare rooms, and candles in blacking bottles.

'Indeed, I am, Mr Dickens, but how extraordinary that I should meet you again so soon.'

'What brings you to Fitzroy Square?'

'Business, Mr Dickens. I am on my way to see Mr Frederick Crouch to discuss the idea of establishing a mutual benefit society.'

'A noble enterprise, Mr Decker. I wonder if I might go with you?'

'You know Mr Crouch?'

'No, but I am in search of some information about his neighbours, Mr and Mrs Henchman.'

'Henchman!' Mr Decker exclaimed. 'Family of Mr Darius Henchman?'

'You know him?'

'I do, I met him at Mr Crouch's. Might I ask why you are interested in Darius Henchman?'

Dickens explained about the disappearance of Posy and Phoebe Miller. 'A confidential matter, Mr Decker. Posy's employers are Superintendent and Mrs Jones — you remember him?'

'I do, I do — that dreadful business — the murder of poor Captain Valentine of *The Redemption*. Mr Jones came in to talk to us about your friend, Mr Penney —'

'Whom I must come to see soon. But you understand that this matter is delicate. I placed the girl, Posy, with Mr and Mrs Jones. I feel a responsibility to do what I can to trace her. I was wondering if any of the neighbours' servants knew Phoebe Miller, and I was thinking if I knew anyone in Fitzroy Square, and here you are like a good angel come to direct me.'

Mr Frederick Crouch was quite delighted to receive Mr Dickens and sorry to tell him that he did not know the Henchmans very well, but they had dined, and Mr Crouch was rather hoping to interest Mr Julius Henchman in the benefit society. 'The bank, you know — useful man to have.'

'And the brother? Mrs Henchman told me he was a friend of Lady Nora Lockhart.'

'Oh, I know Lady Nora — a widow now — her husband was Sir Herbert Lockhart, the judge. She likes her young men. Darius Henchman is supposed to be quite a favourite. I won't tell you what my wife has to say about that.'

Mr Decker laughed. 'Darius Henchman is a great favourite with all the ladies, but I doubt that Lady Nora is taken in by his charms. She's no fool. I know her.'

'Not so much a favourite with the gentlemen, I take it.'

'Not one of mine, Mr Dickens.'

'You have had dealings with him, Mr Decker?'

'In the pawnbroking way, certainly. Quite a regular customer — all kinds of trinkets to pawn.'

'Lily Henchman's trinkets, I shouldn't wonder — she has enough of them,' Mr Crouch added, 'even Lady Nora's — a servant dismissed — suspected of stealing a valuable snuff box. She swore she hadn't, of course.'

'He didn't pawn a snuff box with you?' Dickens asked Mr Decker.

'Not such a fool as that, Mr Dickens. He comes to me in Limehouse — far enough from Fitzroy Square. And my manager in Clerkenwell knows him. I did mention the matter to Mr Henchman. Of course, I was dismissed with a wave of the hand. Pawnbroker, you see. I didn't mention it again — don't want to put our scheme in jeopardy. Let Mr Darius Henchman pawn the whole contents of fifteen Grafton Street and I won't say a word.'

'Short of money, Mr Darius?'

'It'll be the usual — gambling, clubs, women — thank the Lord, my daughters are married,' said Mr Crouch.

'I had a hint — nothing definite — that he might have been seen with the kitchen maid, Phoebe.'

'Oh, I doubt that, Mr Dickens. I shouldn't think Julius Henchman would countenance any dalliance with servants. Plenty of other fish in the sea.'

'I don't know, Crouch, I wouldn't trust that young man with any female — of any age or station,' Mr Decker put in. 'What kind of girl is the kitchen maid?'

'Phoebe Miller — known as Phib. Pretty in the pert manner — a lot of curls and eyelashes. Confident of her charms. She went away in a green dress and cloak, red ribbons, and a fur tippet — on the showy side. Last seen at The Copenhagen Inn with a gentleman, and with Mr Jones's servant, Posy. And, my dear sirs, I want to find her.'

'You think this gentleman might be Darius Henchman?'

'I don't know, Mr Decker, but it's a possibility.'

'I'll tell my managers at Poplar and in Clerkenwell to keep an eye out for Darius Henchman and for the girl.'

'Would you mind, Mr Decker, if I went to see your manager in Clerkenwell — for research purposes, of course?'

John Decker laughed. 'I'll tell him to expect you.'

'And if I see her, I will let you know,' Mr Crouch said.

'Send a message to my office, if you please, number sixteen, Wellington Street. Gentlemen, I am much obliged to you both. Now I must go back to the office. My thanks.'

On his way back to the office, Dickens pondered. Another question: whom did he know who knew Lady Nora Lockhart? For it was at her house that he might meet, by chance, Mr Darius Henchman, who was proving more interesting by the hour.

10: ON THE RAILS

Constable Stemp and a constable from Southampton Police Station were to take the early morning railway mail which would get them with their prisoners to London, Waterloo, in about three hours. Cora Davies and Joey Speed ought to be in two cells at Bow Street by noon.

Where Superintendent Jones and Sergeant Rogers would be by that time was a more complicated question, only to be answered by solving the fiendish puzzles set by Mr Bradshaw's railway guide, a publication which Superintendent Jones was very often glad to leave for Charles Dickens's eagle eye. However, one of the Southampton inspectors turned out to be an expert, advising them to take the morning express with the constables, get off at Reading — on the South Western Line, catch a London South Eastern Line train to Canterbury from whence the East Kent line would take them to Rochester, and beyond that, no doubt, some conveyance could be hired to take them the three miles to Upnor, where Cora Davies had somewhat reluctantly informed them that her ma lived with little Marty, son of Martin Jaggard. Gideon's Cottage. Who Gideon was, Superintendent Jones did not enquire. Though he hoped Gideon was not a six feet tall boxer like that Gideon of London fame, renowned for his right hook. Six feet six and eighteen stone. Jaggard was a featherweight compared to Gideon.

'I want to satisfy myself that he isn't there. I know his paternal feelings are not likely to be much developed —'

Rogers had pointed that out, too, observing that he couldn't imagine Jaggard as anyone's pa — not even the cat's —

'I suppose he had a mother —'

'I don't believe that, either.' Rogers believed in Jaggard as the devil's spawn.

'But it'll be like an itch if we don't do it. We'll wonder if we missed him. A cottage in a country village — somewhere to lie low.'

Several hours and the requisite number of trains later, dusty, and grimy, and not much fortified by a pork pie — gristle pie, more accurately — and a bottle of soda water apiece at Reading, they hired a trap at Rochester Station to take them to Upnor. Superintendent Jones would have to put in his claim for expenses later. Whether Mr Mayne would countenance the cost of the pork pies and soda was another matter. Perhaps Sir George Grey, the Home Secretary, would stump up for his friend, Sir William Pell.

Gideon's Cottage proved to be a neat, weather-boarded affair wherein they discovered Mrs Hannah Davies, who was adamant that Jaggard had not been there, an' that if he had showed his impudent mug, he wouldn'ta got over her threshold — not beyond the garden gate. Not that she was very happy to have the police over her threshold, either, but she let them in and shooed a little black-eyed boy upstairs to play.

Jones could well believe her words about Jaggard. Mrs Davies was a formidable woman — hefty arms, meaty red hands, and a determined chin. She'd have made a fine boxer, but she was handsome in her large way, with a great quantity of black hair. He could see the resemblance to black-eyed Cora. Dickens would have appreciated Mrs Davies, who carried her broom like a weapon — Jones could easily imagine Jaggard being swept into the highway.

Her black eyes flashed. 'I'm a respectable woman, Mr Jones, an' I don't hold with Cora's doin's. London, indeed. Actress — I know what that means. But she would go. Only comes back when she wants somethin', an' I had to take the kiddie, but it's not the child's fault. America — what an idea. Said I wouldn't keep him. Cora'd to stay, I said, but she persuaded me — more fool me. New life, she said. Jaggard goin' to set up in business there. Thievin' business, I'll be bound.'

'She was going with Jaggard?'

'That's what she said, an' that's why I'm keepin' the boy. I won't have Jaggard near him.'

'Cora wasn't with Jaggard on the ship. She was with a man called Joey Speed.'

'She never said — mind, she did keep sayin' "we", so I assumed — she sayin' they'd send for the boy. Who's this Speed, then — another bad lot?'

'I rather think so, Mrs Davies. You'll send word —' Jones gave her his card — 'if you hear or see anything of Jaggard.'

'Let him come here. I'll show him.'

He had to warn her. 'Don't, Mrs Davies, don't get into a row. He's a violent man.'

'He'd not dare.'

'He might, Mrs Davies. I want him for murder.'

She blanched at that. 'Dear God — an' Cora, is she — would he —'

'She's safe enough in custody.'

'She wasn't involved in that?'

'I doubt it, but she was in possession of stolen goods — goods belonging to the victim. Jaggard gave them to her — for America.'

'She's more fool than I thought, but if he comes?'

'Tell him you don't know anything. He'll not take the boy —
he's on the run. He'll not want a child to slow him down.' He
hoped he was right. You never knew what a man like Jaggard
might do. He thought of Sir William Pell's mutilated head.

Mrs Davies turned away. When she faced them again, the
hearth broom was an ancient blunderbuss. 'I'm not afraid to
use it.'

'Try not to kill him — I need him in court.'

'She would an' all,' Rogers said as they went back to the
waiting trap.

'Do you know, I don't care if she does kill him. It'll be all
over then. Self-defence — protecting the child.'

The driver was to take them to an inn. They'd have to stay
the night now. On the way, Rogers asked, 'What do you make
of it — Jaggard goin' to America?'

'Hard to say, Alf; suppose she did mean it and they split up
for safety's sake. Cora and Joey, just an innocent married
couple decided to emigrate.'

'Why'd she use her own name?'

'Mr and Mrs Davies — she'd suppose it wouldn't matter, and
convenient for Speed to be someone else. Those forged notes.
He must be in on the money faking. We wouldn't have known
a thing about her except that someone talked. Someone from
that lodging house, I wondered.'

'An' if Jaggard is goin' to America —'

'He could be anywhere — Liverpool, the Continent —'

'Cora Davies mentioned that new business when we
interviewed her. An associate, she said. Maybe it's true. Just her
and Speed goin' to America.'

'Still in London, then? Jaggard wouldn't mind, perhaps, if it was thought he'd gone to America. Now, Rochester police station, I think. We'd better warn them.'

A grubby little inn not far from the railway station. Lumpy beds, fleas, he was sure, and tough beef. And indigestion. Sam lay awake all night, the soda and pork pie contending for supremacy in his stomach. And Rogers snoring in the other bed.

Home, he thought, not much caring in the wastes of the night where Jaggard was. Home. Magic word. That's what Dickens had written. It was. Elizabeth would be there, waiting, and Eleanor and Tom, and Scrap, of course, eager to know if Mr Jones 'ad found that Jaggard, offering his services. Not likely, thought Jones.

He wondered what new dish Posy would have tried out for his homecoming from the manual of domestic economy, or, more likely, from Mrs Dickens's new cookery book, published in October: *What Shall We Have for Dinner?* Not that he could face anything now, he thought. Kind Mrs Dickens, now a friend of Elizabeth's, had come round to present a brand-new copy to Posy — signed by the author, of course. The other author had never received the dazzling smile and blushes given to Mrs Dickens. Recipes more to her taste than *David Copperfield*, probably.

He dozed, thinking of Posy's little fingers chopping the vegetables for Mrs Dickens's cock-a-leekie hotchpotch, or boiled salmon, perhaps. No pork, he hoped, feeling the acid burn in his chest.

11: DECISIONS

'No water?'

'No, sir, that cistern's failed again — the one upstairs.'

Dickens had gone home to Tavistock House after his meeting with Henry Wills to be greeted by Anne Brown, his wife's maid, who gave him the bad news about the cistern.

'I'll write to Mr Inglis at the waterworks. Someone will have to come and look at it, and I'll write to Mr Austin. He might have some idea. How is Mrs Dickens today?'

'Tired, sir. She's having a lie down. Miss Hogarth is with the little ones and Miss Mamie and Miss Katey are at Gordon Street with Mrs Lemon's girls.'

'I'll go up soon — let me get this letter written.'

Dickens went upstairs to his study. Damn that cistern. It was not the first time — not so much as a tear in the shower bath the other day and all the bother of bringing bath water from the kitchen. Not enough capacity, he supposed. *Neither have I*, he thought, looking at the letters on his desk. And Catherine not well. She wouldn't be. The new baby was due in March — all being well. He hoped he or she would be more robust than poor little Dora. Another girl, he'd like. Six boys were quite enough for any man to deal with, but they were good boys, on the whole, Charley, his eldest, doing well at Eton, and Walter, a weekly boarder at Mr King's school in St. John's Wood.

Mr Inglis of the Clerkenwell Waterworks first, and a letter to his brother-in-law, Henry Austin, who had superintended the restoration of Tavistock House. Then he looked at some of the others. A letter from Mrs Georgiana Morson, matron at the home for fallen women. Mary Ann Church pilfering again. She

had only been at the home since March. A convicted thief —
and still one. He doubted that there was any hope for her. She
liked to steal; she couldn't break the habit. Some you couldn't
help. Mary Humphreys and Ann Davis, too — still in prison
for absconding with clothing and a purse of money from the
home. They were hardened to slyness and deceit, and they
couldn't see further than the immediate desire for the freedom
of the streets.

Freedom of what kind? Freedom to roam, to live on the
margins, to steal, to be trapped in the toils of prostitution, to
be ensnared by a hard-faced brothelkeeper, to be brutalised by
a pimp, to be used by a coining gang — to die alone, riddled by
disease, in a back alley.

But there had been successes. Some had been saved from
that grim fate. Three of the girls were doing well in Australia,
three more on their way there, and another three in South
Africa. Hope and persevere. That was the thing. *Louisa Cooper*,
he thought, glancing at another letter — from Gilbert à
Beckett, the magistrate, who had sent Louisa to the home.
Louisa, who had settled in South Africa. Now Beckett was
writing about another girl whom he hoped Dickens would take
— a poor country girl who had been deserted by her father
and had been tramping and hop-picking. She had been arrested
for trying to get admission to the workhouse at the wrong
time. There was an irony — she had sought shelter from the
very place that ought to have provided it and was taken up as a
vagabond. He would have to go to see Beckett — he owed
him a favour. Gilbert à Beckett had lent rooms in Middle
Temple to one of Sam Jones's constables, who was on watch
for a murderer.

A tramping girl — you saw them often. Coming to London
in the hope of employment, and so often they found it with

the wrong person. Setting aside Mr Darius Henchman for the moment, suppose the "gentleman" at The Copenhagen was someone whom Phoebe, with her desire for freedom from the kitchen, had met. A man who was on the lookout for young girls — virgin girls, fresh girls, who could be sold to high-spending clients. A man in league with a brothelkeeper. A man who made promises of good earnings — that would appeal to Phoebe Miller, who would earn about five pounds a year for scrubbing the kitchen floor and emptying chamber pots. And such a man would ask her if she had a friend. Phoebe Miller might seem a little shop-soiled in her hand-me-down tippet and red ribbons, but Posy — any man or woman in that trade would see at a glance how innocent she was —

He could hardly bear to think about it and turned his attention to his other letters. A note from Elizabeth Jones to tell him that Sam had gone to Kent in search of his murderer. So, not back tomorrow after all. Another day. Every day that they were missing meant less chance of finding them. Probably, the country girl at the workhouse had been saved from a worse fate than Mr à Beckett's court.

Sam not here tomorrow. That was a blow. What to do now? How to proceed? Dickens felt at a loss. They had to find the man from The Copenhagen. He could be Darius Henchman. He thought about Lady Nora Lockhart, widow of Sir Herbert. He remembered him. Died of apoplexy upon finding his lady in a compromising situation with a handsome footman. Judge Lockhart, keen on flogging and hanging. Just as well for the footman that Lockhart had expired on the spot. Kinder folk said he had choked on a chop. Anyway, Lady Nora had lived it down, though now it seemed her reputation was not quite as spotless as an elderly widow's should be. Dickens was assuming she was elderly. Lockhart had always looked as old as the hills in court — and as bald. However, Lady Nora might be in her prime. No fool, though, Decker had said. It would be very interesting to see what she had to say about young Mr Darius.

Not that all this wool-gathering was in the least bit useful. Something must be done. Dickens knew what he ought to do — go upstairs and soothe his wife. He could offer to collect the girls from the Lemon house — a dose of Mark Lemon for half an hour would be a tonic. Mark would have something humorous to tell him about the world's goings-on. *Punch* was much preoccupied now with Mrs Amelia Bloomer. Cartoons showing ladies in trousers smoking cigars and proposing to their hapless swains. He rather hoped that Mamie and Katey would not want to follow the eccentric fashion, complaining that petticoats were their badge of subservience. Not mild Mamie. Now, Katey, his little firebrand… Too young yet, surely.

Too young, too young. Posy was not much older than thirteen-year-old Mamie. Fourteen or fifteen, perhaps. Posy didn't know how old she was. She only remembered the orphanage at Tooting — a place so vile that the man who ran it, Benjamin Drouet, had been indicted for manslaughter. So many of the children had died of cholera, having been left starving and without medical care. Dickens had written about it in *The Examiner*. It was a stain on civilised society, he had said, but the man had been acquitted on the grounds that it could not be proved that neglect had killed them. Posy had suffered enough in her short life — and now —

He made up his mind to do something. He went out to find his sister-in-law, Georgina, coming down the stairs. She was going to collect the girls.

'I was just going up to see Kate,' he told her.

'She's asleep. Leave her.'

'How is she, really?'

'Tired from the move.' The Dickens family had only just moved into Tavistock House, and it had been a trying time. 'She needs to rest, Charles. She is so easily upset just now. Alfred and Frank are being quiet in the nursery, and Henry and Sydney are in bed.'

'I'm going to see Judge Talfourd in Russell Square — I just want to ask him something, then I'll collect Katey and Mamie from Gordon Street.'

His friend Judge Talfourd might well know Lady Nora Lockhart — he'd have known her husband. Talfourd might provide an introduction. There had to be a way of getting into number 10, Fitzroy Square — other than breaking and entering.

12: LADY DETECTIVE

Tom All Alone's, Dickens wrote on his half-sheet of paper. Perhaps. *The East Wind, The Ruined House* — or *The Solitary House* — Mill? Factory? He still hadn't a title for his new book. *Bleak House? Fog. Sooty rain. Implacable November weather.* So it was. He looked out into his garden, a gloomy, dripping scene. The shrubs and bushes transplanted from Devonshire Terrace looked decidedly forlorn. Homesick, perhaps? He looked at his watch. Two hours gone, but something to show for it. *Fog up the river, fog down the river, where it rolls defiled among the tiers of shipping...* Something in that. And the whole was in his head — the plot, the motive, the characters, from the wretched little crossing-sweeper, Jo, to the fashionable Lady Dedlock of Chesney Wold, the house which he imagined dripping and melancholy in the November rain. He made another note: *The waters are out in Lincolnshire.*

And in London. He sanded his paper, put it on his pile of notes, shook his goose quill, and arranged his desk neatly. Time to go. Elizabeth Jones's message said to come at 10.30. She wanted to talk to him — something important, obviously, though not news that Posy had miraculously reappeared, unharmed, and repentant. He looked down at his last paper. *Tom All Alone's* — that ruinous slum he'd known as a child in Rochester. Ruinous slums and criminal haunts everywhere in London. Hidden places where girls were taken, abused, sold into prostitution. No use going over that again.

Elizabeth greeted him fondly and plunged into her tale. 'I had a thought, Charles, about Phoebe's brother, Frankie. How could he have remembered Matty? According to the blacksmith's tale, he was a year old at the time of the drowning, and Matty went off to sea not long after.'

'I never thought of that. You think Matty might have been back?'

'It's possible — the blacksmith said he was close to Phoebe.'

'I ought to go back there.'

'And I'm coming with you. I can't just sit here thinking. Eleanor is at school, and Mollie Rogers will take Tom, and —' she smiled at him — 'Scrap is keeping watch on them Henchmen to see if Darius Henchman is the man he saw with Phoebe. Scrap's not prepared to sit and wait. Mr Jones'll want to know what we've done, he tells me. I agree.'

'Then so do I, and it would help to know if there is anything between Phoebe and Darius Henchman — however slight. Mrs Henchman's servant, Rose —'

'Oh, I met her. She certainly didn't care for Phoebe.'

'She maintained that Phoebe was fool enough to think she might be good enough for Darius Henchman.'

'Phoebe Miller is not a fool. Given what you've told me about the gentleman at The Copenhagen, I wonder if this disappearance was planned.'

'The servant, Joan, at The Copenhagen asked why Phoebe would take anyone to that cottage, and I thought about that. And I've seen the place — there was nowhere for them to sleep. I think you're right. Phoebe had no intention of taking Posy there. Mrs Miller did say that Phoebe didn't always come when she said she might.'

'Might, Charles — she must have told Mrs Henchman or the cook that she had to go home, but she sometimes did not. She was with someone else. Darius Henchman, I wonder?'

'Did Phoebe suggest that she and Posy stop at The Copenhagen?'

'She did — she said she was going to treat Posy to a cup of tea. It seemed innocent enough, and I gave them the money. Posy was so thrilled.'

'It could be, of course, that Phoebe did know that the gentleman would be there, and that he enticed them away, and in that sense, Phoebe is a fool. Eyes dazzled by yellow gloves and a top hat.'

'That could be it. I suppose I'm prejudiced against her now because of Posy — and that business with Scrap at the shop — something hard-faced about that.'

'You think Mrs Miller might talk to a woman?'

'I've every reason to ask about Posy. And I'm taking a basket with me — food and some clothes. That might smooth my way.'

Dickens met Elizabeth at the shop in Crown Street where she had dropped off Tom Brim. Dickens's coachman, Topping, was to drive them. The plan was that Dickens should see Joan again at The Copenhagen. Now he had some idea of Darius Henchman's leisure pursuits, he had thought of the sporting pleasures at the old inn. Boxing, wrestling, for example — very popular with the swells and plenty of money to be won — and lost. He had thought of pawnbroking, too — useful if a man owed money. Topping would take Elizabeth on to Harper's Farm Lane. Elizabeth Jones had not thought it a good idea for Dickens to see Mrs Miller again — or Scrap, especially if Frankie Miller might remember him.

'My lady detective,' he said, bowing to her wisdom. He had noted, too, her shabby brown stuff cloak and plain black bonnet.

She saw him appraising her. 'Just an ordinary policeman's wife, if she asks, but I'll not say. And just the one servant who is my sister's orphan child.'

'But the carriage?'

'Oh, a kind friend, of course.'

The rain had stopped, and Joan was on the steps, beating a rug. Good, he thought, he could speak to her alone. She knew him, and hearing the coins chinking in his pocket, consented to answer his questions. He asked if they might go into the parlour.

'I'm sure that Mr Bartlett won't mind if we sit by the fire for a minute or two. You look cold.' She didn't, but he did notice the angry chilblains on her hands.

'Used ter it, sir, but I don't mind a sit down. Them rugs is 'eavy.'

'You do work hard, Joan, I can see that. I only wanted to ask if you could tell me anything more about Phib's gentleman. I wondered if the name Darius Henchman means anything?'

'Dunno, sir.'

They settled by the parlour fire. 'Have you seen the gentleman here without Phib — at the wrestling or boxing, perhaps?'

'Dunno, sir — it's allus that crowded, an' we get all sorts — gents an' that. I serves the drinks sometimes, but they all looks the same ter me. Drunks all look the same, sir — gents or not.'

'He couldn't be a Matthew?'

'Dunno, sir. Phib's brother woz Matthew — Matty — the one that went away ter sea. Niver liked 'im, neither. Used ter know 'im, years back.'

'Why didn't you like him?'

'Too big fer 'is boots — up ter no good with that Phib, an' niver let on — niver let me in on anythin'. See, them Millers is related to Ma's cousin, the blacksmith down near Belle Isle.'

'So, Phib is a kind of cousin of yours?'

'Serpose — niver liked 'er, neither.'

Dickens asked why, and a litany of complaints followed. Chiefly Phib Miller gave herself airs, 'ad bin spoilt — pretty, see — them lads on the farm, Matty's pals, they all knew what Phib Miller was like — oh, airs, awright, but no better than —

Dickens disentangled from the complex threads of Joan's discourse that Phoebe Miller was — in his words — precocious, not above selling her favours, for a penny or two when she was younger. What those favours were, he did not enquire too deeply, but he got the gist, though he wondered how much came from Joan's understandable jealousy of a girl much prettier than she. He was about to ask more about Matty, but Joan was not to be stopped.

'Yer should ask my ma. She knows all about Phib Miller an' 'er doin's. Yer knows 'er sisters drowned?'

Dickens didn't need to lie. He saw the avid malice in Joan's eyes. Oh, she was very eager to tell. He merely asked, 'Sisters?'

'Phib Miller 'ad two younger sisters wot drowned — drowned —' She waited for his reaction to her announcement which had a good deal of relish in it.

'Oh, dear.' Inadequate, but enough to encourage her.

'Accident, them lawyers said, but my ma knows a thing or two. She'll tell you all about Phib an' that Matty.'

'The one who went away?'

'Run off, I thinks, cos some thought 'e done it — an' Phib —' her eyes glittered — 'tergether —'

They heard Mr Bartlett's voice in the hall. 'Better get on, sir. Ma, Mrs Gall, lives in Shoot Lane — next door but one ter the Fortune —'

Joan hurried away, and Dickens followed. *Milk to gall*, he thought. How much was malicious gossip? He went out to greet Mr Bartlett — to ask him about any toffs who followed the boxing or wrestling. Anyone named Henchman, perhaps, who might have lost money.

Ten minutes or so later, he stood on Maiden Lane, waiting for Topping and Elizabeth. Nothing to look at but damp, empty fields and then the reservoir over by Camden Lane, and to the east where the lunatic asylum and the prison stood side by side; both prisons, he supposed. The fields looked flat and grey under the crushing November sky and a gritty wind came slicing from the east. A bleak spot today, but very often the lanes going towards The Copenhagen from all directions were filled with carriages, gigs, carts, cabs, and crowds on foot making their way to see the boxing and wrestling, to gamble away their wages, or their inheritance, or somebody else's money. Darius Henchman — Mr Bartlett knew him for a gambler. In with a set of young men, all bent on getting a thrill and not always able to pay. Oh, yes, plenty of IOUs and bills passed about. As to women — always a good number of camp followers, so to speak, but no, he didn't remember having seen Phib Miller with Henchman. Only what Joan had said about seeing her with some swell.

The sound of horses' hooves came upon his ear. Perhaps Elizabeth, that lady of natural detective genius, would have prised open Mrs Miller's shell.

13: GALL AND MILK

'Dear me, Charles, that poor woman doesn't know what day it is. I asked about Matty eventually, but she just looked at me blankly as if she had no idea who he was. It was impossible to get through to her. I offered my comforts — some chicken and a new loaf and some butter, and a little cape that was Eleanor's. I asked if her daughter, Sally, might like to try it on, but Sally was out, she said, and Frankie, for whom I offered a pair of Tom's boots. I left them there.'

'Did you get a chance to ask about the dead girls?'

'I told her that Phoebe had mentioned her other sisters — I tried to be tactful, telling her that I'd had a daughter who died, but she didn't respond. She just repeats that Phib's a good girl — so often that I do wonder if in some dark recess of her mind, she doesn't actually believe it, and that she knows that something wasn't right about the drownings. No mother could face that.'

'What about the father?'

'I asked if Mr Miller had any thoughts about Phoebe's disappearance. Honestly, Charles, I might have been asking about a stranger. Not much of a detective, am I?'

'No worse than I — Mrs Miller is beyond our skills, I'm afraid —'

'Not all of us. Mr Topping has something to report.'

'Topping!'

At the sound of his name, Topping turned round. 'Sir?'

'Stop a minute, will you? Mrs Jones says you found out something.'

Topping brought the horse to a standstill at the side of the road, and the new constable turned his red face to them. Topping, groom, stableman, carriage-driver, and messenger, was always red in the face to match his red hair. Something of a philosopher, given to musings about the mysterious ways of the world. Dickens enjoyed him, despite his tendency to accidents. In September, he had fallen off the horse and cut his head, but Dickens had forgiven him. He had been with Dickens for twelve years and that counted.

'The little lad, sir, came out o' the hedge. Wanted ter sit in the carriage. I knew yer wouldn't mind. Asked me if I knew Matty. Asked 'oo Matty was, and the lad said he was Phib's friend. 'E asked where Phib was an' was the lady Phib's friend, too — an' that was it, sir. Not much, I serpose.'

'Excellent, Topping. That's twice the boy's mentioned a Matty — whoever he is, he certainly made an impression.'

'Bit slow, that lad, sir, I think — natural, they call 'em, kids like that. An' seems to live in that 'edge. Scuttled right back in without another word —' Topping's face took on an abstracted air. Dickens waited for the philosophic conclusion. 'Wot a mystery, sir, is nature — yer niver knows.'

'Quite so, Topping, you never do. Now, drive on to Belle Isle — drop us near the Fortune of War and we'll meet you back hereabouts — just by the tile kilns. Mrs Jones, we're off to see a Mrs Gall. I'll tell you as we go.'

Shoot Lane smelt of boiling bones, varnish, manure, decaying fish, and smoke. The Fortune of War — *or misfortune*, Dickens thought — smelt of beer when the door opened and closed as they waited for someone to answer the door of Mrs Gall's cottage, a surprisingly neat one compared with its frowsty neighbours. A canary in a cage at the window opened and closed its beak. It had a message for them, perhaps. Pity they couldn't hear.

Another whiff of beer, footsteps, and a voice asking what they wanted. Mrs Gall, they presumed — a plump woman with a friendly smile and a jug of beer appeared at Elizabeth's side.

'You'll be the lady wot's girl's gone missin' with young Phib.'

'I am — I've just been to see Mrs Miller.'

'No point in that, dearie, she's not all there, poor Alice — niver got over the shock — well, you'd best come in. This yer 'usband?'

'No, a friend, who also went to see Mrs Miller for me — Mr Dickens.'

'Well, 'e's welcome an' all, though I don't know what I can tell you.'

A neat cottage — very different from Mrs Miller's. Mrs Gall was evidently houseproud, judging by the cleanliness and smell of soap, and the Dutch clock on the wall, the scrubbed table, and the rag rug by the hearth where the kettle was boiling on the range, which like the black shovel and tongs shone with polish. And the canary singing in its cage.

They refused a drop of beer and accepted tea. While Mrs Gall was making it, Elizabeth told of her visit to Mrs Miller and emphasised her desire to find the two girls.

'Oh, yes, Joan told me all about it. Phib an' 'er fancy man. I never seen 'im. Toff, supposedly. I don't know, all sorts at The Copenhagen — boxin', wrestlin', gamblin'. Swells, they call 'em. What'd a gentleman want with Phib?'

Dickens didn't answer that one. 'Your cousin, the blacksmith, told me about Matty — the brother that went away to sea after the —'

'Drownin' — there was talk, see. He wasn't a bad lad. Big for his age — knocked Abel down once. That family, allus quarrelling.'

Elizabeth told her about Frankie. 'Surely, he wouldn't have remembered. We wondered, perhaps, if Matty had come back — to see them all and might have been at The Copenhagen with Phib.'

'Nobody said. I go up there once a week or so — ter see how Alice goes on. She never said — not that she would. Never says much, though, an' Sally didn't say. But why'd Matty come back? Bin away years.'

'To see Phoebe? The blacksmith said they were close.'

'True enough — allus runnin' off somewhere together. Can't blame Matty, all them girls. I don't think Matty 'ad much time fer them younger ones.'

'And how did Phoebe get along with her sisters?'

'Nuisances, I suppose. She was meant ter look after them. See, after Frankie, Alice wasn't well — difficult birth an' Frankie ain't — a bit soft — slow, like, an' Phib was the sharp one — 'ad ter take the girls about, out of the 'ouse — lot o' work fer a girl, an' that Liza was a bit — wild, I serpose. Allus runnin' off somewhere. Alice couldn't do anythin' with that one — Abel gave her a few leatherin's.'

'And Phoebe preferred to be with Matty.'

'Both sharp ones — you couldn't blame 'em, wantin' ter be out an' about. There was allus rows — that's why Matty knocked Abel down. Matty an' Phib went off an' left the girls — stayed out all night. Lord knows where. Not the first time, neither. Abel was that mad, he struck Matty. Course, 'e forgot that Matty was bigger than 'im.'

'And did Abel ever strike Phoebe?' Dickens asked.

'Not after that. Matty was there to stop 'im.'

'But he didn't protect the younger ones?'

Mrs Gall looked troubled at that. 'It's hard ter explain, Missis — they wasn't a family, really. I don't know why. Jest all at odds — see, an' then Alice lost other babies. Born dead an' there was a big gap between Matty an' Liza an' Susan. Matty just didn't have no time fer them — an' yer can't blame a lad fer that, can yer?' There was appeal in her voice as she looked at Elizabeth.

'But Matty and Phoebe were close. Do you think he could have come back?'

'I don't know, Missis — why, after so long? Alice don't miss 'im. She never talks about 'im, nor the girls, neither, but then she never was much of a mother, an' Abel, well, he's not much of anythin'.'

Mrs Gall was garrulous enough — and amiable, but the next question was a difficult one. It had to be asked. Dickens glanced at Elizabeth, who nodded slightly. She knew what he was going to ask.

'You said there was talk about Matty after the drowning — and Phib. Was it her shawl that was found about the girls' necks?'

'I know what was said — that's why Matty went, an' Phib inter service, but that shawl, sir, it was an' it wasn't. You know what poor folks' lives is, I daresay, Missis — 'ow they lives from hand ter mouth. Course Phib 'ad worn it, but so 'ad Alice, an' Sally probably. Some clothes is allus in common, boots, fr'instance. Them girls'd take whatever boots fitted, or as near as, or they'd go barefoot. Boots, bonnets, shawls, all in common. Liza an' Susan — one o' them coulda worn it — quarrelled about it — decided to share it — oh, I don't know, Missis — I don't like to think —'

'Your Joan seemed to think —' Dickens began.

'You don't want ter take too much notice of Joan — she's not fond o' Phib, an', well, little pitchers — Joan's a great one fer listenin' at doors. She 'eard the gossip back then an', o' course, she's seen Phib in all that finery. Joan's my girl, but she ain't no beauty.'

'Please, Mrs Gall, tell me what you think.' Elizabeth made a last attempt. 'My little Posy, I can't bear to think that she is in danger. Could Matty be with Phoebe, and could they harm her?'

Mrs Gall looked away, out of the window where Dickens could see the smoke rising from the factory chimneys, and from the tile kilns, and in the silence, he could hear the shouts of workmen, the sounding of hammers, of cartwheels, footsteps going by. Life going on. Two little girls drowned in a pond. Two other girls lost, one perhaps a danger to the other. And the Dutch clock ticking away the time. But the canary was silent in his cage.

They waited. Mrs Gall looked back at them, her eyes troubled. 'I can't say, Missis, it's too big a thing — folk said, but I can't… Poor Alice, she ain't in 'er right mind. I couldn't say it.'

They went out into the grimy street, past the Fortune of War, to the junction where Topping was waiting. Elizabeth looked at Dickens. He knew what she was thinking. Mrs Gall hadn't said, but she had really. And that made it all worse, far worse.

14: A MARKED MAN

'What about Mrs Gall?' Dickens asked when they were back at Norfolk Street.

'I think she's a decent woman who was too loyal to say outright what she really thinks — or knows.'

'Suspicion against Matty and Phoebe, not just idle gossip?'

Elizabeth took a pan off the hob and poured out soup for them. 'Eat this — and there's bread. I made it this morning —' she sat down suddenly — 'oh, Charles, what are we to do? Posy should have been here, making bread with me. When I think — Phoebe's taken her with some man. I know what that might mean. That girl — I half believe that she and Matty are in something together.'

'That family, too — an unhappy lot.'

'Not much of a mother, Mrs Gall said, and a lively, intelligent girl left to mind the children — the mother hopeless, the baby not thriving, and Matty and Phoebe running wild when they could escape. Out all night. And beatings. All the children suffered, by the sound of it.'

'Joan Gall told me that Phoebe was one for the boys — the farm lads. Though Mrs Gall did say Joan wasn't to be trusted.'

'Precocious, I'd imagine, and Matty, a big lad for his age.'

'There was that suggestion at the inquest that a man was seen near the pond. Perhaps it was Matty, not the father, or the father saw something.'

'That's a job for Sam — when he's back. I mean, he could interview Mr Miller — if he has time. The Jaggard case. Oh, how am I to tell him?'

'We've got something, at any rate. Sam will find a way — there's Rogers and Stemp. He might be able to put them on to finding Jaggard. He'll know who investigated the drowning. He can find out what the police thought about the case.'

'Little Frankie — he must have seen Phoebe with Matty — and recently.'

'And not necessarily at the farm cottage. Phoebe could have met him in Belle Isle — Frankie could have been with her.'

'Or at The Copenhagen.'

'In a top hat and yellow gloves — disguised as a toff. Made his fortune at sea, perhaps.'

They heard the door and Scrap came in. 'Marked 'im — Darius 'Enchman.'

'How did you find out?' Dickens asked. Elizabeth went to get more soup.

'Seen 'im. Come this mornin'. Looked a bit rough, I thought. Me, I've a parcel — got one from the shop. Lookin' about me. Lost, see. 'E comes along. Did 'e know a Doctor Strong, I asks —'

'Strong?'

'Thought it out. The diction'ry man. You knows 'im. Copperfield's pal.'

Dickens was glad to hear Elizabeth laugh as he did. 'Of course — I made him up.'

''Xactly — so did I. Anyways, course 'e didn't know, an' it wouldn'ta mattered if there was a Doctor Strong 'bout there. Planned it all — if there was a Strong man, I'd 'ave knocked there an' asked, all polite, of course, for —' He gulped a spoonful of soup.

'Mr Micawber?' Dickens couldn't resist teasing.

'Think I was born yesterday? Everyone knows 'im. The toff goes up the steps an' I stands gazin' at the parcel like it was that Aaron Richard's magic box —' a literary man, Scrap, under Elizabeth Jones's tutelage — the tales of Harun al-Rashid, a favourite — 'an' open sesame, a voice says "Darius". Didn't sound too pleased. Darius, 'e's goin' in. Doesn't look back an' the other cove comes down the steps with a face like sour milk. Pays no attention to me, o' course.'

'Yellow gloves?'

'No gloves. Topper, though, an' 'e was the man with Phib Miller.'

'And he does frequent The Copenhagen.'

'I needs to follow 'im — see where 'e goes and 'oo with. I'll be someone else then, o' course. Not that they ever looks at a messenger lad.'

'You must be careful, Scrap. Mr Jones would not forgive me if anything happened to you as well as Posy.'

'I knows, Mrs Jones, an' I'll watch me step — an' 'is. What did that Mrs Miller tell you about Matty?'

'She didn't respond at all to the name, nor did she say anything about the two girls who drowned.'

'Pretendin'?'

'I don't think so — she's a sick woman. It's no use our asking again, but we did speak to a Mrs Gall who told us that the Miller family was always quarrelling — an unhappy lot.'

'Did this Mrs Gall say if she thought Matty 'ad killed them girls?'

'She knew about the gossip, but she wouldn't say what she really thought. She didn't want to be disloyal — they are her family.'

'But you thinks it might be true?'

'I am going to ask Mr Jones to find out about the case.'

'What next, then?' Scrap looked at Dickens. 'While I'm followin' this 'ere Darius.'

'Tonight, I'm going to the house of Lady Nora Lockhart, a friend of Mr Darius Henchman's. He might be there, so I don't think you need to be out tonight.'

'Could you, Scrap, stay here with Eleanor and Tom? I should like to accompany Mr Dickens. And I wonder if you would bring Tom from the shop later, while I fetch Eleanor from school?'

'If you thinks it'll 'elp? You an' Mr Dickens.'

'I do, but what are you thinking?'

Scrap was frowning. 'But Mrs Jones, what am I to tell Eleanor? If she asks about Posy. I can't lie to Nell, I can't.'

'Then I must tell her myself, and you must tell her what she wants to know if she asks you — I trust you, Scrap. You'll find the words.'

Scrap only nodded, and took the last of his soup, but Dickens saw the light in his eyes. Then he stood up. 'I'll be off, then — gotta bit o' spyin' to do. I'll bring Tom about five — give you time to —'

'He'll find the right words,' Elizabeth said when he had gone.

'He will, and in more ways than one. You've been teaching him to speak better, I've noticed.'

'Eleanor — when they're reading together. She's teaching him — very gently. I want him to improve, but without suggesting disapproval. There'll be a time when he'll be grown up and we'll have to think what he's going to do.'

'Police, he tells me.'

'Yes, I'm sure he will want to follow Sam, and I want him to be educated and get on. But he'll never forget where he came from. I don't want him to be ashamed — just to know that it's possible to be successful and education is one way to do it, but I'm leaving it to Eleanor for now. He has absolute faith in her.'

A wise woman, Dickens thought, Dickens whose shame about his labour in the blacking factory ran so deep that he could never speak of it, except once to his close friend, John Forster, and to Scrap, whom he told that he had worked before he went to school. Scrap had treated this revelation philosophically, as evidence of the unpredictable ways of the world. No, Scrap would not be ashamed. Wise beyond his years. And, he reflected ruefully, Charles Dickens with every gift that fortune could bestow, still concealing his past. He didn't say any of this, however, not even to Elizabeth, merely observing, 'Eleanor will trust him, too. Now, do you really want to come tonight?'

'I do, but not in this gown.'

'You would look lovely in sack cloth, my dear Elizabeth, but perhaps Lady Nora will expect something more —'

'Ladylike — Mrs Henchman's frills and flounces?' Elizabeth suggested. Dickens laughed. 'I saw them. A rather fetching bright green.'

'Arsenic in them, I shouldn't wonder. Tartan when I saw her. Dazzling — in its way. What about that dark red I saw you in once?'

Charles Dickens missed nothing, she thought. How like him to remember what one wore. 'Very well. Dark red it shall be. Let us hope that at least one Henchman will be there.'

'One in the eye for Missis when she sees you glide in with Sir Thomas Noon Talfourd, Judge of the Court of Common Pleas—'

'And Mr Charles Dickens — no less.'

15: IN COMPANY AND ALONE

Dickens was ready to go to collect Judge Talfourd from Russell Square and then Elizabeth Jones from Norfolk Street. Topping would drive them — they could have walked to Fitzroy Square, but it would be pleasing for Elizabeth to drive up to Lady Nora's house in a private carriage. Not that she cared about such things, but Lady Nora might. Mrs Henchman, if she saw them, certainly would. Useful, if they had to confront the ringlets and flouncings again.

Mamie and Katey were up in their room at the top of the house, and he'd been up to look at the pictures with which they had been decorating the walls. The house was quiet. The boys were in bed, Walter boarding at Mr King's, and Charley at Eton — home for the holidays soon. Catherine had taken to her bed with a bad headache. He ought to see if she were feeling any better.

She wasn't. She looked very pale, and he saw the marks of tears. He couldn't do anything — Georgina would sit with her later. *Let her sleep* — knowing he did not want to wake her up. But her eyes opened.

'You're going out.' Statement, but with a note of accusation.

'Yes, with Judge Talfourd — to a reception.'

'Where?'

'Lady Nora Lockhart.'

'But you don't know her — and, anyway, her reputation — I've heard what is said about her. I don't understand you.'

No, nor I you, he thought, but he only said, 'Sir Thomas Talfourd, Kate — you know him well. He is more than respectable. Anyway, it's really for Sam Jones — and Posy. To find out about a man called Darius Henchman, the man Scrap saw with Phoebe Miller.'

'When is Mr Jones back?'

'Tomorrow, we hope.'

'And Mrs Jones?'

That should have warned him. Mrs Jones had become Elizabeth not too long ago, and Catherine had given Posy a copy of her cookery book. 'What about her?'

'Is she to go to Lady Nora Lockhart's?'

Patience, he thought, but he regretted his impetuousness, and his decision to come upstairs. A fool to agree to Elizabeth's request. What would Sam think? Taking his wife to a house tainted with scandal, and, worse, exposing her to the Henchman family. What if Darius Henchman had taken Posy? He'd been dazzled, he admitted it, by Elizabeth's resoluteness and perspicacity, and he had enjoyed her company. That lunch in the kitchen. No use regretting. Elizabeth had already been to the Henchman house and so had he. Be firm.

'She is. Posy is very dear to her.'

'And Elizabeth Jones is very dear to you.'

'She is — as is her husband. Dear friends of ours. Elizabeth Jones is your friend. You know she is.'

'If you say so.'

Catherine closed her eyes. He left the room.

Lady Nora Lockhart — Lady Nora in her own right — her father had been a lord — was delighted to receive Charles Dickens. A handsome young man was summarily dispatched from her side to entertain Lady Sale. He didn't look too pleased. Lady Sale was even more famous than Lady Nora, but well past her sell-by date, which Lady Nora was most definitely not. In her forties, perhaps, but very well preserved. The most arresting blue eyes, sparkling and mischievous.

Judge Talfourd took Elizabeth under his wing — she did look lovely in her dark red with pearls in her ears, her dark hair shining. Simple elegance. Talfourd would look after her — a man of discretion and charm, and as he had reminded Catherine, a knight. For goodness' sake. Sam Jones knew Talfourd, anyway. He turned back to Lady Nora, rather more elaborate in rich blue velvet to match her eyes and diamonds, too.

'That's better, Mr Dickens. You were frowning. Not a reaction I usually elicit on first meeting. Are my diamonds askew?'

'Not at all, Lady Nora. I remembered something I had not done.'

'Always the way in life, I find. The thing not done is the thing regretted.'

Lady Nora turned out to be a shrewd and intelligent woman who talked fluently about his books and wittily about the latest fashions, Mrs Bloomer, in particular.

'You wouldn't —'

'I might — set a few spiteful cats among the pigeons, but I've already done that.' She was smiling, an impudent dimple at her mouth and blue eyes glittering. 'You'll know the gossip. The judge was a fearful old bore, and as old as time when I married him. I doubt he was ever young. Lockhart — I knew that name was an omen. I might have murdered him if he hadn't choked to death.'

'Why did you?' Dickens surprised himself by the intimacy of his question. Lady Nora had a surprising way about her. She was like a glass of cold champagne drunk too quickly which left you breathless and slightly tipsy.

'You mean why didn't I,' she said, laughing. 'Didn't think I'd get away with it. I know too many lawyers, but I know what you really meant, and you can guess very well the answer to that. A little money trouble at home. Lord Forest, my father, was not a prudent man — nor a pleasant one; my mother, sensible woman, died before the crash. My father had but one valuable asset — a beautiful young daughter, penniless, of course, but on offer in the marketplace. To be sold to the highest bidder. Age and character no bar to any reasonable offer. Very decorative, the asset. Very, very rich, the buyer. Assured of the asset's title, pedigree, and fertility. Disappointed in the last. So, to whom shall I leave my money? Plenty of young men about. Plenty of tall, handsome footmen.'

'That was gossip.'

She tapped him with her fan, her smile mischievous again. 'I really couldn't say. I daresay you really couldn't say if I asked you about the beautiful Mrs Jones after whom you looked most anxiously when Sir Thomas took her away.'

Dickens laughed, but he felt the heat at his neck. 'Mrs Jones is the wife of one of my dearest friends —'

'That doesn't stop a great many men I know.'

'I promise you I am not here as Mrs Jones's languishing swain. Mrs Jones's servant girl is missing. She went away with one Phoebe Miller — known as Phib — a servant of the Henchman family. You know them, I think?'

'I do. Poor Lily Henchman — that man is as sour as vinegar. She's a fool, but harmless. The young brother, charming, but all surface. On the make. I like young people, Mr Dickens, after twenty years of servitude. I like young men to fetch and carry for me, to entertain me, to flirt with me, but I am not a fool.'

'I know that by now. Darius Henchman was seen with Phoebe Miller, talking and laughing together. Rather too friendly, the witness thought.'

'Witness — ah, I understand now. Mrs Jones is the wife of the superintendent in the case of Sir Mordaunt Quist. His wife, an earl's daughter — made the same mistake that I did. Marriage à la mode, eh? I never liked him. Of course, my husband thought much of him. A judge, forsooth. Now, that was a scandal, and you gave evidence. Most intriguing, but I see that you are serious now. Tell me about Mrs Jones's servant.'

He told her all about Posy. 'She is an innocent, Lady Nora, and I fear that Phoebe Miller is not.'

'And you fear that Miss Miller has been tempted away by Darius Henchman, and you wish to know about that young man. Debts, drink, gambling, and his brother does not know the half. I haven't encouraged him since I discovered that he tempted one of my maids to steal a valuable snuff box. Of course, I could not prove that, but I believed her — a poor, silly sheep of a thing whose head was turned. Pretty, of course. I didn't sack her, but I found another place for her. With Lady Pancras, who has no visitors — of any kind.'

Dickens laughed. He knew the ancient Lady Pancras — deaf as a post and famed for her ill-temper. 'But you have Mr and Mrs Henchman here.'

'For her sake — it means much to her to be invited. I know what it is to be married to a cold man. And, besides, I rather enjoy that cold man's discomfort at his wife's foolish chatter. Now, you send Mrs Jones to talk to me while you circulate. Mr Henchman is over there. Go and get the measure of him.'

Dickens found that he could not be bothered to make polite conversation with the Henchmen. No letter of recommendation in Julius Henchman's flinty countenance. A handsome man, but a cold one, Dickens thought. He was standing slightly apart from his plump wife, a man of few words, it seemed, who was obviously irritated by his wife's twitterings about a dinner invitation which Dickens evaded by hinting that his wife was unwell just now. Not that Mr Henchman seemed the slightest bit interested in entertaining Mr Dickens, or anybody for that matter. Dickens didn't mention Phoebe or Posy. He could not have borne to see Henchman's fishy eye turn to ice at the mention of servants. Mr Crouch appeared at an opportune moment to talk business, and Dickens slid away.

He saw Lady Nora deep in conversation with Elizabeth, and sight of sights, Mr Decker, the pawnbroker. He liked Lady Nora even more at that moment. They were all three laughing. Elizabeth Jones looked beautiful, too.

'Conspiracy?' he asked.

'Just idle chatter about my neighbours, Mr Dickens. You know Mr Decker, of course — he is well acquainted with my neighbours. I'm sure that Mrs Jones will tell you about them.'

'I will indeed, but now I must ask Mr Dickens to take me home. It has been a great pleasure to meet you, Lady Nora.'

'And you, my dear. I shall expect you again — with the gallant Superintendent Jones.' Her teasing blue gaze turned on Dickens. 'And you, of course, Mr Dickens. I wouldn't leave you out.'

Talfourd was in deep conversation as they passed. Dickens signalled his thanks, and he and Elizabeth went out to walk the short distance to Norfolk Street. Lady Nora's observations about Darius Henchman and her advice to Elizabeth that she ought to talk to her former maid who might have some knowledge of Darius's friends preoccupied them as they walked. Sam, Elizabeth said, would advise on that, and they laughed about Lady Nora's comment that she would be entranced to meet Superintendent Jones of Bow Street, who must be a remarkable man —

'To have such a remarkable wife — I heard her,' Dickens said.

'You'll come in? Scrap will want to know everything.'

'No, I ought not to. Catherine —'

He met her candid eyes and she saw the misery in his. She had seen it before, sometimes when he was caught off guard — two points of darkness in the brilliant light. She only knew about his marriage what she had observed herself; she knew that it was different from her own. Faults on both sides, no doubt, but she was fond of him. She couldn't help it.

'Tomorrow, then — when you can —'

Footsteps behind them and Sam Jones's voice asking, 'And where have you two been?'

Elizabeth's eyes lit up as he came to them and took his wife's outstretched hand.

Dickens left them. Very glad to see Sam. No, he wouldn't come in. He'd come to Bow Street tomorrow. He'd to go to the magistrates' court to see about a girl for the home.

'Something up?' Sam asked, looking after the retreating figure.

'I'm afraid so.' Elizabeth's joy dissolved. She would have to tell him.

Dickens walked away to turn left along Tottenham Street, past the window of Mr Dodd's shop where he and his family had first lodged when he was a small boy lost in wonder at the sight of the teeming city. And then into Gower Street, where his mother had opened a school in the north part — a school to which not a single young lady had come. And then the blacking factory, and the first knowledge of shame. Scrap would be spared that, for he had Elizabeth Jones and Eleanor Brim. To be loved — that was the thing, to be cherished. His mother had never made him feel that.

He didn't know where he was going, but he found himself in Keppel Street, where his father had died in March at the house of Doctor Davey at number thirty-four, and Catherine had been in Malvern for the water cure for her headaches. And Dora, his baby girl, had died in April.

That was the damnable thing about London. Everywhere he went the past came, too, dragging like a chain. The present a blank tonight, empty of hope. And the future? Tavistock House was but a step away, but he turned into Russell Square

A girl emerged from a shop doorway and grabbed at his coat, a haggard white face in the gaslight, two hectic spots of red and a tawdry satin dress, cut so low that he could see the bones of her, green feathers in her hair. He smelt the gin and rottenness on her breath as she whispered her hoarse words of invitation. He pushed her away, suddenly angry and despairing. How dared she? But that's what they did, what they were trained to say and do. That's what their pimps made them, the ones who took innocent young girls from the streets. She fled, cursing him in the foulest language. Oh, it was hopeless. Iron-hearted London.

He went up to Tavistock Square, where he saw lights in his own house. He opened the gate, dread in his heart. Bereft, and suddenly intensely lonely.

16: THE TRAMPING GIRL

Things looked better in the morning. They often did, he reflected, thinking on the anxieties of haunting, sleepless nights when night's black agents swooped upon their prey. Well, they'd swooped away now. Time to be up and doing.

First, he took up his pen to write to Judge Talfourd, inviting him and his wife to dine. Talfourd was fond of Catherine. He always made much of her, and it might help if Talfourd were to make reference to Lady Nora Lockhart as a particular friend. He wrote to Mark Lemon, too, with the same request. Kate enjoyed the company of old friends. Lemon could always make her laugh. Mrs Bloomer might come up in the conversation.

Alfred, the crossing-sweeper, whose pitch was outside the iron gates of Tavistock House, greeted him cheerfully. Dickens asked about his chest, which was often "somethin' chronic" in the cold weather, and received the intelligence that things wasn't so bad; howsumever, Alfred could do without the east wind, but the rain was awright as it made folk glad ter 'ave the street cleaned fer 'em, though the damp got on the chest. Still an' all — receiving Dickens's tuppence — yer'd ter give yer feathers a shake an' get along the best way yer could. Business looked up in winter, fer the families woz at 'ome an' yesterday he'd taken more than a shillin'.

Dickens went on, giving his own metaphorical feathers a shake. *More than a shillin'*, he murmured, an' get along the best way yer can. A lesson, indeed.

In her cell at the magistrates' court, Dickens contemplated the tramping girl. A poor, ignorant, ragged girl. She still had some of the freshness of the country girl about her, and hopeful, innocent brown eyes. A pretty girl of about sixteen, he judged. She had been on the tramp for three or four years — she couldn't remember exactly. Her father — she didn't know where he went — just woke up one day an' 'e was gone, an' the farmer wanted the cottage. Went ter be a milkmaid on another farm, but then she wasn't needed no more. Picked fruit sometimes, an' a girl told 'er 'bout London. That's where Ma 'ad gone — an' she thought p'raps she'd find 'er...

Dickens regarded the little face, which looked sad and bewildered. She was, perhaps, remembering a cottage where a mother had lived, but somehow, somewhere, she had lost her, and the father who had left her without a word. He felt she was truthful; there was a gentle manner about her which impressed him.

He asked her where she had come from, and his ears pricked up when she said Bull's Cross. That was north of London. 'Can you remember how you came into London?'

There was a long road through a place called Holloway, where she'd slept in a shed and had eaten a few apples, for which she was very sorry. She'd had water from a horse trough and the next morning she had limped on. She showed Dickens her bruised ankle which had been hurt when she had a fall. Some boys had thrown stones at her. There was another long road where she'd seen some chimneys and some queer pointed roofs.

The tile kilns, Dickens thought. So, she had been on the Belle Isle road.

And she had seen a blacksmith and asked for water, which he had given her, as well as some bread and a penny.

'And on Friday afternoon, did you —'

She looked blank. She didn't know what day it was when she had started her journey. Dickens had worked backwards from the day of her court appearance on Tuesday, and her night in the police cell on Monday after she had tried to get into the workhouse. She knew that she had spent two nights by the canal on an abandoned barge and the next day — Dickens thought that must be the Sunday — she'd gone to look for the workhouse. By then she was starving. She had offered the watchman at the workhouse her penny. She thought you could pay. He said he'd see, but then he sent her away. She didn't get her penny back, and the policeman had said it was a likely story —

'On that road from the blacksmith's, did you see anyone? A young man, perhaps, with two young ladies?'

'There was a carriage, sir, near the canal, an' a gentleman looking at the 'orse's leg, and two young ladies sittin' in the carriage.'

It took a good deal of patience to elicit any detail about the carriage and the people. The carriage was black with red on the wheels — in the middle — red circles. The gentleman wore a black coat and a top hat. Dickens didn't want to feed her information about the girls' bonnets and cloaks. He knew she would want to please him. If he said a brown bonnet, she would agree.

She had rested at a gateway into a field — her foot was very sore. She thought she might sleep under the hedge. No one noticed her. The gentleman seemed to be angry at the horse — called it a brute. She didn't know what Dickens meant by a gentleman's voice — it was just angry. She knew about that. She couldn't say much about the ladies —

''Cept fer a feather, sir — noticed a green feather —'

Did it come from a bird? she'd wondered. She knew hens and geese, and crows, and sparrows. Blackbirds, too — blue eggs, they had. Pretty. Was it a peacock? she asked Dickens. She'd heard of them up at a great house where —

She broke off to look at him sorrowfully. 'Where I lived once in the cottage — home, sir, I remember it now — home —'

That nearly did break his heart. She had just tramped on and on, not thinking, not remembering, only surviving, not knowing any why or wherefore, until his questions had opened up a forgotten past — the memory of a place called home. He felt sorry that he had caused her pain and he thought of Posy, lost and bewildered, tramping unknown streets, or worse. Too many lost children, abandoned, unloved, uncherished. He left it at that. She looked too dazed to take any more. He promised her that she would be looked after — she would not have to tramp the streets again. A kind lady would come for her, and she would have some new clothes and some good food. He made to go. He would have to speak to Gilbert à Beckett to tell him that Mrs Morson would come for the girl.

'Red ribbons, sir,' she said with that heart-breaking smile, 'saw 'em.'

17: JOHN THE BAPTIST

Cora Davies and Joey Speed were committed for trial on charges of possession of stolen goods and forged notes. They were to be held on remand in Newgate.

'Serves 'em right,' Sergeant Rogers said to Sam Jones.

'So it does.'

Cora Davies had been adamant in her denial that Jaggard intended to go to America with her, but she had to admit that the jewels in her possession were stolen property. Joey Speed stuck to his story that he did not know that the notes were forged, and that he did not know the name of the man to whom he had sold the jewels. The evidence of the notes, and the property of the murdered Sir William Pell, and the fact that the prisoners were connected to Martin Jaggard, the coiner and suspected murderer, convinced the magistrate that both should be sent for trial. Sam Jones was glad to have them out of the way. Transported to Australia, he hoped. His intention had been to go to Clerkenwell to the lodgings of Joey Speed's ma to find out if Jaggard had been there. The notes, the very skilful forgeries, confirmed that some new business was afoot. Cora Davies had said so — a new associate. But now —

Sergeant Rogers looked at his chief and saw the anguish in his eyes. He wasn't thinking of Jaggard, Rogers knew.

'Scrap told me everything. That girl, Phib Miller, must have taken Posy with this gent in the top hat and yellow gloves.'

'Look about you, Alf — how many top hats and yellow gloves, do you see?'

It was true. You didn't notice most times, but now Rogers looked, there seemed to be yellow gloves everywhere. 'Mr Dickens,' he said, 'when's he coming?'

'In half an hour. I had a note this morning.'

There had been no time to do much for Elizabeth this morning as he had to be at the magistrates' court first thing, but last night, she had told him, and he had known that she knew very well that Posy might be impossible to trace. Elizabeth had told Eleanor. She had known that they couldn't keep it a secret any longer. And they couldn't lie; they couldn't invent a family for Posy — someone she'd gone to stay with. In the morning, Eleanor had looked at Sam with grave eyes. She knew about loss — she had watched her father die.

'Will you find her?'

He dared not promise. 'I will do my best, and I have Mr Dickens to help and Sergeant Rogers and Constable Stemp.'

'And Scrap. Scrap told me that he's been looking. He said that you would all do your best.'

'Of course — Scrap will find clues. All my men will be looking. Mama and Mr Dickens have already been to Phoebe's house and to her employers. And we know that they were with a gentleman. I think we can find him.'

'And you'll tell me everything — you won't pretend.'

'I will not pretend, my dearest girl.'

'And Tom, what shall we tell him?'

'That she has lost her way, but that she is with her friend —'

'I'll tell him. I won't pretend, but I'll explain that sometimes people do get lost, but that — they do get found, don't they, Papa?'

'They do. And very often.'

'Phoebe wasn't Posy's friend.'

'Why do you say that?' asked Elizabeth.

'She didn't suit Posy. She was silly and spiteful, and teased her about the butcher's boy. She said he liked Posy and that she could tell that Posy liked him, which she doesn't. He's a nasty boy — he teased Posy and pinched her, and I saw him kick Poll. She barked at him.'

'You should have told me.'

'I told him off and said I'd tell the butcher if he did it again and he had to leave Posy alone.'

Elizabeth glanced at Sam. Eleanor had a strength of character and she could see through pretence. Suffering had made her a wise little person. She would deal with Tom — it was best to leave her to it; Tom was her brother whom she had looked after throughout their father's decline, and for whom she still felt responsible. Tom had never known their mother. Eleanor and Tom had had a life together before Elizabeth and Sam Jones. Elizabeth knew by instinct when she was not needed, though she ached to kiss the child she loved as deeply as she had loved her own dead daughter, and tell her it would be all right, but it might not be, and they would all have to face that. They would all need strength of character.

And poor Sam, who had looked so weary when they had gone into the house. He had gone to Bow Street from the Rochester train. His face had turned white when she told him. She had longed for his coming, longed for his comforting arms, but it was she whose strength had been needed first.

She had bidden him goodbye in the early morning. 'Am I to go to see Lady Nora's former maid?'

'Only Lady Nora knows about that?'

'Charles and Mr Decker. Lady Nora and I had a very quiet talk with Mr Decker, who knew about the snuff box. He remembered you — the case of Captain Valentine.'

'Ah, yes, he can be trusted, I'm sure.'

'I would say so. I shall go then?'

'Yes, I know you want to do something.'

'Anything, Sam — we have to find her.'

Dickens came to Bow Street, as punctual as clockwork. He saw immediately the strain in Sam's face and anxiety in Rogers's usually cheerful countenance.

'Anything new?' asked Jones. 'Elizabeth and Scrap have told us what you've got on the Miller family, and that drowning. I'll look into that — speak to whoever investigated. Inspector Fall of N Division will know. And Darius Henchman — what do you think?'

Dickens told them about the tramping girl, the carriage with red wheel hubs and the black horse with one sock, and that he was going to Clerkenwell to ask the manager at Mr Decker's shop if he had seen Darius Henchman recently and whether in the company of a young woman — green feather and red ribbons.

'Elizabeth said she spoke to Mr Decker at Lady Nora's reception. Darius Henchman sounds like a possible candidate, given what Scrap said about seeing him in conversation with Phoebe Miller.'

'He's a regular at The Copenhagen, too —- gambling on the boxing and wrestling — losing money, and a lot of IOUs flying about.'

'Rogers and Stemp and I are off to Clerkenwell, too, in search of a Livvie Slack — known to be acquainted with Martin Jaggard. A lot of coining goes on in Clerkenwell.'

'You didn't find him, then.'

'No, but we've put away Cora Davies and one Joey Speed, who had forged notes on him. He admitted he'd sold some of

Pell's jewellery, for which he was given the forged notes. Didn't know the man who bought the jewels, of course.'

'He got the jewels from Jaggard?'

'He wouldn't say so — too frightened, but the magistrate drew his own conclusions. Speed knew he'd be going down for possession anyway. I'll come with you to the pawn shop while Rogers and Stemp look for Livvie Slack.'

'I'll get Stemp, sir — we've to change into plain clothes. I'll come back in a few minutes.'

'We'll maybe find out more about Henchman —'

'Oh, we will if that carriage is his. He'll have more than a few questions to answer. Your witness — very handy.'

'Where did Speed say he sold the jewellery?'

'At John's, so he said, and I'm wondering which one. He couldn't remember, he said — a likely story.'

'I know Mr Foster at The St. John of Jerusalem in St. John's Square. I shouldn't think he would be harbouring forgers.'

'Oh, some of them look very respectable — quite the swells.'

'I know, but Mr Foster is an author — of *Ye History of Ye Priory of St John of Jerusalem* — yes, *Ye History*. Ye honest innkeeper, Mr Foster.'

Dickens was glad to see Jones smile as he asked, 'And being an author and scholar precludes him from consorting with the criminal underworld?'

'Very droll, Sammy my boy — my consorting, as you put it, is purely in the interests of helping the police with their enquiries.'

'And I'm grateful — truly. For what you and Scrap, and Elizabeth have done so far.'

'Your wife, Mr Jones, is a prodigy of excellence in the detecting line. She realised that the little boy, Frankie, was only a baby at the time of the drownings.'

'She's going to see Lady Nora's former maid — but that's all, Charles. We don't know enough about Darius Henchman. When he realises questions are being asked, and if he is the guilty party, I don't want him knowing too much about my wife. You know, and I know, and Elizabeth knows, why a young man might take away two young girls — one of them an innocent —'

'I know, Sam. You didn't mind my taking Elizabeth to Lady Nora's?'

'No, no — she said she went in with Judge Talfourd. So far, she's hedged about by powerful people, and the Henchmen — Lord, I'm doing it now — it's what Scrap kept saying — know that I'm a superintendent at Bow Street, but still —'

He was interrupted by the entrance of Rogers and Stemp, the latter bearing an uncanny likeness to some Old Testament prophet in his shabby greatcoat, moth-eaten comforter, and lugubrious countenance. *The end of the world*, thought Dickens, and more than nigh. He couldn't help smiling as he realised that Stemp's disguise was to be that of an itinerant preacher, evidenced by the battered shovel hat and dog collar. Non-conformist, of course. Stemp had a streak of the Puritan in him. Boys would probably throw stones at him, but Stemp wouldn't care. Treat them to a bit of hell fire, probably.

'Very alarming, Mr Stemp.'

'Meant ter be, Mr Dickens. While they're chuckin' their rotten veg at me, I'll be watchin' fer Livvie Slack an' whatever fancy-man she's in with.'

Rogers was, disappointingly, just a labouring man — with his boy. Scrap had appeared with a sooty face and a mangy fur hat jammed over his hair — as unlike the messenger boy outside the Henchman house as it was possible to be. Broken boots and ragged trousers completed the wretched portrait of abject poverty. Scrap, hearing of the Clerkenwell connection to Darius Henchman, had, with his practical logic, pointed out to Superintendent Jones that he was, after all, the only one who had actually seen Darius Henchman. 'Topper an' yeller gloves ain't no use as a description,' he had said.

They went on their way, Stemp having been helped into his sandwich board which bore the legend: *Vengeance is Mine.* Dickens noted that the words, *Saith the Lord,* were missing. Stemp's vengeance would be quite enough for any sinner.

'The Old Baptist's Head,' Dickens said when they had gone.

'Stemp?'

Dickens laughed. 'Prophet in his own time, but no, as in the pub in John Lane — though the sign there has a look of Stemp in his most recent incarnation.'

'And there's The Jerusalem tavern in St. John Street.'

'John 1, John 2, John 3 — very biblical.'

'Den of thieves, probably, in Clerkenwell. Come on, we'll try your Mr Foster first — just in case.'

The archway of the old Priory of St. John of Jerusalem still stood, and within its solid walls was to be found Mr Foster's inn. Mr Foster, scholar and author, had adorned the wall with a large oil painting of knights setting out for a jousting tournament. Inside was the coffee room where there was, allegedly, a chair in which Doctor Johnson had sat when he was writing for *The Gentleman's Magazine*, founded by Edward Cave in 1761. Cave's portrait by Hogarth, allegedly, was up on the wall. Goldsmith had been a regular here, too, and David Garrick. Crimson upholstery and suits of armour completed the medieval theme established by the oil painting.

Mr Benjamin Foster, a suitably Falstaffian figure of a man, was delighted to welcome his fellow author and to offer coffee, or there was his renowned Chivalrie gin. Dickens hoped it hadn't been aged since the time of the knights — or even Doctor Johnson. However, they declined the offer of refreshment. Dickens knew that Sam was anxious to get to the matter in hand.

Mr Foster did not know of a Joey Speed, and he certainly did not welcome forgers into his house. Dickens forbore to glance at Doctor Johnson's chair. Men of letters and men of business were Mr Foster's customers. He would, of course, be honoured to entertain Mr Dickens and his friend, Superintendent Jones, to a comfortable dinner at any time. However, The Old Baptist's Head would be worth their while trying — Mrs Younger entertained a more varied type of customer, he explained with a wink, as he pressed a copy of his olde crusaders into Dickens's hand.

The Old Baptist's head on its charger looked a bit weather-worn, not at all like Stemp, resembling if anything a faded piece of mutton served centuries ago. Traces of the old inn were gone, the black and white timbers replaced with stucco. Probably not the place for men of letters.

Mrs Younger, an amiable woman in her forties with a capable chin and hands, was able to tell Superintendent Jones and his colleague, Mr Dickens, that Joey Speed was an occasional customer. In fact, he'd been in a week or two back — came in to see a guest they had staying — a French gentleman from Paris.

Speed, forged notes, a Frenchman from Paris. That was interesting. 'What was the Frenchman's business?' Jones asked.

'Jewellery, I believe, sir. Joey Speed had some to sell, I imagine. Lot o' folk deal in gold and jewellery roundabout here. I saw money change hands.'

'Notes?'

'And cash — I heard the clink of coins as well, but I didn't see what Speed was sellin'.'

'The Frenchman's name?'

'Mister Tait — oh, I'll have to look in the book — just a minute —' she reached under the bar counter to retrieve her register of guests — 'now, a couple of weeks ago. Yes, here he is. Mr Tait.' She showed them the entry: *M. Jean Baptiste Tête, jeweller, Paris.*

'Mr John Baptist Head,' Dickens said, *'tête* — it means head.'

She looked at him, astonished. 'Oh, I never thought — he spelled it out an' I thought it was like French for Tait — it was the way he said it, an' I just called him Mr Tait.' Dickens repeated the name in a French accent. 'Oh, sir, what a fool I am. Do you think it was a false name?'

'I should think so,' Jones said. 'Did he pay his bill?'

'Oh, yes, sir, no trouble about that.'

'And the bank accepted the notes?'

'Just a five-pound note, sir — I put it in the till. It's long gone now. Are you talking about forgery?'

'Possibly, but keep it to yourself, Mrs Younger, if you please. If it was a forgery, then I'll need to investigate the possibility of more forgeries in circulation. How long did Mr Tête stay?'

'Two nights, sir — there wasn't much to pay.'

'Now, tell me what he looked like.'

''Bout as tall as you, sir —' turning to Dickens — 'similar build, very dark hair and eyes, moustache, short beard. Well-dressed — smart, you know. Very charmin'.'

'You don't know where he was going?'

'Into the city, he said, on business.'

Jones warned her again to say nothing about forgery, but to come to Bow Street if Mr Tête appeared again. 'Don't alert him, Mrs Younger — just let me know as soon as you can.'

Out in the street, Jones explained to Dickens the significance of the Frenchman and Speed's possession of the forged notes. 'There was a forging operation broken up in Paris — coins and notes. One man escaped. He was a Belgian.'

'Escaped to London, maybe? Passing himself off as a Frenchman.'

'And a few years ago, there was a to-do about Belgian banknotes being forged in London and sent to Belgium. Thousand-franc notes. They were detected because the paper wasn't right — more opaque and slightly green. Speed's notes were very nearly right, but Stemp, being suspicious of Speed, and the connection with Jaggard and coining, had a good look in daylight. The paper was too dark.'

'Belgium, Paris — suggestive. You think Jaggard is moving up in the world?'

'Why not? There have been forgeries of Austrian notes, Norwegian notes — make 'em in London and distribute them through your continental associate. The question is: where?'

'And why kill Sir William Pell?'

'Jaggard needed money or valuables to recruit his French or Belgian partner, Monsieur Tête, masquerading as a jeweller. Monsieur Tête gets the jewels in exchange for samples of forged notes which Jaggard's crew, no doubt, are intent on copying. What could be easier?'

'And Jaggard would have known all about Pell's wealth.'

'Or made it his business to find out. He simply walked out of Pell's house one day and didn't come back. No one had seen or heard of him until he turned up one day, some weeks before the murder. Saw Pell, but Pell didn't say anything about it —'

'Casing the joint?'

'Don't know, but it's an odd detail. The other servants hadn't liked him, but Pell didn't bother about such matters.'

'Mind on higher things.'

'He probably didn't notice Jaggard had gone. Even a valet's just a servant to some rich folks.'

'Jaggard would have resented that.'

'So, he would — his mind was on higher things, too, as in how to get rich. I was struck by the violence of the attack.'

'Something happened, perhaps, when Jaggard called on him?'

'You could be right, Charles. Now I think about that violence, there was hatred in it.'

'Hatred for a man who didn't see him. Galling for a man like Jaggard. All that ego — that monstrous sense of self. He didn't seduce any of the maids, did he?'

'Now, that is an interesting thought. The maid who took Jaggard's fake card to Pell had been dallying in the mews with her sweetheart. And more than dallying, it seems. She hadn't been in service at Pell's when Jaggard was there, and she maintained she believed the stranger was from Pell's acquaintance. He gave her two shillings — that kept her quiet, too. It might be worth questioning her again. Could be a lead to him, but now, let's get after Darius Henchman. Stemp and Rogers can look after Livvie Slack for now. And, later, I'll get Inspector Grove onto the Frenchman — see if anyone else came across him hereabouts.'

18: SILVER AND GOLD

They did not need to go to Mr Decker's shop for as they were about to cross the road, a carriage passed them, a carriage with red hubs on its wheels drawn by a horse with one white sock. It turned into the archway next to The Old Baptist's Head.

They stood in the archway leading to the inn's stable yard and watched as a young man descended and turned to help his companion, a slight, well-dressed young woman in a dark green bonnet and matching cape. The young man was well-dressed, too, in his top hat and yellow gloves. A wretched-looking boy of about ten years or so darted out — probably wanting a penny to hold the horse, but the ostler clipped him round the ear and he ran past them, screeching abuse. The man and woman went into the inn.

Dickens and Jones went back into the inn by the front door. Mrs Younger stared to see them back again.

'A young man and a young lady have just come in. I want you to find out where they are sitting and to come back and tell me if you know the gentleman.'

Mrs Younger returned to tell them that the couple had asked for a private room and lunch. Mrs Younger had established them in a quiet corner of the parlour where they would take lunch. She did not recognise either of them.

'I need to talk to them, so I would be obliged if we might not be disturbed. They may not need lunch.'

Jones's face was stern as a hatchet as they went in. If it were Darius Henchman, he was going to have a hard time — he might be laughing now, but in a few moments, he'd be quaking in his boots.

Jones wasted no time. 'Mr Darius Henchman?'

The young man looked up. Dickens saw a soft, appealing face surmounted by long, fair, curly hair — a handsome young man. Young — and foolish, no doubt. Maybe criminal. Red lips and good teeth, little moustache. Weak chin, though. Frockcoat and embroidered waistcoat. The top hat and yellow gloves were on the table. The young lady looked up, too. Very pretty, with glossy ringlets and very dark eyes. Well-dressed in her dark green mantle and bonnet.

'Yes, who wants to know?'

'Superintendent Jones of Bow Street and Mr Charles Dickens —' Jones ignored the look of astonishment — 'in search of your sister-in-law's kitchen maid, Phoebe Miller, and her friend, Posy — seen in your company at The Copenhagen Inn, and by the bridge over the canal in Maiden Lane. Your horse, one white sock, was lame. Those two girls are missing. You can tell me what you know here or at Bow Street.'

Darius Henchman couldn't speak, though his face turned very red. The young woman simply stared. There was nowhere for them to go. Superintendent Jones towered over them. Dickens stood still, too.

Jones gave Darius Henchman no quarter, firing his questions as from a loaded pistol. Darius Henchman sweated but stuck to his story that he had seen the girls in the lane by The Copenhagen where he was waiting to meet Miss Hormel — indicating his companion — they were to take a drive into the country, but Miss Hormel had not come. Phoebe had told him that she was going back into town, and would he take them in his carriage.

'And the other girl — did she want to go?'

'She did look a bit bewildered, but Phoebe whispered something to her, and I said I'd take them, but, as you have said, your witness saw me by the carriage — the horse had picked up a stone.'

'Where did you take them?'

'Phoebe told me that she had an appointment at a hotel to meet a friend.'

'Which hotel?'

'She didn't say the name — just Union Street, where I dropped them near the station, and then I went in search of Miss Hormel.'

Jones looked hard at the young woman, who seemed perfectly composed. 'And where were you to be found?'

'At my lodging, monsieur.'

Good Lord, Dickens thought, *French*, but Jones kept his countenance. 'Where?'

'In Fitzroy Street with Mrs Barn —' she stumbled over the name — '*excusez-moi* — my English — Mrs Barn-ham —' She pronounced the "h". 'You may check. I have been there for several weeks.'

'And you came from France?'

'Yes, from Paris. I wish for a change — I have money from my aunt. I was her companion, but *hélas*, she is dead. I wish to see London, and I meet Mr 'Enchman in the Square and we become friends — there is nothing wrong in that, I 'ope.'

'Nothing in the world, Miss Hormel. May I ask why you did not keep your appointment with Mr Henchman at The Copenhagen?'

'I have some business to arrange at the bank and I miss the time, but all is well now. Mr 'Enchman, he forgives me, as you see.'

'Clerkenwell, Mr Henchman — what brings you here?'

'Just business.' Darius Henchman was trying very hard to retain his composure, but his cheeks were still red; Dickens could see the pulse beating in his cheek.

'At Mr Decker's premises, perhaps. His manager seems to know you well.'

Henchman steeled himself to assert his authority as a gentleman of means. 'It is my business, I presume, if I wish to purchase a few trifles from a reputable dealer.'

'And pawnbroker. There is the matter of a snuff box belonging to Lady Nora Lockhart.'

Henchman mastered his anger, though an even deeper flush gave him away. 'Stolen by a maid, I believe. And, yes, I have pawned a thing or two — one sometimes finds oneself in a pecuniary difficulty. It is common practice and not a crime.'

'No, indeed, Mr Henchman. Very well, if you can tell me no more about Miss Miller and her friend, we will bid you good day.'

Dickens bowed and said, smiling, 'Good day, Mademoiselle Hormel.'

A self-possessed and knowing face smiled back with a flutter of long eyelashes. A calculating gleam in those dark eyes. She saw a gentleman and liked it.

Very knowing, and not as young Mr Henchman imagines, Dickens thought as he followed Jones out of the parlour.

There was no time to discuss the matter once they were out in the street. Jones was anxious to find Rogers, Scrap and Stemp. He wanted Darius Henchman and his lady to be watched.

They threaded their way through a muddy maze of little streets up to Bridewell Walk — the nuns, whose convent had stood hereabouts, had long departed. Here was grovelling poverty, filth, vice of every kind, starvation, fever, and dereliction. Houses simply tumbled down without warning, the residents moving on to any rotten stable, or shed, or workshop, or cellar that might accommodate them — ten or twenty or more — until that collapsed in a rain of dust and debris. No prayers could answer that degradation, except those for light, air, and sanitation. Clearly no one above was listening, Dickens thought, nor anyone below — he had given evidence to the Metropolitan Sanitary Commission. Clerkenwell had somehow been missed by the commissioners.

There were ragged children everywhere, barefoot, pinched with cold, homeless, probably — nothing to do but steal for their bread, and a gang of boys watched them from behind the railings of the churchyard — like a row of prisoners, all hard eyes and snarling mouths. The same wild beast look of the child who had run from the inn yard. What was horribly chilling was the banging of their heavy sticks on the railings — a drumbeat of menace. The sound set Dickens's teeth on edge.

They hurried on to the inappropriately named Bridewell Walk, which had stood once in the shadow of the prison which had housed vagrants and prostitutes. Now it lay in the shadow of what was called the New Prison, not far from the workhouse and the Middlesex House of Correction. If the authorities thought that such stern neighbours might serve as a warning to the denizens of Clerkenwell, they were mistaken. The Lamb and Dove looked very busy — no sermons there. There was a labouring man with a boy lounging by a wall opposite.

'No sign of Livvie Slack,' Rogers said. 'Some old dame came totterin' out an' she's in the pub now — I assume it was Speed's ma, but no one else out front.'

'No one out the back except some kid sittin' on a windowsill. Looked right at me — nasty-lookin' cove.'

'There's a lot of lads hangin' about,' Rogers said. 'Stemp hasn't seen Livvie Slack. He's still walkin' the streets — no one's botherin' him now — a few stones were thrown and sticks bandied about, but they scarpered when he threatened 'em with damnation.'

'Right, we'll leave Livvie for now. Things have come up. Mr Dickens and I need to get to the pawn shop. Darius Henchman is at The Old Baptist's Head taking lunch with a lady. I'll get Stemp to keep his eye on them. You and Scrap to King's Cross — Union Street. A hotel — I don't know which one, but Phoebe Miller told Henchman that she had an appointment there. He said he only gave them a lift from The Copenhagen.'

They saw Constable Stemp, who looked thunderous as he stalked towards them — very much in the part, but he grinned as he saw them and told them he hadn't come across Livvie Slack. Jones sent him off to wet his whistle at The Old Baptist's Head and to keep his gimlet gaze on the lunching couple.

'Lemonade, I should think, Mr Stemp — you'll needs be a tee-totaller.'

'I might give a warnin' about the evils of drink, Mr Dickens,' Stemp said, arranging his eyebrows into the expression of a man about to consign his fellow mortals to the fiery furnace, and stumping by Dickens and Jones as if he had warned them of impending damnation.

The manager of Mr John Decker's silver-smithing and pawnbroking business had not dealt with Mr Darius Henchman for some time, but he had seen him that very morning going into the goldsmith's shop in Jerusalem Passage — something to sell, he hazarded. Mr Shadrack Argent bought jewellery to refashion into his own designs.

'We need to think about this,' Jones said as they went out.

Dickens pointed to the coffee house on the corner. 'There.'

They found a table in a conveniently dark corner — Lunt's Coffee House had been in business since the eighteenth century. Tallow candles, the smoke of thousands of pipes and cigars, and sea coal fires, and a gravyish smell in the air gave the place a dark brown atmosphere in which they could sit concealed. An obliging waiter skimmed to them to promise hot coffee and skimmed back again with his tray before they had time to look about them.

Jones drank some of his coffee and began, 'Darius Henchman seen with our girls in that carriage — maybe innocent, and now with a Frenchwoman in Clerkenwell; a presumed Frenchman gave a false name and exchanged some forged notes for some of Sir William Pell's jewellery from Joey Speed in Clerkenwell; Martin Jaggard, Cora Davies, Joey Speed and Livvie Slack — all in the coining business; all four of them connected to Clerkenwell —'

'Darius Henchman with a French lady seen going into a goldsmith's shop in Clerkenwell —'

'Exactly — there may be no connection, but to be on the safe side, you go to the goldsmith's. If Darius Henchman is involved in something nefarious, then I don't want him knowing that I've been asking. You'll find a story to tell Mr Argent and find out about Henchman. I'll go along to the police station to tell Inspector Shackell about Phoebe and Posy. He knows Clerkenwell. He'll know Livvie Slack — and about Jaggard.'

'Give him my compliments — I still owe him two bob for the cab he got for me that time.'

Jones remembered vividly the case of a missing governess from last year. 'Ah, yes, the day Mrs Curd threw her pot of beer at you. Duck this time, if Mr Argent proves tetchy.'

The silver-bearded Shadrack Argent inhabited an eighteenth-century house turned into a spacious shop in which glass cases piled up to the dark ceiling displayed his gleaming golden treasures and his silver. The glass cases which formed the counter showed gold watches, snuff boxes, rings, chains and bracelets and enamelled boxes. It smelt of money as well as sea coal and cigars. The workshop was in the brick vaulted cellars, remnants of the old priory.

He was a perfectly temperate man with amiably twinkling eyes and an air of composed wisdom who was quite ready to oblige Mr Dickens — whose books he had read with great pleasure. Dickens thought too late of Fagin, his thief and fence, hanged in Newgate, and of Oliver Twist, had up before Magistrate Fang for the theft of Mr Brownlow's pocket handkerchief at a bookstall a stone's throw away in Clerkenwell Green. Mr Argent, however, made no reference to that work, observing only that if Mr Dickens wished to purchase some golden trinket, he would give him a very good price, indeed.

Dickens had his story ready — it was one that had served before. 'It's research, Mr Argent, for my journal, *Household Words*. We like to inform our readers and appeal to their imagination — I thought that jewellery-making might appeal — how you fashion your treasures. The lump of gold into a chain, for instance — a necklace for a lady — a gift from a gallant lover. I'm writing a piece on pawnbroking, so I have been to Mr Decker's premises — when I saw a beautiful chain there, I wondered how it was made and he mentioned you.'

'You would wish to see my workshop?'

'Oh, indeed, but, perhaps, I might look at some jewellery and pick something with romance in it so that you could show how it is made —' he glanced down at the counter — 'nothing as prosaic as a watch chain for a gentleman — a ring, perhaps —' pointing to the gold ring which lay next to the chain, and hoping it might have belonged to Darius Henchman.

'Ah, those have just come in. No romance there, I'm afraid. A young gentleman needing ready cash, I imagine, came in this morning to sell — not to buy, though his lady was very pretty. French. He tried to sell me another chain, but it was merely pinchbeck — he seemed surprised. You'd be surprised, Mr Dickens, by the number of folk who try to pass off fakes. Some very good ones, but I always know.'

'How?'

Mr Argent picked up the chain. 'This one weighs about six ounces, worth about six guineas and ten shillings. I gave the young gentleman five pounds.' He placed the chain on his brass scales. 'Now, here are four and a half sovereigns to balance — see, this chain balances exactly. Pure gold.' He felt under his counter. 'Now, this one you see is lighter, so I know that it is made of silver and gold. And, for the purest gold, the customer should always see on the invoice the carat weight — if the invoice says only gold, then there is no guarantee. There are chains made of gold, silver, and copper — a customer might not know, but I know. There is jewellery made of base metal washed in gold — sold as gold in cheap shops, and there is jewellery made of zinc and electroplated with gold. Caveat emptor, as the lawyers say.'

'Indeed — and the ring here, is that genuine?'

'Oh, yes, I gave the young man its carat value. It is a gentleman's ring, though — the young man took it from his little finger.'

Dickens took the ring. It was heavy, but he saw that the initials were not those of Darius Henchman. He felt his heart quicken, but he did not say anything. Sam Jones would have to deal with this. He carried on as if he had not noticed anything.

'And such base pieces washed with gold or electroplated, who would make those?'

'As I say, cheap jewellers — many of those are honest enough, but there are criminals, of course, who try to sell to such as I, and those who set up as jewellers, using stolen bits of gold — shavings, clippings of money, wire — make some quick money and vanish.'

'Round here?'

'This is Clerkenwell, Mr Dickens. There are hundreds of little workshops — they come; they go. I have been here for thirty years and never have I sold that which is dishonestly described, or indeed, forged. This light chain is worth about three pounds.'

'And the pinchbeck one the young man brought in?'

'A few shillings at most, but someone might buy to sell on at a profit. As I say, there are many so-called jewellers in Clerkenwell.'

Dickens thought about Monsieur Jean Baptiste Tête. 'And do people often come in off the street to sell?'

'Oh, yes — especially if they need ready cash.'

'But a businessman, would he make an appointment?'

'Oh, yes, though we sometimes get a traveller looking to establish a connection.'

'From abroad, perhaps?'

'Certainly, but not of late.'

'Most interesting, Mr Argent. I shall certainly come back to see your workshop, if you could oblige me — or my secretary.' Dickens added the detail in case he had to send someone else to do more research. It would make a pretty article for *Household Words*, though Sam would prefer him to keep his distance.

In the passage, Dickens paused to put on his gloves. Mr Foster's crusaders fell out of his pocket. A little, shabby-looking thing, a bundle of tatters, shot out from a doorway and picked it up. Dickens thanked it and offered a penny. A pair of eyes glittered, snake-like, darting, calculating; a hand snatched and then it was gone. Whatever it had been — boy or girl — there had been something almost inhuman in that glance.

Dickens looked at the engraving inside the blue cover. *Engravers*, he thought, very necessary for the forging of banknotes. "This is Clerkenwell", so had said Mr Shadrack Argent. Forged coins, forged gold chains, stolen silver to be melted down, banknotes to be copied, no doubt. He went out of Jerusalem Passage and looked about him. Smith's clockmaking works, Winch's foundry for casting metal, finishing shops where wheels were cut, rings turned and dials silvered, warehouses, jewellery shops, goldsmiths, silversmiths — Nemiah Silverlock looked prosperous — instrument makers, more clockmakers, coin dealers, pawnbrokers, and in the dingiest of alleys, the dolly shops where the very poor pledged the clothes from their backs on Friday and redeemed them on Monday morning. You had to dress to look for work, but you had to eat on Sunday, and Saturday for that matter, but the children could go barefoot like the wretched child he had just seen, and there'd be dozens like him, hundreds probably.

And an empty engraver's shop which still bore the legend: *Stamps, Seals and Dies, Arms and Crests Engraved on Metal or Stone. Coffin Plates.* The improbably named Blucher Death had been the proprietor. Gone to his maker, perhaps.

In this teeming, hissing, hammering, grating place of machinery and steam engines, and tools, and vice, and ragged humanity, and gold, and silver, and jewels, there was a place, no doubt, for the establishment of a secret, prosperous new business where in some hidden vault, money was literally to be made.

And what had Darius Henchman to do with forgers and coiners — and murder? The initials on the ring he had sold were 'WTP' — William Talbot Pell, perhaps.

19: THE RING AND THE FLOWER

'Very friendly, they was,' Constable Stemp reported at Bow Street. 'Well, she was. That young man looked a bit overcome — she ain't as young as 'e thinks. What they call a siren, if you asks me.'

No one did, but they looked on Stemp as if as at an oracle. Dickens didn't look at Jones, who merely said, 'Go on.'

'A lad, Mr Jones, that's wot 'e looked like, an' she all lips an' teeth. I thought she might eat 'im, never mind 'er lunch. She's an appetite, that one — wine, too,' he added in his Old Testament mode, 'an' 'e 'adn't much appetite fer 'is food — somethin' upset 'im, mebbe, or someone —'

'No doubt — she needs investigating.'

'Lost 'em down the New Road. They was goin' towards Euston, so I thinks they was goin' ter Fitzroy Square, but the carriage wasn't ter be seen at the Henchmen's —' Stemp was doing it now — 'not at the lodgin's in Fitzroy Street, but 'e's bound ter go home sometime if yer wants me ter watch, sir.'

'Yes, good notion, Stemp. In the meantime, Sergeant Rogers will pay a call on Mrs Barnham. I'd like to know more about Miss Hormel —'

Rogers and Scrap came in. 'No hotels in Union Street, sir — not as such. A pub that looked a bit down at heel, but there was a boarding house all locked up. Name of Barnes on the brass plate — an' that hadn't been cleaned recently — blinds down as well. For sale notice.'

''Ad a look round the back — could see from top o' the wall — nothin' in the yard and blinds down at all the windows.

Some old crone comes out o' the yard next door an' tells me to scarper.'

'Thought we'd better, sir. Better to go back in uniform. I've a feelin', sir, you know what an empty house might mean. The old dame said she thought we were — then she stopped, looked us over, and told us to clear off.'

'Someone had been there. I know what it might mean. It happens. Girls taken to an unoccupied house to meet whoever is to take them elsewhere, or kept there —'

'Prisoners,' Dickens said.

'Exactly — empty house in some obscure street. A kindly woman to reassure them until they're collected. No one to hear anything. Covering their tracks from The Copenhagen, maybe.'

'And Darius Henchman deep in it — he took them to Union Street. And there's the ring.'

Jones turned to Rogers and Stemp. 'Mr Dickens heard from a goldsmith in Clerkenwell that Henchman had sold him a gold watch chain and a gentleman's ring — initials "WTP" — which I have retrieved from the goldsmith.'

'Good God,' Rogers said, 'Pell — William Talbot Pell.'

'Could be. I've sent Feak with the chain and ring to see Pell's valet. He'll surely know them.'

'Darius Henchman got them from the French woman who got them from the Frenchie who got them from Speed who got them from —'

'Jaggard — very probably. However, we'll have to wait for Feak to come back. Stemp, you go and keep your eye on the Henchman house. Scrap can watch the mews. Come back quick as you can if that carriage returns. Rogers, get off to Fitzroy Street. Find out all you can about Miss Hormel.'

Jones remained in his chair when the others had gone. Dickens waited. Sam's face looked very strained, and he understood. If Jaggard… Dear Lord, the thought was hardly bearable. A murderer, and a violent one. Darius Henchman had that ring. Darius Henchman with Phoebe. Flirting.

'Barnes,' Jones said at last, 'Miss Hormel —'

'Oh, Lor, she nearly said it — pretended it was her poor English, and then made a to-do about pronouncing Barnham. Did she see that brass plate? Did she meet Darius Henchman there? But what's all to do with Jaggard? I can understand the jewellery, but —'

'Interests, Charles, Jaggard is a man of many parts. When we raided his house and my constable was shot, I noticed several young girls, and children. I know they use 'em in the coining business — useful little fingers, but Livvie Slack's a prostitute. Cora Davies, actress at The Hoxton and then she met Jaggard — money to be made, and in more than coining.'

Dickens could find no answer to that. He stared out of the window as if that would bring back Feak. 'I rather hope it will be Pell's ring — you could bring in Darius Henchman then. He'll have to spill the beans.'

'Interesting what Stemp said about Miss Hormel. I wonder if he has any idea of what he's into — whether he's just Hormel's tool.'

'She seemed very knowing to me, and I thought she was older than Darius. She put him on to sell the ring? Linked to Mr Jean Baptiste?'

'Then she's a fool if she's connected in any way to Jaggard. But then they wouldn't have expected to meet us at The Baptist's Head. They wouldn't imagine we could be on to them — which we wouldn't have been, except for Posy.'

'Perhaps they don't know that Posy belongs to — oh, good God, Sam — if it is Jaggard and he finds out that Posy is a servant in the household of a police superintendent —'

Jones just looked at him, his face bleaker than ever. He knew the answer to that. Jaggard was ruthless, probably a murderer, and bent only on his own desires for money, for power. The only tenderness he had shown was to advise Cora Davies to take their child away, but that did not mean that he would have any mercy for a policeman's servant.

'Let's not get ahead of ourselves — we don't know yet —'

'But you think it could be —'

'You can see the links for yourself,' Jones said wearily, 'and sit down, for God's sake. He'll come.'

It was Sergeant Rogers who came back first from Miss Hormel's lodgings where the landlady was Mrs Barnham, Mrs Barnham who had plenty to say about Miss Hormel, who'd been with her for about a month. The most important thing was that Miss Hormel was no longer her lodger. Miss Hormel had returned to France — it seemed that she was homesick. She had packed her bags and left last Friday morning. And Mrs Barham had been glad to see the back of her — such goings-on. A French gentleman calling at all hours — Miss Hormel's brother, supposedly. Now, that she did not believe, and she was sure that he had been in Miss Hormel's room — the parlour was for gentleman guests, including so-called brothers. Mrs Barnham had seen him in her hall early one morning — just arrived, he'd said, but she knew a thing or two. Two of 'em on the go, she had, and that young man was a silly fool about her. Mr Darius Henchman, he was — moneyed young man, and didn't Miss H know it.

The Frenchman was not as tall as Rogers, Mrs Barnham had said in answer to his request for a description — slight build, very dark hair and eyes, moustache, short beard. Well-dressed — smart. Brother and sister, she didn't believe. A landlady saw all sorts. They were a lot more than brother and sister.

'John the Baptist,' Dickens said.

'The Frenchman who bought jewellery from Joey Speed,' Jones said to Rogers.

'An' if that ring —'

There was no "if" about it. Feak came at last with the news that all the servants had recognised the ring as one worn by Sir William Pell. Jones sent him back to enquire about any possible relationship between Jaggard and any maidservant, including the girl who had taken Jaggard's card.

'Grafton Street?' asked Rogers.

Jones thought. 'Not yet. Stemp and Scrap are keeping watch. I don't want Henchman warned that the police have called. I want to surprise him with the ring in my hand. Union Street now. I'll get someone to send a message to us if Stemp reports that Henchman is home.'

Rogers took them to the shut-up house. They made a lot of noise in the yard and sure enough, a woman with a menacing eye appeared like a very large genie from, no doubt, a very large lamp. Like Mrs Davies in Upnor, she was armed with a hearth broom which weapon she lowered, seeing Sergeant Rogers's uniform. Still, she asked belligerently what they were doing in Mrs Barnes's yard.

Superintendent Jones told her. And she told them about Mr Robert Thornhill — a very pleasant gentleman who had come from the house agent to make an inventory, and who had borrowed the key, having forgotten the key at the agent's office. He had not given it back, but he had come again last Friday with some ladies who were taking the lease — a lady with two daughters, she thought — a well-dressed lady who seemed to know Mr Thornhill very well — a foreign lady, she thought.

Yes, they all went in an' they stayed a longish time — till dark, anyway, when she went in to see to the supper. Fish, see, wouldn't wait. Measurin' up, she supposed, but, queer thing was, they never came back. An', no, she 'adn't seen Mr Thornhill since. Then earlier today, there was a boy on the wall lookin' at the yard. Thievin' little wretch, an' with some labourin' man — looked poor as dirt. She'd 'ave got a policeman, but they ran off — she'd 'ave to see the house agent about that — empty house, bound to attract thieves. There were sticks o' furniture left an' the blinds —

No, she didn't see no carriage. Mr Thornhill came in a cab, but where the ladies came from she didn't know. The girls went straight in. Just a glimpse — see, Mr Thornhill saw her comin' out of her door and she asked about the key which the lady was usin' ter open the door an' let the girls in — only saw 'em side on — young, she thought. Nicely dressed — green feather in one of the bonnets. Saw that. Couldn't say what the older lady was wearin' — somethin' dark, but quality, did they see?

Oh, they saw all right. Superintendent Jones saw Mademoiselle Hormel's smart dark green pelisse and Dickens saw Phoebe Miller's bonnet with its green feather. But they did not see Mr Robert Thornhill. He was certainly not the French John the Baptist.

'Can you describe Mr Thornhill?'

'Tall, broad-shouldered, beard, darkish skin — been abroad, maybe. Light-coloured eyes — blue, pr'aps. Top hat, dark coat and trousers. Very gentlemanly.'

There was no difficulty in opening the back door, which led into a scullery then the kitchen, where there was evidence that someone had been there recently — a kettle on the fire, dregs of tea in a pot and a tray with cups and saucers. The parlour contained a few bits of furniture — enough to reassure a girl as innocent as Posy that it was all perfectly respectable. Cold ashes in the grate. A fire in here, too, perhaps to welcome them, and cups of tea, of course.

'Didn't sound like Darius Henchman,' Dickens observed as they looked round.

'Nor Mr Jean Baptiste, or Jaggard for that matter, but the lady could well be Miss Hormel — she had arranged to meet Darius Henchman at The Copenhagen and didn't turn up. Other business in hand, perhaps.'

'An' who's this Robert Thornhill?' asked Rogers.

'Not a name I know,' Jones said, and seeing Dickens's thoughtful face, asked, 'You recognise it?'

'I thought I did when she said it, but it could be the name of any one of thousands. All sorts of people write to me, asking for help, for money, for advice, for me to preside at a dinner, to chair a meeting, to sign a petition. I'll think about it.'

Rogers went off to see the house agent, just in case there was an innocent Robert Thornhill who had unwittingly shown the house to a charming French woman with two daughters.

'Let's have a look upstairs,' Jones decided, 'just in case there's anything…'

There were closed doors leading from the landing — rooms for the lodgers who had departed — and at the end of the corridor a door ajar. This room had been used, evidenced by the unmade bed, the smell of sweat and hair oil, and the open door of the wardrobe. A jug stood on a washstand, and a bowl with water in it and the scum of soap on it.

'A man,' Dickens said.

'Cuckoo in the nest. Someone knew the place was empty. Waited here for instructions. Things are moving, I'd say, all perhaps waiting for the arrival of the Frenchman and the approval of the forgeries. Nothing to say the Frenchman hasn't been here, waiting, too.'

'Mademoiselle Hormel told him?'

'Convenient place to hide. And Jaggard could meet them here. Two strands of business very conveniently brought together.'

'For some time, too, Sam, there was tea, the fire, they'd boiled a kettle — turned on the water?'

There was a bathroom next to the open room and a water closet which smelt of urine. *No water up here*, Dickens thought, but there was something else — something small and blue on the floor. He picked it up and backed out to hand it to Sam Jones.

A little flower made of velvet — a flower that had been sewn onto a bonnet ribbon by a sweet girl who had thought she was going to a friend's cottage in the country. Sam Jones had seen it being sewn on, and Elizabeth Jones had told Dickens that she had given it to her sweet girl.

There was nothing to say. Dickens and Jones parted at Tavistock Square. Dickens did not dare to be late for his dinner. Jones went on to Bow Street. There were constables to be sent back to Union Street. Someone might have seen them

— some other neighbour, housewife, street-seller, baked potato man, muffin man, shoe-shine boy, cabman or waterman, or idler with nothing to do but watch. And later he had an appointment with Inspector Fall of N Division, who'd know all about the drowning of Phoebe Miller's sisters.

Constable Stemp waited the long night through. He watched the grey dawn wreathe itself about the house. He watched the lights come on in the basement. He watched the milk girl go down the area steps with her cans and heard voices. He watched a yawning girl come out to polish the brass door furniture. He watched Mr Henchman senior go away. And Scrap watched, too, in the mews behind the house. But no carriage returned to the Henchman house. Darius Henchman did not come home.

20: MESSAGES FROM THE SEA

Dickens was lying awake again, brooding on the last letter from Mrs Morson at the home for fallen women. About one Martha Williamson, who had secreted away a bonnet and gown, intending to abscond. Dickens had hoped to give her a second chance, but she had run away, and was now, according to Mrs Morson, about to serve two months for her theft of two gowns, two petticoats and various other articles of clothing.

Another failure. It grieved him. His desire had been to give these women at the home the means of returning to happiness; to give it into their own hands by educating them, teaching them to read and write and to acquire the domestic skills that no one had ever taught them. Martha Williamson's sly and sullen face appeared before him. She wouldn't be going to Australia to live a new life — except as a transportee, probably.

Good Lord, Australia. That was it.

He couldn't wait until morning. He crept out of bed, careful not to disturb Catherine, who was sleeping peacefully. No tears on her face this time.

The dinner had gone well. Mark Lemon had been on good form, complimenting Catherine on her cookery book and the excellent leg of mutton, responding heartily to Dickens's teasing about his supposed farming enterprises. Lemon pastured cows in Westbourne Grove to provide milk for his children. When he had lived out there, he had been listed as a cow-keeper in the trade directory, much to the amusement of Dickens, who would insist on asking about Lemon's sheep and pigs — which were, he claimed, part of Farmer Lemon's extensive acres, and fed on a diet of mangelwurzels. Mrs

Dickens, he told them, had a very good recipe for braised mangelwurzels.

Bloomerism in Chipping Sodbury — a headline repeated by Mark Lemon — produced unaccountable hilarity, as did Catherine's straight-faced observation that she had heard that gardening was popular there. Catherine had been on good form, too.

And Talfourd, who had a talent for enjoyment, was always a genial guest; Talfourd, who took people at their best, was attentive and gallant to Catherine, whose laughter Dickens was glad to hear. He had not heard it for some time. And Mrs Lemon and Lady Talfourd were the most good-humoured of ladies.

He had kept the conversation away from crime — and punishment, giving Mark Lemon a brief warning look when he attempted to ask about Superintendent Jones, whom he respected and liked, especially after he, Wilkie Collins, and the superintendent had grappled with a wild-cat actress who had entertained murderous designs on Dickens. Yet, from time to time, listening to the ebb and flow of talk, he had thought about that name: Robert Thornhill.

Downstairs, he looked through the letters on his desk, the ones dealing with the home for fallen women. Yes, a letter from Lieutenant John Hoskins Brown, the Registrar of Merchant Seamen, who had given him the information about the best ship to take some of the girls to Australia — and the best captain, and here he was: Captain Robert Thornhill, master of the *Duke of Bedford*, which had set sail for Melbourne on October 25th, carrying Ellen Glyn, Emma Spencer and Rosina Newman from the home to their new lives.

And that Robert Thornhill at the boarding house in Union Street had been a tall, broad-shouldered young man with darkish skin — once a sailor, maybe. A chance in a thousand, no doubt, a chance in a million, but suppose the sometime sailor, Matty Miller, had used the name of a sea captain — a captain under whom he had served. And, if he were involved in some nefarious business, which the meeting at Union Street seemed to suggest, then he would not use his own name — and there was the matter of his drowned sisters. Turned to crime, perhaps.

Lieutenant John Hoskins Brown had assured him that the *Duke of Bedford* was a fine ship — the girls would be travelling intermediate class, there being no steerage class, and that was a good thing for them. They would have their own cabin, better than mixing with the rougher sort. Dickens had heard tales of disorder, fighting, drunkenness — and worse, flogging of women and other abuses. And one captain had been prosecuted for raping one of the passengers. The girls from the home had seen enough of that in London. He wanted them safe. Brown had spoken highly of Captain Thornhill, a gentleman, formerly Commander of the East India Company ship, *Thomas Grenville*; an experienced sailor, Thornhill had travelled to India and China as well as Australia. And always an orderly ship, the lieutenant had declared. Mr Dickens's girls would be safe aboard the *Duke of Bedford*.

He wanted Posy safe, too. He'd go down to the Registrar's Office in Lower Thames Street to see Lieutenant Brown — anything was worth a try. If Matty Miller had gone to sea, it would have been on a merchant ship. Brown would surely find him in the register, even if Captain Robert Thornhill didn't come into it. He might find out something about him — whether he was returning to the sea, for example. He thought of Elizabeth Jones's visit to Lady Nora Lockhart's former maid. That was a long shot, too, but worth trying. He wondered if she had found out anything about Darius

Henchman. Sam Jones had been going to see Inspector Fall of N Division to find out what the police had thought about Matty and sister Phoebe and that drowning — it would be interesting to know if Matty Miller had been suspected by the police, not just the gossips.

Lieutenant Hoskins Brown, at his desk by ten o'clock, was most obliging. While his equally obliging clerk searched the records for Matthew Miller who had possibly sailed with Captain Robert Thornhill, perhaps as early as 1845, the Lieutenant expiated once more on the merits of Captain Thornhill, the handsomeness of that fine Indiaman, the *Duke of Bedford*, teak-built, well-ventilated, and carrying an experienced surgeon. Mr Dickens's young ladies would have a comfortable voyage. The ship had left Plymouth on November 1st, and the weather was fair, it seemed.

Dickens nodded appreciatively — and he was pleased, but he was more interested just then in Matthew Miller, to which subject he returned when it was polite to do so, observing that he did not know if the young man were still at sea.

He was not, the clerk returned to tell him. Mr Miller had left the service in 1849, but Mr Dickens might like to get in touch with a Lieutenant Barnes who —

Barnes — Dickens concealed his astonishment, but good Lord, how that name rang a very loud bell. Bells, more like. *Five, at least*, he thought, his mind running on shipping. The clerk, however, was still talking. Lieutenant Barnes had served under Captain Thornhill from 1845 to 1847 and was on the list with Matthew Miller, and as the lieutenant lived only in Cartwright Street, a step or two away — serving on *The Minerva* — back from Calcutta only yesterday, Mr Dickens could easily—

The smart young man in the uniform of a lieutenant — clearly, a man who had risen in his profession — was astonished to find Mr Charles Dickens on his doorstep, but Dickens was invited into a cheerful parlour, shipshape as an officer's cabin, where an equally neat and pretty young woman was about the business of unpacking a sea chest. Mr Barnes, it seemed, had been away for six months. He was busy with a chuckling little boy on his knee, a little boy clutching a toy ship in his plump hand.

When the young lady, having also expressed her astonishment at the advent of the author in her parlour, departed with her reluctant boy and his ship, Dickens had the chance to explain his purpose.

Frederick Barnes remembered Matty Miller very well. 'Used to come and stay at my mother's. No family left — except for a sister in service. He was fond of her, I know — but what's this about?'

Dickens told him. Barnes was astonished. 'What on earth was he up to in my mother's house? You know she's dead? I haven't been able to do anything about the house. It's been empty for more than six months.'

'Meeting his sister, we think. Name of Phoebe — known as Phib,' said Dickens, and Barnes nodded. 'You seemed to suggest that he saw his sister when he was home from sea?'

'Oh, yes, he'd go to meet her. I don't know where. I suppose on her day off.'

'I'm much concerned about the other girl, a young servant of friends of mine. You see, Mr Barnes, I placed her with them. She was from the orphanage at Tooting.'

'Oh, I remember that. It was in the papers — you wrote about it. A dreadful business. All those children dying, but I don't see —'

Dickens explained that he was concerned for the girl's safety, that she would not run off, and that he believed that Matthew Miller and his sister had taken her for some nefarious purpose. The girls had been taken to Mrs Barnes's empty house by a French woman whom the police suspected of being involved in various crimes.

'You think Matty's up to no good?'

'Tell me about him, Mr Barnes,' Dickens said. 'Tell me if you think he could be up to no good.'

Frederick Barnes invited him to sit down. He looked troubled. 'I haven't seen him since '49, when he left the service. Said he was sick of the sea. He was a kid when he started, only fourteen, though he was big lad. No family, he said, except the sister, Phib. I was that bit older — I felt sorry for him. I'd my mother, you see. It makes a difference. A sailor needs a family — I've my wife and children now — something to work for, someone to come home to, but Matty — well, he stuck it, but it's a hard life, cruel, sometimes. The sea hardens a man.'

'It hardened Matty Miller?'

'Think of tempered steel, sir — the metal is toughened, but it will still yield when it needs to. As if it knows, sir, but, say, the temperature wasn't right, the hardness remains, but it's brittle, liable to break. Matty Miller got hard, but he couldn't bend under the discipline. He left Captain Thornhill's service. The captain was a gentleman, but firm, sir, and punishment was stern. I thrived, but Matty resisted. He resented the captain — any of the officers, in fact. I don't know what he wanted to do, except to make his fortune…'

'And how might he do that?' asked Dickens, sensing there was more.

'Crimps, sir, you know what they are. I read your piece in your magazine — all about the docks — and the sailors.'

'I do. Crimps who squeeze every last farthing from sailors who come ashore. Offer them lodgings and rob them blind.'

'And sell them to unscrupulous captains. Matty got into trouble that way — turned up at my mother's back in '48 with nothing on him but bruises. Somewhere in Limehouse. Near the docks, I suppose. Not that he seemed to mind the beating — he thought it was a good business to be in. Easy money, he said. I put him right about that and got him onto *The Messenger* under a captain I knew. When I saw him in '49, he told me he'd left the service — didn't say when, but he looked pretty prosperous. I wondered — not that I asked. I knew somehow that he'd go wrong. I think I always knew it. Knew that he'd break. Easy money, he wanted.'

Dickens thanked him for his time. It was enough. An embittered young man, prone to violence, resentful of the discipline of the seafaring life, but ambitious for money. It was easy to see how such a man might turn to crime. Hardened, Lieutenant Barnes had said. Hardened, even as a boy, brought up by those cruel parents, poverty and ignorance, a hopeless nursery in which the seeds of ruin are sown. Phoebe Miller, hardened, too, and the distinctions between right and wrong confounded and perverted in both their minds. He remembered what Phoebe had said to Scrap about the money in the stationery shop till.

These crowded streets as much a prison as that Tower, he thought, making his way past its implacable bulk, back to Thames Street, and seeing the river swarming with ships and masts, watermen, lightermen, colliers, dredgers, steamers, and the wharves teeming with dockers and colliers loading and unloading all the world's goods. From Australia, China,

America, India. He thought of Lieutenant Barnes's kindly hazel eyes, troubled by the memory of a young man he had tried to help. A good heart, the lieutenant. The sea was a severe mistress, but Barnes was, indeed, Damascus steel to the core — a poet in his way. In his heart, Dickens wished him joy, and his pretty wife and the little son who would not be ruined by ignorance and want.

He dropped a coin into the upturned cap of a disabled sailor sitting on the pavement. The man looked frozen and wretchedly poor, and very sick. Dickens saw the hectic red in his thin cheeks — the familiar sign of tuberculosis. There was nothing else in his cap. He could understand, too, why a young man wanted to insure himself against this.

21: HARD AS NAILS

At Bow Street, Jones and Rogers were discussing the non-appearance of Darius Henchman and wondering if he were somewhere in the company of Miss Hormel. Dickens had told them what the Henchmans' maid had said about his staying out all night, and Scrap had seen him returning early in the morning. So, perhaps it wasn't so unusual. Constables Semple and Dacre had returned to the precincts of Union Street to ask their questions in the light of day. And, as Rogers had discovered, the house agents had never heard of a Robert Thornhill, at the mention of which name, Dickens entered, fresh from his encounter with Lieutenant Barnes.

'You have news,' Jones said, noting his eager eye. Dickens had hurried from somewhere important.

'I do — I have been investigating a merchant sea-captain, one Robert Thornhill. I remembered him from —'

'Blimey,' Rogers interrupted, 'that's a queer thing. I asked the house agent about Mrs Barnes — just wondered why they chose that house. Nothin' particular about her except her son was in the merchant navy — the agents were waiting for him to come home from sea.'

'Blimey, indeed,' Dickens said. 'Thornhill is captain of the *Duke of Bedford*. I remembered because three of our girls from the home are on board now — sailed on October 25th. Anyway, I had correspondence with the Registrar of Merchant Seamen about the girls, so I went this morning to Lower Thames Street. Found Matty Miller and his former shipmate, Lieutenant Frederick Barnes, son of the very Missis of Union Street.'

They would have been less surprised had he conjured a Christmas pudding from a top hat — both had seen that feat from Dickens the magician, but to produce those two names created a sensation at which Dickens could not help but grin broadly. Rogers looked at him, open-mouthed.

Jones couldn't help smiling, but his voice was dry. 'So, tell us — and be quick about it. We've enough suspense about without you tearing our nerves to shreds.'

'Mr Jones, you are in a wounding mood, I see, but I will be brief — as woman's love —'

Before Jones could comment on that piece of irrelevant philosophy, Dickens gave them the essential details, forbearing to include the pretty wife and the kindly hazel eyes, and the chubby, laughing baby with his toy ship. And he forbore to add the scrofulous sailor he'd seen in the street. He was tempted, but behind Sam's smile was the anguish of the missing Posy and the burden of Jaggard, the murderer, and the connection between the two cases. 'And Barnes told me that Matty met his sister, Phib, when he was home from sea — Barnes didn't know where, unfortunately.'

'So, the so-called house agent could well be Matty Miller.' Jones was cautious.

'Could!' Dickens couldn't help himself. 'He knew that house — he could have known it was empty.'

'All right, like Barkis I'm willing. That do you?'

'It will.'

'American dollars, sir,' Rogers said, 'you remember. Jaggard—'

'I do now — tell Mr Dickens.'

'Inspector Bold — you know, at Wapping — knew of Jaggard in connection with the coinin' of American silver dollars — sellin' 'em to emigrants was the racket. Jaggard had taken over some abandoned mill down by Kidney Stairs. Limehouse, Mr Dickens. Gone, o' course, by the time Mr Bold got there. Only a badly burnt child left behind —'

'Burnt by the molten metal, I suppose.' Dickens had heard such stories. Little children maimed when pouring the hot metal into the plaster coin mould, often through clay pipe stems. Delicate fingers were good for that, so what use were burnt fingers to the likes of Jaggard?

'Right — tipped over when they all scarpered.'

'Limehouse, near the docks — where he could have met Jaggard. Fancied a life of crime. When was this racket going on?'

'Back in '48 — '49.'

'When Matty Miller was crimped. In 1849 he left the service.'

'Interesting — not that it matters where they met —' seeing Dickens's face — 'for the moment anyway, but I've news, too, which will, no doubt, add to your conviction. I spoke to Inspector Fall of N Division. He wasn't satisfied at the time of the drownings, but Matty and Phoebe were adamant that they hadn't seen those girls. They were always running off, it seemed. The parents didn't know where any of them were half the time. The magistrate wasn't keen on pursuing that line of inquiry, and the farmer spoke up for the lad —'

'What about the father — any use speaking to him?'

'Inspector Fall thought not. He'd only tell the same story, and we can't accuse Matty and Phoebe — the inquest found accident, but Fall did find out about the violence at home. None of them seemed to get on. Always at odds. He didn't think there was any real feeling about the drowned girls, though Phoebe Miller did a lot of weeping and wailing about which Fall was very sceptical. The father was a brute — beat his children, and Matty did have a temper —'

'As Frederick Barnes suggested. He resented a flogging on board, but the beating by a crimp taught him that crime pays.'

'Right, but wonderful as your news is — Rogers and I naturally pay tribute — my two constables are still asking questions in Union Street, and I'm off to Clerkenwell now and Joey Speed's mother. We'll not be welcome, but I want to know where Livvie Slack is and who with.'

'We?'

'Thee and me. Rogers is off to The Copenhagen. I want to know if anyone saw that carriage in the lane. There was no mention of it when you asked your questions.'

'The landlord's boy saw them walking towards the lane — just the two of them, but Joan Gall said she saw Phoebe with her toff in the gardens, so was it Matty in the garden?'

'And Darius Henchman was telling the truth? He was on the road waiting for Mademoiselle. Phoebe told him that she was going back into town, and would he take them in his carriage—'

'Was going — was going, Sam. She'd met Matty, who told her where to go — to the hotel in Union Street. She knew what she was doing. Taking Posy to The Copenhagen was deliberate.'

'And Miss Hormel had no intention of meeting Darius Henchman at The Copenhagen, but she sent him there, and Phoebe was to look out for him, I'm guessing.'

'Phoebe Miller knew what kind of man he was. She flirted with him — got him in her pocket, so to speak. Scrap saw him giving her something. Money, maybe — a little bit of blackmail. We don't know how far she'd gone with him. He called her Phoebe. I remember that from our meeting with him. She thought she was going up in the world. Not kitchen maid Phib anymore. In with a well-dressed French lady, too.'

'They intended to use him in some way, I'll wager.'

'Matty Miller in the top hat and yellow gloves.'

'Very clever — and from a distance, one mistaken for the other. Just in case. Well, Rogers might find out something from the girl, Joan — or that lad sweeping that you mentioned. Now, let's be off to find who knows what about Livvie Slack — and Jaggard. Cora Davies said she didn't know who Livvie had set up with. No one particular, she said, but I'm wondering. She's a good-looking girl, and hard as nails.'

22: GIN PARLOUR

Eyes, the colour and size of a boiled lobster's — and a bad one at that, gin-soaked, half-dressed, and with a dirty, puffy face, Mrs Speed ought to have been named Mrs Slack. She resembled the badly made bed from which she had obviously just risen. She would have shut the door in their faces, except that Superintendent Jones of Bow Street shoved it back very hard and planted himself on her threshold.

'Out here or inside — your choice.'

She cursed half-heartedly and tottered after them into her parlour — or bedroom. It seemed to serve both purposes, and that of a public house taproom, the flavour of gin and fried fish pungent in the mouth and nose, and bad lobster, and the familiar staleness of unwashed clothes and persons, and smoke from sea coals and her pipe burning on the table.

She picked up her pipe to take a greedy drag and then looked at them through the smoke with red-rimmed eyes. 'Wha' d'yer want now? Yer've got my lad — 'e was twisted. 'Ow could 'e know them notes was forged? 'T'ain't right —'

Jones had no intention of debating with her. 'Livvie Slack — where is she?'

'Oh, it's Livvie yer after now, is it? Can't leave us poor folks alone. I dunno where she is — I ain't 'er keeper.'

'Some man, is it?'

'Not your business.'

'Oh, it is, Mrs Speed. And murder's my business — and Martin Jaggard who came here to see Cora Davies, your Livvie's pal. Where is she?'

She sat down suddenly, as if the air had been knocked out of her, and reached for her cup. Jaggard's name had obviously given her a fright. She took a deep swig, and another. Dickens caught a stronger whiff of gin and stale clothes as her crumpled skirts swished about her, and he saw bare feet, misshapen and very dirty. She looked a poor, hopeless creature — and ancient, though she could only have been in her forties — if that. Gin did that.

'I ain't anythin' ter do with 'im. That woz Cora's business.'

'And your Joey's, and Livvie's — is she with Jaggard? Tell me here or at Bow Street.'

She looked from side to side like some ragged trapped animal. 'I daresn't, sir. She'll know an' then 'e'll know. Joey an' Cora, they're safe enough, but wot about me? Serpose 'e comes back? Wot use will you be then, Mr Bow Street copper? An' 'im? 'Ooever 'e is.'

'Just tell me where Livvie is. If anyone asks, I came about Joey.'

'Went off Friday — said she woz meetin' a lady on business fer — well, I ain't sayin' 'is name — I've not said — yer can't say I 'ave.'

'I won't, but what business?'

'Yer knows wot business Livvie's in — she said there woz girls to be picked up.'

'Where?'

'King's Cross, she said. Hotel, she said — way the toffs live.'

'Let's have it clear: Livvie and her friend, let's call him, are setting up another brothel?'

Another swig. Dutch courage. 'Tha's right. 'Igh class, Livvie said, clean girls. Why not 'ere, I says — time I woz paid fer all me trouble. Not good enough, she says. Woz good enough when she an' that Cora wanted —'

'Where?'

'Dint say — said it woz ter be on the quiet yet. She woz goin' inter business with some Frenchie —'

'The woman she was meeting?'

'Serpose — I dunno nothink more, Mr Copper. Surely, yer can leave me be now.'

'I will, but first I need to see Livvie's room, and Joey's.'

'Upstairs — two rooms on the first floor, but she ain't left anythin'. I've looked.'

They left her muttering to herself, lost in fumes of smoke and gin. They heard the sound of drink being poured into the cup as they mounted the rickety staircase, dark and damp as a tunnel. As a lodging house, it didn't offer much, but perhaps the bedrooms were more salubrious. Lodging house was a loose term, they knew now. Mrs Speed's lodgers were prostitutes — and not of a high-class kind.

The room on the right was empty apart from the double bed, a chest of drawers and a washstand. The walls were blotched with damp, but it looked clean and there was a rug on the bare floorboards. Livvie Slack had standards, maybe — and ambitions. Jones remembered her, a tall, rather handsome girl with golden hair who'd scrub up well enough — better than Cora Davies, whose voluptuousness was running to fat. She'd become a battle-axe like her mother, though without the honest courage.

'She has —' he began. A door slammed upstairs, and feet clattered down. He signalled to Dickens to peek through the crack of the door. A glimpse of two angry eyes, and then she was gone.

'Woman,' Dickens said, 'dressed for outdoors.'

'Go after her — see where she goes.'

Dickens saw her going up Bridewell Walk, past the Lamb and Dove. She turned the corner and he hurried after her into a passage, where she stopped suddenly to face him. He couldn't see much of her face, but he heard the belligerence in her voice as she spoke.

'You followin' me? Saw you back there. I ain't —'

'No, no — I wanted to ask about Livvie Slack.'

'Missed your chance there — she ain't about no more, an' I ain't —'

'I'm sure, Miss —'

'Stooks — Polly, an' I ain't into that game, so clear off —'

'A girl's gone missing —'

'Your daughter?'

'No, a servant of a friend who disappeared with a girl called Phib Miller or Phoebe, possibly.'

'Don't know her, an' Livvie's gone off an' so must I — I've gotter get —'

'I would like to talk to you — just for a few minutes. Is there somewhere — in the church, perhaps?'

Her eyes narrowed suspiciously. 'You a parson? Cos if so, I ain't interested. I've enough to do in this world without thinkin' o' the next — hell's here in Clerkenwell, Mister Parson, an' I need savin' from that, not fer heaven — two bob's more use than prayers ter me.'

Dickens wanted to laugh at her robust philosophy. She spoke true, but he just handed her his card, which she read slowly before looking at him again very closely.

'Blimey — Charles Dickens. My ma said about you — said you knew Clerkenwell all right. Oliver Twist — caught right here in Clerkenwell, an' that Sikes, she said — an' them thievin' lads. See 'em every day, she said. Read a lot, Ma. Blimey, to

155

think — an' I can't tell her now. All right, the church, it is — no prayers, mind.'

And more than two bob, she shall have, thought Dickens as he followed her along to St James's Church. He had a feeling that she would tell him something about Livvie Slack — now she knew he wasn't a parson. Thank the Lord for Ma — a very discerning woman, no doubt.

Polly Stooks stopped in the churchyard and faced him again, pushing back her bonnet so that he could see her face more clearly than in the dark passage.

'Just so you know, Mr Dickens, that I ain't on the game — no man'd want this —'

A dark purple streak coursed its way from her forehead, down her cheek to her chin — someone had cut her. It was ugly, like a badly sewn seam, and it dragged down her left eye so that she looked as if she had had a stroke. The other side of her face was unmarked, and he could see that she had once been a very pretty girl.

Then, horribly, he heard a hellish chorus of chanting voices. He whipped round to see the gang of boys whose banging of the church rails had so chilled him. It was hard to tell what they were saying. He picked out the words cock alley, cock dolly, cock polly, witch-bitch, and worse. Crude and menacing.

Dickens was about to raise his stick, but Polly was quicker. She flew at them, grabbed one by the ear and shook him as if he were a collection of rags — which he was. 'Clear off, you little bleeder, or I'll give you a touch of this —' she pointed to her scar — 'an' your insides'll be eaten away.' She dropped her tormentor and he fled, screeching. The others followed with wild yells and more curses and more banging of their sticks on the rails.

She turned back to Dickens. 'Little buggers — they think I'm a witch cos I've got this, but they're frightened of it. It's all they are frightened of. I tell 'em it'll poison 'em to death. An' don't you be sorry for me,' she continued as he was staring, 'I'm all right as I am. We don't all want a man to make us happy. I ain't goin' ever to be a fool about some drunken bastard with his fists an' his knife. Most women I know are miserable as sin — an' no parson can change that. Now, come on. I ain't got all day.'

As bracing in her own way as Lady Nora Lockhart. Soda water rather than champagne, he thought, and no doubt, much too good for the kind of men she'd know — Joey Speed, for example, and Jaggard. Livvie Slack was the fool. And Phoebe Miller.

They sat in one of the box pews at the back of the church; the white plaster ceiling and plain glass windows gave light. It was cold, but without the seeping damp of many churches. St James's was new. The old one had been the site of another nunnery — a thought which amused Dickens when he thought of where he had been. Pious days — a long time ago. There was an enormous pulpit at which Polly Stooks looked with disdain. Perhaps she had heard promises of heaven preached from there.

Better be equally bracing. 'Where's Livvie Slack gone to, and with whom?'

Polly laughed. 'Whom, eh? I don't think her fancy man's a whom — Jaggard's his name — once the property of Cora Davies. She's in quod for possession, an' Joey Speed. Boated, they'll be — all the way to Australia, an' Cora thought she'd make her fortune in America.'

Sunlight spilled like gold from the windows. Dickens felt as if sovereigns were being poured into his lap.

'An' Livvie's in with him now — more fool her, no doubt. Thinks she'll make her fortune, too. Mind, she's cleverer than Cora, an' harder.'

'A fortune in the forging business? Or something else?'

'Somethin' else — settin' up a high-class brothel, Livvie said. Didn't ask me — you can see why, but I heard enough, enough to get my sister out of it, but I'm too late, I reckon. Couldn't keep away, our Emmie. Don't know where she is — that's why I was there, but no sign.'

'You don't know where this brothel's to be?'

'I wish I did, Mr Dickens; I only know that Livvie's got in with some Frenchwoman — very la-di-da. Saw them in Livvie's room, an' Livvie lookin' at her like she was Queen Victoria.'

'And Jaggard, did you see him?'

'Came in a cab — very much the swell in his silk waistcoat an' perfume, all of a swagger, an' off they went — last Friday. I'd gone after Emmie — told 'em she was needed at home — Jaggard just shrugged. He didn't care. Said he could get plenty more girls, and now Emmie's gone after 'em — an' I don't know where.'

'Did you ever see a young gentleman with them — top hat, yellow gloves?'

'You mean Matty Miller — oh, God, you said Phoebe Miller — her brother, you think? An' this servant girl with 'em — you know what that means?'

'I do. Tell me about Matty Miller.'

'Emmie told me about him. Came with the Frenchwoman. Emmie said they was very thick. Don't know anythin' about him 'cept he'd been a sailor an' knew Jaggard from way back.'

'Any other gentlemen? Another young man named Darius Henchman or a Frenchman?'

'No, don't know of those. I only know what Emmie told me.'

'How old is Emmie?'

'Seventeen. Head filled with nonsense — she might be two years old. I don't know what Livvie wanted with Emmie. She's no oil painting — no scar, o' course. They'll want her skivvyin' — mark my words, an' she thinkin' she'll meet some duke.'

'What about Jaggard? You know him?'

'No, only saw him a few times. Gent, Emmie says, but then she's easily impressed. Dresses like a toff, but he's a bad 'un, I know that much. Cora an' Livvie came ter Mrs Speed's. There was talk that they were wanted for some game or other. Coins an' forging, I heard, but Emmie said it wasn't true — she would. But if Jaggard, Cora, an' Livvie were in somethin', then bound to be crooked. Next thing, Cora's off ter America with Joey Speed and Livvie's off with Jaggard.'

The brothel a cover for the forging, Dickens wondered, but where had they gone? That was the important thing. Pity Polly Stooks couldn't tell him.

'Would you let me know if you hear anything of Emmie? My office address is on the card. I really do want to find my friend's little servant.'

'Good of you, sir — there's many folks wouldn't give a toss about a servant.'

'What do you do for a living?'

'Nothin' just now. I had a position at the engraver's, Mr Blucher Death in John Street — dead now, an' me out of a job.'

'Extraordinary name.'

'German, I think, or 'is pa was. He was a good sort, Mr Death.'

'What did you do there?'

'Writin' engraver — Mr Death taught me. Said I had promise. Coffin plates mostly. Did my ma's — wanted her to have her name on it. Not much else I could do for her. Cancer, it was. The burial club paid for the coffin an' the funeral. She's buried here. Unmarked grave, o' course, but her name's there. I know that. 'S'important. Her name, Mr Dickens. Poor folk may not have much, but a good name's worth somethin' —'

He saw the glint of tears. 'What was her name?'

Polly blinked in surprise, but her wounded mouth smiled. 'Ann, Mr Dickens. Folk called her Annie, but I put Ann — Ann Stooks. A good name, an' that's why I've gotter find Emmie. Emerald, Ma called her — thought it'd make her — oh, well, you know.'

'And you are Polly.'

'Paulina, Mr Dickens, but folks can't be bothered. Polly — like a bloody parrot.'

'Is there anyone else at Mrs Speed's who might know something?'

'The girls has all gone — Mrs Speed's a wreck — the drink, see, an' now Livvie's gone, the place ain't worth livin' in. There's one or two might know if I can find 'em.'

Dickens thought of the danger Polly might be in if she did find Jaggard. 'Mrs Speed seemed very frightened at the mention of Jaggard. This coining business — there's some ruthless types in that, and those notes and jewels Cora and Joey had, they were stolen from a man who was murdered.'

Polly blanched at that. 'Jaggard involved in murder? How d'you know?'

'I was with a policeman at Mrs Speed's.'

'Lookin' for Jaggard?'

'Yes.'

'Oh, my God, an' Emmie's gone with 'em — a murderer —'

'The police don't know that. It's just that Jaggard once worked for the murdered man. You must be careful, Miss Stooks. Just ask about Emmie and if you find anything, come to me, I beg you.'

She looked at his card for a long time and he saw that she touched her scar, which appeared livid purple against the white of her face.

'Does it hurt?'

'Like hell, sometimes. Thoddy Cragg did this to me with a burin.'

'An engraver's tool.' Dickens knew that from his work with those who engraved the illustrations for his books. 'He was an engraver?'

'Worked for Mr Death. Ran off after he'd done it.'

'Mr Death's shop is empty. What happened to the stock?'

'You're thinkin' about forgery, Mr Dickens — an out-of-work engraver, an empty shop with some good stuff to thieve. Thoddy Cragg's a bad lot — that was his lad I chased off, an' the gang he's in.'

'Why did Thoddy Cragg attack you?'

'Cos I kicked him where it hurt most. You can imagine what he was tryin' ter do. Said I'd asked fer it. He was that mad when I kicked him, that when I tried to get away, he took up the burin an' gouged it down my face. Mr Death tried to stop him, but Cragg pushed him outta the way. Never saw him again.'

'He'd have known Livvie and Mrs Speed and Joey Speed, perhaps?'

'I daresay — they all drank at the Lamb. An' with that Jaggard. Thoddy Cragg should have taken his gibface to Ma Speed's an' paid for his pleasure an' his gin. Could have had both for a bob or two.'

'Was he?'

'What?'

'A gibface — I know what it means.'

'You get about, don't you? He was — ugly beggar. Big jaw like a bloody anvil an' I didn't want it anywhere near me — nor any other part of him.'

'Well, consider the idea that he might be in with Jaggard and be very careful, Polly. Cragg will remember you and that kick. Now, I've got to go. But I owe you two bob.'

'No, Mr Dickens — I wouldn't want —'

He took her hand and opened it — a rough, reddened hand, but a good hand. She stared down at the golden sovereign. 'Don't say anything — just keep your promise only to ask about your sister. No other names.'

He left her then, still staring at the coin. *Worth every penny*, he thought.

Superintendent Jones was waiting patiently in Livvie Slack's room. 'I was just thinking that you'd been kidnapped.'

'Sorry, Sam, but it was a long and interesting conversation with Miss Polly Stooks, who was a writing engraver at the premises of a Mr Blucher Death — now dead.'

'As a — I presume.'

'As a burin — an engraving tool, about which I will tell you on the way to wherever we are bound.'

'The Lamb and Dove — a lad called Jacko Cragg whom I discovered upstairs seemed to know more than he was telling.'

'Cragg! We'd better sit down for a minute. I've just heard that name. What did he know?'

23: BIRDS OF A FEATHER

Jacko Cragg, a sharp-faced, tattered imp of a lad with the restless, darting eyes of the habitually hunted, and the vicious mouth of an old lag, had spat at Superintendent Jones's penny in exchange for his name and sneered at another penny for information about Livvie Slack. Those hard eyes wanted more. He agreed to sixpence. He seemed to think that the superintendent was a customer. Jones did not enlighten him and kept his patience, refraining from taking the creature by its ear and giving it a good shake. He watched the boy take a bite at the coin. Knew something about forging, then. Copying his elders, at any rate. Not his betters.

Livvie Slack 'ad gone — dint know where — off wiv a nob from the city — settin' 'er up as a duchess in a mansion near the queen's 'ouse — palace it's called. Made o' gold, Livvie said. No, 'e dint know no name — bang-up toff, a lord, 'e thought — topper, see. Gas pipes. Shiny boots. Jacko Cragg's feet were bare. His shoes of mud and filth.

Jones did not mention the name of Jaggard, but he assumed that the well-dressed "nob" — the lord in the tight trousers — was he. Jacko Cragg could certainly tell a story — a fairy story, however. What else?

Jacko's too old eyes met his. Livvie want a bad-lookin' bite fer cock alley — done up champion. Coulda prigged 'er 'imself. Needn't 'ave paid, Jacko Cragg — got it fer free all the time. No thrupenny uprights fer Jacko Cragg. *All of four feet*, Jones thought, and unlikely to grow much taller — or older.

Plenty o' jewels, Livvie 'ad — diamon's. Ring as big as an egg wot the lord give 'er. But plenty more fish in the sea fer Jacko

Cragg. No, he dint live in the attic where Jones had found him asleep — dossed there sometimes. Old Ma Speed downstairs dint mind — did erran's. Gin from the Lamb, coal from — well, never mind that —

Dint live nowheres 'xactly — dossed in places. Oh, Ma in the work'ouse. Jacko Cragg want goin' ter no spike. Not bleedin' likely. Work'ouse — beat yer 'alf ter death an' made yer work. No freedom, see. A man wanted his freedom — entitled, see. Jacko Cragg 'ad 'is own business ter mind. Oh, Pa?

Only at that question did Jones detect a hesitation in the fluent narrative. The eyes shifted again — this time to the open window. Pa want at 'ome jest now. Away on business. No, dint know when 'e might be back — anyways, wot business woz it —

Then he was gone, leaping up and out of the window with the agility and speed of a monkey. Jones saw him scuttling down the roof, jumping onto another with practised ease, and vanishing down a drainpipe.

No point in haring after him. Jones had a good look round the attic. Under the bed he found a very interesting stash of goods — stolen, no doubt.

'Nearly done brown, Mr Jones,' Dickens observed at the end of the superintendent's tale, 'Jack the Dodger, come to life.'

'All the patter — mouth like a sewer.'

'All gammon?'

'And spinach — until I asked about Pa —'

'Mr Thoddy Cragg, drunk, would-be rapist, and sometime engraver.'

'And customer at the Lamb and Dove, from where young Jacko gets the gin for Ma Speed.'

Neither lambs nor doves were in evidence in the packed bar of the pub — a good many cackling crows, draggled daws, and light-fingered magpies, no doubt. The bruisers, the bullies, the bludgers, the dippers and their dolly-mops, the dragsmen who robbed coaches, the fences and fakers, the lags and the lurkers, the pitchers, the smashers and the shofulmen passing their false coin. You could go through the alphabet and find a pack of them for each letter. A skulk, more like. Dickens was thinking of foxes, and then of ravens, an unkindness thereof. A good many hard hearts here — and hard heads.

But Jones was through the door, squaring his shoulders. Look like a bully and they'll take you for one. Dickens wasn't sure what he was supposed to be. Coiner? Smasher? Expert in the Yellow Trade? At least, he knew the language. He might pass. He arranged his face into a suitable scowl and gripped his stick. Should have worn his green emergency disguise spectacles. Pity for the blind man. Somehow, he doubted it. Jones shoved his way through the crowd, looking neither right nor left. Dickens stared ahead, ignoring some of the rather menacing stares, keeping a firm grip on the stick. Last time he'd been in a miserable Clerkenwell pub, he'd found himself in the middle of a fight between some card sharpers.

The landlord heard the tone of menace in the single word Jones's steely whisper imparted and, seeing Jones's equally steely face in the grimy light of his bar, merely nodded and pointed to another room beyond, to which he followed his visitors and shut the door.

'Police. Bow Street.'

'You said "Jaggard" — I thought you was —'

'And let your customers hear the word "police"? Who did you think I was?'

'Jaggard's a dangerous man, sir — thought p'raps he'd sent—'

'Owe him, do you?'

'Stayed upstairs a few months back — paid with forged coins. I knew, see, knew they wasn't right. Told him. Should have kept my trap shut. Said I needn't say anythin' — between us, he says, all smooth and gentlemanly — like the toff he isn't — but when a man tells you it's a secret an' he has a knife, you can't help agreein', sir, an' you can't help wonderin' if he might be back. Saw him, see, last Friday. Livvie Slack goin' off with him. Good riddance, I thought, but when you said —'

'I'm sorry for that. Now, these coins — did you keep them?'

'Didn't know what to do 'cept keep 'em in the safe upstairs. If he came back, I could swear I ain't told no one.'

'I need to see them — if anyone asks, we're the customs.'

'I'll get 'em.'

While they waited, Jones showed Dickens the two counterfeit shillings he had found under Jacko Cragg's bed.

'There were some clippings off gold coins, a couple of grains in a paper, some pieces of gold wire — stolen to sell on, I should think. In business on his own, Jacko, maybe?'

'Shadrack Argent mentioned that — it's the way some so-called jewellers get started. They even sieve the water from goldsmiths' premises to get the grains. The Dodger's a fly one.'

'These coins, though, suggest to me that he knows about the coining business. The "nob" must have been Jaggard. A bit too clever, I'd say, thinking I'd swallow all that nonsense about duchesses and lords.'

'That's the trouble with these lads — think they can get one over on anyone; they know it all. They know too much, certainly, but not enough to know where it all ends —'

'A man's entitled to be free, he said — a man. Lord, he was about eleven years old and hard as nails, fancying himself as a customer of Livvie Slack's.'

'Free to starve, to be riddled by disease, free to walk right into Newgate and not come out again.'

The landlord came back before Jones had time to comment on this despairing notion — not that there was anything to say. Dickens had said enough and written enough about the plight of abandoned children left to scrape whatever living they could in the streets, to live by cunning and brutality, to thieve, to abuse and be abused. To know nothing of kindness. Crime and disgrace, but not the child's — not even Jacko Cragg's. England's.

Jones took the coins, advising the still nervous landlord that he could tell anyone who asked that he'd spent them in Town — they were long gone, and no questions had been asked. The landlord would be safe enough, though if he did hear anything more of Jaggard then he was to come to Bow Street, and there was one more thing. 'Thoddy Cragg — know him?'

'Thievin' bastard, an' his lad. Thoddy worked for Mr Death, engraver in John Street — slashed a girl there. Don't know where he is now.'

'Seen him with Jaggard?'

'Oh, aye, birds of a feather. Cragg knows Livvie Slack an' some o' the other girls — lot o' drinkin' when Jaggard was here — Jaggard, the gentleman, buyin' the drinks.'

'And the lad, where's he to be found?'

'Anywhere an' everywhere, sir — there's dozens of 'em, swarmin' like rats, pinchin' whatever they can an' worse. I don't know — gang of 'em dosses in a cellar near the church in Bowlin' Green Lane. Bad lot. Folk are scared to death of 'em.'

It was dark when they came down into Clerkenwell Close. That fugitive sunshine which had illuminated the church had fled. Fog was descending and the misty, cadaverous gaslight lent a livid ghastliness to the pinched and weary faces passing like spectres, and it threw the entrances of little alleyways into deeper darkness, in which more shadowy forms shifted. Occasionally there was the flare of a light, the sound of footsteps running, laughter or a scream. A dirty window showed the light of a tallow candle and a white face staring, horrified, into the wild world. Dickens looked at Jones and saw that he was haggard, too, the bones of his face set into stone.

'Let's get out of here,' Jones said. 'We'll pay a quick visit to Inspector Shackell. He'll know about Jacko Cragg and his father and that assault on your Miss Stooks. And then the Henchman house. Jaggard and his lot have vanished, but Henchman can tell us where he got that ring. And anyone who knows him can tell me who his friends are.'

Roaring drunk, bloody and bruised, but not unbowed, swearing on every saint in the book that he was 'innothent' and that it was 'murther bein' done', a prisoner was being manhandled to the stairs by two policemen, one whom had lost his hat. Dickens's old friend, Inspector Shackell, was watching with a kind of humorous resignation — obviously the man was a regular guest of Her Majesty. They heard the slip and strike of boots on the stone steps, and the voice gradually died away.

'Patrick Quilp, Mr Dickens,' Inspector Shackell said with a smile, 'not as much a horror as your Daniel Quilp, but a thorough nuisance all the same. A bucket of cold water ought to shut him up. Now, what might I do for you, Superintendent Jones? No sign of Jaggard or Livvie Slack, I'm afraid.'

'Went off with Jaggard, so I hear from a young devil named Jacko Cragg who escaped before I had a chance to find out more.'

'Monkey up a drainpipe, that one — there's packs of lads just like him. Jacko's the snakesman — can get in anywhere. We cleared out a nest of 'em from a cellar a few weeks back. Mr Fagin's still about, Mr Dickens. The place was home from home — fireplace, kettle, frying pan, bit of bacon, straw palliasses. Stolen property, of course. Up before the beak and three weeks in the House of Correction, and a whipping. No sign of Fagin — whatever his name is, or Jacko, but the other lads'll be out now and somewhere else.'

'Behind the church in Bowling Green Lane, according to the landlord of the Lamb and Dove. Can you keep your eye out for Jacko Cragg? He knows something. I found two fake shillings and some bits of gold under a bed at Mrs Slack's, where I found Jacko, incidentally, and the father, Thoddy Cragg, is an out-of-work engraver.'

'Not been seen since he attacked a girl with an engraving tool. I want him for that.'

'I met the girl, Polly Stooks — her sister's missing. Polly thinks she's gone after Livvie Slack and Jaggard — setting up a brothel, but she doesn't know where,' Dickens told him.

Inspector Shackell looked very grave. 'Jaggard, Mr Jones, you want him for murder. Cragg's a violent man, an' that lad's a piece of work — I know you feel for 'em, Mr Dickens, an' so do I, but some are that hardened, they'd skin their own grandmothers for a shilling. There's a dangerous crew about — lot o' lads with sticks. Sticks weighted with lead, and they're not afraid to use them on anyone who gets in their way. Jacko Cragg's in with them. It wouldn't surprise me if he went after his pa, and when he tells them about a stranger asking questions —'

'There was a boy in the yard at The Baptist's Head,' Jones said. 'We thought he was just waiting to earn a penny, but now—'

'And I met one outside Shadrack Argent's shop — and Jacko Cragg was in the churchyard, spewing filth about Polly Stooks — a little fiend in rags,' Dickens added.

'Imp of Satan, he is — capable of anythin' — and his mates.'

Dickens felt the chill of his words, remembering the menace of those sticks beating on the railings. He and Sam had been followed, and Jaggard might well know now. He couldn't feel very much just now for Jacko Cragg, young as he was, or Phoebe Miller for that matter. It was Posy he thought of as they went out. In the hands of Jaggard and his crew.

24: THE OWL SHRIEKS

William Herring's face looked shrunken in the light of Constable Stemp's lantern, his eyes starting from his head. The man with him, holding on to Herring's arm, was equally pale. Stemp's face was in shadow, but Sam Jones's face was even more haggard. In profile his face looked fleshless as if, in the minutes it had taken them to rush from the Henchman house to Quickset Row, he had aged a hundred years. Sergeant Rogers and Constable Feak were looking down, their lamps angled onto the ground.

It was a scene from a nightmare, the fog creeping in corners; the frozen figures; the lantern in Herring's shaking hand casting sickening, lurching shadows on the walls, their own shadows, monstrous, misshapen, rising and falling, pushing and jostling for a better view. Dickens wanted to seize the lamp from the trembling hand. The terrible tableau on the ground; the chattering monkey perched on top of the wall, his shadow a grotesque half beast, half man; a shadow with a white face beside it — how could —? But then the lantern dropped with a clatter and the face was gone. Stemp picked up the lamp and kept it.

The shriek of an owl — that fatal bellman — and the hideous high-pitched screaming of a peacock came from the menagerie next door — like something mortally wounded. Dickens felt he would have strangled the peacock if it had been in the yard. A dog barking — or a fox, maybe. William Herring, the owner of the menagerie, had all sorts of creatures for sale and for exhibition. He was a taxidermist, too, had stuffed Dickens's pet raven, but even he, accustomed to death, seemed completely undone. The jeweller, in whose yard they stood, had thought, hearing screams, that some animal had escaped and had fetched Mr Herring, not wanting to investigate himself — he'd once had a rather trying encounter with a large South African cat.

What they had found had sent them hastening for a policeman, who had found the dead man's card and had sent his colleague to Bow Street, where Sergeant Rogers was waiting for the superintendent and he, having heard, sent to Stemp — if Mr Jones came to Grafton Street, he must not go to the Henchman house, but must be brought to the yard behind the jeweller's shop next to the menagerie on Quickset Row.

There was nothing to be done for the two motionless forms on the flags of the yard. Darius Henchman had been stabbed. The blood bloomed black on his chest in the lamplight, and someone had inflicted an ugly wound on his face. Mademoiselle Hormel had been strangled, and they lay together as if in some last embrace — a suicide pact? wondered the horrified Mr Herring. Superintendent Jones did not believe that at all. This was murder — the gash on Darius Henchman's face told him that. And it had been done because, greedy and stupid, they had tried to sell Sir William Pell's ring, and a stranger had asked questions in Clerkenwell, and there had been a lad in the yard at The Baptist's Head, and a lad at Mrs Speed's, and a lad who had looked at Dickens with hard, inhuman eyes. Someone had lured them to a jeweller's shop with promise of more profit, no doubt.

'We need Doctor Woodhall,' Jones said. 'Rogers, you see to that, and Stemp, you stay here with Feak until they come and then do what's necessary. Take statements from these gentlemen. Mr Dickens and I will get off to the Henchman house.'

'Mr Dickens,' said William Herring. 'I didn't know you.'

'I am sorry, Mr Herring, that you had to endure this. Please, go inside and take some brandy. I'm sure your neighbour could do with something.'

The monkey, hearing a kindly voice, hopped down from the wall onto his master's shoulder, and put his little hands over his eyes. He had seen enough.

Dickens saw the anger drain from the man's face. He watched it turn white as if he were turning into a wax figure of himself. Julius Henchman had been furious at the incursion of Superintendent Jones, who had knocked at his door far too peremptorily and refused to accept the maid's information that Mr Henchman was not at home. He was even more furious at the presence of Charles Dickens. What business was it of his? Superintendent Jones did not answer that question. He simply broke the news.

'Stabbed?' he repeated. 'Dead? Murdered with some Frenchwoman — a prostitute, was she? Enticed him into — oh, what a fool he was — I told him —'

'What?'

'To watch his step — too fond of the ladies. Just a silly fool — no harm —'

'I don't know that she was a prostitute, Mr Henchman, but I do know that he was with her in a pub in Clerkenwell, and that they sold a ring to a goldsmith there, and a watch chain. You will see that the ring bears the initials "WPT".' Jones held out the ring.

'I've never seen it before.'

'It belonged to a murder victim, Sir William Pell — it was stolen.'

Julius Henchman turned even paler. 'Murder? Darius wouldn't — this Frenchwoman — surely, she gave him the ring to sell. How would Darius be in possession of stolen goods?'

'I must tell you, Mr Henchman, that the probable murderer of Sir William Pell is Martin Jaggard, seen in Clerkenwell with a prostitute, Livvie Slack, who is involved with setting up a brothel with a Frenchwoman — the Frenchwoman who is now at the mortuary with your brother.'

'It's monstrous — Darius wouldn't — couldn't — he is a gentleman — stolen goods, a brothel — I can't believe it. It's a mistake — he has been foolish, no doubt, but consorting with criminals —'

'He may have been drawn into something he did not fully understand. He did not know, perhaps, what kind of people he was mixing with, but they are criminal, and I want to know who might know what Darius was doing out all night last Friday —'

'You have watched my house?'

'I have. I wished to question your brother about your kitchen maid, Phoebe Miller, who has disappeared with my servant girl, Posy. Both seen in your brother's carriage and in the company of Miss Hormel at a house in Union Street near King's Cross, where your brother dropped them off.'

'The kitchen maid. Mr Dickens came to ask about her, but Darius had nothing to do with —'

'He did — he was seen with her at The Copenhagen Inn —'

'I told him — I mean —'

'Told him what, sir?'

'Not to — to — go too — not to meddle with the servants. He's — was — just a foolish —'

'More than foolish, Mr Henchman. He appears to have been involved with some very unsavoury people. I suppose you understand what the abduction of two young girls might mean?'

'Well, of course, I've read — but Darius wouldn't — he is a gentleman —'

'Where was he last Friday night?'

'I don't know. He did not always come home — he was a young man — he only — he didn't deserve — I can't tell you —'

'You must, Mr Henchman, you must tell me anything you know about your brother's life or friends. There are two young girls in dreadful danger — you know now what Darius's folly has led to — murder, Mr Henchman, and it is my duty to investigate it.'

'But what has it to do with Mr Dickens? I don't understand.'

'An innocent girl, Mr Henchman, scarcely more than a child, an orphan from Mr Drouet's scandalous establishment — you have heard of him, I take it?' Dickens interrupted.

'Of course.'

'This little girl I found starving in the streets. I placed her with Mr and Mrs Jones, where she was safe and cared for until Phoebe Miller took her to The Copenhagen and met your brother there — your brother who dropped them off near an empty house from where his lady friend took them away.'

Julius Henchman could not answer.

'Did your brother have debts?'

'He sometimes — he never meant — I mean, he only — just cards —'

'Martin Jaggard is a coiner and forger. We have reason to believe that he is in the business of forging foreign banknotes. He has dealings with a Frenchman who was also seen at the Frenchwoman's lodgings in Fitzroy Street. This is a conspiracy, Mr Henchman, and your brother was connected to the principals. Now, tell me a name — someone who might have known where he was.'

Henchman looked shattered. 'Conspiracy — I don't understand — I don't know, I tell you — just fellows, he said, fellows he went to clubs with, or to the races, or the wrestling. He liked sport — the theatres — just a young man. No harm —'

'Great harm has been done, sir,' Dickens said, 'and great harm may yet be done. You must know something of your brother's life. What did he do for a living?'

Something relentless in Dickens's tone made Henchman answer, 'He had been studying for the law — but I'm afraid it did not suit him. He wanted something more stimulating. I thought he might go into business — I have a friend in the wine trade who was willing to give him a chance.'

'Not banking, as in your profession.'

Mr Henchman looked positively alarmed at the thought of his brother in the banking way. No doubt, Julius Henchman knew that the young man could not be relied on. 'No, no, Darius wanted nothing to do with banking. It would not have suited Darius at all. He would have found his way, I am sure, but now — I can hardly believe — I can't tell you anything more. I need to —'

Henchman looked a broken man, but Jones was determined to finish. 'Just one more question, Mr Henchman —'

They heard the door handle turn and Mrs Henchman's querulous tones outside, calling for Rose. 'Oh, there you are. I have a dreadful headache. I am going upstairs. You might bring me some tea. Is Mr Henchman at home?'

'Yes, ma'am — in the drawing room, I think.'

'Tell him, please, that I am resting. I shall not be down for dinner.'

They heard the rustling of skirts and footsteps going away, and all the while, Dickens watched how the waxy pallor turned almost yellow and the perspiration on Henchman's forehead created the impression that he was melting. He looked almost terror-struck.

The footsteps came back. Mr Henchman seemed not to be breathing. The room was full of silence, a silence so tight that Dickens thought it must crack and the house fall to pieces. The door clicked shut with a sound as loud as a pistol shot. He heard Mr Henchman exhale the ragged breath of a man who had passed through an ordeal and was somehow saved.

'Last Friday, Mr Henchman. You did not go to your daughter's house as arranged. Where were you?'

'Just my club — a business appointment.'

'Murder, Mr Henchman. I do not wish to waste my time verifying that information.'

'If you must know about my private business. A lady — an acquaintance — a friend, I mean.'

'Name?'

'Is it really necessary?' Henchman looked up and saw that it was. 'Mrs Amelia Wand — she lodges at Number 3, Arbour Square. My wife doesn't — she needn't — it is only —'

They knew perfectly well what Mrs Henchman needn't. Jones merely said that he would ask Mrs Wand for confirmation of Mr Julius Henchman's visit to her on the last Friday night.

'Darius — what? When can I see?'

'Tomorrow, Mr Henchman. Doctor Woodhall of King's College Hospital will conduct the post-mortem tonight. I will send a man to take you to the hospital. There will be an inquest, of course, probably in the afternoon. The verdict must be murder and the inquest will be adjourned pending enquiries by the police. Of necessity, I will come back, and you can tell me if there is anything you recall about your brother's life which will assist me in finding the murderer.'

Julius Henchman did not answer. They left him, a man in pieces. His life had been one of easy success and pleasure. His wife irritated him. She talked too much — not that he listened, and her extravagance angered him. Her money, she'd say, because that oaf of a father had left a fortune in trust for her and her heirs. Mostly, he kept out of her way, except when his digestion was upset. He had been fond of his younger brother and tolerant of his spendthrift ways and flirting — no harm, no harm. A man was entitled to enjoy himself. What else was money for?

But a common prostitute in a back yard. His own dalliance with Mrs Wand was discreet, and she was a lady, in her way. It made a difference. Expensive, though, damn her, always wheedling for more, suggesting that she might pay his wife a visit. Well, it would have to end. But only after the police had seen her. He had been with her, but he didn't want her spilling too many beans. He'd better write to her — warn her. He'd keep her sweet until — after… Good God, into what coils had Darius entangled himself? No harm, he had thought. No harm in a little business on the side.

But there was harm. Murder had hammered on his respectable door, burst in, and left its indelible bloodstain on his carpet — and his curtains, his brand new 'sociable', his wife's porcelain shepherds and shepherdesses, smirking in their pastoral landscape. He sat on, staring at his white Carrara marble chimney piece as if the blood soaked there. In the fitted grate the fire burned brightly, but he felt no warmth. He was a frightened man.

25: SHADOWS IN THE FOG

The world had stopped. Time had stopped. The acrid smell and taste of sulphur — and the devil. Night and fog thickened into dense black as if they'd walked out into a wall. They were in the street but had no idea which way to turn. Dickens reached out and touched Jones's sleeve, which felt damp and cold.

'I'm still here — a piece of me, at any rate.'

'Good. Don't move. Let's get our bearings. Now, there's a lamp just —'

As if from a distant world concealed in that awful thickness, they heard light footsteps and hoarse breathing, but from which direction they could not tell. Curiously flapping footsteps. Coming slowly. Jones felt for his truncheon and pulled Dickens behind him. Theft was common in the fog. You'd feel a breath at your neck, a hand at your pocket, or the cold kiss of a knife at your throat. You wouldn't see a thing, but when the breath faded, you'd know he was gone. Or it might be worse. The strangling garotte might choke the life out of you or the knife carve deep. Dead in a minute. And in the gutter.

The footfall stopped. The breath nearer now. Someone was there — the stink of him. Close enough to strike. Jones raised his truncheon. A hand reached out. The gleam of a blade — brief as lightning. Jones struck out and heard the sound of wood on bone. A yelp. Then a strike back and the truncheon fell with a clatter. A swish of air. Jones reached out to grasp an arm. A rip of cloth. A twist. Footsteps halting away. And Jones left with a ragged sleeve in his hand.

'Who the hell —'

'Opportunist,' Jones said. 'It happens in the fog. Garrotting, stabbing.'

'Unless we were followed. Someone saw us at the jeweller's?'

'Damn this fog. We need to get to Doctor Woodhall — though it'll take the mortuary van hours to get to the jeweller's and back. Still —'

'Sam, Sam — where's Scrap? We forgot him in the rush to Quickset Row. If he's still there —'

They felt their way to the end of the terrace, where there was the faint light of a gas lamp. Dickens knew that there should be an alley leading to the mews behind the houses. At the corner, they groped into emptiness and felt their way down once they had found the solidity of brick wall. They heard no more heavy breathing or footsteps, but faintly came the sound of a horse snorting in the darkness. Stables, then, and now a little halo of greenish light, fading and reappearing as the fog swirled about it.

Jones, leading the way, felt the grain of wood under his hand. Double doors — a carriage house. They inched along and saw more light flickering. From more doors, they presumed. And then there were open doors, firelight and lamplight, and a groom inside, washing down a carriage.

'Police,' Jones said. 'Mr Henchman's carriage house?'

'Next one — but the carriage ain't there. Stable lad's gone off 'ome. All locked up.'

'Have you seen a lad about — scruffy little urchin?'

'Up ter no good?'

'No, he's a lad we know and he's missing. He had some information for me.'

'Lot o' comin's an' goin's — seen a lad 'angin' about last couple o' days, but then there's allus lads about, lookin' fer work. Seemed 'armless enough.'

'But you said up to no good. Why did you think that?'

'Sometimes you get a feelin' about a lad or a fellah — lookin' about 'em. A few weeks back, fer example, a stranger asked about Mr Darius Henchman — which house was it. I told 'im — 'e seemed pleasant enough, but then, I dunno, 'e seemed a bit too curious. Were the Henchmans well-off? Was Mr Darius moneyed? Did 'e 'ave a lady friend? Course, I said I didn't know anythin' — not my business. 'E went off round the front — debt collector, I wondered. You know the sort — all old pals, offerin' a flask o' drink, a tip, an' slippin' in the questions as if yer was an idiot.'

'What did he look like?'

'Oh, tall — well-dressed — yer knows — topper, fancy cravat, gloves — yeller, they was. Remember that. Niver saw 'im again, so I didn't mention it ter Mr Julius Henchman. Not that I wanted ter — cold fish, that one. Told Mr Darius — 'e jest laughed, said 'ooever it was wouldn't get no change from 'im.'

Matty Miller? Jones wondered, but he only asked, 'Can you lend us a lamp? I'll get it back to you. Superintendent Jones from Bow Street. I'd like to have a look about.'

The groom lit two dark lanterns with a spill from his brazier and picked up a third. 'I'll come with you.'

They rattled the doors of Mr Henchman's carriage house, but no familiar voice called out. They searched along the mews to the very end, which came out into Fitzroy Street, but there was no sign of Scrap. Jones told the groom to keep the lad with him if he turned up — to tell the boy that Superintendent

Jones and Constable Dickens had been and would send someone to fetch him.

'Which way you goin', sir?'

'Up to the New Road — Quickset Row.'

'Mr 'Erring's up there, sir — jest foller the noise — peacock screechin'.'

They worked their way up Fitzroy Street with the aid of the lanterns, which at least allowed them to see their own feet. They heard nothing but their own breathing. No peacock called. The silence between them was as heavy as the fog. Separated by an anguish which could find no words, not even from Dickens, who always thought he could cheer up Sam Jones with a quip or a teasing comment on the old coat he was so fond of. But this — Posy missing and now Scrap, possibly, and the dark pressing on them as if sealing them in a tomb. And a shadow in the fog with a knife. Dickens had seen that blade flash — a serpent's tongue in the night.

Scrap leave his post? Unlikely — but they forgot sometimes that he was a child. He could be as much swayed by emotion and impulse as any other child, or any other human being, for that matter. How often had he rushed off without Sam's say-so? He remembered a night in Limehouse, and Sam telling him that he might be inimitable, but not immortal.

Posy was Scrap's friend; he cared about Eleanor Brim more than anyone; what hurt Eleanor had to be put right. Eleanor loved Posy. Posy must be found — could be found, Scrap would believe. Suppose he had seen something, someone near the Henchman house…

But, no, no. Stemp, seeing the fog, would surely have told him to stay, or maybe Stemp had said to go back to Sam's house. The fog had not been so thick when they had rushed to Quickset Row. That was it — Scrap, safe, fed by Elizabeth

Jones, sitting with Eleanor and Tom by the fire. Dickens opened his mouth to speak, to reassure, but seeing Sam's face emerge, grey as stone in the brief ray of a gas lamp, stopped him. Sam seemed a stranger, and then the stranger's face dissolved into the dark as they crept on.

Save it, Dickens thought — let Stemp say the comforting words. Let Stemp be there waiting for Rogers and the mortuary van. Scrap had sense — he'd have seen the fog falling, known that the best thing was to get to Norfolk Street and wait.

The New Road seemed more familiar; more lights and the sound of a horse's hooves clip-clopping slowly. Figures looming out of the fog. Two men in top hats cursing, but lightly, humorously, one telling the other to watch his step. 'No feet,' the other replying, holding his hands before him. Bumping into a woman with a basket, the smell of beer and fish — a good-humoured, 'Care ter take me 'ome, sirs?' Laughter in the dark; light spilling from the pub on the corner; singing; the sound of a train coming into Euston Station just up the road.

And Stemp, solid and imperturbable at the back gate of the jeweller's yard, explaining that the mortuary van had not yet come, and telling them that he had told Scrap to get to Norfolk Street before the fog came down too thick.

Stemp, hearing about the shadow in the fog, and the knife, seeing his chief's face, said, 'The van'll come, sir, I'll wait. Feak can go to Grafton Street. You get back to Norfolk Street with Mr Dickens. Jest ter be sure. But he'll be there, sir.'

Elizabeth Jones was sitting with Eleanor Brim by the fire, waiting for news — Eleanor who could not sleep in her bed, but who, at last, was asleep on the sofa. Elizabeth, who had found out from Lady Nora's former maid that Darius Henchman had asked to borrow a silver snuff box. He'd promised to bring it back. He wanted to have one made just like it, but Lady Nora had found out and said she was a silly girl and must keep away from the foolish young man who would only get her into more trouble. She missed Lady Nora, an' though she knew that Mr Darius 'ad been wrong — still 'e was a very 'an'some gentleman. No 'an'some young gents called on Lady Pancras.

Nothing useful at all, Elizabeth reflected, just a silly, simple girl, head turned by a silly young man. She wondered if Sam had found him. What about the Jaggard man? And where was Sam in this fog? It was late, very late. She should take Eleanor up to bed — she would sit with her until —

She heard the key in the lock and went out quickly. There might be news that Eleanor ought not to hear. By their faces, she knew that there was.

And there was no way that Jones could hide the truth from her — murder and the possible connection between Jaggard, Matty Miller, Darius Henchman and his French woman that he dreaded to explain. He had promised Eleanor not to pretend — though he would have to. But Elizabeth — he could not lie to her.

And in the gaslit hallway into which the black fog had crept, Dickens and Jones watched her face shrink into white bone as they whispered the news of the murders. She could only nod her understanding of the terrible implications of the story and her acceptance of the fact that they would have to go out again.

At the door, she caught Jones's arm. 'Wait. Where's Scrap?'

Sam Jones hesitated. Dickens had to answer. A half-truth, he thought — if Scrap could not be found, then she would have to be told, and she would know that they had lied if they said they knew he was safe. 'He was at the Henchman mews. We're going there now on the way to Bow Street.'

She understood. She knew every minute change in her husband's face. She knew every nuance of his every word. She knew when it was impossible to speak. She'd lived through enough cases.

She touched his face. 'I know. You'll do everything you can. Look after each other.'

The street was strange again. Out of house and home and no idea what to do for the best. Sam Jones shook himself. 'We need men — and lamps. I want that place scoured. Shouldn't you go home?'

'Do you know, Mr Jones, I thought I heard a voice asking a question — a queasy sort of question. I answer the unseen with a firm no and beg said question be not asked again this night.'

Dickens turned to go and heard a faint chuckle as Jones stepped to his side. 'Comedian.'

'Comical, pastoral — and all the rest.'

'Always in your debt.'

'Never. Bow Street, then?'

'We'll go by Grafton Street — see if we come across any beat constables.'

The blurred yellow of a bull's eye lamp showed a constable at the corner of Fitzroy Square. Ordered to search the mews. The smell of meat and fish, and sawdust, and the slip of cabbage leaves underfoot announced the proximity of Fitzroy Market by Tottenham Court Road. The constable looking about the silent stalls, told to search the few sheds and hovels still there. Some rum neighbours, the Henchman family.

The fog was thinning, and they made better progress, catching a constable near the church in John Street. Constable Doublett, discovered coming from an alley in Gower Street, recognised his chief and Mr Dickens, and went off smartly. He knew Scrap very well. His normally cheerful countenance blanched at the news. 'I'll know him, sir, an' I'll get Semple. He'll be near the workhouse — in your street, sir.'

In Clarke's Buildings, the old, rented houses for unmarried officers just up in Whetstone Place, Inspector Grove mustered a group of men for Superintendent Jones. Some to be sent to Quickset Row. When it was lighter, they could search the jeweller's yard and Mr Herring's premises for any clue, any trace of the murderer. Others to the mews and the surrounding streets. Constables Semple and Dacres to assist at the market. Those sheds and hovels interested Superintendent Jones — very near Grafton Street. Very handy for someone who wanted to hide — or to hide a victim.

Dickens marvelled at Sam's calmness. He addressed the men firmly — their duty was to try to find the boy. Some of them knew Scrap, and those that did not were ready to follow orders. Inspector Grove had picked his men wisely. There was Jaggard, Jones told them, possibly connected with two murders — the murder of a man whose house Scrap had watched with Constable Stemp.

Dickens, invited to address them, felt strangely shy — he who had addressed audiences of thousands, hesitated, found his voice, and told them what Scrap meant to him, and to the superintendent.

'Just a lad, gentlemen, but a good lad who came from nothing and had nothing until we found him — and he has paid us back a hundredfold, nay, a thousand, by his loyalty and courage. He's found his way into our hearts. You are single men, I know, but one day you'll have a lad of your own — try not to have six, like me. They do cost, I can tell you —' They all laughed at that. 'Just a lad, sirs, but worth more than any lawyer over there at Lincoln's Inn, or any judge in Chancery, or any lord in Parliament, or any Duke of anywhere, or any prince in the palace itself. Solid gold — no coining there.'

Of course, they cheered him, these two-pounds-a-week men. They'd do it for Charles Dickens, but most of them would do it for the superintendent, too. They'd seen his face as he came in. They knew all about Jaggard and about the little servant girl, Posy.

Back at Bow Street, the night inspector lit a fire in Jones's office, brought tea and bread and butter. Inspector Jolley, who never smiled, did so now, encouraging them to take something.

'Good for you, Charles, dukes and lords, eh? They'd walk on water for you.'

'And you. I saw that. But what now? Matty Miller at the Henchman mews —'

'Knew all about Darius Henchman from his sister.'

Dickens watched Jones's face. He looked more like himself, as if the warmth had breathed life into his face, which had seemed so drawn when they had looked down at those bodies. The fire — and Elizabeth. She had known that they had somehow forgotten Scrap. He'd seen it in her eyes, but she had touched Sam's face to tell him that she understood. A remarkable woman. Sam would not come to harm while she lived to love him. No harm, no harm, Julius Henchman had said. Darius Henchman was beyond hurt or harm now, but there was still harm being done —

Jones interrupted his thoughts. 'Conspiracy — they wanted someone respectable, a gentleman —'

'What for?'

'Joey Speed was used to get the sample forged notes from the Frenchman, but they needed someone of a better class to sell Pell's jewels, to change the sovereigns — no questions asked. All Henchman needed to do was to make small purchases and pass the money on to Hormel, but they took some of the loot for themselves, and then somebody found out about us.'

'And that somebody lured them to the jeweller's in Quickset Row. In any case, perhaps they were no longer needed. All the jewels sold, and the sovereigns got rid of.'

'Where else did you say Darius pawned his goods?'

'Mr Decker knew him in Poplar and in Limehouse — always pawned his stuff at a distance from Grafton Street.'

'Limehouse where Jaggard forged his American dollars. Inspector Bold will know the pawnshops and the jewellers' shops. Round Kidney Stairs, maybe. Darius Henchman wasn't supposed to sell them in Clerkenwell.'

'Bold — when?'

'When —' Dickens knew what he meant. Jones looked at his watch — 'Half-past three. There's nothing else we can do now except wait for light. Rogers should be back then. I'll have to look at the bodies. The inquest tomorrow. I know you said — but this is not a question. You should go home — get some sleep. If I look anything like you do —'

'Fresh as a spring lamb, Mr Jones, you are.'

'For the slaughter, more like. Mr Mayne will soon be asking questions, no doubt. Now, go — before Mrs Dickens sends out a search party.'

'If you get word of...'

'I'll send.'

'No matter what the hour.'

'No matter.'

26: A STITCH IN TIME

Up Bow Street and then into Drury Lane, across Bloomsbury Square where the clock of St George's told him it was four o'clock, and the other clocks told the same tale, the voices of the night speaking to the abandoned, the trampers, the vagrants, the outcasts, the orphans, the wakeful mad — telling that they were irretrievably lost to time and hope.

The dead of night, Dickens thought. Not so dead. There were invisible companions, he knew, the houseless nomads for whom sleep was always an absence, and home unknown; the restless sleepers in doorways and backyards, dreaming of warm fires and faces, waking to find only a pillow of cold stone; the dead waking and walking in the crooked ways of unseen life and death. The fog was still with him, a thinner, more spectral companion whose clammy breath he still felt on his neck, and whose whispering fingers still wreathed themselves about his face, even his gloved hands, and his wrists — the lightest of manacles, but there was no escaping them. He felt the chill of them, listening for a flapping footstep, or hoarse breathing at his ear. But there was no one, just the muffled forms in the doorways and shifting shadows by the ghosts of gaslight. Shadows which vanished at his approach.

In Russell Square, Talfourd's house was in darkness; up in Gordon Street, Mark Lemon would be telling jokes in his sleep; in Tavistock Square, his neighbour, Frank Stone, painting lovers in his dreams; Mr Cardale, his other neighbour, writing a sermon in his head, dreaming of the damned. Well, they were real enough out here. City of dreadful night.

And somewhere in this endless darkness, in this limbo of lost souls, there was Scrap, awake, perhaps, on watch, listening, or asleep, or —

Dickens stopped. A noise. The sound of someone running a stick along railings. It stopped and he waited. A someone, he thought, not a gang. The sound came again, eerily magnified, but it was hard to tell where it was coming from. The fog distorted everything. Again, that rippling metal sound — haunting music of the night, sounding the presence of something menacing. It set his teeth on edge. He could taste metal. A stick weighted with lead?

He'd seen children running sticks along railings. Mischievous, enjoying the noise, but not in the dead of night. He slipped closed the shutter of the dark lantern Jones had given him. He had no choice but to creep forward, using the railings of the houses to guide him, dipping in and out of shadow, finding himself in dark deeps after passing a gas lamp. He didn't hear the noise again. He turned the corner and stayed still. Nothing to see but the fog. He inched forward. He could see the faint light from his own porch. Only yards away, but an immeasurable distance if someone were there.

And then the loud clang of the stick on iron. A pause. Then another. And another. Three tolls of a hollow bell — a warning in the fog, and he a ship at sea. Suddenly angry, he took his own stick and banged it very hard on the railing to which he was clinging. There was an answering bang. He waited, hardly daring to breathe. Not a sound. No footsteps. No hoarse breathing at his ear, just the sound of his own heart. He didn't move. Then he did hear footsteps, but this person was not hiding. The steps came on, measured, firm, steady as clockwork — two and a half miles an hour, those steps were ordered to do.

The light of a bull's eye lamp and a tall figure in a tall hat, a glint of white buttons.

'Constable Flint?' Flint was a man he had often met on his beat about Tavistock Square and its environs.

'All well, Mr Dickens?'

'I heard someone making a racket with a stick on the railings.'

'Drunk, probably. I'll take a look as I go on. Scarpered now, I'll bet.'

Dickens hoped so. He went through the gate, but he heard nothing more, and slipped into the house. The lamp low, and the house silent. The sleepers all wrapped in their secret dream lives. Something so strange, he always thought, in being surrounded by familiar faces asleep. No one knowing he was there. A ghost in his own house, coming in with the fog — and the whiff of danger. Could it have been? He felt shaken. That hollow sound of ringing metal in the dark — a threat in it, and that answering clang had felt like the last word in an argument. And he hadn't won it.

He should change, take a shower — but there might not be any water. In any case, suppose he missed a message — he didn't want the whole household roused. He crept upstairs to his study, where the remnants of a fire gleamed dully. He put on some sticks and coal and gave it a shot of air with the bellows. His desk waited silently for him — everything in its place — just as he had left it hours before. The letter from Lieutenant Hoskins Brown telling him about the ship and Australia. He sat by the fire, half-dozing, half-dreaming.

Eyes — Mrs Speed's boiled lobster eyes; Jacko Cragg's, hard as stones; Mr Herring's eyes, starting from his head. A monkey's eyes, tragic and pleading. Blood on a white shirt; the bulging eyes of a strangled woman. A face with a purple scar;

Elizabeth Jones touching his own face; the sound of sticks knocking on metal; a shadow with a white face on the wall —

Knocking. He came to. Someone at the door — he sprang to his feet, then realised someone was knocking at the study door, which he flung open to reveal John, his manservant.

'Oh, sir — I'm sorry, I didn't know. I saw the light and wondered —'

'No, I'm sorry, John — it was too late when I came back. The boy's missing, Scrap. I'm waiting for news. I need to take a shower and change. Is there any water?'

'Just about, sir. Shall I make tea while you dress?'

'Yes, yes, but keep your ear open for the door. What time is it?'

'Just after six — it's getting lighter.'

'I'll be ten minutes.'

And he was — enough cold water to douse himself and a quick change in his dressing room. He did not want to disturb Catherine. He'd leave a message for her with John — he'd tell her about Scrap. She'd understand that. He remembered her shock on the night Scrap had come, and her concern for Posy before he'd mentioned Lady Nora. Talfourd had made her laugh about the gossip, but he had defended Lady Nora, telling Catherine she would like her. 'All nonsense,' he'd said, 'she's a thoroughly nice woman.' Dickens wasn't so sure about that — Lady Nora was a thoroughly attractive woman. Not always the same thing, but Talfourd had done the trick.

He drank his tea in the study and watched the darkness lift as if a stage curtain were rising. He started as if scalded when he heard the knock at the front door. He went out to the top of the stairs, not daring to go down, feeling the ice at his neck and sick dread in his heart. John was opening the door. He heard his own name. Not Sam Jones's voice. Sam would have come if…

He went down, stiff as if he were made of wood. Constable Doublett was in the hall. Dickens couldn't tell by his face.

'Mr Dickens, sir, Mr Jones sent me. We haven't found him. Feak is still at Grafton Street, but there's no sign. Mr Jones has gone to see the bodies with Sergeant Rogers, but he says, now it's light, you might want to —'

John gave him his coat and stick.

Doublett noticed the workshops in Warren Street just above Fitzroy Square — they had been mews, but the carriage folk had moved out and little businesses took their place. It was worth a look, Dickens thought. A lad could find a hiding place down there — if — if he needed somewhere. It looked promising — little buildings divided up, sheds and hutches, a few carts. Several were opening up, but no one had seen a boy, and then Doublett's lamp picked out blood on the closed door of Mr Reuben Sawyer's carpentry workshop. Bloody fingerprints — small ones. Enquiries sent Doublett hastening down to Cleveland Street where Mr Sawyer had his lodgings.

In the lamplight, Dickens contemplated the fingerprints and waited. Not a sound from inside, but there was comfort in the sound of voices, doors opening, the sound of a hammer, a dog barking. Then Mr Sawyer came with his keys, a thin, anxious-looking man with uncombed hair and a shabby jacket. And, as if by some magic, Constable Stemp was there, too.

There, on a pile of straw, curled up, like the child he was, his face very innocent in sleep and very pale in contrast to the blood matted in his hair.

'I didn't see 'im,' Mr Sawyer said. 'I only went in the yard — 'e musta —'

'It doesn't matter,' Dickens said, kneeling by the sleeping form, feeling that there was a pulse, and very, very gently turning Scrap to him, hearing him mumble and seeing the cut on his face where blood had congealed and the bloodied hand. Not life-threatening. A knife, though, had done this.

'Scrap,' he said, 'my boy, can you wake up?'

Two blue eyes opened. 'Misser D — where'd you — someone jumped me —'

Doublett went off to tell Constable Feak to spread the word, after which he was to hasten to Bow Street, and to King's College hospital, if necessary — to find Mr Jones and bring him to Norfolk Street.

Stemp carried him. Stemp who had appeared as if by magic and said nothing, only picked up the injured boy. Scrap was light and weighed nothing in his strong arms. Dickens knocked lightly twice. There was a light upstairs and then Elizabeth was there to receive him and examine his head.

'Don't tell us yet, Scrap. We'll wait for Mr Jones. Just let me see.'

Elizabeth bathed the matted hair and applied witch hazel. Dickens thought it looked as though he'd knocked his head. Fallen, perhaps — fleeing from whoever had jumped him. She bathed the cuts on his face and hand and applied more witch hazel. The cut on the hand was just a scratch, though it had bled a good deal. The cut on the cheek was deeper. Elizabeth took a stout sewing needle from her work basket, threaded it with purse silk and stitched the wound.

'One for each inch,' she said, deftly tying the silk in a double knot to bring the edges together. 'Two for two inches.' She repeated the process and placed a strip of plaster across the wound on each side. Scrap didn't make a sound.

'There now, brave boy. No moving about, though. Toast and tea next.'

When she had gone to the kitchen, Scrap closed his eyes. Dickens arranged the blanket over him. Let him sleep. Time enough when Sam came to find out what had happened. He thought of the knife in the dark. A knife that had killed Darius Henchman; a knife that had killed Sir William Pell. Jaggard had killed Pell. Jaggard was ruthless, Sam had said so, a man to whom power and wealth meant everything, and life nothing. He'd rid himself of anyone who got in his way — a thing to toss on the dust heap.

Elizabeth came back. 'You eat it,' she said, handing Dickens the toast. 'When did you last eat?'

'Do you know, I can't remember — oh, no, Inspector Jolley made us tea and bread and butter. He smiled — I remember that.'

Elizabeth smiled, too. 'You brought him back — I knew it. I really did.'

'And Posy?'

'That's the difference. There is dread about my heart. I'm full of doubts. I didn't feel that after you'd gone. I just knew — the same as I would know if anything happened to Sam, or the children. I knew that Edith would die — my only child. I knew. And you — I think I'd know. A light would go out and I'd know —' Seeing his face. Brisk suddenly — 'Now, eat that toast — I've to get the children up.'

'What will you tell them?'

'Only that Scrap's had an accident and he's asleep for now and mustn't be disturbed. I'll take Eleanor to school and Tom to the shop — I'd better tell Mollie that Scrap's all right. Scrap'll know what to tell Eleanor.'

Dickens ate his toast and drank his tea. He heard the sound of low voices and footsteps on the stairs, and Elizabeth promising that they could see Scrap later. He dozed. He was aware of the clock ticking in the hall and coals spitting on the fire and Scrap muttering in his sleep. He'd heal, in heart and mind. Elizabeth would see to that, and Eleanor Brim. Watch and wait. Sam would come.

He heard the key in the lock and Jones was beside him, looking down at the sleeping boy with his plastered face.

'He's all right — Elizabeth stitched him up. His cheek will heal.'

'Knife?'

'I'd say so. Someone jumped him, he said, but that's all. Elizabeth told him to wait for you.'

Scrap woke, saw Jones, and sat up. ''T'ain't nothin' — jest a scratch. I got away.'

'From whom?'

'Dunno — see, Mr Stemp said to get off before the fog came down too quick. 'Eard a carriage comin' into the mews. Waited, but it wasn't 'Enchmen's. Nothin' else doin', so I makes my way up into Grafton Street an' it 'appens — jumps me. Feels the knife on my face, shoves it off, but feels the cut. It caught my 'and an' I kicks out — got 'im on the shin an' 'e lets go. 'Ears the knife drop. I scarpers back down the mews, finds my way out, but I can 'ear 'im runnin' or tryin' to. Queer, as if 'e was limpin' or the sole of 'is boot was loose.'

'Did you smell anything?'

''E stank. I knows that. O' fish an' somethin' else, now I remembers.'

'He did, I remember that,' Dickens said. 'I'll have to think … asphaltum — pitch — used in engraving and etching on the steel plates.'

198

Sam reached into his pocket, took out the ragged sleeve and passed it to Scrap, who sniffed and said, 'That's what I smelt.'

'Quite a bouquet.' Dickens sniffed it. 'Ink, acid, too — used to create the lines in the plates.'

'Asphaltum — that's what I thought. Thoddy Cragg, perhaps. Did you hear anything? His voice, maybe?' Jones asked Scrap.

'Drums — well, that's what I thought. Folk beatin' something.'

'On metal?'

'Bangin' on wood — a door, mebbe. Jest ran — lost 'im, anyway. Fell over something 'ard, bashed me 'ead an' sees an open door. In I goes an' that's it.'

Elizabeth came in with more tea and toast for Scrap. 'Two plates of egg and bacon in the kitchen. No, you've time. Charles says that you, Samuel Jones, have only eaten bread and butter since breakfast yesterday. I've made coffee. Don't let it get cold. Then you can go. Scrap's staying here.'

A predictable, 'But —' from the injured party.

'No — your battle scars have to heal. If the wound opens, it'll get infected then it'll be the doctor with his scalpel.'

27: LIMEHOUSE CLUES

'Those that touch pitch,' Dickens remarked as they went out into the already tired morning. It had got up late and seemed to be changing its mind. The light was grey-green, hardly day at all, but, after the compulsory breakfast, Dickens and Jones were on their way to take a steamer to Wapping Stairs, where they would find Inspector Bold of the River Police.

'Shall be defiled,' Jones completed the quotation. 'That's Jaggard — pitch. He's like a disease, corrupting everyone he comes into contact with.'

'I think Cragg was already gone — and taken his child with him.'

'And ours.'

On the steamer, they watched the misty vapours coiling on the water; fog still hung about the riverbank, making the buildings ghostly and shivering and the lights hazy; it hung about the masts of the great ships, mingled with the smoke from the steamer stacks. At a distance they heard the mournful sound of a foghorn and the answering blare of a steamer's hooter. Barges passed in funereal procession, lights wavering in the murk. They passed the collier boats crowding at the entrance to Whitefriars Dock, where once they'd been caught in a flood. The water looked as uninviting as it had then. Dickens remembered with a shudder those few moments under the heaving water.

'What did Doctor Woodhall say?'

'Nothing more than we saw — Henchman stabbed in the heart and Miss Hormel strangled — manually. He broke her neck. He'll be able to tell us more later. I'm thinking Jaggard.

She'd trust him — didn't mind Darius getting it, and Jaggard could get close enough to her to do the deed.'

'They might have been lovers.'

'I wouldn't be a bit surprised. Something compelling about Jaggard — a power about him. I saw for myself. Handsome, I suppose — well-dressed. Swarthy complexion and good white teeth. Looks after himself, I daresay.'

'I wonder who he was — before he took to crime.'

'Pell's valet. Though, I see what you mean — before that — I don't know. Mayne passed on the case to me. I knew Jaggard as a coiner, head of a vicious crew — but nothing of his antecedents.'

They watched a woman with a little boy in her arms, gripping the rail and pointing out the Tower and Traitor's gate, and the child laughing and pointing, too.

'Imp of Satan, Shackell said about Jacko Cragg. Rogers thinks the same about Jaggard. Couldn't believe he ever had a mother,' Jones said.

'And those other lads, the ones we saw in the graveyard — same ones Scrap heard?'

'Recruited by Jacko Cragg, I'll bet.'

'I heard something in the fog earlier — on my way home. Someone banging along the railings. I met Constable Flint of D Division — told him.'

'You didn't see anything?'

'Not in the fog, but I've told John to be careful and send Topping to Bow Street if anyone appears.'

'I'd best put a constable at your house, though — to be on the safe side. Those lads we saw — brutal-looking lot, and if they're working for Jaggard…'

'I know. And in the jeweller's yard, I thought I saw —'

'What?'

'A face — an impossible thing, I thought at the time. A face in the shadows on the wall — I mean on the top. And then Herring dropped his lamp, and it was gone, and that peacock started up. Perhaps, I imagined —'

'Someone followed us to Grafton Street — someone with a flapping shoe.'

'With a knife. And Scrap heard that same sound and that drumming noise.'

'It worries me, Charles. Jaggard has eyes everywhere.'

'Wild eyes. Inhuman eyes. Watching us.'

At the police station, Inspector Bold, solid as a stone tower, and with humanly enquiring eyes, greeted them with one question: 'Jaggard?'

Jones gave him the details and explained their purpose. Bold remembered the old windmill at Kidney Stairs to which he escorted them with Jones's godson, Constable John Gaunt.

A man and wife lived there now, she a fishwife and he a pure-finder. That stinking trade in dog dung for the tanneries. A shilling a bucket, the stench of which met them as they came upon the half-ruined place. The smell of fish hung in the air of the room in which they found a man with a patch over one eye, and there was the smell of blood, too. The fishwife was slitting herrings and taking out the guts, which she tossed into a pot on the brazier which was their fireplace. No Carrara marble here, nor any 'sociable', just three rough stools and the deal table where the fish scales glinted in the light of the smoking oil lamp, and a wooden bunk in the corner where a boy was sitting, taking the fish from a basket to hand to his mother.

The boy, a lad of about twelve, showed them his scarred hands. 'They don't 'urt no more.'

The fishwife spoke up. "'E was only a child, sir, an' that gang, they was a vicious lot, an' see, we didn't know wot was goin' on until 'is fingers, an' then they was all gone. Still, the place was empty an' in we came. Ain't seen anythin' o' that Jaggard since.'

'Can you remember any of his associates who stayed behind when Jaggard left?' Jones asked the boy.

'There woz Tipper wot broke 'is leg.'

'Mr Tipper?'

'Dunno, sir, but when they all went off, Tipper, 'e fell down the stairs ter the river an' couldn't get up. They jest left 'im. In a bad way, 'e woz, an' some folk took 'im ter the 'orspital — 'ad 'is leg off.'

'And do you know where he is now?'

'Sells metalware in the street — dunno where 'e lives but seen 'im about the market. Talked to 'im, sometimes. Wooden leg now.'

'The market's at the top o' Rose Lane,' the mother told them.

Tipper wasn't hard to find. They knew him by the wooden leg leaning by his rough deal table, heaped with an assortment of rusty metalware: old pans, skillets, tin plates, rusty fire irons, some chains, locks and bolts, hinges, hammers. No one was buying.

Tipper looked like a man in pain — he'd taken off his leg to ease it, probably; a pale face with deep creases in which the black dirt stood out, but he flushed in anger in response to Bold's query.

'Bastard Jaggard,' he spat, 'left me ter die there in the stinkin' mud. My woman went with 'em. Niver saw any of 'em agin. Bastard Jaggard makin' a fortune an' me a shillin' a day if I'm lucky. Cadges the stock from cooks an 'ousewives or pays the mudlarks. 'T'ain't any sort o' livin'. Waste o' bleedin' time.'

'How'd they get away?' asked Jones.

'Boat — jest Jaggard, my girl an' a couple o' lads. Rest scattered. There woz a lad got 'is fingers burnt. Jaggard didn't care. Not about me neither. Dunno where they went, but Jaggard'll be makin' money — be sure o' that.'

'What do you know about him — where did he come from?' Dickens asked, thinking about his and Jones's conversation.

'Said 'e woz a gentl'man's son — a gent 'imself if 'e 'ad 'is rights.'

'Did you believe him?'

Tipper looked thoughtful. 'All sorts of folk say it, sir — there's a fish seller hereabouts wot says the same — father a parson, a holy gent. Shows me a bible — says 'e'd niver part with it. I dunno, 'e don't look much like a gent, but they ain't many gents 'ereabouts. Jaggard now — 'e is different. Ain't like anyone else I ever met — clean fer a start, dressed up — it's as if — I dunno, yer can't 'elp yerself. Somethin' about 'im wot makes yer do wot 'e wants. An' the women, sir, they goes fer 'im — my woman couldn't 'elp erself, I suppose —'

'Did he say anything about his gentleman father?'

'Said the name Jaggard — lawyer, 'e said. Rich cove, but the rich cove'd get it one day.'

Dickens glanced at Jones, whose expression showed that he knew the lawyer, too. His glance told Dickens to go on.

'Still alive, the rich cove?'

'That I can't say, sir. See, Jaggard told me cos once I said my pa 'ad ended in the work'ouse. Dead now. Asked 'im about 'is ma an' pa, an' that's wot 'e told me. Ma a fine lady. Clammed up then. That's wot 'e did — took 'imself away somewhere in 'is own 'ead. Yer couldn't — yer didn't dare — yer didn't know wot 'e'd do.'

'Lads,' said Jones, 'what kind of lads were with Jaggard?'

'Always lads about. Jaggard 'ad a way with them, too. Used 'em in the coinin' an' fer distributing, an' fer —'

'What?'

'Say, if someone crossed 'im, tried ter muscle in, them lads'd put the frightners. Jaggard, 'e could make 'em do anythin'.'

'And you — what did you do for Jaggard?' asked Jones.

'Makin' the moulds, mixin' the acids — yer knows all about coinin'. I've paid the price. Wished I'd niver, but wot's a poor man ter do? My woman — she wanted... I'd 'ave bin better off in quod with food ter eat, an' a roof wot don't leak. An' my leg still on. Though I feels it still, twitchin' an' achin' in the damp.' His laugh was bitter, and he kicked the wooden leg viciously. 'No bloody use. Bloody 'urts. Bloody murder.' Tears in his eyes. Nose running. A child in his pain.

Tipper could tell them no more. He had no idea where Jaggard might be, or his own woman. Dickens gave him a shilling and they left him gazing at his palm as if the moon had landed there.

Sam Jones had flushed Jaggard out of St Giles's. Tipper's woman, whose name was Annie, might have been there, but she might have moved on. No sense in thinking about Annie Taylor, whoever she had been, but Jaggard, the lawyer — very interesting.

Bold departed, promising that John Gaunt would investigate any likely pawnshops or dubious jewellers' shops. Dickens and Jones went to board a steamer.

'Lawyer Jaggard,' Jones said, 'it never occurred to me.'

'Sir Titus Jaggard, once a judge, the scourge of the Old Bailey. Face like an iron mask. Suited the black cap very well.

Flog 'em, hang 'em — quartered them if he could. Long retired.'

'But victim of a particularly violent robbery a few years back. Thought to be a revenge job — someone's relative he'd sentenced to hang. Never found who it was.'

'Sir Titus attacked?'

'He wasn't in the house at the time, but the manservant was bound and gagged, then stabbed. The robber just knocked at the door in the middle of the night — urgent message for Sir Titus, he said. The manservant opened the door and the attacker walked in, cool as you like — cool as Martin Jaggard.'

'No other servants?'

'All asleep upstairs on the top floor. No one heard anything. The manservant found dead the next morning. But whoever it was must have known where to find the goods — went through the drawing room, the master's study, even his bedroom, and helped himself to all sorts of valuable trinkets — none of which was ever recovered.'

At Wellington Street, Dickens opened the Law List. Sir Titus Jaggard was still alive. Address in Bryanstone Square. However, neither *Burke's Peerage* nor *Burke's Landed Gentry* gave any further information.

'Not an inherited title,' Dickens said. 'No handy son to inherit a country seat — or grandson, for that matter, gone to the bad. No daughter dead in the workhouse, leaving an illegitimate child brought up by the parish. Said child —'

'Yes, I get your drift, Mr Twist. Who'll know?'

'Talfourd — he's been about since the 1820s. I'll ask.'

Jones flicked through the pages of the Post Office Directory. 'One other Jaggard —' he stared at Dickens — 'good Lord, I wonder about you — Mrs Maria Jaggard, workhouse matron at The Strand Union —'

Dickens stared back. 'Good Lord, Norfolk Street.'

'Right under our noses — well, mine at any rate —'

'Heavens, Sam, mine, too. It is extraordinary. When I was a lad, we lodged on the corner of Tottenham Street. That monster of a workhouse haunted my dreams, casting its looming shadow over the street. Lord, it was a place you certainly walked by on the other side — ran by, in fact. I used to see the children marched out in their brown cloth.'

'Nothing's changed. It gives me a chill to see them. When I think of Eleanor and Tom, if we hadn't found them… No wonder Jacko Cragg has turned to crime rather than the workhouse.'

'Perhaps Jaggard spent time in one.'

'He told Tipper his father was a lawyer, but he could have simply stolen the name. It suits him.'

'The workhouse, though, Sam — the parish boy's progress. Or *The Heir of Gauntley Grange* — to be found in *Reynolds Magazine*. Two and six — not worth tuppence —' the publisher, George Reynolds, was not a favourite of Dickens — 'bastard son steals fortune. Unmasked by —'

'No Grange — no country seat.'

'Ah, slight impediment, I admit, but still —'

'Tales of the Workhouse, more likely. Let's find out.'

28: DUTY DONE

The stench of hides from the leather cutter's shop, the scent of wood shavings and sawdust from the carpenter's, the sound of glass breaking and the glazier's roar at his apprentice darting away with bloodied hands, the thundering roll of barrels at the Bromley Arms, the cheers and boos of the crowd watching the boxing matches, the smell of hops and ale, the sudden tea leaf fragrance from the tea dealer's shop — Sam Jones had only to mention the workhouse and Dickens remembered the street, the shops and the people. He remembered snow thick on the pavements and soldiers with wooden legs, fugitives from the French wars, begging on the pavement.

And The Strand Union itself, then the Cleveland Street Workhouse, which the child Dickens had seen from the window of Mr Dodd's grocer's shop. The smell of dust and dung, and stone chippings, and the clanging bell punctuating the day — the harsh call to wake, to work, to sleep. Most of all the high walls and the forbidding gate with its admonitory legend: *AVOID IDLENESS AND INTEMPERANCE.* Easy enough to say over your port at the Founders' dinners when you had just come from the bank which paid you a handsome salary for settling your sleek, overfed paunch in a leather chair and dozing over your papers.

The workhouse had seemed to him a prison, a place of terror from which you might never come out, except in a rough coffin carried by drunkenly staggering bearers. He'd listened, of course, when people talked of the graveyard in there and the paupers dying of hunger and disease, and some being sent to the anatomists for dissection — cut up for what? he had wondered when told what the word meant. Not that he asked, but his dreams had been haunted by homeless legs making their halting way along dark streets and bodiless arms waving from house tops. Dancers of death.

The reputation of the place had not improved by the time the Dickens family moved back to lodge with Mr Dodd at the corner of Norfolk Street when Dickens was sixteen. The graveyard had more inhabitants. Not surprising. The stench of the cesspits told the same story about that. The place was still notorious, according to a report he had read recently. Gruel was still served with husks of bran or pig meal. No change, just more decay.

'Catch is the master,' Jones told him. 'Rat-catcher, they call him.'

They negotiated the great wooden gates, let in by the keeper who recognised Superintendent Jones of Bow Street. And then there was the stink of misery and the shouts of the lunatic paupers as they passed their ward and the moans of the sick in the infirmary. And cries from the lying-in ward. Dickens had read the reports about the wretched conditions in the wards, the damp, and the overcrowding. *We cry that we are come to this great stage of fools*, Dickens quoted to himself. Born only to suffer.

The Ratcatcher was civil enough, a large, well-fed, brute-eyed man with no more pity in his face than any rat — less, perhaps. The rat's eyes looked suspiciously at the superintendent from Bow Street and even more suspiciously at his companion whose face he thought he knew, but whom the superintendent from Bow Street did not name. Naturally, he was eager to assist the superintendent. Mrs Jaggard could certainly be fetched from her duties — a good woman, of course, a high reputation with the governors, hard-working, though with a kind heart —

The superintendent did not bother to answer, and his companion remained silent, but his eyes seemed somehow too piercing to the Ratcatcher — a man who saw too much. His words trailed away to the somewhat lame conclusion that the paupers was lucky to —

'Mrs Jaggard, sir, if you please.' The superintendent from Bow Street's face was as unnerving as his title. Catch went without a word.

'To catch a thief,' Dickens murmured.

'She may be blameless.'

'With a testimonial from the rat and the stench in here, and that pauper found dead on the steps of a pub and her new-born child dropped in the street.'

Jones knew the case of a young woman who had been an inmate, and had left, it appeared, of her own free will. And had died the same night. Consumption, and the miscarriage, of course. The child born dead, lying on the stones of the alley. The girl had been nothing but skin and bone. He couldn't help thinking that whoever had watched her go had been at best negligent, at worst downright uncaring. But he didn't answer Dickens as the door was opening to let in Mrs Maria Jaggard.

Handsome, tall — rather imposing. *Crocodile*, Dickens thought, noting the wide mouth opened in what was meant to be a smile. It did not reach the hard eyes. *Jaggard*, thought Sam Jones, noting the resemblance to handsome Martin. It was there in the high cheekbones and dark hair and the wide, red-lipped mouth. And in the calculating green eyes.

She came with a swish of black skirts and a clinking of the keys and chatelaine at her waist, where the steel chains carried her steel scissors, pins, needles, thimble — a small knife, probably. All the better to stab you with. *Miss Murdstone*, Dickens thought, though better looking. Gaoler, certainly.

'Superintendent Jones, Mr Catch says you wish to see me. I can assure you that the girl wanted to go — to her mother, she said. We could not stop her. Her death is very unfortunate, but we can hardly —'

And the dropped child, Dickens wanted to say, but Jones interrupted with a brusque, 'No, it's not about that. I'm here about Martin Jaggard, your relative.'

That was a risk, but it paid off. Jones could tell by the surprise she could not conceal. He watched her recover herself enough to ask, 'I don't know who you mean.'

'I think you do. Don't waste my time. I'm investigating robbery and murder, and the abduction of two young girls.'

'I don't know anything about those things. I don't know anything about Martin Jaggard.'

'You share his name — there are only two people in the directory with the name Jaggard. You know him. What is he to you?'

'Nothing.'

Nothing will come of nothing, Dickens thought, King Lear having been on his mind, and wondering what this nothing meant. Sam was certain that she was connected to the man.

'You had better explain,' Jones said firmly.

She knew that she must. Her face hardened. 'My brother's child — all he left to me after squandering all his legacy from our father, who left a pittance to me. My father was a gentleman of good breeding, but one with no love for his daughter — only his spendthrift son. I have no idea what happened to my brother — he vanished years ago. Debts, drink, gambling — any of those. He'll be dead, I'll warrant.'

'Martin's mother?'

'As immoral as he, worse. It was she who dragged my brother into the gutter. And the coward left her with me. She didn't last long after he disappeared, and I was left to bring up that child. I did my best and found him a situation with Sir Titus Jaggard, a distant connection of my father's. He said he would take the boy into his service, provided he was never told of any family tie. He would take him as a boot boy under a different name. He was not entitled to the name Jaggard, in any case. He had to make his own way in the world. He was old enough at eleven to work for his living.'

'And you agreed to that?' Dickens asked.

She gave him an icy look. 'He was not my child. I had my own way to make.'

'And he stayed with Sir Titus?'

'I have no idea. Sir Titus had no wish for my acquaintance. The boy would be fed and clothed, taught the ways of service. I did my duty.' The red lips closed into a hard line.

The same duty that she did for the paupers under her tender care. Dickens was familiar with that stern sense of duty, rigid as a straitjacket, cold as steel, and sanctimonious as the Sunday Trading Bill — that measure designed to deny all earthly pleasure to those who had that one day off. Souls must be saved while the lawmakers dined and rode in the park, and the workhouse masters and matrons dined on roast beef.

'Martin Jaggard's name has been in the newspapers — a notorious criminal. Did you never think of your nephew?' asked Jones.

'I never think of him. He went into the service of Sir Titus under the name of Martin Todd — his mother's name. I was glad to be —'

'Rid of him?' Dickens asked.

She was unmoved by the question. 'I did my duty. Sir Titus Jaggard is nothing to me. Martin Jaggard is nothing to me. I have made my way alone in the world, and I will not allow Martin Jaggard to ruin my life. He is Martin Todd, the illegitimate child of a wicked slut. No wonder he has turned out to be a criminal, but he is not my concern, and you cannot make him so.'

Jones knew that he could not. Apart from the earlier shock of hearing the name, she had soon recovered her composure. She knew of Jaggard, that was certain. No doubt she had seen his name in the papers and suspected, but she had severed all ties with him long ago. What Martin Jaggard had become was not her responsibility. Perhaps it was not, but it accounted for his claim to be a gentleman as Mr Tipper had told them, and his desire for power and riches. Perhaps it accounted for the ambition to send his child to America. More likely that Rogers was right, and the man had no paternal feelings. He had just been preparing a sanctuary in America to flee to if he ever had to.

One more question. 'You are Mrs Jaggard — a courtesy title?'

'It is. For the matron of this establishment. Jaggard is my name. Martin Jaggard stole it. When you find him, Superintendent, and you bring him to the gallows, he will be Martin Todd — a thief and a liar from birth, as his mother was.'

Jones knew that she would say no more. She gave a curt nod to acknowledge Jones's dismissal. With a defiant swish of black skirts, the rattle of her chains, and her mouth a gash of red, she was gone. She was too composed to slam the door, but its decided closing indicated that she was finished with them.

'Not a lady one would want too near the knives in an ill-humour.'

Jones grinned. 'Close as an oyster and not to be opened again.'

'The parish boy's progress, eh?'

'Magician, you are — I wonder what happened to him at Sir Titus Jaggard's.'

'I'll go and see Talfourd.'

'Good. We'll talk later, for I must go back to Bow Street. The inquests on Darius Henchman and Miss Hormel are later — no need to advertise your presence. It'll be adjourned — pending further enquiries. The police have reason to believe that Mr Darius Henchman and Miss Hormel were connected to Martin Jaggard, the notorious coiner and suspect in the murder of Sir William Pell.'

'Ah, very suggestive — it'll send a shiver up the rigid spine of Julius Henchman, no doubt.'

Sam hurried away. Dickens thought he would try Talfourd in Russell Square — at least leave a message. Then he remembered. There had been a pawnbroker in a crooked little lane off Ogle Street — the sort of narrow lane you were hurried past by whichever adult was holding your hand — suddenly in a vice-like grip. You looked, even if the grown-up averted his or her eyes. The place was somehow secret, tainted, as if you might catch something down there. *Poverty, perhaps*, he thought now, remembering the people sliding furtively into the darkness, clutching sacks to their ragged breasts, faces drawn with shame and hunger. He'd once seen a lodger from the next-door shop slipping into the lane — a yank on his arm and the man was gone. Gruel Place, that was it. He remembered thinking it was Cruel Place. Grabham was the name, though he hadn't been able to read it then. They — the adults — had whispered 'Grabbem', so he had thought.

Of course, he'd had to look at "Cruel Place" and he had wanted to know about "Grabbem" — a goblin, he had imagined, a figure from a picture book with bony hands, a pointed nose, and wicked eyes. They'd had a little servant girl in those early days when they'd first come to lodge at Mr Dodd's, and sometimes she'd taken him out. It had been easy enough to slip from her grasp and dart down the crooked lane to see the shop into which the ragged people went. He'd soon been yanked back from the door — and glad to be so. It was too dark and there were noises of wild laughter and weeping. He never went there again.

Gruel Placewas still the narrowest and darkest of passages — more so now, and it still smelt of effluent, was still muddy, and still led nowhere, and there was still wild laughter. Laughter from the dark. Always sinister. A madman in on a joke — a very black one. There was the shop with three tarnished golden balls over the door, just above the sign that read *Grab awn roker* — like some secret goblin command. Outside the shop was a selection of goods — not very tempting, or useful. A drunken three-legged stool, a birdcage, an old portmanteau, and a broken-down cart with one wheel, on top of which were a battered violin and a drum — some kind of regimental drum, judging by the faded coat of arms. The minstrel boy long gone, it seemed.

He remembered the sound of the shop bell from before, jangling a warning to curious little boys. He could see nothing through the filthy door window, and he had to struggle with the damp wood. However, the bell remained silent. He looked up. The clapper had been jammed with a piece of red flannel cloth. Torn from the red flannel petticoat that dangled from a pole just inside. He hoped nobody wanted to redeem it.

A pair of feet in felt slippers on the counter, and the sound of snoring that indicated deep sleep. Where the body was, he could not make out in the gloom. He stood by the door, wondering what kind of noise ought to be made to wake the sleeper.

He had not actually been inside the shop as a child, but he imagined it wouldn't have changed in thirty-odd years. He negotiated the red petticoat and sundry other articles of mildewed clothing which hung like ghosts on various poles, shirts, dresses, a selection of mouldy top hats, an opera cloak which would never hear music again, a green-stained hunting jacket, and many more items which were so malformed that it was impossible to say what they had been. He stepped by a rusty mangle across a floor littered with baskets stuffed with books, kettles, teapots, fire irons. There was an old saddle on the floor and a few riding whips, stirrups, and a pair of boots, one with a bunion-shaped bulge in the foot. Still, if you had no shoes at all, you'd accommodate that, and the lack of a sole. A pair of wooden legs was propped against the boots. They looked as uncomfortable as Mr Tipper's. Perhaps the owners had pawned them in despair. He spied in the corner a spectral sedan chair, out of which two more wooden legs poked. Was there a trade in second-hand legs? he wondered. Behind the counter, shelves rose to the ceiling, packed with assorted parcels and pledges. The tickets which dangled from some of them were so torn and dirty that it was clear that the articles would never be redeemed. One-way tickets only.

The smell was a pungent flavour of soot and oil, damp, rotten vegetables, old clothes, horse — sweat and dung — and cheese and pickle. As he approached the counter, he saw that the sleeper had dined, for there were a half-eaten pickle, some bits of bread and some cheese rind on a pewter plate. That all looked as if it might have been there for thirty years, except for the mouse which was enjoying a little repast. That looked very young, though old enough in experience merely to give him an enquiring glance before continuing to eat. There was the smell of beer from a pewter tankard.

The sleeper lay back in a worn velvet chair, which like the pewter looked as though it had come from some noble house, long decayed. A rusty broadsword lay at a little distance from the plate with a collection of rusty nails, some hammers, and a horse collar with a set of bells.

Dickens could not resist. The bells gave a pleasingly loud tinkle. The mouse fled, the sleeper snorted, fell back in the chair, his feet dropping from the counter, and a pair of indignant eyes glared at him.

'Closed fer lunch,' the hoarse voice said.

'Mr Grabham?'

The speaker, a kind of malevolent goblin, struggled to sit upright. 'Shelved, ticketed, awaitin' in the storeroom.'

'For redemption?' Dickens asked, keeping a straight face.

The speaker emitted a rusty chortle and glanced at the rusty nails. 'Dead as. Never to be redeemed — the ol' bastard. Hell's too good fer 'im. Somethin' I can do fer yer, sir? Now yer've woken me up.'

'My nephew, a rascally knave, has taken my gold watch — young fellow, fair hair, moustache, yellow gloves, top hat. He frequents the Bromley Arms — betting and all that. I wondered —'

The muddy eyes looked at him suspiciously. 'Toff? We don't get no toffs 'ereabouts. No gold watches 'ere. See fer yerself.

Domestic goods, only — if yer needs an 'ammer, I got a good selection.'

The goblin picked one up. It looked lethal, but Dickens persevered. 'He has a friend — tall, very gentlemanly, green eyes.'

'Told yer. Can't 'elp. Good day ter yer.' The slit of a mouth disappeared, and he put up his feet again, the hammer on his chest. Closed for business.

If the goblin knew anything about Darius Henchman or Jaggard, Dickens knew he wouldn't get anything out of him. He must live on something — certainly not the contents of his shop, but you never knew. He still might be doing business with the very poor. He might be fencing jewellery and gold, but he'd never tell, and the evidence would be passed on very quickly. There'd be no gold watches on these premises.

Of course, the door refused to budge. The mysterious legend on the inside of the door commanded him now to '*rekor nwa barG*' — gnomic, indeed. Barge, maybe. He pulled at the handle with his foot on the bottom of the door. He was aware of a snickering in the gloom behind him. A face rose, as from the deep, pressing itself to the window outside, a face that understood the mystery. A devil's face, lean and hungry, predatory, malevolent, with hard black eyes like stones. Not Jacko Cragg. A stranger, but that face would know him again.

When he got out, Gruel Placewas empty, except from somewhere came the sound of a beating drum.

The minstrel boy off to war.

29: DEAD TO THE WORLD

Death has knocked on the door of a royal palace. So reported *The Morning Chronicle.* Apparently, the King of Hanover was dead — fifth son of mad King George. Formerly the Duke of Cumberland on a pension of eighteen thousand pounds a year. Fierce opponent of the Reform Bill and 'universally hated', according to his obituary.

No one will miss him, Dickens thought, reading on. A woman had died at Euston station, a wretchedly poor creature. Tuberculosis, the report told. No one would miss her — because no one had come forward to claim her. No name. And a child found dead in a back alley — starved to death. Dead, your Majesty. Dead, my lords and gentlemen. No name, no family, no friend to succour him. No one would miss him.

Person or persons unknown. Wilful murder by… That was the verdict of the inquests on Darius Henchman and Mademoiselle Hormel. This Sam Jones had reported. Julius Henchman would bury his brother at Highgate, perhaps, or Kensal Green, or Norwood, any of those green open spaces where the dead lay under the sky, waiting, as the seasons passed, for the Day of Judgement. Darius Henchman — the judgement on him was folly, heedlessness, a sense of entitlement. Perhaps, he would have grown out of it, become a sober citizen, a grave lawyer in his suit of black, rising to his feet before 'M'Lud'. Too late. The waste of it.

Too late for Mademoiselle Hormel. If that were really her name. No one would come forward — certainly not Mr John Baptist Tête, of whom no trace had been found. Back in France, Dickens wagered, or Belgium, waiting for his consignment of forged money. William Pell's jewels a nice little bonus. Sam had been on to the French and Belgian police. It was all he could do.

They had no idea where Mademoiselle Hormel had gone after taking Posy and Phoebe Miller from Union Street. And they wouldn't know until they found Jaggard and Matty Miller. Mademoiselle Hormel would be buried by the parish — in that pestilential graveyard in Paddington Street, the one you went into by Paradise Street where the paupers were buried one on top of the other, their bones jumbled together, waiting in the dark to be reassembled on the Day — no seasons in Paradise Street, the sky obliterated by the blank wall of another workhouse. That glossy-haired woman in her smart green costume with her beating heart and fluttering lashes. Alive — even if a thoroughly corrupt young woman. Very much alive, then dead in a minute or two and to be buried in a cheap deal coffin. An unmarked grave, uncheered by any gleam of promise — of reward above, of rest, of sleep. Dead to the world. Person unknown.

However, Sir Titus Jaggard was known. Talfourd had told him. A sick man — heart attack after the robbery. His treasures had never been found. Talfourd did not know of any family. Sir Titus was never a sociable man. Dead to the world. Still bad-tempered, apparently. Few friends — Pell had been one —

Perhaps that was how Martin Jaggard had come to work for Pell, Dickens had said. Could be, Talfourd thought. Both collectors — silver and coins for Sir Titus — that's why he was so devastated by the robbery.

Talfourd didn't think that Dickens could just call — better if Talfourd wrote to prepare the way. Not that Sir Titus would definitely see him — very careful of the dignity of the law. Not much sense of humour. Talfourd grinned at Dickens as he said that.

'Ah.' Dickens had grinned back. 'Magistrate Fang. Friend of Sir Titus?'

'One of the few, I'm afraid, Magistrate Laing of Hatton Garden. You gave him a drubbing in *Oliver Twist*.'

'My youthful indiscretions.'

'He was a pompous ass — still is. Not to mention Sir Peter Laurie.'

'Lord, Talfourd — the evidence for the prosecution. Laurie said Jacob's Island didn't exist. I had to put him right.'

Talfourd laughed. 'You would. Remember that case of the tailor —'

'Oh, the one whom Laurie told to get his hair cut. He wasn't surprised that the tailor was accused of attacking women — a man with such hair was capable of anything. Be a man, he told the tailor. Pompous ass, too. I suppose Laurie was another of Sir Titus's few friends.'

'Made of the same coin, but I'll write to Sir Titus for you.'

'You wouldn't come with me? He'll not like my hair.'

'Guarantor of your good character? I've my own character to think of.'

'Caesar, you are, above suspicion.'

Now all he had to do was wait for Talfourd's approach to bear fruit. Otherwise, Sam Jones and he would simply have to go and knock on the door and ask about Martin Todd, the former boot boy, who was going about his criminal avocations under the name of Martin Jaggard. Sir Titus Jaggard could hardly refuse Superintendent Jones of Bow Street — unless he were too sick a man to see anybody. In any case, he might be like Mrs Jaggard of the workhouse and know nothing more than that his former boot boy had gone into service with Sir William Pell. And murdered him.

He heard voices on the stairs, laughter and quick feet skipping up. Mamie and Katey. More laughter. Lally and Betty Lemon round from Gordon Street. A tea party for the girls. Annie and Minnie Thackeray, too. Georgina's voice and Catherine's heavier tread. Lemon's wife, Nelly, with her.

They wouldn't need him. Ladies only, Katey had told him firmly with that familiar spark in her eye. He was not to disobey. But milder Mamie had kindly suggested that he might come up after a time, if he were to do some conjuring. He'd be sent for, Katey added.

Family life. He sometimes felt it crowding in. The Responsibilities. Mark Lemon had only five to his eight, soon to be nine. He would like another daughter this time. A hundred and fifty pairs of double-soled boots on the stairs sometimes, always jumping a bottom stair with that final clatter. And that was just Walter who was at school, not leaping downstairs. The little boys would have been consigned to the nursery while the girls — ladies, he should say — commandeered the schoolroom. The boys wouldn't mind. They got on all right — most of the time. No sound of quarrelling from the nursery.

Martin Jaggard — that unwanted boy. Lonely, probably, resentful, bitter, brought up by a woman who wanted only to be rid of him. Uncherished. And then sent to be a boot boy. No doubt kicked about by bigger boots. Footmen's slippers, the cook's shoes, the coachman's wellingtons, the gardener's boots, and his fingernails thick with boot blacking. Well, Dickens knew all about that. No wonder Jaggard was always clean and well-dressed. But shackled by the chains of the past, the past fated and immutable because it was the past. The past engraving its mark on the future forger. But had the workhouse matron and the judge made him a murderer?

Impossible to say. They were part of it, no doubt. Perhaps Jaggard was his mother's son, though they only had Mrs Workhouse Jaggard's evidence for the mother's wickedness. She might have been an innocent maiden, seduced by a rotten gentleman. Jaggard his father's son? Or nobody's child. Or everybody's child. Cruelty, neglect, beating, ignorance, want, all the parents of monstrous, misshapen murder. Like Matty and Phoebe Miller — the natural affections perverted and stunted. Like Jacko Cragg and that face at the pawnshop window, and those boys in the graveyard. Like wild beasts — they might have been nurtured by the wolf or the bear.

These depressing thoughts were interrupted by a knock on the door. Two shining, pretty faces appeared. The summons had come. Summons to magic. He took the packs of cards from his desk and some matches. He was rewarded by Lally's big smile. Katey was smiling, too. Such innocence — and trust. He heard them skipping up the stairs, and then there were boys' voices. They wouldn't want to miss the show. Katey was magnanimous; he heard her giving permission, and then a cheer and the familiar sound of boots coming down from the nursery. Home, sweet home today.

"Magician," Sam had said. Would that he could conjure Posy home. As he closed his study door, a piece of paper fluttered to the ground, a piece of paper on which he had written: *Dead, your majesty. Dead, my lords and gentlemen. Dead, right reverends and wrong reverends of every order.*

30: MESMERISING

'Brandy?' Dickens asked. 'Smelling salts? Arsenic tonic? Strychnine?'

'Don't tempt me — I might use the latter for nefarious purposes.'

Sam Jones had been to the house of Sir Titus Jaggard, where he had gone alone since the distinguished judge had turned down Talfourd's suggestion that he might be gracious enough to meet the distinguished author. The judge, it seemed, did not care for fiction of any kind, tragical or comical, and he certainly did not read cheap magazines intended for the masses. Furthermore, he had nothing to say to anyone about any former or present servant. It was not his habit to discuss his household with strangers.

'That put me in my place,' Dickens had told Jones, who steeled himself for the interview.

Now in Wellington Street, Jones accepted a cup of tea. 'Pompous ass,' he said.

'Nothing doing?'

'Nothing at all from him. I was allowed into the presence — I think he expected me to touch my forelock. He is a sick man — he'd be better if his temper improved.'

'Grim as a gargoyle?'

'And as ugly. No wonder Martin Jaggard turned into a monster — he worked for one. I touched on the blood connection. That didn't go well. As far as Sir Titus is concerned, the connection was so distant as to be meaningless. The boot boy, Todd, had no significance for him. Yes, he had allowed him to leave and take up service with Sir William Pell

— if the boy wished to advance his career, then Sir Titus could see no objection.'

'You didn't mention the murder?'

'No, because I had no wish to be cross-examined as to evidence, and I didn't refer to the robbery, either. No wish to hear about police incompetence. I said that I wanted Martin Jaggard in connection with a missing young woman whom I believed knew him.'

'Waste of time.'

'Not entirely. I spoke to the housekeeper — been with Sir Titus for years. Bad-tempered, certainly, but she knew how to humour him. Anyway, she remembered the boot boy — handsome lad, but sullen, very quiet — not like a lad at all, but a quick learner and biddable, but knowing, somehow, as if he had his reasons for what he did. Taking everything in as if he were waiting, she said, but she didn't know what for.'

'Opportunity, I suppose, for something better, and then friend, Sir William Pell came along.'

'Rose to the position of under footman and then it seems that Pell offered to take him on, young as he was — about seventeen then.'

'Never had him down as a philanthropist — wanted him for his bumps?'

'It's odd when you think of it. Pell took him on as his valet — at that age. Handsome lad, the housekeeper remembered.'

'Pell a confirmed bachelor — makes you think.'

'It does, and the murder was particularly violent. Hatred in it, I thought.'

'What did the servants at Pell's house say about Martin Jaggard?'

'They didn't like him — kept himself to himself, but was always in the laboratory with Pell. They didn't like that. The inspector on the case at first wasn't much concerned about the relationship, because Jaggard was known by then as a coiner and a violent one. Money and jewels were motives enough for the inspector.'

'But he was Todd at Sir Titus's house.'

'So he was. But Pell's butler called him Jaggard. Took the name when he left Sir Titus? Probably took a few valuables as well. I don't suppose Pell cared what he was called.'

'A nice piece of revenge on Sir Titus who had denied him the name of a gentleman. So, something happened between Martin Jaggard and Pell which led to Jaggard's walking out and later to murder. Or was he dismissed? Revenge again?'

'Remember you asked if he'd seduced any of the maids? I thought it probable, given what I'd seen in St. Giles's, but Feak didn't hear any talk about Jaggard seducing serving girls. It's a small household. I wonder if the servants know any more about Pell and Jaggard — stuff they don't want to talk about…'

'Queer fish, Pell, phrenologist, mesmerist — the two are connected. For example, the mesmerist can touch, say, the organ of tune and the subject will sing and dance. What was going on in that laboratory, I wonder? Perhaps the servants did have suspicions about Pell and Jaggard.'

'It doesn't matter much. All right, we know more about Jaggard's background, we have an idea what made him, even that Pell might have corrupted him. But we also know that he wanted money to set up his new forging business and he knew where to get it. The first inspector might have been right. It was murder for the money and valuables. What matters now is where he is, and unless there is somebody at Pell's house who knows that — I'll send Inspector Grove to speak to them again — we are no further on.'

'My friend, Doctor John Elliotson, is treasurer of The Mesmeric Infirmary — I wonder if he knew Pell. It would be interesting to know what Elliotson thought of him — whether Pell was one of them — wanting to use mesmerism to alleviate suffering. That's the Infirmary's aim. They have several mesmerisers and they open every day for patients. There's a lady mesmeriser, and they are getting ladies on the committee.'

'Very progressive. Perhaps Pell didn't want anything to do with lady mesmerisers. You believe in it. You've practised it yourself.'

'I have — it can work. I told you about my friend, John Leech. I used it on him when we feared for his life, and the Infirmary claims success with palsy, neuralgia, epilepsy. There was a man back in May who could hardly swallow; he was cured. Of course, years ago, they were accused of fraud and told that they were unfit to associate with reputable medical men, but now they have the support of all kinds of people — dukes, earls, bishops, members of the clergy, professors.'

'But there are still a lot of charlatans out there — those who say they can predict your future when you're in a trance, or by looking at your handwriting.'

'I daresay Pell was interested in that, too. It might help to know more about him.'

'Perhaps Pell was an outsider — up to no good with his mesmeric skills, practising on his valet.'

'It's a powerful thing in the wrong hands.'

'Tipper said Jaggard could make them do his bidding. When I think of those lads, too... Tipper said he could make them do anything. They're a black-hearted lot, and when I think of what Jaggard's done ... and might do yet... Yes, go and see Elliotson. You might find out what Pell was up to and if there was any talk about his valet.'

'Maybe Jaggard outdid the master. Realised what power he had. Saw his own future.'

'Pell didn't see his. But I see my future — a meeting with Mr Mayne. I somehow don't think that talk of mesmerism and clairvoyance is going to impress.'

'Tell him that the Archbishop of Dublin is a Vice-President of the Mesmeric Infirmary — with the Earl of Stanhope.'

'Now that I will enjoy. Mayne's a Dublin man. Useful, ain't you?'

'Always ready to oblige.'

'Conjure a murderer for me, will you, while I'm gone?'

Dickens put on his coat. A call on Doctor Elliotson might not do much, if anything, but it was something. Something to do for Sam Jones — and for Posy. They hardly dared mention her in the context of Jaggard, but she was there in that pause when Sam had thought about what Jaggard had already done and might do yet. That was a very chilling thought.

Elliotson was no charlatan. Dickens knew him to be dedicated to the cause of mesmerism as a healing treatment. But, in the hands of someone without any human sympathy, someone who regarded it as an exercise of power, then it could do harm. To have that power over another's will… He had known it himself — relished it, he knew, but he had wanted to save Leech when there seemed to be no other hope.

"Yer didn't know wot 'e'd do." That's what Mr Tipper had said. Jaggard certainly seemed to have power over his minions. Such power that blazed in the blood — like a trail of gunpowder catching fire. Nothing could stop it.

31: THE NIGHT WATCH

Doctor Elliotson was out of town, so Dickens made his way to Bow Street, where he found Jones and Sergeant Rogers. Dickens stopped dead when he heard the name on Superintendent Jones's lips.

'Abel Miller?' Jones was asking Sergeant Rogers.

'The very same. Something queer at the old chemical factory at Belle Isle. Lights seen — folk hanging about. Report of kids and women. One of Fall's constables went to investigate. Met Abel Miller, who claimed he had been given the job as night watchman and he'd moved 'em on. Just dossin' there, he told the constable. Course, the constable didn't know about the Miller case, but when Inspector Fall read the report, he was very interested, the factory having been empty for years.'

'Abandoned chemical factory, children and women, Abel Miller, Matty Miller, Jaggard,' Jones said. 'Just the place for a forging operation.'

'Inspector Fall's goin' to have a look tonight — message says that you're welcome.'

'What time?'

'Eleven — the inspector's thinkin' that the folks of Belle Isle should be in their beds by then, an' if not, the factory's far enough away to watch on the quiet an' go in if he needs to.'

'Right, tell Stemp and Feak, and tell Doublett to keep watch on Mr Dickens's house. Nothing to do now but wait.'

A clear night, for once. Starlit and very cold. Not much of a moon, just a thin shaving of silver, but they'd have to be careful.

Stemp went on ahead — in his labourer's garb and a heavy ragged coat. Just a tramping man. No need for a parson tonight, Dickens thought, unless... Thinking of the guns carried by Superintendent Jones and Inspector Fall. Feak followed, driving a cart. Just a carrier out late. Fall's men went out to go up to Belle Isle by different routes — up the Holloway Road from where fields led to the back of the factory. The police van would take another four up beyond the blacksmith's, from where a lane took them into the grounds of the factory. Fall would walk up Maiden Lane with his sergeant. Dickens and Jones were to follow. They would approach the factory site by a path across the field.

The place might be a den of coiners and forgers, so stealth was vital. Fall had thought of the women and children. They'd try to take whoever they could if there were a stampede. Of course, the place might be empty. They might look fools if there were no one there, but Fall was prepared to take the risk. He didn't believe in the tale of Abel Miller as a night watchman. He didn't believe in Abel Miller as anything at all — except perhaps as a father who knew how his little daughters had drowned, and who didn't care.

By eleven o'clock, all the men were in place. Dickens and Jones watched the lights go out in the houses of Belle Isle. They heard the last shouts of the drinkers from the Fortune of War, the sounds of hooves clip-clopping away. The stragglers from The Copenhagen, perhaps. Then there was silence, except for the keening of the wind through the grasses. An east wind, bringing stinging sleet. An east wind slicing over the listening earth.

All was quiet, the listening earth, the faintly breathing grasses, the silent, lightless factory across the field, but they knew that in the dark, still as the shadows of statues, Inspector

Fall's men were waiting for his signal. Stemp and Feak were waiting, and they were, too. Fall would decide when. A brief flash of his lamp, repeated by the sergeant, and taken up by the constables on the village side of the factory, answered, too, by Superintendent Jones. A series of brief glimmers — someone making his way home to an outlying cottage or farm. Nothing to arouse the suspicion of anyone inside that dark building, or anyone hiding in the jumble of derelict outhouses and sheds.

Constable Doublett was inside the gates of Tavistock House, the carriage sweep behind him and the empty street in front. At the back of the house, Mr Topping, the coachman was watching the garden. Mr John Thompson, Mr Dickens's manservant, was in the hall. No one would get in the house. Doublett had spoken to the beat constable, Flint, who would keep an eye out for any strangers lurking, and there were beat constables in the alleys behind the house. Doublett's rattle would bring help if he needed it.

No fog, thankfully, and the gas lamps illuminated the road outside the gate. Doublett heard occasional footsteps — hurrying, purposeful not stealthy. No flapping step — Superintendent Jones had warned him about that. He heard laughter — a cab drawing up somewhere and cheerful voices bidding goodnight. The horse and cab going away at a smart pace.

Mr Thompson came out with a tin mug of coffee. 'Keep you warm.'

'And awake — though the cold's enough for that. Thank you, sir.'

They stared out at the street, but there was no one. They heard the clocks strike midnight, St Pancras New Church nearby, St Giles in the Fields further away, and beyond the sounds echoed, then died away on the twelfth stroke, leaving a deeper silence which Doublett felt in his heart. He wondered what was going on at that abandoned factory. Something, he hoped, which would bring the case to an end. And bring back Mr Jones's little servant. All sorts of kids missing in London — happened every day, but this one… What did the Bible say? Something about the fall of a sparrow. A little bird, but important. Someone's lost lamb. That's what his ma would say. He thought of her now — she kept house at the police barracks. The lads, she'd say, good lads, serving them the soup or the stew, shaking her head over the tale of another lost child.

Thompson, who had not spoken, waited for the young man to finish his drink, took the empty mug from him, and bade him goodnight, telling him that he would come out again later.

Silence again. Then something, he was sure. The faint sound of ringing metal as if… He opened the gate. It came again. Someone was running a stick along railings somewhere out there. He opened the gate slowly, quietly and went out, holding his lamp high and peering into the darkness, his rattle ready in his other hand.

There it was again — that metallic ringing. It was coming from behind now. He darted back inside the gate. Somewhere to the left. He moved under the trees. Something dropped on him, arms tight about his neck. Shocked, he dropped his lamp. Something that stank and wriggled and gibbered in his ear. Foul breath and nails digging into his cheek. He raised his rattle, but an arm struck it away. Such was his fury, that he yanked at the arm so hard that the thing screamed and then fell, darting away. He saw it, a horrible monkey-like thing scrabbling up the tree. He heard it in the branches. He picked up his lamp and shone it upwards, but he couldn't see anything. Then something leapt the other way — over the railings. He heard the swift pad of feet as it ran.

He dared not use his rattle. He thought of Mrs Dickens and her children in the house. And the neighbours. Whatever it was — an animal, surely — it had vanished. Too big for a monkey. An ape, perhaps. Rich folk got all sorts of strange pets from menageries and dressed 'em up. That arm had a sleeve on it. The stink of it, though. Give him his ma's cat any day.

Scrap heard the clocks, too. Wide awake and restless in his bed. Something he'd not asked about. That drumming he'd heard in Grafton Mews. Mr Jones had looked at Mr Dickens. They knew about that. It meant something. But what? Someone with the cove that jumped him? Should have asked, but Mrs Jones came in and he forgot, but it troubled him now.

Something he'd heard in Clerkenwell when he had been watching Ma Speed's house round the back. Someone had watched him. He'd known it — felt eyes on his back. Sneaked a look, but there had been nothin', 'cept — and he remembered it now — a kind of drumming. Didn't think much about it then. Someone foolin' about.

But he thought now, 'e'd been followed. He sat up. Followed to Grafton Mews. An' they knew where he was now, mebbe. An' that lad sitting on the windowsill — he'd not forget that face. Jacko Cragg, Mr Jones had called him. Nasty piece of goods. Looked like a monkey, sittin' cross-legged up there.

He knew he wouldn't sleep now. Couldn't sleep on his back. Scrap liked to curl up, bury himself in the pillows. But his cheek hurt and that kept him awake. Midnight, the clocks told him. Think of something else. But he couldn't — he could only think of that Jaggard and of eyes watching, and that devil's tattoo. And of Posy — still missing.

He got up, put on his clothes, and crept downstairs, checked the bolts on the front door — they wouldn't come that way. That's what he thought. If he'd been followed. He went through to the kitchen, checked the bolts on the back door, pulled up a chair, surrounded himself with bottles, took one in one hand and the kitchen poker in the other. Bolt upright, armed, and dangerous. The garden door was always locked at night, but there were walls to climb.

And in the silence of the night, his sharp ears caught the sound. A drumbeat at the back gate. Soft at first, then louder, more insistent. Scrap stood up. He was ready.

'Scrap, what on earth —'

Elizabeth Jones stopped. She heard it, too. Scrap turned with his finger on his lips. She saw the bottle in his hand and the ones on the floor. The children, she thought. Hearing this. It was so menacing — coming nearer, it seemed, louder, telling them that it wouldn't be stopped. An army on the march. But the garden door was locked. They couldn't —

But it had to be stopped. She took a bottle from the floor. Scrap's eyes were wide as he saw her slide the bolts. They waited then. The drumming had stopped. She opened the door. They listened again. Nothing now. Elizabeth took one step and looked across to the garden door. And it was there, a white, impossible face staring back from the top of the door.

As one, she and Scrap threw their bottles. They crashed and splintered on the path, the noise reverberating. The face vanished, then feet were running, sticks beating a tattoo on the doors in the alley. Then silence again.

'Mama.' Another face, white, too, with enormous eyes. Eleanor was there.

32: CONFLAGRATION

A doomsday crack. The earth heaving. Monstrous thunder. Stars bursting. The heavens falling in great glittering showers of light. The earth rent. Hell's furnaces opening. Hell breathing out great sheets of flame roaring upwards to meet the falling sky. The world's end now, it seemed. And in the red glare, Sam Jones's astounded face. And Dickens half falling, catching Jones's sleeve, both staggering backwards with the force of the blast, feeling their ears ringing, struck dumb, staring. Half-standing and seeing the figures frozen in the act of running. Screams and yells, and burning, burning, fire consuming the abandoned factory. A circle of fire, blazing to the very sky.

Jones found his voice. 'Gas, gas explosion.'

They started forward. The air rained glass. The stars were glass under their feet. They could feel the heat, the fire leaping up, tearing at the sky. Great crests of towering flame. Another crack, as though the world were split in two and more flames pluming and smoke billowing. *Those outhouses*, Dickens thought, as another explosion rent the sky. Dear God, who had been in that place? No one could survive this. Stemp, Feak? Where were they? Fall's men?

Fall came up beside them. 'We'll not get any closer — there might be more explosions. We'll skirt round. See if there's anyone…'

He stumbled away across the field. Dickens saw him and his sergeant surrounded by so strong a glare that they seemed ablaze themselves. He and Jones went the other way. By now, there was shouting, voices coming from the village, figures running, stopping, crowding at the field gate, crimson faces gaping like spectators at the fireworks, feeling the heat, drawing back, flinching at the next crack as the sheds and outhouses burst apart, and somewhere at a distance another blast and more flame leaping. Dickens thought of the varnishing factory, the tallow factory, the blacking works, the houses in the village. Dear Lord, phosphorous — Lucifer's matches —

A man came up to them. 'Police?' he asked.

'Yes.'

'There was folks in there — kids — lads, I think, couple o' women. Trampin' folk, we thought.'

Another joined them. 'Chemicals, sir, an' a paint store fer Brown's in one of the —'

An ear-splitting blast drowned him out. Glass burst like shot and cascaded down on them. White sheets of flame soaring.

The second man's face was suddenly lit up, clear in a kind of wild daylight. 'Matches works. Over 'ere, sirs, by the trees — shelter.'

'Anyone gone for the fire engine?'

'Policeman, sir — 'ad a cart. Went fer the Islington Green one. But there ain't nothin' —'

Feak, thought Dickens, *he's safe*, but the man was right, no single engine could deal with this.

'Parish engine's no use,' the man continued, 'but there was police in a van — gone up ter Holloway fer their engines. There's three up there — water plug in the lane just there — they might —'

There was a great roar and shouts of, 'See, see 'im.'

Silhouetted against the red glare, they saw a column of flame — someone was burning, someone blown out of a shed or outhouse, and then a figure leaping at the burning column, a figure with a blanket or coat, flinging it over the burning thing, and leaping back as devouring dragons licked at him, trying again to damp out the flames on the thing on the ground. A great timber falling and the rescuer retreating, vanishing into the smoke. The thing on the ground gone, too.

The sound of horses' hooves coming at a gallop. The cry went up: 'The engines!' Coming into the lane, the crowd scattering, the sheen of gas lamps in helmets. The rattle of chains. The unravelling of the hose. Men clamouring to work the pump levers — volunteers always needed. The chief fireman organising, another lifting the nozzle, the water dazzling in the red blaze and going up in a great fountain to descend on the nearest sheds. Another engine and the same process repeated. Figures in a dumb show, from where Dickens and Jones stood.

And from over the field, another engine from Holloway coming along the path, the horses steaming and snorting, stopping at the pond. More men charging to man the pump levers, and at last, the nozzle pointing to the factory walls, the great arc of water descending. The third engine coming. More men and Dickens and Jones manning the levers, hatless, black in the face, seeing Fall's men doing the same, thinking of nothing but the action of their arms, not knowing how long until the deafening crash came.

The whole building collapsed into a wreck of sharp angles. A dense cloud of black smoke billowed forth. Plumes of dust and glass soared and fell. Torrents of water continued to fall on the smoking heap of debris. The flames dying down, the great beast tamed, licking its paws now.

An unexpected silence, the air filled with smoke and the stench of burning wood and plaster, and paint and burning varnish. Choking smoke and dust. And then the crowd cheering the firemen.

Two men took their places, ready to pump if the fire blew up again. They stumbled away and met Inspector Fall, holding up his lamp in search of them, his face black, too, and his eyes red-rimmed.

'Your men?' asked Jones.

'All accounted for — just one got blown off his feet from one of the blasts. He's all right — just a few bruises and scorches. The firemen think the explosions have stopped. Your men?'

'Constable Feak went in the cart to get the Islington engine. I don't know about my sergeant or Constable Stemp.'

'Safe enough to have a look about now.'

'No one?'

'Shouldn't think so. It'd be a miracle if anyone survived that. Saw just the one who came out in flames. We'll have to wait until it's light. Not long now. The firemen will go in soonish. Do you want to get away, Superintendent Jones? I'm thinking you won't want it known you were here. I mean, if Jaggard's dead in there, it won't matter, o' course, but if he isn't, then —'

'I might think he's dead and call it off. He'll think he's safe. You're right, Mr Fall, I'm obliged to you for that.'

'No need for Mr Dickens to be mentioned. And your men could have been anyone. All smoke-black faces now. We'll have dozens of witnesses for the inquest.'

Inspector Fall went away to speak to the chief fireman. Another blackened face loomed up as they made their way towards the sheds and outhouses. Sergeant Rogers.

'Sir, I've found Stemp and Feak's waitin' with his cart.'

No one spoke as the cart rolled back down Maiden Lane. It was enough to wonder about the bodies in the wreck. Dickens looked back at the lurid sky. It looked like sunset on a winter's day, or a bloody sunrise. It was neither, but morning would come and bring with it dreadful news.

Dickens got off the cart at Tavistock Square.

'Tomorrow,' Jones said.

Tomorrow, and tomorrow, and tomorrow.

33: BODIES OF EVIDENCE

'Five bodies, so far — six, if you include the one that came out — the one that Stemp here tried to rescue.'

'Man, I think, but I couldn't get near enough.'

'Abel Miller, I wonder?' Rogers said.

'Might have been. They're at the Islington Mortuary. Not much chance of identification, according to Fall. I'll spare you the details, but Fall will let us know. It was gas — collected in the cellar. Of course, the place hadn't been used. That and foul air. Someone probably went down with a candle —'

'Bloody fool,' Stemp said.

'Glassware, chemicals left there and what Jaggard's crew might have been using. Asphaltum, sulphuric acid, batteries. Went up like a bomb, and that paint store. Jaggard's lot, I'm sure. When it cooled a bit, the firemen went in wearing their protective jackets with those pipes to let in fresh air. Fall had to wait, but the firemen found steel plates, and copper ones — all twisted, but they knew what they were, and a mangled wreck of a printing press. Fall's men picked up bits of paper that had blown about — mostly ash, but some they deciphered. Fall's sent some fragments over. Belgian notes, I think. Fall will send the rest later.'

'Jaggard there?' asked Dickens.

'I don't think so — he was directing other business. Tell your tale, Doublett.'

Dickens gaped as he heard Doublett's story of the railings and the creature that had jumped from the tree and vanished.

'You didn't say — just wished me goodnight after I told you about the fire.'

'Didn't want to worry you, sir. No point — some escaped animal — ape, I thought. You know how people keep queer pets. And whoever was banging on the railings hooked it.'

'Not an ape, Doublett, a child.'

'A child, sir? What kind of child would —'

'One in league with Martin Jaggard.'

'Jacko Cragg,' Dickens said, remembering Jones's description of the boy shinning down the drainpipe.

'I'd say so, and they were at my house beating their devil's tattoo on the garden door. Scrap couldn't sleep. He was in the kitchen, and he heard them. Elizabeth found him with a bottle and the kitchen poker, ready to do battle if anyone got in. They opened the kitchen door when it was quiet, and my wife saw — ' he looked at Dickens — 'an impossible white face on top of the garden door. She and Scrap hurled their bottles across the garden and heard them run away.'

Dickens thought of the drumbeat in Gruel Place but he didn't say anything. They knew already that they had been followed.

Sam Jones did not mention Eleanor, either. Elizabeth had coped with that. There were sometimes drunks in the back alley, making a nuisance of themselves. Scrap had reassured her that they'd frightened them off. Elizabeth thought they had got away with it. Jones hoped so. And, he thought, now that Jaggard's business was in ruins, he wouldn't be sending his lads again to frighten his family and Dickens's. He'd know the forging operation would be discovered, and the bodies. And if he was dead, then those lads might well be back in Clerkenwell.

'What now?' asked Rogers.

'I'll bet that Jacko Cragg is back in Clerkenwell — we should find him.'

'I agree, we'll have to look for him, but in the meantime, I want Mrs Jaggard here — in handcuffs, if you have to. I don't care. Just get her here and in a cell. I want to know who she knows that knows Martin Jaggard — family, anybody — any connection. If he's alive, I want him.'

'Sir?'

'What is it, Doublett?'

'Talkin' of family, my ma, she has relations in Clerkenwell. I wonder if I could lodge there, you know, as someone else —'

Pastoral, comical, tragical, thought Dickens. Doublett was something of an actor. He'd made a convincing law student in the last case. He didn't say it, but he could see that Sam was remembering.

'Jacko Cragg know you again?'

'Doubt it. All coppers look the same to them. In any case, I'd just be — a sailor, maybe.'

'Go and talk to your mother — see if it's possible. Rogers, Stemp, go and get Mrs Jaggard, if you please.'

Dickens picked up some fragments of charred paper from Jones's desk. He could decipher some of the scorched letters. Foreign, certainly. 'Paper,' he said.

'What?'

'You said the paper was wrong on the notes in Joey Speed's possession. What about this?'

'Hard to tell until we get —'

'John the Baptist couldn't have brought tons of paper over from France or Belgium.'

'Speed's notes were Bank of England notes. John the Baptist would have brought samples of French or Belgian notes in

242

exchange for the jewels. Jaggard would want samples to copy, if that's what he was about. Speed's banknotes were early trials by Thoddy Cragg, maybe, before the foreign ones came, and Speed kept them. No wonder he wouldn't talk. He wasn't meant to have them, I'll bet.'

'This paper, though, where'd they get it?'

'A bank which issues its own notes, maybe. Some provincial banks still do, but we can hardly go to every bank that produces its own and ask if they've got any spare paper lying about. And I don't care much now. Jaggard will know that it's all gone up in flames — probably with his cohorts. We'll have to wait for some idea of who was in that factory. It's Jaggard we want, and the whereabouts of that brothel.'

There was a hurried knock at the door. Constable Feak appeared, red-faced and breathless. Constable Feak who had been on duty at Grafton Street.

'Shootin', sir — Mr Julius Henchman — suicide. It looks like.'

On the way out, they met Rogers and Stemp, who were bringing in Mrs Jaggard. She looked grim and opened her mouth at the sight of the superintendent. Jones ignored her. 'I've no time for her now. Put her in a cell and keep her there until she tells you what she knows about Jaggard.'

Then they were in the street and rushing up to Oxford Street.

'Grief?' Dickens asked when they stopped to cross the road.

'Unless he knew something.'

Dickens looked at the buildings on the other side. London and County Joint Stock Bank. 'Henchman was a banker.'

Rose opened the door. She simply pointed upstairs. 'Study,' she said.

Dickens noticed Mrs Plum standing at a distance with the other servants, a boot boy, and another couple of maids.

'Your mistress?' Jones asked.

Rose sniffed. 'In her room — she just collapsed. The doctor gave her something to calm her down.'

'Then you should be with her,' Dickens said. He'd noticed her clipped tones. Her eyes were dry, though her nose, sharper than ever, was red — where had it been poking?

She went upstairs without a word. Jones turned to the waiting servants. Mrs Plum looked very solemn, the maids open-mouthed, eyes alight with curiosity, and the boot boy looked as if he'd seen a melodrama and enjoyed it.

'I'll speak to you all later. Wait in the kitchen. Go with them, Feak.'

Julius Henchman was slumped over his desk, a gun by his hand, and blood on his head and on the papers before him. The blood which would have gushed from his mouth. His safe was open. Something in those papers which caused this act? *Or grief for his brother*, Jones thought briefly as he approached the doctor, who was lifting his hands from a bowl. Red water dripped from his hands. His assistant gave him a towel and that turned red, too.

'Shot himself. No doubt about it. They all heard it — forty-five minutes ago. The cook looked in — only one with any presence of mind. She sent the boy for a policeman and sent a maid for me. No one else in the room. No visitors.'

Another one that didn't waste words, Dickens thought, or sympathy. 'Did you know Mr Henchman?' he asked.

'No — family doctor is Smithson, Princess Street, number five. If that's all, I'll send the mortuary van — post-mortem at the Middlesex Hospital. I'll write it up, but it's obvious. Circular wound in the right temple — two inches deep. Corresponding wound on the other side — exit wound. Right-handed — asked the cook. Pistol. Barrel discharged. Blew his brains out.'

Jones had already seen that in the mess that was on the desk — the mess that he and Rogers would have to search through to find what was in those papers. He thanked the doctor, who was out of the door in a moment, followed by his mute attendant.

'He's probably right, but we'll have to talk to the servants just to get the facts straight about the timing. Doctor Smithson's my doctor. I'll see him, too — anything about Henchman's state of mind and so on, the usual thing.'

'Depressed by the murder of his young brother?'

'Bank, you said.'

'I did and now I think of it, when we interviewed him and he thought Mrs Henchman was coming in, I thought he looked terror-struck.'

'Afraid that his wife might find out about Mrs Wand.'

'But you only said one more question. You hadn't asked what he was doing on the Friday night, but you had mentioned conspiracy and forgery —'

'And he looked shattered then.'

'Julius Henchman wasn't so terrified when you insisted he tell you who he was with on the Friday night. Uncomfortable, yes, and that spark of annoyance about his private business. He said that Darius never meant — and then he stopped.'

'Never meant it to go so far? Which bank?'

'London and County Joint Stock Bank, Lombard Street. Branch in Oxford Street. I noticed it earlier.'

'They don't print their own money. There might be something in these papers when we've dried them out. Ask someone for a key, would you? I'll need to lock this room after the body's been taken away. Send it up, and you stay in the kitchen while I look in the safe. We can guess at the state of Darius's financial affairs. It would be interesting to see the state of Mr Julius Henchman's.'

'What am I to do in the kitchen?'

Jones couldn't help smiling. 'Oh, the usual — get 'em to tell you the secrets of their hearts.'

Mrs Plum was in the kitchen, making tea for the servants. She sent the boot boy with the key and invited Dickens to take a cup.

'What a business. Poor Mr Darius and now this. I never thought … but Mr Henchman was that upset. Havin' to look at the body — I thought he'd never be the same, but I never thought he'd — not do a thing like that, but then you never knows. He wasn't what you'd call one for showin' his feelings, but then inside — mebbe felt things —'

'How true, Mrs Plum.' Dickens gazed at her admiringly. 'You never do know, and the girls, here, all very shocked. I mean, living —'

'Oh, no, the girls don't live in — see, Mr Henchman — well, I think the girls better go home. They've had enough for one day.'

One of them spoke up. She looked disappointed. 'But that policeman, 'e said ter wait —'

'Ah, yes, Superintendent Jones. Have you anything particular you want to say to him? He is busy at the moment, but —' smiling benignly — 'you can tell me, and if it is important, then I am certain the superintendent will want to see you. So do tell me.'

'Not 'xactly — only I was brushin' the stairs, an' then I 'eard it — ooh, ever so loud it was, an' Rose ran down from Missis's room an' I ran an' Mrs Plum came up an' we stood a bit, an' Mrs Plum peeped an' she closed the door quick, like, an' said ter the boy to get a policeman an' —'

'How long ago?'

'About an hour. Hall clock struck twelve. I was preparing the lunch,' Mrs Plum explained.

'It was, it was. I was on the stairs.'

'An' I goes fer the doctor — the other maid wanted her tuppenceworth — jest in Conway Street. Nearest, see, I thinks, an' the doctor comes an' up 'e goes, up ter see the body — dead, see — dead, 'in't 'e? An' there'll be an inquest. Me an' Meg, we'll 'ave ter give evidence, see.'

'I am sure you will, and I am obliged, and I will certainly tell the superintendent everything. Now, you can go off home — your duty is done.'

They went, albeit reluctantly, and the returning boot boy was dispatched to wait in the carriage house in the mews with the groom who had played no part in the drama but that of a latecomer who had missed the climactic moment.

'They aren't bad girls, Mr Dickens, but Mr Henchman don't mean much to 'em. They didn't know him except as someone who passed 'em on the stairs or served at table, an' he wasn't one for noticin' servants. He'd not be able to tell you which was which — not that I mean — an' I am sorry —'

'I know you are, Mrs Plum — you have feelings, of course, but you can't help being truthful. I know that, too. I think you were about to tell me something which you didn't want to say in front of the maids.'

'Let my tongue run away there. We had a footman, but he was let go. Girls is cheaper, you see, especially when they don't live in. The laundress comes, of course, an' Rose does for Mrs Henchman. I think Mr Henchman would like to have got rid of her. Rose is a nosy piece, but Mrs Henchman has her own money. There was rows — he wasn't very nice to her — though I shouldn't speak ill — the truth's the truth.'

'Were there financial problems, Mrs Plum?'

'I don't know, sir. Mr Darius had no job. I daresay he was an expense, an' the daughter married to a curate. Poor as charity, I think, an' Mrs Henchman supports them. It's a funny thing, now I think of it. She's a rich lady, pays for all the trinkets an' new furniture an' that. You can tell he don't like it — but it was Mr Henchman who wanted to cut down, an' he said the maids had to live out an' got rid of the footman. Though, he likes his food just so. Rose heard — he said Mrs Henchman wanted him to live like a pauper when she spent money on rubbishy things. I think he wanted money from her, and she wasn't for payin'.'

'Is this a recent thing?'

'Last few months or so. The kitchen maid — oh, Phib, sir, I forgot to ask.'

'No news, I'm afraid, but she wasn't replaced, I take it.'

'No, I was told one of them girls would help — not that they're much good. Still, I'll not need them now, I suppose. Just Mrs Henchman to do for now.'

Dickens left her and stood in the hall and watched the mortuary men bring down the body in its shell. Not a kind man, a man who couldn't get the money he wanted from his wife and punished the whole household. Apart from Darius, of course. Two of a kind. Self-indulgent, self-centred, and fundamentally heartless.

Jones had various papers in his hands. 'Debts,' he said. 'Unpaid bills, bills of exchange — creditors on the march.' He pointed to the desk. 'Something more in those, perhaps.'

'And Mrs Henchman seems to have held her purse strings very tight of late. The timing's right, by the way. They heard the hall clock at midday.'

'Suicide, then. No doubt. Desperate thing to do. Back to Bow Street and I'll set things in motion. I'll need to see the coroner.'

'I'll try Doctor Elliotson — just in case he knows anything at all about Sir William Pell and his valet. Any rumour, gossip — anything.'

34: THE TANGLED WEB

'One male corpse with the remains of a tattoo — part of an anchor on part of an arm.'

'Sailor?' Dickens asked.

'I've sent someone to your Lieutenant Barnes to ask. Another male — nothing to identify him, but Fall sent this —' Jones showed them a bit of charred wood which might have been a handle. The metal was undamaged, but Dickens recognized the sharp point on the blackened metal.

'A burin. Thoddy Cragg?'

'Could be. One other, again no way of knowing who he was. There was part of a boot — a bit of sole hanging off. Scrap's attacker, maybe. The man who was burnt to death outside was Abel Miller. There were remnants of clothing and another boot. The blacksmith identified the hat which had been blown off and escaped the worst of the flames. Abel always wore it. It makes sense that he was there if his son was there. We know Matty Miller had been back. We know Abel Miller's family was in poverty. Matty Miller had quarrelled repeatedly with his father, but Abel Miller could be trusted to keep his eye on the factory and its environs while the others were setting up there. He'd be paid.'

Dickens was struck by something almost mechanical in Sam's tone. He was looking down at Fall's report and giving them the facts, and there was tension in the others. There was an unnatural woodenness in Stemp's face, as if he were steeling himself to hear something dreadful. Rogers was red. His eyes looked dry — from the smoke, probably, but he seemed to be opening them very wide, as if to prevent himself from closing them. His hands held on to his pockets. Dickens could see the white knuckles. His own hands were clenched, too. He felt hot about the collar, but he didn't dare ask. They all wanted to know but dreaded to know.

Jones had stopped. He looked up and caught Dickens's eye. Dickens nodded. *You'll have to tell us*, his glance said.

'Two females. Nothing recognisable about the fabrics, so we don't —' he cleared his throat. His voice had been hoarse from the smoke, and now the words seemed difficult — 'we can't be sure — except there's a ring on one of the hands — a wedding ring, so I'm wondering about Annie Taylor — Tipper's woman. She might have worn one. I don't know if Phoebe Miller had a ring — we can find out from Mrs Plum. Or Matty might have given it to her. The bones of the second supposed female are — suggest someone taller than —'

Stemp had the courage. 'Those girls, Mr Jones, 'e'd not use 'em fer coining — 'e'd want — sorry, sir, I can't put it another way. Yer know what I'm gettin' at.'

'I do, Stemp, and I think that you are probably right. We all know what he might keep them for.'

'Emmie Stooks.' Dickens found his voice. 'Polly Stooks said that she was not much to look at. She thought Jaggard would use her as a skivvy. She might — Polly's tallish. Her sister might be —'

'Polly Stooks won't know her. Just a collection of bones. We'll have to wait until we find that brothel, then —'

'I'll tell her, then. Polly won't want her buried on the parish. Their mother's grave is in that church in Clerkenwell.'

'That reminds me. Doublett's gone to lodge there. Looking out for Jacko Cragg.'

'No kids at the fire?' asked Rogers.

'Not as far as I know, but they're still sifting through those sheds and outhouses. I'm thinking about that brothel and where it might be. Oh, and Mrs Jaggard — Rogers, tell us what you found out.'

'Piece of work, she is. Nothin' to say at first. We had no right — the usual thing, but Stemp persuaded her.'

Stemp looked very solemnly at his chief, but there was a lift at the corner of his mouth. 'Only told 'er, sir, that she wasn't goin' anywhere, an' I'd bring 'er some bread an' water, an' 'oped she didn't mind rats, an' cells was busy so she might 'ave ter share. Did she mind drunks?'

They all felt better, and Rogers smiled. 'That did it. I don't think she does know anything about him. Went on about her name bein' besmirched an' all that, but I asked about family, and she did confirm Jaggard's mother's name — the one that died — the wicked one. Louisa Todd's the name. Father made artificial limbs down Wapping way —'

'A lot of wooden legs in Wapping,' Dickens observed.

'Where Mrs Jaggard's brother met her — he was a navy man before —'

'He was dragged into the gutter,' Jones said.

'That's what she said. We've found all the Todds in the Trade Directory. No limb-maker. Mrs Agnes Todd in Coram Street, two barristers, one in The Temple, one at Thavies Inn, doctor in Spring Gardens —'

'An' there's eight artificial limb-makers — the Strand, Grosvenor Square, Oxford Street, Covent Garden, Cork Street.'

'Not making wooden legs for common sailors. Mr Gray in Cork Street — made the Marquis of Anglesey's leg — very ingenious, apparently.'

Stemp looked at him. 'The things you know, Mr Dickens.'

'Blackwell in Covent Garden making spring crutches, the latest in legs, surgical instruments, trusses — big concern — business, not the trusses.'

Jones did chuckle at that. 'Try the Todds first — let's get them out of the way. Start with Coram Street. A Miss Louisa Todd reported missing — you know the drill, and then we'll try Wapping. Bold will know the wooden leg-makers.'

'Wooden legs in Gruel Place at that pawnbrokers',' Dickens said when the others had gone, 'and he was well supplied with nails and hammers. And I heard someone drumming in the alley. One of Jaggard's lads, I suppose.'

'You didn't say —'

'Well, we knew we were being followed, and then the news came about Julius Henchman.'

'The pawnbroker's name isn't Todd?'

'I didn't get a chance to ask.'

'We'll stick to Wapping first — that's where the father made his legs. Your pawnbroker will still be there.'

'And his legs, I daresay, unless there's a demand for used wooden legs. He looked as if he'd been there since the flood — and most of his goods. Anything about the bank?'

'Ah, yes, I found out from a clerk here. The London and County has branches all over the place, having taken over a good many provincial banks over the years — acquired Jeffreys in Chatham, Hector and Lacey in Petersfield, banks in Arundel, Chichester, Epsom —'

'Where Mr Julius Henchman's daughter lives with the curate.'

'Now, that is interesting. When the banks were taken over, their notes were taken out of circulation — consigned to the fire, I imagine —'

'And the paper?'

'Same — unless someone was careless, or forgetful, or pensioned off, or in awe of the boss. Mr Julius Henchman, director from headquarters, or his brother with a bona fide card announcing him as Mr Julius, carries out an inspection. Makes off with the wastepaper for the sake of security and passes it on to Jaggard — for a fee, of course.'

'There's a paper mill at Epsom.'

'Yes, there is — a contact there, maybe, bribed to sell paper. It's been done before. I'll contact the Epsom police. Not that it matters just now, Charles. Julius Henchman's dead, and his brother'

'What did his doctor say?'

'Nothing wrong with Julius Henchman except indigestion. Depression? Good God, no. Henchman had no feelings. Didn't get on with his wife. Smithson treated her for nerves, especially after Darius's death. Julius Henchman was fond of the lad, but he wouldn't kill himself over it. Then, confidentially, Smithson said a man like that would only kill himself over debts.'

'And the police asking questions about murder and forgery.'

'Smithson will testify at the inquest that the man was in good health, not depressed and so on. I'll give evidence about the debts. That's as far as I can go, but when we find Jaggard, any involvement by both Henchmans will emerge, no doubt, and the police at Epsom will make enquiries. It's a loose thread to be tied up later.'

'Lord, what a tangled web we weave —'

'With a damned great hole in it where Jaggard should be. Did you get to see Elliotson about Pell?'

'I did. It's what we thought — not part of the medical circle. Pursued his own interests. Secretive, though. Elliotson doesn't know what he was up to in the latter years. Could have been looking for the philosopher's stone. Mad enough, Elliotson said.'

'Lead into gold. Refused to give Jaggard the secret?'

'Refused him something, I'll bet. His money, for sure. But no gossip about his servants, but then Pell was virtually a recluse anyway.'

'Another loose thread. And another — what was Henchman spending on Mrs Amelia Wand? She might be of interest at the inquest. Grove saw her and she confirmed he was with her on that Friday night.'

'Poor Lily Henchman — this will all be an ordeal for her.'

'She might be glad to be rid of him — of them both, and she's got her own money. I know it sounds cynical, but I don't want a verdict of suicide brought about by grief at the death of his brother. I'll need to tie it in with Darius's doings when the inquest is resumed on the murders.'

'Nice little love nest in Arbour —' Dickens began.

They stared at each other. 'Square,' Jones added, 'just above Wapping. What was Julius Henchman doing in Wapping? Long way from home. A trip to Inspector Bold, I think.'

'Wapping, wooden legs, and Mrs Wand — magic in the web of it.'

35: WOODEN LEGS IN WAPPING

Inspector Bold greeted them with the news that they had not found any pawnbrokers who knew of Mr Darius Henchman as a customer, except Mr Decker, of course.

Jones told him that the young man had been murdered and about the explosion in Belle Isle.

'Forging business, it looks like. Blown to bits, I'm glad to say. Though I suspect Jaggard is still in one piece.'

'Think he'll come here? Back to his old haunts. Take ship?'

'To the continent, maybe. We think the notes he was forging were Belgian. He had dealings with a Frenchman — or he could have been Belgian, but he's nowhere to be found. Gone home, I should think. However, neither of us has enough men to scour every steamer.'

'Jaggard could be gone already. Stowed away, even. He'd get taken on as crew. He's hard enough.'

'There are two things of interest. Julius Henchman has committed suicide — financial problems there. He might have been involved and we do know he visited a lady in Arbour Square.'

'Just up the road. Paying a visit, are you?'

'We will do. The other thing is that Jaggard's mother was from hereabouts. Dead now, but her father made artificial limbs. You don't know the name of a Todd in connection with that trade?'

'Wooden legs for sailors — made by carpenters mostly. One in Gravel Lane — name of Toddy. There's a Todder family in Dry Salt Alley.' He turned to Dickens with a smile. 'You remember where Mr Ajax Cheese has his shop —'

'I cannot forget — I shall never forget. How is that dauntless man?' Ajax Cheese had played a part in the case of a missing banker earlier in the year.

'Still selling cheese and giving away his medicines. Mr Todder, however, is in prison. Assault and battery — with a wooden leg, as it happens.'

'His?' asked Jones.

'No, the other fellow's. He was a carpenter, but not a Todd. Plenty of carpenters around, of course. I'll find out who makes wooden legs. What was the name of Jaggard's ma?'

'Louisa Todd. Jaggard was illegitimate. Father, a gentleman, we're told, a naval man. Jaggard was Todd before he purloined the name Jaggard from a distant relative.'

'Judge, Sir Titus Jaggard,' Dickens said.

'The hanging judge — remember him, all right. Jaggard might find himself on the squeezer at Newgate. Pity it won't be his namesake with the black cap on. Be years back, though, this Louisa Todd —'

Constable John Gaunt came in to see his godfather and Mr Dickens. Bold asked, 'Any carpenter named Todd you know of? In the peg-leg trade — other than Toddy in Gravel Lane.'

'Can't think of — oh, there's that woman, Miss Tiddy — her name's really Miss Tilda Todd.'

'The doll maker?'

'Wooden dolls have wooden legs,' Dickens said.

John Gaunt took them to Dry Salt Lane where the paint manufacturers operated, and the saltpetre dealers had their warehouses. *Just the place for an explosion*, Dickens thought, eyeing up a brazier in the street, the gas lights, and the oil lamps and tallow candles in the dirty windows. There was light in Ajax Cheese's shop window, but they crossed into another alley where Miss Tilda Todd made her dolls. Mr Cheese had been heroic, but somewhat inclined to wander into the realms of literature at the sight of Charles Dickens. *Another time*, he thought. *No time*, thought Sam Jones.

'Tiddy Doll, they call her,' Gaunt told them.

'The gingerbread man? Curious name for a woman,' Dickens said. Tiddy Doll was a legendary maker of gingerbread who had featured in one of Hogarth's cartoons.

'Who knows? Maybe from Tilda and Todd. Anyway, Miss Tiddy's the name on the door. She is a bit eccentric. I've met her a few times. Kids name-calling, a few broken windows. Now she keeps a guard at the door.' Gaunt grinned at them. 'You'll see. He stands in the hall — never moves a muscle.'

A very tall soldier in the uniform of a heavy dragoon with a red mouth and magnificent moustaches stood to attention inside the door. He didn't move a muscle. His wooden mouth was firmly closed, as were his very straight wooden legs.

A woman carrying a basket of material in one hand and a yellow wig in the other, answered Gaunt's query about Miss Todd with a sharp, 'Miss Tiddy. Upstairs.'

'They make the clothes down here, and the wigs. Carpenter out the back. Wooden dolls upstairs,' Gaunt explained as they made their way up.

The smell was of paint and glue and wood chippings, and there was the buzz of a wood turning lathe from somewhere. A girl passed them on the stairs with a basket, out of which a quantity of painted faces peered blankly — looking irresistibly like severed heads just come from the guillotine.

Gaunt knocked on the open door. Jones stayed at a distance. He just wanted to listen. She knew Gaunt, and if there was anything to be known, he'd find it out. He couldn't help grinning as he listened to the conversation that followed. Of course, Dickens went in after Gaunt. He couldn't resist Tiddy Doll.

'Miss Todd, good day to you,' Gaunt was saying.

A silvery voice like music from a distance answered, 'Miss Tiddy, sir, if you please. Always a pleasure, Mr Gaunt, and you've brought me a customer, I hope —' Miss Tiddy stood up, a little doll-like figure in a white dress, but she wasn't young — 'Oh, my, my, my — now here's a taking, girls. It's Mr Dickens. I know you, sir, come to write us up, have you? Tiddy Doll's girls. Take a bow, girls, give him a smile. He might take you home.'

On the worktable, the girls did not move, but at least twenty painted blue eyes gazed and ten little red mouths puckered at him. Quite unnerving. Tiddy Doll's eyes gleamed, and a peal of silvery laughter followed. Silver ringlets bobbed under an elaborate lace cap and two little hands clapped. A miniature old lady, that's what she was. A model of your ideal grandmother with a silver lace shawl on her shoulders and little fingerless lace gloves on the hands. And as clean as polished silver. Something about the eyes, though, not quite a grandmama's. Pale as moonstones, far-seeing eyes of a curious otherworldly transparency. Water in moonlight.

The shelves were filled with heads — bald heads like the inmates of the asylum, unspeaking mouths, pale as ghosts, unseeing eyes, jumbles of arms and legs — miniature corpses waiting to be reassembled. Not that they came to life, he thought. Those blue eyes — no speculation in them.

'A moment, if you please, I can't leave her —' The old lady took up her brush of red paint and they watched while her nimble fingers filled in the pencil-drawn mouth on the doll on which she had been working. When she had finished, she turned the face to them. 'There, now, that's a kissable mouth — a little innocent, of course, but kissable —'

There was something grotesque, Dickens thought, in the sightless eyes and little point of a nose above that vivid mouth. Not kissable at all. Like kissing a corpse. It had no legs, either. They were waiting on the table — little jointed wooden legs with modelled calves the colour of flesh. Better than Mr Tipper's leg. Tiddy Doll was an artist.

'I go in for beauty, you see. What's the use of ugliness in a doll? People are bad enough. Dear me, what ugliness there is out there. What hard eyes. Blue eyes go well — pretty blue eyes. Brown, sometimes, warm brown, black for a wicked doll. Sometimes they are — you never can tell. But, never, never cold green eyes.'

Outside the door, Jones felt a shiver at his neck, but he didn't move. Dickens waited to see what might come next.

'The gentleman outside, won't he come in? No need to be shy. There's room. I'd like to see his eyes.'

No choice. Jones went in. She looked him over. Her pale eyes might look faded, but he had the impression that she saw a great deal. There were sparks there.

'I like grey eyes — wise eyes. Eyes you can trust.' She turned to Dickens. 'I like your eyes, too. Dark blue, I think. Changeable, like the sea. Storms, sometimes. Eyes that see a lot. Eyes that see everything. Honest eyes, but pain there, too. It is a hard world and no mistake, Mr Dickens. And young Mr Gaunt. Hazel eyes — very nice eyes. No harm in them. Never green eyes.'

'Miss Todd,' Dickens began.

'Miss Tiddy will do. We don't use Todd now. Not now. Remember that, Mr Gaunt.'

'Why is that, Miss Tiddy?' asked Dickens.

'Someone had a sister —' They didn't speak. She would take her time. Sparks in her eyes still.

Looking at Jones. 'No names, Mr Policeman. No cruel names. No jagged names to cut yourself on, but I'll tell you a story. The girls all know it, but they won't tell. The story of a green-eyed man who came from over the sea and drank deep at the Safe Harbour, where a blue-eyed girl caught his roving eye, a carpenter's daughter, who wanted a gentleman to woo her, and so he did, and away they roved, drinking deep all the while. Scattering gold wherever they went until all was spent, and in a ditch they died, but not before a boy was born, a boy with green eyes and a hard heart. A boy who wanted to know, a boy who asked, but there was only Miss Tiddy, and she could not answer. She never knew a blue-eyed girl or a green-eyed man from over the sea. She was only Miss Tiddy Doll, who never knew a man who made wooden legs in Wapping by the river that flows to the sea where all the secrets lie, deep within the shells whose voices tell them to the fishes.

'And the green-eyed boy who was really a man with a cruel mind behind his red-lipped smile went away, and the blue-eyed girls did not sleep well that night, and Miss Tiddy sang an old song to them all night until they slept without dreaming of the green-eyed man, who walked with a swagger to the end of a rope.'

In the silence that followed, Miss Tiddy smiled to take the chill from her words. The twenty blue eyes stared, and the red lips stayed closed, keeping their secrets.

Sam Jones opened his mouth, but a lace-mittened hand stopped him. 'No, sir, you'll have to dream the end of the story for yourself.' She pointed to Dickens. 'He'll help you. He knows all the stories that were ever told, and dreams of many not yet told. He will know when you take your walk to Arbour

Square, where a lady lives who bought a doll from Miss Tiddy, a doll with black eyes and a fine velvet dress. All in black, that doll. Black magic, you see.'

Sam Jones felt that same chill at his neck. Arbour Square. There was magic in the web of it. Good Lord, what was he thinking? Those silver eyes, though. He did not look at the other two.

'Downstairs, there's a blue-eyed doll for him, and a brown-eyed doll for you, Mr Policeman. Three shillings each. You can pay the blue-eyed maid. Mr Gaunt does not need a doll yet. He has no children. It'll be a boy, Mr Gaunt, when he comes.'

John Gaunt blushed and Miss Tiddy Doll laughed her silvery laugh, picked up a paintbrush and dipped it into blue paint. They went downstairs, followed by the strange, silvery words of an old song:

'*Weep on, weep on, your hour is past,*
The fatal chain is round you cast...'

Whether Miss Tiddy Doll was singing, it was impossible to say. It sounded like more than one voice. But it couldn't be. Yes, it could.

Dickens and Jones bought their dolls from a blue-eyed maid. Dickens had to buy two blue-eyed darlings — he could hardly go home to two daughters with one doll. Two dolls, uncannily like Lady Nora Lockhart in their blue velvet. And another in Elizabeth Jones's dark red dress. Warm brown eyes.

Mamie and Katey were a bit old for dolls, he supposed, but they could give them as presents to Lemon's daughters. No, they couldn't. He looked up the stairs as they approached the door with their parcels. Wrapped in silver paper. The strange music still fell on their ears. '*Breathe not his name,*' one voice sang now. She'd know.

Jones glanced at the stern-faced guardsman and stopped before he opened the front door. Gaunt, still rather red in the face, looked at him. 'What was that all —'

'He'll know, trust me, but before we say anything more, I'll tell you what I do know. And that is that I think you should keep a close eye on this place, John. Mr Mustachios, here, will be no use at all — begging his pardon — if someone is determined to get in.'

'Jaggard's the green-eyed man?'

'Yes, I worked that out. Mr Dickens will give me the finer details, but do you know the carpenter who's out the back?'

'Yes, a decent man.'

'Tell him that there's thieves about — a bad lot. Warn him.'

'She'll know,' Dickens said, still gazing upstairs.

'Don't mind him,' Jones said. 'He has these moments. Now, take the dolls, for God's sake. We can't go to Arbour Square with a bundle of dolls in our arms. See the carpenter and get back to the station and tell Bold where we've gone.'

'But —'

'I know you want to know, and you will. We'll come back for the dolls. The safety of these women is more important now. Constable Dickens —'

Dickens snapped to attention. 'Superintendent.'

'Go on before me. I'll meet you at the church just above the square, near the police station.'

'St. Thomas's.'

'That's the one.'

Dickens went out and up towards Old Gravel Lane. Jones gave him a few moments before turning in the opposite direction. *Eyes*, he thought, *eyes everywhere*.

36: BLACK VELVET

The fatal chain. A shining, silver link in that long, loose chain of iron that bound them all — Dickens thought of Miss Tiddy Doll and her connection to Martin Jaggard. But a chain suddenly pulled tight, the links appearing above the mud like a long-buried anchor chain made of rings small and large, but all part of it, inextricably woven together. He and Sam Jones had to break it by finding the missing link.

'Praying for guidance?' Jones asked as he slid into one of the back pews next to Dickens.

'Good Lord, what a strange encounter. Gormed, I was.'

'So I saw. So was I — talk about casting a spell. However, let's piece it together. The first green-eyed man is Jaggard's father and the blue-eyed carpenter's daughter is Louisa Todd, Jaggard's mother, and the story's just about what Mrs Maria Jaggard told us at the workhouse. And the green-eyed boy, our Jaggard, went to see Miss Tiddy. She knew he was dangerous. Intuition — or something —'

'Second sight. Those eyes — I told you there was magic in it.'

'I'll take anything we can get. Wooden legs in Wapping — Miss Tiddy's father. And she knows Jaggard's red lips and his swagger.'

'To the rope — clairvoyant, she is, and that song — the fatal chain.'

'You know it?'

'Oh, yes, one of Thomas Moore's Irish lyrics — new edition, illustrated by my friend, Daniel Maclise. And those last words, another song. The next line is: *Where cold and unhonoured his relics are laid.* Coincidence, eh? Or the mysterious ways of fate.'

Jones grinned at him. 'Don't you start going all mystical on me, but I hope she's right. Cold and unhonoured in Dead Man's Walk. But what gormed me the most was Arbour Square.'

'Mrs Wand. Black magic, you see.'

'And I don't believe in coincidence. Julius Henchman, Amelia Wand, Jaggard's aunt, all connected. Amelia Wand and Jaggard?'

'The tangled web.'

'If Mrs Wand is wearing black velvet, I'll believe in anything,' Jones said as they walked round to Arbour Square.

But they were not to know yet. Number three, the corner house, was in darkness. It was a handsome four-storey Georgian house of red brick with a shiny brass plate which announced the house as The George Private Hotel. A rather ladylike house with a neat, freshly painted set of railings over which they peered to look down into the area. Someone might be in the kitchen downstairs, but there were no lights. Dickens followed Jones up the white steps and Jones knocked sharply on the door. The brass fittings were very shiny. A well-kept house. No one answered his summons, even though he knocked again, hard enough to wake the dead. They heard the sound reverberating in the empty hall, but no one came.

'Police station,' Jones said, as they walked back across the road. They paused to look back, just in case a curtain twitched, or a brief light showed.

'Henchman spent his money there?' Dickens said.

'No wonder he was in debt.'

Fifteen minutes later, they came out of the police station where an anxious constable, eager to assist the superintendent from Bow Street, had informed them that Mrs Wand had gone to Belgium — so he had been told by the next-door neighbour. Mrs Wand had been resident in the square for two years or so. Jones had asked what was known about her. Respectable private hotel, she kept — professional men, lawyers and so forth. Servants? Oh, yes, girls came and went. There'd be a cook, he supposed. And a laundress? Sam Jones knew exactly what to ask. A laundress would know what went on in the bedrooms of a respectable private hotel.

In answer to Dickens's question about Inspector Grove, Jones said, 'A maid let him into a parlour and there she was. He just assumed she was lodging there. She was a very charming lady, he said, quite ready to answer his questions about her friend, Mr Julius Henchman, whom she said used to stay at the hotel. They were good friends, apparently. Grove was quite taken with her — he's a bachelor — and he had his answer to the question about the Friday night. Mr Henchman stayed there. Mrs Wand had dined with him. There was no reason to suppose any connection with Jaggard.'

'Belgium,' Dickens said.

'Yes, indeed. I wonder if Mr John the Baptist stayed at the private hotel when he wasn't with his mam'selle in Fitzroy Street.'

They made their way back to the square. The house was still in darkness, but in a little street behind, the constable had assured them that they would find Ma Cobb, the laundress.

Up to her eyes in suds, crimson in the face, little blue eyes casting a professional eye on their cuffs — more blue eyes, but plenty of speculation in them. Waving them in with a wrinkled red hand, Ma Cobb looked gormed as she backed into the hot room where a fire blazed and sheets and articles of clothing steamed and hissed. Those flannel bloomers looked reassuringly real, Dickens thought, no magic here.

'Yer wanter know about Mrs Wand's hotel, Mr Copper?' she asked. A knowing smile, though, that she couldn't conceal.

'Private hotel,' Jones responded. 'I want to know what was private about it. Professional gentlemen, I was told.'

'She's gone off. I goes at nine to get the laundry. No need, says she. Didn't know when she'd be back. Somethin' urgent, she says, in Belgium. Fam'ly business — relations there, she says, so I don't suppose it matters if I tells ye. Let's say, a lonely gentleman needs a bed fer the night — a warm bed. More than one night if 'e 'as the chinks. Charges a pretty penny, Mrs Wand, pretty pounds, yer might say. All very private, though — nothin' common about Lady Melia. But there's a lot o' dirty sheets ter wash — pity she's gone. I've my livin' ter make an' it ain't my business wot toffs spend their money on.'

'Girls?' asked Jones.

'Oh, aye, done up like maids in the day an' plenty o' fine feathers at night.'

'Where did they come from?'

'Dunno — where do girls come from? The streets, I'm guessin'. No 'omes ter go to. An' only the work'ouse fer 'em? No thanks. Mrs Wand brought 'em, usually, an' some fella came with 'em sometimes. Thorn'ill, 'is name was. She treated 'em well, though — fine clothes, good food — better than the streets, I'd say. Better than washin' dirty sheets, I can tell yer.'

'Any new ones recently?'

'Two — one a cheeky madam, all 'oity-toity. 'Ands give 'er away. Kitchen maid, I'd wager, servant, anyways — them red 'ands — not a lady's, for all the airs she gave 'erself. I —'

'Did she wear a ring?' Dickens interrupted, remembering, hoping not. If Phoebe were in that conflagration, then — oh, Posy...

'Nah. Mrs Wand'd give 'em the paste when she dressed 'em up, an' take it back in the mornin'.'

'The other girl?' Jones asked, betraying nothing but professional interest.

'Little thing. Wouldn't say boo to a goose. Looked at the other one as if 'er life depended on 'er. Younger, I'd say. Servant, I'd guess. Wanted a better life. Kitchen's an 'ard graft, I can tell yer.'

'Now, as to the gentlemen. Mr Julius Henchman — he came to the hotel?'

'Ol' fish face — regular, 'e was, only Mrs Wand fer 'im — got the chinks, though. She robbed 'im blind, I'd say. Sometimes she would an' sometimes she wouldn't — that'll be the story. 'Ad a wife at 'ome, I daresay — maybe she'd tell.'

'Any others, you remember?'

'Furrin' gentl'man used ter come. Spent a lot o' time with Mrs Melia — not when ol' fish face woz 'ere, o' course. Turn an' turnabout, see. Serpose 'e 'ad the chinks as well. Very gentl'manly.'

'When did the new girls come?'

'Dunno — picked up the laundry last Saturday an' they woz there, eatin' their breakfast, an' the toity one lookin' at me as if I'm dirt under 'er feet, but I sees those 'ands —'

'Anyone else?'

'Nipper came with a message. Cocky little bugger — turned up in the yard. Told 'im to clear off, but no, 'e ad ter see Mrs Wand, an' funny thing is, she came out an' took the note. Give 'im a shillin'. Puts it in 'is mouth an 'ops it over the wall — like a bloody monkey. A shillin', an' me on a shillin' fer all them sheets.'

'When was this?'

'Yesterday.'

'He didn't say who the note was from?'

'Tol' me ter tell Mrs Wand that 'e 'ad a message from Mr Jay.'

'You've never seen a Mr Jay?'

'Nah, don't know 'im.'

It was enough. Well, not quite. Dickens had to ask. 'Did Mrs Wand wear black velvet?'

'Oh, all the time. Quite the lady, Melia Wand. 'Enchman liked it, she said.'

Easier on the eye than poor Lily Henchman's red ribbons and tartan.

Inspector Bold had heard the tale of Miss Tiddy from John Gaunt. He'd make sure the beat constables would keep an eye, and he'd speak to the inspector up near Arbour Square.

'True what the old dame said, then? I could hardly understand what Gaunt was tellin' me.'

'Oh, yes, though the black velvet lady, Mrs Amelia Wand, has vanished. A private hotel, of sorts.'

'Oh, one of those. Accommodation house, eh? Belgium, you say?' He saw their bleak faces. 'You think —'

Jones answered. 'I'm afraid we do. Taken to Belgium — or France. To a licensed brothel — and an introducer's fee for Amelia Wand.'

They all knew about the continental trade — girls taken away by 'auntie', told they'd be 'actresses', sold to a licensed brothel, examined for venereal disease, and kept as virtual prisoners. Amelia Wand would want to be rid of them, but she might as well make a profit while she was at it. Jaggard would want rid of them, too, and of Amelia Wand.

Where was Livvie Slack in all this? Jones wondered. Mr and Mrs Slack on a steamer to Calais, or Antwerp, or any of a dozen other continental ports? By the tidal train from Folkestone or Dover. The enormity of it overwhelmed him.

Inspector Bold was promising to be on the alert for Jaggard when Dickens said, 'Swaggering to the rope. Rope Walk above Kidney Stairs where —'

'The windmill is,' Bold finished. He looked at Superintendent Jones. 'Look, I'll send my men down there and there's men from Arbour Square. I'll ask the inspector there to get in that house. See if there's anythin' to be seen. You two should get off. Jaggard could be anywhere. There's nothing you can do in the dark.'

'And those lads, Inspector Bold. I don't know if any were in the fire, but there was certainly one at Mr Dickens's house and one at mine on the night of the fire — beating a tattoo on the back gate, so they might be with Jaggard.'

'Jacko Cragg took the message to Mrs Wand. Jacko Cragg knows where Jaggard is. Doublett's in Clerkenwell. Maybe Jaggard's there with the lad,' Dickens said.

'Doublett knows about Mrs Speed. Jacko Cragg dossed there. She'd not know if Jaggard was in one of those empty rooms. Good, then we will be on our way. I'm obliged — as always, Inspector.'

'And, I've thought, Mr Jones — Mrs Wand went off this morning. The Antwerp Packet doesn't go until Thursday, from St Katherine's Wharf. You've got time.'

'Home,' Dickens said when they had boarded the steamer to take them to Waterloo Bridge, 'home, Sam. Bold's right. She can't have gone yet.'

'Ghent, Bruges —'

'Someone with a newspaper — there. I'll ask.'

Dickens was back in a trice. 'Borrowed it. Now, sailings — sailings —' turning the pages — 'Ghent — sailed this morning, nine o'clock.'

'Good — Ma Cobb saw her at nine o'clock.'

'Next one on Wednesday. Bruges — tomorrow nine o'clock. Next one Thursday. Le Havre from St Katharine's on Thursday and Sunday. Calais from London Bridge Wharf Thursday and Sunday. Boulogne Wednesday and Sunday. The General Steam Company. They handle the Belgian trade.'

'Ostend?'

'Wednesday.'

'Stemp, Rogers, Feak, you, me, anybody to St Katharine's dock at first light — continental boat quay. The Bruges boat. I'll see Mr Mumford, the superintendent of the dock police. He'll give us some men.'

'Two girls and a woman in black velvet. We'll find them. I believe in Miss Tiddy. She knows.'

Past London Docks where the great ships waited for the wind to carry them to India or China, or Australia, or New York. Dickens thought of Cora Davies on *The Excellent*. Past St Saviour's Dock on the south side where Jacob's Island lay — that putrid ditch where Bill Sikes had lost his brutal life, that vile slum in which Sir Peter Laurie had not believed. As real, however, as the stench of Belle Isle where this story had begun. Now Saint Katharine's Basin, watching the steamers at the long wharf. The steamers which came and went to and from Antwerp, Ghent, Bruges — had it arrived? Making ready to depart tomorrow, carrying a woman in black with two girls to a new life in Belgium, a life that did not bear contemplation. Or somewhere else? Calais? Boulogne? Or somewhere they had not thought of?

Dickens stole a glance at Sam Jones watching, too. Dickens knew what he was thinking.

37: RAIL, STEAM AND SPEED

Laughter pealing from upstairs. Feet running and then four girls on the stairs and four pairs of eyes wondering at the silver parcel in his hands. Pa was good at presents, though it wasn't Christmas yet, and Katey had had her birthday in October.

Four girls and only two dolls; it was too late to hide the parcel, which he handed to Mamie. Katey looked appalled when the wrapping came off. 'Wooden dolls, Pa?' He knew she would have preferred a paint box.

'Oh, but they're lovely,' mild Mamie said, 'lovely velvet dresses.'

Lally and Betty Lemon agreed — they were younger, only nine and seven to Mamie's fourteen and Katey's twelve. Betty stroked the blue velvet.

'Betty can have mine,' Katey declared.

'Ah, I'm sorry, little Betty, but I bought them from a rather remarkable lady. She'll know if —'

Three pairs of eyes stared. Katey raised an eyebrow. Dickens wanted to laugh. His friends would recognize that. Katey Dickens was very like her father.

'Well, not know exactly… Of course, I don't mean — but I cannot tell her that one has been given away because a naughty little girl wanted something else.'

'Little!' Katey looked down at him from the stairs, eyes all sparks. Lucifer Box, Dickens called her.

'Get away, all of you. Play with your dolls.'

They knew he wasn't cross and scampered away. He went upstairs to the nursery, where Catherine and Georgina were

273

with the little boys. All seemed well, he thought, settling down to play with the trains.

Later, he picked up a fallen piece of paper in his study. *Dead, my lords and gentlemen. Dead...* Had he written that? It was his handwriting. He didn't remember. A message from the future? From that strange, unearthly woman, Miss Tiddy Doll, insubstantial as a ghost, come from the shadows with her warning. Perhaps it was catching, all this soothsaying. He would not have been surprised to find that she had vanished tomorrow, flown away with all her doll attendants, her prophetic work done.

Dead, indeed, my lords. Sir William Pell, Miss Hormel, Darius and Julius Henchman. And whose were the bones in that ruined factory? They might never know. Posy, Phoebe Miller. It did not bear thinking about. Sam's hollowed-out face when Inspector Bold had repeated the word "Belgium", and they had all known what it might mean.

But there was hope, surely. The boat to Bruges tomorrow. They might just find them. It was possible.

But he knew that Sam had his doubts, and that all the words in the world could not assuage those doubts until Posy was safe back at Norfolk Street. Words, words, wild and whirling words. He took up his pen.

Then he was absorbed, spinning new words, a world away from Wapping, in a place *where the heavy drops fall, drip, drip, drip, upon the broad, flagged pavement, called, from old time, the Ghost's Walk...*

Away to Chesney Wold and Lady Dedlock, haunted by a secret. The secret of a child born out of wedlock.

Sam Jones was seemingly absorbed in little Tom Brim's wooden trains, but his mind was on different rails, on the London Bridge train to Folkestone and then the tidal train to Calais — or Boulogne. London to Newhaven by the South Eastern Railway, then to Dieppe; train to Hull from where the steam ships went to Belgium and Holland. There were ways to get to the continent other than by steamer from St. Katharine's Wharf. And a steamer with possibly two hundred crowding passengers, not to mention the cattle, the sheep, and the pigs. A hundred tons of cargo. The livestock trade, a horrible thought. But he had sent Rogers to see Mr Mumford. There would be plenty of men to watch.

He was aware of eyes on him. Scrap's. His face with the black scab. Dangerous, but he knew that Scrap would not be satisfied to stay out of it. In any case, his sharp eyes would pick out Phoebe Miller and Posy. No one like Scrap to shove through a crowd. He could come down to the wharf.

As for Eleanor, who was gazing at him, too, that was more difficult, but if she knew that Scrap was coming... Though there might well be a painful truth to tell. He had promised. Scrap caught his eye and busied himself with teaching Poll the dog to shake hands, drawing in Eleanor, who became absorbed, too. Poll, that good-natured beast, obliged, though she rolled her eyes at Jones.

Elizabeth came in to take the children upstairs, squeezing his shoulder on the way out. Scrap tidied up the toys and put them in their box.

'Tomorrow,' Jones said. Scrap did not smile that heart-warming smile which usually accompanied the knowledge that he was needed. He just nodded. Jones told him what he wanted. 'I knows. I'll be careful. I'll see 'em.'

If they are there, thought Jones, but he didn't say that.

There was a great cheer coming from somewhere, and a great jostling crowd of passengers and bags and boxes. Porters calling, shoving through, carrying boxes that would crush anyone but porters. Cows bellowing, sheep bleating, shouts from the dockhands and deckhands and sailors. All the general mayhem of the travelling public: turning in the wrong direction like lost sheep, open-mouthed, bleating, baffled and bewildered, shoved out of the way, tripping over luggage, feeling in their pockets for tickets, quarrelling about who had them. Bad-tempered faces in the early morning cold, anxious faces looking about, cheerful faces looking forward to the voyage. Toppers, tipsy bonnets, caps, shawls, scarves, red-tipped noses, eyes blinking in the grit of a bitter east wind. The sound of funnels blowing off, engines throbbing, impatient to be away, and bells signalling departure. Another great cheer. No faces they knew.

But Stemp found them. He was to have charge of Scrap. Not to take his eyes off him.

'Elephants,' he said, jerking his thumb to somewhere distant. *Bombay?* Dickens wondered.

Of all the livestock which had haunted Jones's restless dreams, elephants had not been of the company.

'Not white, I hope,' Dickens said, momentarily imagining a line of white elephants caparisoned in countless gorgeous colours with silken-clad rajahs riding in howdahs on top.

'Just come in from Calcutta on the *Ann Mary*. Fer Astley's circus, they say. Folk wantin' ter see 'em come off on the crane, an' then they walk 'em along the wharf ter stretch their legs. Crowds, see, more than usual. Mr Rogers in one waitin' room, Constable Feak in the other. Mr Mumford's men with 'em, an' our men along the wharf and by the boat.'

'Which one?'

'Cream an' black funnel. *Magician*,' said Stemp. Jones stared. 'Name o' the boat, sir.'

'It would be,' said Jones, shaking his head.

Stemp cut a swathe through the crowd, Scrap keeping up at his side. A warning bell rang — time to board.

Jones took Dickens's arm. 'Come on, Wizard of the North.' And they plunged into the surging tide of people.

The surge narrowed as the passengers funnelled up the gangway of *Magician*. Dickens glimpsed Stemp's broad shoulders and his large head above the swell. He couldn't see Scrap, of course, but his eyes would be everywhere. There was a momentary stay in the rush as someone stumbled on the choked-up gangway and he saw Sergeant Rogers gripping the handrail. Then the crowd closed in again, and he was blinded momentarily by a pair of huge shoulders blocking his view and distracted by the need to extricate his boot from under a heavy foot. He slid in front of the giant, whose meaty hand was raised in farewell — to a giantess, perhaps.

He had no idea where Sam Jones was, but when he looked up, he saw that Stemp was on the gangway and before him was Scrap, darting through towards a tall woman, in front of whom were two other female figures. He saw Stemp yank the woman back by the arm. He heard her scream. Then Scrap was holding on to the smaller of the other two females and Rogers was there.

Then he was through, just barging and shoving, not caring about the protests or the bruises he might have next day as people tried to hold him back, angered at his pushing to the front of the queue. 'Police,' he shouted, and some people moved out of the way. Sam Jones was already just stepping onto the gangplank and Stemp was dragging the tall woman. Scrap had the smaller figure by the arm, and Rogers grabbed the other figure and down they came onto the wharf, shifting along to find a space away from the gangway.

But the tall woman was struggling and cursing, lashing out with her carpet bag, and Stemp was trying to haul her away. He wouldn't let go. Rogers's captive was screaming, Rogers trying to drag her away from the gangway, and the crowd pressing forward, shouting and screaming, too, at the sight of women being manhandled by the coppers. The press was suffocating. It was as if the crowd were being pushed forward by some other force, but Dickens managed to squeeze through. It was Scrap he was making for. He reached out to seize the smaller girl just as the tall woman's bag swung backwards. The girl vanished. Scrap tottered. Dickens grabbed him just as he heard the splash.

'Posy!' Scrap shrieked. The tall woman broke free, and she was off, kicking her way through, all fists and feet. The sound of a police rattle, Stemp roaring, Sam Jones holding onto the other girl, still yelling, fending off an irate woman with a murderous-looking umbrella. Rogers vanished, and Dickens was looking down, seeing the billowing dress and the churning water, not thinking, just jumping, the water a shock, the clothing in his fist, coming to the surface, dragging the stuff dress with him.

Strong hands grabbing, hauling, the thud of his own body and another landing by him, and a brown face bending over him, concerned.

'Gotcher, sir. All right?'

Dickens coughed. 'The girl?'

'Safe. 'T'was but a moment — saw it 'appen. Yer wasn't in but a few seconds. Yer'll do.'

He would — dredged from the deep, wet, certainly, breathless, indeed, frozen. No hat. And Posy? He looked at her. Shocked, speechless, but safe.

'Lend me your hat, would you?' he asked the dredgerman.

Faces at the top of the iron ladder. Sam Jones handing Posy to Rogers, reaching a strong arm down to pull up him up. A blanket over his head. Voices. 'Copper saved 'er.' 'Nah, a sailor.' 'Toff, I saw.' 'Nah, bobby, said 'e was a bobby.' 'Give 'em room, boys.'

On dry land. Hustled through the crowd, hearing a cheer, shouts of, 'Well done, copper.' 'Bit of awright, copper.'

A sudden halt. Arms on either side of him, still holding him. Raucous gales of laughter. Applause, more cheering. A sudden, hot stink of dung. He thought he heard the sound of a trumpet. He had to look. The most preposterous sight. Stemp without his hat. Constable Feak gormed. Mr Mumford's jaw dropped almost to his chest, his top hat askew. A man bent double, apparently weeping with laughter. A gaggle of lads pointing. One face looking in his direction. A face he'd seen close-up through a grimy window.

And an elephant with a tall woman in his trunk. Not white. Grey and massive. Heroic, too.

38: DUMB SHOW

Posy, still speechless and shaking, and Dickens, also uncharacteristically mute and still damp, with the dredgerman's hat pulled low and the blanket over his shoulders, went in a cab with Scrap to Norfolk Street. Scrap with his arm about Posy, holding her tight, but not speaking either. Livvie Slack — she who had been seized by the elephant as she was charging across its path, pursued by Stemp — was with Phoebe Miller in a cell at Bow Street.

Cork bobbing up. That was Charles Dickens. Thank the Lord he could swim. Jones was glad he hadn't seen it happen. Stemp's roar had made him look up from the struggle with Phoebe Miller, the umbrella, and the protesting crowd. Oh, she'd screamed for help, of course, and cried "murder" — he'd felt like slapping her impudent face.

Phoebe Miller had stopped screaming — eventually. Now she was dumb and sullen. She wasn't going to peach on Martin Jaggard. She wouldn't respond to the name Amelia Wand, and she had nothing to say about Matty Miller, but Sam Jones saw the shock in her eyes when he told her that he believed that the body of Matthew Miller was amongst the dead found after a fire at an old chemical works in Belle Isle.

Livvie Slack was somewhat dishevelled and stunned by the elephant's attentions to her person, and sufficiently humiliated to bawl her execrations at the gentle beast and his partner, who had done nothing but stand impassively — though Dickens had sworn, laughing under his blanket, that Mrs Elephant had a twinkle in her eye.

Jones didn't know if elephants possessed a sense of humour, but they certainly would not forget the shrieking harpy who had tripped at their feet, pursued by the roaring Stemp. He'd had to laugh himself, despite everything. Livvie Slack dangling upside down, her skirts over her head, and her bloomers on display — laundered by Ma Cobb, no doubt, and crying out for help. No one had moved for a minute or so, and then the doubled-up keeper had stopped laughing and ordered the elephant to 'drop it'. The most obedient and obliging elephant did so. Sam heard the thud of her head on stone as she dropped. Stemp had hauled her up, none too gently. The crowd had cheered again.

'Pity it wasn't a tiger,' Stemp said afterwards. 'Woulda taken 'er 'ead off.'

Livvie Slack had been spitting feathers — literally. Her bonnet had been crushed and the jaunty feathers of the would-be travelling lady had somehow ended up in her mouth, which refused to say anything more. Nothing to say about Martin Jaggard's whereabouts, an' she didn't know no bleedin' woman in black velvet. Never 'eard of no Melia Wand — bleedin' conjuror, was she?

'A very fine diamond, Miss Slack,' observed Jones, looking at the ring on her wedding finger.

That gave her pause for thought, and she handed it over without a word. One of Sir William Pell's treasures, Jones hoped.

Jones left them to contemplate their futures. Posy might well know where they had been after they had quitted Arbour Square the previous day. That is, if Elizabeth could get her to speak. He thought about that white face and terrified eyes. Elizabeth would know what to do when they arrived, apart from drying them off and giving them food.

At Norfolk Street, Dickens was swathed in blankets and eating soup. He felt all right. He hadn't been in long enough to swallow any of the Thames's filth — he'd probably escape cholera, if not a cold in the head. He'd been given brandy at the quayside, and now he felt the soup warming him from the inside. Elizabeth Jones had taken Posy upstairs to wash her down with hot water and to put her to bed with hot bricks. She still had not spoken. Dickens thought that even the drenching had not really registered. She looked very frightened, and he could not help wondering what had been done to her. Nothing terrible — perhaps that would have been done when she had been made a prisoner in a brothel in Belgium. Where was Amelia Wand? he wondered. Mumford's men had searched *Magician*. But she had not been on board, and they'd searched the Rotterdam boat and the one for Hamburg, even *The Nautilus*, bound for Constantinople. Telegraphs were sent to the police in Folkestone and Dover.

But she could have slipped away, having seen the police in either of the waiting rooms. They would not know until Posy could speak, or if Sam Jones had persuaded Phoebe Miller or Livvie Slack to give evidence.

He heard the front door. Sam Jones came in with Elizabeth and Dickens asked how Posy was.

'Very frightened. She only says that she is sorry, and that she couldn't help it — she thought Phoebe was her friend — sorry, sorry, she says.'

Elizabeth sat down and they saw the tears in her eyes. 'I've left Eleanor and Scrap with her. I don't think we are the right people just now. I know you want to know, Sam, but it's too soon, and when I think of what she went through at that orphanage, I think she thinks we'll blame her, as if all the memories of those hideous adults have come back, and she'll be punished. I know it's irrational and we've never —'

Dickens understood. 'What secrecy in the young under terror, no matter how unreasonable.'

'I won't ask,' Jones said. 'Those two harpies in the cells can answer. Phoebe Miller knows about Matty. She might —'

'However hard she is, I suppose she's a victim, in her way. Those parents had no idea how to treat their children. That poor little Frankie, blue with cold and hiding in the hedge all day, and speechless Sally. What hope is there for them?' There was no answer to that. Elizabeth continued. 'Posy might tell Scrap and Eleanor. She trusts them, and Eleanor saw off that wretched butcher boy who teased Posy. Scrap will know what you want, but he'll be careful.'

'I know he will, and it really doesn't matter. Posy is back and safe. We'll find out where they were before they went to the boat, and if we don't and Jaggard's away to Belgium with his black velvet madam, then Mr Mayne can demote me to constable. I don't care just now. At least the forgery's shut down —'

'Quite exploded,' Dickens said.

'Sky high, indeed, and if Jaggard starts again in Belgium with Mr Baptist's Head, then that's their business.'

'Are you going back to Bow Street?' asked Elizabeth.

'That I'm not. They'll send if they want me. Inspector Grove's in charge. What about you, Neptune, are you going home?'

'If I can walk.'

'You'd better put your clothes on. We've enough scandal.'

'They'll be dry enough, Charles, if a bit worse for wear —' Elizabeth gave him a smile, which said more than her next words — 'though, you're used to a swim, I daresay. I remember last time in that flood.'

'Don't remind me.'

Dickens dressed in the kitchen by the range. The clothes were almost dry, but were distinctly shrunken and crumpled. His coat was still very damp, but it would do. No hat, of course, but the dredgerman's. Still, a handy disguise for the street. He hoped no one would recognise him. The important thing was to get into his house without being seen — or smelt.

Elizabeth had gone when he returned. 'Well, me old salt?' Jones said.

'Droll, Samivel, very droll. I do feel a bit —'

'Shrivelled? Come on, I'll walk you to Tavistock Square. Oh, and here's your hat — the dredgerman picked it up. Fish in it — no rabbits.'

Dickens laughed. 'Souvenir, eh? I'll wear the dredgerman's for now. Heavily disguised as a stranger.'

Outside, in the street, Jones stopped and looked up. There were stars tonight, far off, mysterious. The heavens remote and unfathomable. The earth below, equally so sometimes. Evil and good — what did it mean? No answer in heaven or earth. No answer to anything.

He looked at the man beside him who was looking at him, a look both wry and tender.

'You shouldn't have — but I'm glad you did.'

'If I'd thought for a moment — but I just saw that dress billowing up. And that churning water. I can swim. Maybe if I couldn't, I wouldn't have.'

'It doesn't matter. You did, and Posy is safe.'

'They were there, Jaggard's lads. I saw a face — the minstrel boy from outside the pawnbroker's shop.'

'Here, there, everywhere — and nowhere.'

They walked on in silence until Dickens asked, 'What's the story?'

'Funny you should ask that. Folk thought a policeman had gone in, but it was a stranger, and do you what, he wouldn't give his name. Just took a peg of brandy and went off in a cab. Person unknown. Just a topper in the water. Toff, mebbe. Nothing else to tell, m'lud.'

'Dumb as a drum with a hole in it, sir.'

39: BROKEN DREAMS

A woman by the name of Madame Amelie Wand had been picked up at Folkestone, where she was waiting for the tidal train. She was travelling alone. Spoke only French, it seemed, but her protests in that language had gone unheeded. Her passport declared her to be Belgian — forgery, probably, thought Jones. However, it didn't matter to him whether she was Belgian or Chinese, she was coming back to London in the company of two constables.

Not that she'd say anything in any language, but Ma Cobb was a witness to the presence of the two girls in her house, and to the fact that she spoke perfectly good English. He'd have Ma Cobb brought to have a look at her, then she'd have to say something. Jones had not questioned Posy — he'd wait for Scrap to find out what he could. The other two harpies, Livvie Slack and Phoebe Miller, still wouldn't give anything away.

No news from Inspector Bold either. Nothing of note at the Arbour Square house. Except one detail which had given Jones a sensation of another icy finger at his neck. There had been a wooden doll in the parlour — a wooden doll in a black velvet dress. Dickens wouldn't be surprised.

No Jaggard, no boys — well, there were plenty of 'em, homeless, houseless, their lives spent on the run, in alleys, yards, wharves, by the river, mudlarking, thieving, scavenging, fighting, and not one who'd say, "Oh, yes, I know Martin Jaggard."

Clerkenwell, he wondered, then Dickens came in. 'What news on the rialto?'

'You all right?'

'Lively as a trout in a lime basket. There was distinct flavour of fish about my person this morning. Posy?'

'Asleep when I left — peacefully, according to Elizabeth. Mrs Wand is on her way. Picked up in Folkestone, gabbling away in French. Rogers will fetch Ma Cobb to identify her and Phoebe Miller, who may talk then. In plain English, I hope.'

'Nothing incriminating at Arbour Square?'

'Only a wooden doll dressed in —'

'Black velvet, of course. Signs and tokens, eh? Gives you a bit of a shiver up the spine.'

Jones smiled at him. 'Throwing yourself in the Thames does that. And, of signs, your Lieutenant Barnes confirmed Matty Miller's tattoo — an anchor. The one on the arm looked as if it might have been. So, unless he turns up... The other man could have been Thoddy Cragg. Some small bones — could have been children, but not confirmed.'

'Emmie Stooks one of the women?'

'Possibly, and the other could possibly be Tipper's woman, possibly anyone, anyone at all.'

'Ought I to warn Polly Stooks that...'

'I suppose you should. I ought to go to Clerkenwell to see Doublett. I doubt Jaggard will be back there. I'll see Shackell, too.'

The livid scar stood out on Polly Stooks's cheek. Her face turned deadly pale when she saw Dickens at the door of her small cottage. She knew.

He explained that it could not be certain, but she knew. Emmie Stooks had not been at the hotel in Arbour Square, so where else could she be? Polly had known that Emmie Stooks would not have been recruited by a French lady for some high-class brothel.

'Workin' at the coinin' or forgin', or whatever that Jaggard was up to, an' Thoddy Cragg in it. Took on our Emmie to spite me. I'm glad he's copped it. Hope he — no I don't, because that would mean — poor Emmie —'

'They wouldn't have known anything about it. It was so quick — the whole place just exploded.'

'In bits, though, Mr Dickens, all in pieces. Seen it once in Clerkenwell. Fireworks factory blew up. Three people burnt to death. I'll never forget that. The flesh roasted off their bones — that's what folk said.'

'Don't dwell on the horror, Polly, I beg you. She wouldn't have known anything.'

'She'd have known that her dreams were ended — put to pourin' acid, or stirrin' pitch — filthy stuff, an' she thinkin' — that Jaggard, was he there? Hope he carries on burnin' in hell.'

'We don't think so. The police are here in Clerkenwell.'

'I haven't seen him — nor them lads, Mr Dickens, nor Jacko Cragg — burnt to death, that little fiend?'

'No, he was seen afterwards.'

'Pity — oh, I know he's just a kid, and his father was a rotten bastard, but he is wicked, that one. An' my poor Emmie, just a girl with foolish dreams. We all have dreams, Mr Dickens. That's all we have, all Emmie had, an' I shouted at her, told her she was a fool to think a toff would — just dreams, all vanished in fire and smoke —'

She touched her scar, and in that unconscious gesture, he saw how her dreams had vanished, too, scored out of her book of life by an engraving tool.

'Is there anything…?' he began.

She gave him a faint smile. 'No, Mr Dickens, not now, thank you. Let me be alone. I want to think. You'll let me know what — she must come home and be with Ma. Emerald, eh? Dreams — huh. Ah, well…'

Dickens promised. He left her, gazing into the fire, into the land of dreams and shadows. Voices now forever silent, caresses forever stilled, bright eyes forever closed. Poor Polly. Poor Emmie. Dreams she could never dream again. Dreams shattered by that other fiend, Jaggard.

He went out into the unchanged streets through which all the degraded lives stumbled on in their broken shoes. What a dream this life was, the saddest dream that ever was dreamed. *Ah*, he thought, *how little we can do in such a dream after all.*

Sam had said he didn't care, but, of course, he did. That was why he had come to Clerkenwell. Jaggard wasn't here, Dickens was sure. Where Jacko Cragg was, so was Martin Jaggard. Dickens gripped his stick and strode on. Little to do, but something, surely, though he was blessed if he knew what.

He turned the corner and almost collided with a man. He stepped back smartly, ready to beg his pardon. An eye winked at him. He closed his mouth, bowed, and went on. He did not look back. Constable Doublett in a slightly shabby suit. Vanished without a word.

Dickens walked on towards the coffee house where he had arranged to meet Jones. *Vanished*, he thought. Clerkenwell was that sort of place, all those winding alleys and passages, all those stones upon stones of centuries. The ancient priory, ancient vaults, all those ghosts, the Knights Hospitallers, the kings and queens, Elizabeth I's actors, the men of letters. And the countless, nameless multitude vanished into unknown graves. But, somewhere, maybe, breathing their dusty breath through cracks in wainscots and doors, and watching.

Jones, very real and substantial, however, was watching for Dickens. They didn't go into the coffee house this time but walked away to take the long road back to Bow Street. Dickens told him about Polly Stooks, and of his encounter with Doublett. 'I nearly spoke to him, but then I realized who he was. A wink and a bow and I walked away.'

'He knows what he's about. I'll leave him for another twenty-four hours, just in case there's anything. Shackell's men haven't seen or heard of Jaggard or his lads. Vanished into thin air. Oh, I don't know…'

'It's this place. Something about it. Even the buildings have a furtive air about them, as if they're about to sneak away into some dark alley. Always that feeling of being watched.'

40: INTERROGATION

Sergeant Rogers was waiting with news. Ma Cobb had given her evidence about Mrs Wand. Ma Cobb had laughed heartily when told that Madame could not speak English — Mrs Melia knew enough English ter count 'er pounds an' shillin's from all the English toffs at The George Private Hotel. She had told them all about the doin's at Arbour Square — dirty sheets an' all. And she recognized Phoebe Miller as one of the girls she had seen at Mrs Wand's house on the Saturday morning. Oh, aye, she 'adn't forgot Miss Toity.

Ma Cobb didn't know Livvie Slack, however, which pleased Livvie mightily. 'Ad she ter tell 'em again? She didn't know no Melia Wand. They should ask that little tart in the next cell. Little cow, she woz.

When thieves fall out, Sam Jones thought, listening to Rogers's recital.

Rogers continued. 'No love lost between Livvie and Miss Phoebe. Each of 'em tryin' to get out of it by blaming the other. Phoebe Miller claims she didn't know that they were going to a brothel. Livvie Slack had kept them prisoner, trapped them into going on board.'

'And I'm the *Flying Dutchman*,' Jones said. 'So, she's an innocent dupe. Then she won't mind telling us where she was kept prisoner by Livvie Slack. Let's have a listen.'

Phoebe Miller certainly had been crying, but she gave them a defiant look when Dickens and Jones entered the cell. Her feathers, like Livvie Slack's, were very much ruffled. Her pert face was smudged and her clothes very much crumpled. Dickens thought that she looked very young. He thought of

Polly's words about dreams. He thought of that wretched cottage, the half-witted mother, and the brute of a father. Phoebe Miller had had her dreams, too, but he thought of Posy's terrified eyes and hardened his heart.

'Did your brother have a tattoo of an anchor on his left arm?' asked Jones.

The question surprised her into a 'Yes.'

Jones went on in the same cold tone. 'Then I must tell you that one of the bodies found in the fire at the old factory in Belle Isle is that of a young man with part of a tattoo on the arm we found. Mr Matthew Miller, your brother, a former sailor on the *Duke of Bedford*, under Captain Thornhill. Matthew Miller engaged in a forging operation in that factory. Furthermore, the body of a Mr Abel Miller was also found there. Your father?'

She wouldn't look at them, but she nodded.

'The forging operation run by Mr Martin Jaggard whose associate Miss Hormel met you in Union Street, where a Mr Thornhill let you into a lodging house formerly owned by a Mrs Barnes, mother of Lieutenant Barnes who knew your name. From there you were taken to the hotel in Arbour Square and from there to the ship. You met, by design, Mr Darius Henchman at The Copenhagen Inn, and prevailed upon him to take you to Union Street. Mr Darius Henchman and Miss Hormel are dead, murdered in the yard of a jeweller's shop by Thoddy Cragg, an engraver in the forging business —'

She kept her eyes down, but her face turned so white that the black smudges appeared as grotesque patches on her face. Dickens thought that she probably didn't know. Jones went on, relentless in his itemizing of the facts, facts made more horrifying by the chilly tone of professional indifference. He glanced at Rogers, whose face was expressionless. It was their job, he knew, but the girl seemed like a cornered animal, hunched in her seat, the knuckles of her red hands white. She looked as pitiable as little Frankie in his hedge —

Jones never took his eyes off her. He covered everything from the death of Sir William Pell to that of Julius Henchman. 'Martin Jaggard is a murderer, a thief, and a pimp, who is quite prepared to leave his minions to hang for their part in his wicked schemes. You tricked an innocent girl into a wicked scheme for her violation, and no doubt you knew full well what kind of people you were —'

Phoebe stood up suddenly as if she were about to flee, her mouth open, her eyes wide. The chair went with a crash, and she backed into a corner, her arms flailing. Then she screamed and she went on screaming. Rogers took hold of her, and she collapsed into his arms. He sat her down and she put her head on the table and sobbed. Dickens thought it was the most dreadful thing he had seen. Phoebe was a broken doll, but he didn't dare move. He saw pity in Rogers's eyes as he looked down at the beaten girl. He heard Sam continue in that same hard, even tone and he felt chilled. Too far, surely. He hardly recognized Sam's hatchet face as he went on talking.

'No one can save you, except yourself, and that by telling me where you were taken after you left Mrs Wand's hotel in Arbour Square. Where you met Livvie Slack and with whom.'

She looked up then, straight at the policeman. 'Fuck off,' she said.

In Jones's office, they stood, shaken to the core. Dickens took out his flask of brandy and passed it round. They needed something.

'What a performance,' Rogers said.

'I was completely taken in — I honestly thought we'd —'

'Me, you mean — that I'd broken her on the wheel. I knew, though. She looked at me before she stood up. A look so brief as to be almost unnoticeable — but it was there, that moment of calculation. She thought I'd leave her alone, send for a doctor, but I asked that last question.'

'Little vixen,' Rogers said. 'I honestly thought we'd need a doctor.'

'Send someone for Mrs Feak, will you? Just to be on the safe side. Make sure the vixen has a cup of tea and a blanket.'

Rogers went. Mrs Feak, mother of Constable Feak, was a nurse. And she'd seen everything. She'd know how to deal with Phoebe Miller.

'Lord, Sam, she must be made of adamant. After that list of deaths, murder, brothels. I was ready to confess, I can tell you.'

'You thought I was going too far.'

'I will confess to that, but I knew you had to do your job. It's not my job. I'm just the amateur — not for me to judge you. She's just a girl. I honestly thought —'

'So did I, and I would have put that question gently if I hadn't seen that look.'

'She won't tell us, nor will Livvie Slack, I suppose.'

'That's what they learn — never talk ter the coppers. They can't touch yer an' they don't know nothin'.'

'She was frightened, though. I saw how white she turned when you mentioned the murders of Darius Henchman and Miss Hormel. I wonder if she did know about those.'

'She's hard-faced enough, and Livvie Slack. Mrs Amelia Wand now.'

Amelia told them. Perhaps it was something to do with the screaming she had heard from the next cell. She had flinched when Jones, Stemp and Dickens came in. Her face was very white above her black velvet cape. Perhaps it was to do with the papers Sam Jones held in his hand — retrieved from her portmanteau, or perhaps it was to do with the doll from the house at Arbour Square which Dickens placed on the table, positioned so that its hard black eyes looked at her. And the silence as Dickens arranged its black velvet dress in neat folds. Amelia Wand stared at it as if mesmerized. It looked horribly like her.

'I know where you got this, from a relative of Mr Jaggard's. A bit of intimidation, was it? Mr Jaggard's aunt was not to tell any policemen that she had seen him. Mr Jaggard afraid she knew where he was?'

'I don't —'

'Oh, but you do. Jacko Cragg came with a message from Mr Jaggard telling you to get out. I want to know where you were the night before the steam ship was to sail. I must tell you that Mr Jaggard is wanted for the murder of Sir William Pell, Miss Hormel —'

Oh, she knew that name. Her face took on the wooden stiffness of the doll's, her eyes seeming to shrink into her head. The doll was more likely to rise and walk than Mrs Wand.

'— and Mr Darius Henchman, brother of Mr Julius Henchman, a frequent visitor to your house of accommodation in Arbour Square. Mrs Cobb, your laundress, knew him very well. A business associate, perhaps — he seems to have paid you a good deal of money, as these papers show. Very careful accounting, Mrs Wand, for all those gentlemen who stayed overnight. Mr Henchman will not, of course, be returning. He is dead, but you know that. No doubt, Mr Jaggard knows it.'

She would know, thought Dickens, remembering the sound of drumming heard by Scrap behind the Henchman house.

Jaggard would know. Spies everywhere. He knew everything. He would know all that had happened on the quayside. He probably knew exactly where Mrs Wand was. Would she tell them where Jaggard was?

She did not seem able to speak. Jones continued. 'Mr Matthew Miller who brought the girls to your hotel is dead, too. You may have known him as Robert Thornhill — no matter, you knew him. An associate of Mr Jaggard.'

They waited. The name Jaggard seemed to reverberate round the cell, its hard consonants bouncing from the walls, setting their teeth on edge, causing Mrs Wand to put her hands over her ears as if she heard it echoing, too.

Jones said no more, but he watched her. They all watched her. And waited.

She licked her dry lips. They could hear her breathing. Would she, like Phoebe Miller, scream herself into hysterics? Her mouth opened slightly. If a doll could speak, its voice would be a small, dry, wooden thing making words out of sawdust and chippings.

'Quag Lane — a house near the marshes.'

41: THE MARSH LANDS

Their hearts sank. Quag Lane, off the East India Dock Road, just before the entrance to the docks. Ships. Quays. Warehouses. 'Stowaway,' Inspector Bold had said. And above the docks, the marshes, an empty wasteland, criss-crossed by a web of channels, streams, ditches, bogs, and dykes, reaching up to Bromley in the north where Quag Lane ended, and to the east where the River Lea wound its way to the Thames at Bow Creek. River craft, rowing boats, fishing boats, dredgers, hay barges, grain barges, dung barges. A barge might take the Lea Cut into Limehouse Cut. Another barge might come out of the Limehouse Basin into the Regent's Canal. And the Free Water Clause allowed barges and lighters to enter the docks free of charge. To the north-east and more marshlands, flat and full of water, then West Ham. Docks there. A river port at Stratford. Paper mills. Silk mills. Breweries. Barges, barges.

And more rivers: the Channelsea at Stratford; the Ravensbourne which wandered through Bromley to Deptford, from where Sir Francis Drake had set off round the world; its tributary, the curiously named Quagga; Pudding Mill River at St. Thomas's Creek. A dozen ways to escape, unless he drowned — the only comforting thought that occurred to Dickens as he contemplated the map which Inspector Bold had spread out on his desk. Jones, Sergeant Rogers, Gaunt and Stemp followed the inspector's finger.

Bold pointed to Quag Lane, and they could see the unhelpfully vague words "Marsh Lands" which designated the empty regions above the East India Dock Road. The customs houses clustered along the road beyond the junction; they saw the New Iron Bridge which crossed the Lea. There were a few scattered houses at the beginning of Quag Lane, but they petered out and the road was a blank until it reached a calico works and a place called Bromley Hall. There were a few houses by the East India Tavern, but nothing at all on the marshes.

'She didn't say exactly where?' Bold asked.

'Just near the marshes — they arrived at night and left when it was still dark. She swears she doesn't know. Anything habitable at all, across the marshes?'

'Oh, yes, a few cottages — fishermen, sluice gate keepers, reed cutters — folk who want a quiet life.'

'Slucius Dry,' John Gaunt said.

'What?' Jones and Dickens asked in unison.

'A who — tell them, Gaunt. Mr Dickens'll like this.'

'Lives on the Marsh Lands, has an old reed cutter's cottage by a sluice gate. Drinks at the East India sometimes. Calls himself Sir Lucius an' the wags call him Slucius.'

'Dry?' asked Dickens, who did like the irony.

'That's his name, Sir Lucius Dry of Bromley Hall. Reckons he's descended from the lords who once owned the place. It's part of the calico factory now, but they say it was a Tudor house and there was a monastery there before the Reformation.'

Dickens thought of Jaggard. Plenty of people who claimed a distinguished ancestry. Mr Tipper's fish man, for example. John Gaunt, whom he always called Johnno Gaunt, and whose father had taken him to see the remains of the Savoy Palace on the Strand. Descendants of the great duke, perhaps, the Limehouse Gaunts. John Dickens, esquire — quite a pedigree, the Dickens family. The Marshalsea Dickenses of the debtors' prison. Not that they ever went back. Not a thing referred to again.

Sir Lucius Dry could be the Arch Fiend or the Archbishop of Canterbury, or even Jaggard himself, but he only asked Gaunt if he believed in Slucius as a decayed gentleman.

'He speaks Latin — not all the time. Spouts it off sometimes. The locals think he's a wizard.'

'Just what we need to guide us over those marshes,' Jones said.

'He knows his way about them, certainly. I doubt there's anyone who could find his cottage — even in daylight.'

They were all aware that darkness would come soon. They hadn't much time. Bold had been thinking, 'I suggest that Gaunt and Mr Dickens might see if Slucius is in the tavern — he knows Gaunt, and Mr Dickens might be doin' a bit of research, p'raps. Keep it friendly, eh? The lord might be a bit on the shy side. Folk from the marshes ain't a talkative lot. But he might know of any strangers visiting the marshes. Meanwhile, Mr Jones, we can take a look at the few cottages. The one on its own there —' he pointed to a solitary house on the left of Quag Lane and to one a little further up — 'and that one. We'll work our way back to the ones near the tavern. We'll take the wagon as far as the tavern. Not very comfortable, but quicker than walking. And we'll need some more of my men.'

Slucius Dry was certainly not the Archbishop of Canterbury, nor the Arch Fiend, but he looked a strange and isolated figure, nursing a pot of ale, sitting alone in one of the quieter corners of the tavern, which was full of noisy dock workers and sailors carousing and singing. He wore a heavy coat, caped like a cabman's and underneath seemed to be swathed in all kinds of wrappings. *Very cold and damp on those marshes*, Dickens thought. And of no known colour. Ditch brown, perhaps. He wore a thick hood in the same indeterminate colour which gave him a somewhat monastic air.

John Gaunt addressed him politely as Sir Lucius, at which the man looked up and bowed his head briefly. Eyes, rather startling in their intensity. An unusual amber colour. Aristocracy in the thin, high-bridged nose? In the long face and chin — admittedly covered in rough stubble. It was the sort of face you might see in a Tudor portrait. Something of the martyr about him. Dickens imagined him unbending even before the pyre.

He accepted the brandy that Dickens had paid for at the bar and sipped it as he listened to Gaunt's explanation that Mr Dickens wanted to write about the Marsh Lands.

He might be a marshlander, but he knew that name. 'Sir,' he said, 'an honour.' His voice was slow and rather hoarse, like someone unused to speaking. 'You wish to explore the marshes?'

Dickens couldn't tell if Slucius were surprised, suspicious, or disbelieving. He improvised. 'An article for my magazine, *Household Words*. Something descriptive. A strange sort of place, remote, yet on our doorstep, so to speak…' The sort of man who made you talk too much.

'Strange, indeed. *Terra Incognita*.' A deep voice, too. Not the voice of a humble reed cutter or a sluice gate keeper.

'Who lives there?'

'Cattle, mostly. Some oxen. The dead, of course.' He looked straight at Dickens. 'Those multitudes unknown, unshriven, doomed for a certain term to walk the night —'

'For foul crimes done,' Dickens responded. The ghost of Hamlet's father. A well-read man, Sir Lucius Dry.

The ghost of a smile for Dickens's reply. 'Very few people — a hard place to make a living, a haunted place. There was a priory once, before the Tudor heretic. Who can know what spirits walk there now?'

'Strangers?' asked Gaunt, somewhat discomfited by talk of spirits abroad on the marshes.

'Sometimes. Fugitives from family, from debts, from life itself. From the law.' He looked knowingly at John Gaunt. 'That is what you are after, young man, is it not? Someone on the run.'

Another soothsayer, thought Dickens. Gaunt merely nodded.

42: DESCENT INTO THE UNDERWORLD

They might have stepped off the edge of the world. Dickens looked at the marshes stretching endlessly ahead, dissolving into mist and vaporous wraiths rising from the water. The hissing of the wind, the reeds clicking, the mud oozing, sleet whipping their faces. An owl shrieked and they saw it, a white phantom thing drifting away on silent wings, something in its claws.

A place between life and death — a few lights behind, already fading; darkness and mist falling before them. A mere strip of dwindling daylight on the horizon, silver darkening to pewter. No moon to guide them, but the immensely tall figure moved ahead of them, sure-footed and certain of his direction, feeling for the flat stones which made the path through the marshes. From time to time, Dickens felt the squelch of mud under his boot as he missed a stone, and the suck of water at his stick.

Sir Lucius — Dickens thought of him with his title — stopped at a wooden plank that formed a kind of bridge across a stream, which gleamed dully in the dying light. Sir Lucius went over easily. Dickens followed, not looking down, Gaunt's lamp lighting his way from behind.

'*Ad inferos descendere*,' the voice said as Dickens stepped off the plank.

Now they were certainly going down deep into the marshes — only a plank across a stream, but like crossing the Styx to the underworld, thought Dickens. It seemed darker now, the mist rising and Charon beside them, an unearthly ferryman, his face wreathed in vapour and the Latin words somehow sounding fateful. Not fatal, Dickens hoped.

They followed the black figure as if he were their own shadow going on before them, his cape flapping like wings in the misty darkness. Sir Lucius stopped and pointed. They could see it, a huddled shape, dark against the greyer sky.

'Cow byre,' whispered Sir Lucius. 'I have seen lights.'

There were no lights now. Dickens could not imagine Amelia Wand here, but Jaggard and those lads —

As if on cue, the sound came, at first as faint as the heartbeat of a dying man, or the reeds ticking in the wind, and then like the pulse of fearful blood in the veins. It was coming now, the menacing beat of a drum. The minstrel boy at war. And his army — the beating of stick on stick. The sound was all around them. The Devil's tattoo.

'*Diabolus*. Let us depart.'

They turned away, the sound of the tattoo fading. *They saw Gaunt's light*, Dickens thought, but they wouldn't know who was there, only that they must be frightened off. Over the plank bridge and Sir Lucius led them away in a slanting direction.

'The iron bridge takes us to the road,' he told them. 'It will be quicker. *Terra firma*, also.'

It was a long walk down the East India Dock Road. There were traffic and people coming from the warehouses and the docks, shouts, and cheerful voices. No one looked at them. Even Sir Lucius Dry seemed more ordinary now, though his long strides and flapping clothes gave him the appearance of some stalking bird. The marsh might have been a different planet — the moon, perhaps. Too dark, though. Some undiscovered world — dark and forbidding, whipped by icy winds. That was it. Quite terrifying. But they would have to go back to the Marsh Lands.

Jones and Inspector Bold, Sergeant Rogers and Stemp were waiting for them in the porch of the tavern. Dickens told them about the boys scattered about the marsh near the cow byre.

'How many?' asked Bold.

'Too dark to see. More than one, certainly. I heard that drum, though, so the one I saw at the quayside must be there.'

'We only need one. No sign of Jaggard?' asked Jones.

'No. Nothing at the houses?'

'My men are still looking,' Bold answered. 'We'll take a couple with us to this cow byre.'

'Sir Lucius will take us.' Bold raised an eyebrow at the title and looked doubtful, but Dickens explained, 'I think they must have seen our light coming.'

'I can find my way in the dark, Inspector, if you wish,' Sir Lucius offered in his gravely courteous tones. Just as well he hadn't said it in Latin, Dickens thought, or quoted from *Hamlet*. That would have put off the practical inspector. But Sir Lucius Dry was a reader of men's faces, and their hearts, probably.

They went in the wagon to the iron bridge, where Bold left one of his men to guard it.

Once they were across, Sir Lucius said, 'Lights out.' They followed him from stone to stone and they came to the plank bridge and from thence into the deeper darkness. There was no human sound, except their breathing and the eerie sounds of the marsh. *A thing with a life of its own, a submerged serpent waiting for its prey*, Dickens thought, as they crept on, across the slithering mud which seemed to pulse and bubble, exhaling its vaporous breath into the biting air, sucking at their boots;

through the rattling reeds and hissing grasses; and by the whispering waters where other mists rose and curled.

Then there was a light in the distance, away by the cow byre, and they crept forward, well-spaced-out, crouching in the reeds and grasses until they could see that the door of the byre was partly open, and light flickered out. Rogers and Gaunt melted away to investigate the back of the rude building. Dickens and Stemp remained in the shadows with Sir Lucius Dry.

They could hear voices and laughter, and then the drum started, and the chanting:

'Jag, jag, jag, jag, raise the flag
To jag, jag, jag, Mr Jaggard
Madanbad, madanbad, jag, jag, jag
'Ard, 'ard, 'ard, 'ard, Mr Jaggard
Madanbad, madanbad, madanbad...'

It was horrible. There was a wildness in the last words, and savagery, a devilish glee. *They're capable of anything*, Dickens thought, an army of demons on their dreadful march. The air seemed full of menace. Sir Lucius's face was grimly set; his eyes two gleaming pools deep under his brow. He was not frightened.

The drumming reached a crescendo, the words *jag, jag, jag* rising to a scream, then ceasing, and in that pause Dickens heard the sound of a gun being cocked. The drum started again, low and insistent, and the voices joined in, whispering the terrible words, then rising and rising.

Jones and Bold advanced, holding their guns in the air. One of Bold's constables charged and kicked the door open. Bold fired into the air, and they rushed through the door. Yells and howls from within. Dickens and Stemp moving forward. Inside, a lad running up a ladder, another diving behind a hay bale to be hauled back by Jones. Rogers and Gaunt breaking through the rotten wood, Rogers catching a hurtling body heading for the gap. Dickens tripping one up as he darted by, Stemp snatching him up. Two running off into the dark. It didn't matter. Their haul was five, handcuffed, cursing, and screaming, a ragged, stinking, drunken, cocky bunch with the savage eyes of Jacko Cragg, whom Dickens did not see. No sign of Jaggard either. But he recognized the minstrel boy from Gruel Place older than the rest, his chin jutting, mad, black eyes staring at him, insolence in his smile, foam at his mouth. Terrifying, if it were not for the handcuffs.

'Mr Jaggard?' Bold addressed them.

They took up the name, chanting, '*Madanbad, madanbad, jag, jag, jag…*'

There's a madness about all of them, Dickens thought. They seemed hardly human, all filthy with matted hair, wild, unfocused eyes, and snarling mouths.

Sir Lucius Dry was standing by the door as the policemen dragged out the howling, cursing boys. The lads looked at him. He loomed over them like a pillar of black cloud, shadows behind him, his cape blowing in the wind, his hawk nose a blade in the lamplight, and his golden eyes on fire. *Lucifer*, Dickens thought, *the dark angel*.

Sir Lucius raised his hands and spoke: '*Omen infaustium, triste.*'

That shut them up. Everyone else pretended that they had not heard. Sir Lucius did not speak again. They followed him to the plank bridge and there he pointed the way to the iron bridge. They had their lights, and the boys were cowed now, and suddenly sober, their eyes terrified.

Dickens stopped to bid him farewell. Sir Lucius accepted the proffered coin with a grave bow and a blessing: '*Omnia bona salute.*' Sir Lucius Dry, sluice gate keeper, scholar, and apparition, disintegrated into the misty darkness.

43: THE DODGER

Dickens sneezed. A dip in the Thames and a night on the marshes. It was bound to happen. Still, Mr Von Liebig's nutritious beef tea and a mustard poultice immediately after he had got home, and a deep sleep in his dressing room, had staved off the usual hideous aches and pains that accompanied his frequent colds. *One sneeze doth not make a dead man*, he told himself, though the smell of beef and mustard was a bit overpowering. Still, it beat smelling of fish.

A dreamless sleep. He had expected to dream of Slucius Dry and Miss Tiddy Doll. His last thoughts had been of those two seers with their peculiar eyes looking into some far distance. The world was full of the oddest creatures, and always crossing his path. He'd seen the old woman from Berners Street last night, another ghostly figure dressed in white, with a ghastly white plaiting round her head like a bridal wreath, who always curtseyed to him as he passed, and there was Mrs Joachim, who'd lived not far from his own house at Devonshire Terrace, another white lady, whose father had been murdered, and whose lover had committed suicide whilst sitting with her on the sofa. White ladies at every turn, and a black velvet one. She was real enough.

Stranger than fiction, truth, so Byron had said. Byron, whose natural son had been up before the beak. An Italian with nothing in the world but the rags on his back and a claim to an illustrious name, so Iacchimo Guiccioli had told the magistrate. He thought of Sir Lucius Dry with his noble martyr's face. He believed in the title, if not the man who had seemed to dissolve into darkness. What had he said to those boys? Something about the devil and ill-omens — not that the meaning had mattered. It was the sound, as if Sir Lucius had cursed them. They had got the message. Not that they had remained terrified for long.

They had recovered somewhat by the time they had been put in the cells. They had claimed that Mr Jaggard had gone to America. And, of course, they didn't know nothing about no murder.

Dickens, Jones, Stemp and Rogers had left Inspector Bold to it. He'd keep the boys overnight, but he didn't think they'd tell him anything more. They probably did believe that Jaggard had gone to America. Bold couldn't haul them before the magistrate for playing the drums and sleeping in an old cow byre.

And even if he did, Dickens thought now, as he sat at his desk in Wellington Street, they'd no doubt be whipped, sent to the House of Correction for a few weeks, and be let out to return to Clerkenwell or wherever, to terrorise someone else. No one would claim them, and he doubted they could claim any distinguished heritage. Of course, you never knew, Jacko Cragg might be the descendant of a Plantagenet bastard. Or just the offspring of Thoddy Cragg, deceased, the only marks of his existence a scar on a young woman's face and a child so neglected and brutalized that he had run wild and mad, inhabiting a world far below any world which could be described as human.

Jacko Cragg — had he been one of the escapees? Dickens hadn't seen him when he entered the byre, but that did not mean he wasn't there, the climbing monkey. Or was he with Jaggard, clinging to the skirts of the toff's coat like an unwanted pet? Unlikely. Jaggard would kick him away. America, then? Probably. Poor Sam was to go to see

Commissioner Mayne this morning with the bad news that Jaggard was still missing. No doubt Mr Mayne would raise a haughty eyebrow in wonder at the lack of progress, given the resources at Superintendent Jones's disposal. Not to mention the journeyings to and from Southampton, to Rochester, Limehouse and Clerkenwell. Perhaps Inspector Bold was the better man for the job, etcetera, etcetera…

Dickens sneezed again, took a sip of his beef tea, and bent to his papers. Schools were his theme — or the lack of them. All those lads with not an iota of education. Ignorant as the beasts of the field. More so. The beasts of the fields lived ordered lives and looked after their young. In the guise of the fictional Mr Bendigo Buster, Dickens was advancing that eminent gentleman's theories of education, Mr Bendigo Buster whose boast was that he took in *Household Words* only to differ from its editor, who was a sentimental idiot. England, argued Mr Buster, that practical, sensible nation, was rightly bringing up her boys "in the gutters, growing up to manly independence, they swear well, fight like bricks, and have game in 'em."

Dickens was on his way now, pen flying, recalling all the sights he had seen in Clerkenwell and Wapping, in Whitechapel, and in Westminster itself in Devil's Acre, just behind the sacred walls of the abbey.

"Go down into Westminster. What do you find there? Freedom!" cried Mr Bendigo Buster, bursting with admiration for the "Young Bricks, by thousands upon thousands, left to themselves, herding and growing together, in the gamest manner, like so many wolves… Rule Britannia…"

He had almost finished expatiating with his keen satirical pen, the point of an arrow, skewering the evils of ignorance when Jones came in.

'Luncheon,' Dickens said. 'You have a lean and hungry look, my ancient, as one who might consume the leather of his boots should food not pass his lips. Mr Stagg, I think, and not another word.'

Dickens was right. Mr Mayne had said all that he had foretold and more. Commissioner Mayne was, he had said, very glad that Inspector Bold was on the case. Bold, he had heard, was a man of practical common sense —

'Mr Bendigo Buster,' Dickens said, grinning, as they went into Mr Stagg's Ship Tavern.

'Who now?' asked Jones, fearing some other lunatic offering to look for Jaggard in a crystal ball. Eccentrics were all very well in their way, but sometimes you did just want practical common sense and a sighting in the real world.

'Oh, someone I've invented. Just writing about the evils of ignorance and the scandal of all these children living like brute beasts. Last night —'

'I know, little savages. Not that I did more than tell Mayne that we'd traced Jaggard's crew and Bold had them in custody. Anyway, enough of Mayne. It's not good for my temper or my digestion.'

'Which will be settled in a few minutes by one of Mr Stagg's pies. His gravy will soothe your troubled soul, as will this pale ale.'

Mr Stagg, who could be relied upon for his pies and for his always giving them a table by the fire in a little nook, came with steaming steak and kidney, perfect shortcrust pastry, silken gravy, mashed potatoes, and greens. And a mustard pot, the contents of which Dickens declined on the reasonable grounds that he had already taken enough. 'Poultice,' he said to Jones. 'Preventative.'

'Cabbage leaves, some say,' said Jones, tackling his greens. 'Poultice, that is.'

They ate in companiable silence for a while until Jones began, 'Last night —'

'"Wondrous strange" — Hamlet's words. Sir Lucius Dry quoted them.'

'He would. This morning I wondered if I had dreamt him. I didn't mention him to Mayne, nor Miss Tiddy Doll, nor you, for that matter.'

'Not a fanciful man, Mr Mayne, though truth, I thought this very morning, is so often stranger than fiction.'

'Here's a truth from Inspector Bold. It's what I came to tell you. He sent me a message. Near the tavern, a lodging house where Mrs Wand and the girls stayed. A cab came to take them to the boat, so the landlady said, but she didn't take much notice of a cab driver, of course.'

'Jaggard, the driver?'

'Could be — in any case, the woman's a useful witness for the case against Mrs Wand and Phoebe Miller, and Livvie Slack.'

'She was there?'

'Oh, yes — the landlady described her. I shall be very glad to present the landlady to Miss Slack.'

'I was thinking, will Posy be able...?'

'Hard to say. I'll leave it to Elizabeth and Scrap to decide. Posy looked better when I went in to see her. She gave me a smile and she didn't look so frightened. I think she'll be all right.'

'Not harmed?'

'Elizabeth doesn't think anything physical was done to her. I think Posy would have told her, but we'll wait.'

They finished their food, and Jones took up his tale again. 'Another thing concerning Bold. Something was delivered to him early this morning. A gift from Slucius Dry, I imagine. I ought to say Sir Lucius, I know. It suits him. He sent a boy, trussed up like a chicken, delivered in a sack, too terrified to speak. One of the escapees — the others knew him.'

'Not Jacko?'

'No, one Billy Whittle. About nine years old. He was hardly able to tell what had happened, except he was took by the divil on the marshes, an 'e wouldn't go back for all the tea etcetera. Anyhow, Gaunt patted him on the shoulder, gave him food and drink —'

'Softened him up.'

'He did. And the boy talked. Not that he was very articulate, but the gist is that Jaggard took them all to the marshes, left them with plenty of beer and baccy, told them to stay put until he came back. John Gaunt worked out that this must have been after the fire. The lad has no idea of time. They thought the light was Jaggard coming back and went out to drum him home, but they saw a very tall figure in the distance. Knowing they weren't to let strangers anywhere near, they beat their sticks and frightened him off.'

'So the America story might not be true.'

'Billy Whittle contradicts it, but you never can tell. You know how they make up any tale on the spur of the moment, or Jaggard told them to put it about that he was going to America. I suspect that Jaggard said he was coming back, but didn't intend to. They're a liability now. He wanted them out of the way. They make too much noise. He'll want to be very secret now.'

'Anything about Jacko Cragg?'

'He went off with Jaggard after he left them on the marshes. Gaunt, who is a sharp young blade, asked what Jaggard was wearing. The answer was just ordinary clothes. And a big heavy coat.'

'Cab driver at the lodgings, picking up Mrs Wand and the girls. A boy on top — who'd notice?'

'That's what I thought. Jacko Cragg might be useful to him while he's still in hiding. Messenger boy. I'm wondering if he's waiting underground, waiting for the moment to act. When we're less vigilant. And he knows we can't have men everywhere. Jacko Cragg can do his errands, unless he's found a lair where someone's willing to hide him. Money in it for some old coiner. I'm thinking if Tipper might know some former comrade. You gave him a shilling — he might talk to you.'

'And he's no fan of Martin Jaggard. Am I to tell him that his woman is probably dead?'

They could not tell Tipper anything. There was no sign of the stall or its keeper. Dickens, wearing his long coat and a rather parsonical low-crowned hat with a wide brim, asked around the market. No one asked why Tipper was wanted, nor did anyone know where he was. Those who did know Tipper thought he might have given up. Business wasn't so good. Work'ouse, one said. On the tramp, offered another.

The latter unlikely, Dickens thought, not with that painful wooden leg. It was conceivable that Tipper had given up — he had seemed very tired of the ironmongery business. He could have sold his stock for scrap and gone off to drink away his profits. No one knew where Tipper lived.

He caught Jones's eye and shook his head. They had already decided that if there were no information at the market, they would go to the windmill. It was well to be cautious, Jones had thought. They should not be seen together. And Stemp was in the crowd, too. Dickens had seen him at his elbow, a seafaring man this time, idling about the market looking at the stalls.

The fish wife had not seen Tipper, nor had the boy with the burnt fingers. The father was out at his noxious trade, but he didn't know Tipper anyway. No one knew him, really.

'Kept hisself to hisself,' the woman told them, 'poor divil, in terrible pain with that leg. Said 'e'd drown hisself one o' these days.'

'Would he have gone into the workhouse?' Dickens asked.

''E'd rather die, I should say, an' I think the same. The herrin's an' the pure findin' mayn't be a gentl'man's trade, but we ain't proud, an' we can get our own bread. My lad's not goin' in no work'ouse. We can do better than that.'

'Does your boy go to school?'

'Night school, sir, at the ragged school. Learnin' ter read, sir, an' write. See there, 'e's got his name writ down.'

The boy's eyes shone as he held out the slate for Dickens to see. The name was there, however imperfectly scrawled in the chalk: *jony rigg*, he read, *the winmil*, *kidny stares*. It was a start, he thought, giving the boy an approving smile, better than a coining den, and, no doubt, more than anything Jacko Cragg would achieve.

Jones waited during this exchange. He had another question. 'Where did Mr Tipper keep his stall?'

She looked blank at that, but the boy knew. Sometimes, he had helped Mr Tipper move it into an alley where he kept it.

'Gave me a farthin', now an' again. Course, 'e took his stock away on 'is back an' in sacks.'

The alley was at the top of Rose Street, just by the market next to the grocer's shop. The boy offered to take them, but

Jones declined. He had no wish for this boy to be seen by Martin Jaggard. Dickens gave him a sixpence. A very engaging lad, he thought, and a brave mother, too.

Stemp had disappeared when they left the windmill. They stood for a few moments, looking down at the foreshore where the mudlarks were scavenging in the mud and in the water, girls as well as boys, some up to their waists in the river, looking for anything to sell — coal, old rope, bones, rusty tools, nails. Tipper wouldn't be down there — not with a wooden leg. There were as many boys there as in Clerkenwell, all stunted, all pinched faces and feral eyes.

A fight broke out as they watched. A small boy had found something, and a gang of bigger ones was determined to have it. Something valuable, perhaps, a coin or a silver spoon. The small boy darted away, scrabbling up the steps and past them, emitting a wild shriek. The yelling gang pursued him. Then they were gone into the alleys.

'Would we know him?' asked Jones. 'They all look like him. All rags and hair.'

'Scrap would know him.'

Jones looked at him. 'Soothsayer, are you?'

'I can see far enough ahead to know he'll be waiting for the call.'

'He keeps dropping very heavy hints that he's feeling tip-top now and he's thinking he ought to pay a call on Zeb Scruggs.'

Dickens smiled at that. Zeb Scruggs was a dealer in old clothes, to whom Scrap went to borrow his various disguises. The street urchin was his speciality — as he had been one. 'I honestly don't think you can keep him out of it.'

'I know, but Limehouse is a dangerous place, and we know what Jaggard is capable of. I know I asked Scrap to come down to the wharf. That was a risk, and I took it. Even after that night in the fog. My responsibility.'

'Ours, Samivel, I've encouraged him just as much as you have.'

'Dangerous for you, too.'

'My responsibility. I choose to come with you, knowing full well the risks, and Scrap knows, too. I told him once that he should remember the motto, "one for all and all for one". He understood.'

Jones laughed at that. 'The three musketeers, eh? I know you're right.'

'And Scrap started it by coming to me when Posy was missing. You can't leave him out now. He's got sense — he'll be careful. And he'll look like any of those lads down there. You've just said it. All rags and hair. And he'll sound like one. Quite the actor, Scrap.'

'Charles Dickens, what a comfort you are to me.'

''Umble servant, Mr Jones, Superintendent.'

Stemp was already there. He had heard what was said in the windmill and sloped off, emerging from the alley as Dickens and Jones arrived. He shook his head and wandered on casually along Rose Lane. They followed until they came to the busy Commercial Road, where they slipped under a warehouse archway.

'It was there,' Stemp said, 'and all his goods, just left anyhow. The sacks was there.'

'Just walked away from it, maybe — he seemed very despairing about it,' Dickens said.

'Odd, though, that a former confederate of Jaggard in Limehouse should disappear. Pity we don't know where he lives.'

'I sees a lodging house down there — wreck of a place. Worth a try?'

Jones was staring out into the busy road. 'Yes, but you need to be careful, Stemp. You know what lodging house keepers are like — too many questions and they're suspicious. Just ask who the stuff belongs to and whether it's for sale. Where can you find him to do a bit of business. We'll go and see Inspector Bold before we go back to Bow Street.'

Dodger, to the life, Dickens thought, noting Scrap's old cut-down coat, the sleeves rolled up to the elbows to show the filthy arms, the crushed top hat perched rather rakishly on his head, the shabby corduroy breeches, the bare legs above the old boots tied with string. *Keep him out of it. Too late for that.* He didn't look at Jones.

Constable Doublett and Rogers were waiting at Bow Street, too. Doublett had heard talk at the Lamb and Dove from a loquacious Irishman called Patrick Quilp.

'Sober, I hope,' Jones said.

'Mostly — I had to treat him to a jar or two. He knew Thoddy Cragg and the lad. Talk is, Cragg's dead. Quilp knew about the fire — everyone knows, it seems. Cragg wasn't a popular man. I didn't know anything, of course, but Quilp mentioned Jaggard. Forger, he said, at the factory in Belle Isle that had burnt down. Gone to America — taken Cragg's lad with him. Good riddance, so most folk are saying.'

'Did Quilp know Jaggard?'

'By sight and reputation, I gathered. Lot of talk in the pub. I get the impression that Quilp's a regular. Listens in, but harmless, I think, if too fond of his tipple. He did say that Jaggard was supposed to live in Limehouse. "Bejasus

Limehouse" were his words, and it was his opinion that a shower of rain would wash the gentleman off him.'

Dickens laughed. Doublett's imitation of the Irish Quilp was very good. 'The discerning Mr Quilp being so often in the company of the gentlemen customers of the Lamb and Dove.'

'Quilp's evidence ties in with what we heard at Limehouse, but I doubt Jaggard's taken that boy to America,' Jones observed. 'And an old coining confederate of Jaggard's is missing in Limehouse. One Mr Tipper, and I'm wondering if Jaggard has taken up residence with him.'

'At knife point, I should think,' Dickens said. 'Tipper was no friend of Jaggard's.'

'True enough — I wouldn't put anything past Jaggard.'

'Saw that Jacko Cragg on the windersill at Ma Speed's house,' Scrap piped up. The street urchin back in force.

'And?' asked Jones, knowing only too well what was coming.

''Ow yer goin' ter find 'im?'

'Mr Stemp is down in Limehouse, and Mr Bold's men, and Doublett is going down there now — handily dressed as a sailor.'

'Mr Doublett ain't seen Jacko Cragg. I could go with 'im.'

'Dangerous, Scrap,' Dickens said, thinking to help Jones, 'you've already had one brush with a knife.'

'I'm still 'ere, Mr D., an' I'm only goin' ter foller the kid, an' that Jaggard ain't goin' ter be paradin' round the streets fer all ter see. 'E'll be lyin' low till 'e can get a ship.'

Jones looked at Scrap, who understood the warning in his eyes and nodded his acceptance. Scrap knew that Mr Jones trusted him not to take unnecessary risks. Mr D. 'ad told 'im somethin' once about some musketeers wot's motto woz "one fer all, an' all fer one" meanin' that yer 'ad ter remember the others. It wasn't just about you.

Rogers, who had listened and knew full well what was on Jones's mind, offered his thoughts. 'Mr Dickens, what about Mr Meteyard, the butcher? I'm wondering if Doublett and Scrap could lodge there. Out the back — there were outbuildings.'

'And the dog,' Dickens said. Sampson Meteyard, father of Henry, a barrister and friend of Dickens and Jones, kept a shop in Gun Street in Limehouse, and he had a very large dog, a Newfoundland named Mug who had once saved Dickens from two very menacing sailors. Scrap had stayed there, too, when on the hunt for a murderer. Sampson Meteyard and Mug wouldn't let anyone get to Doublett and Scrap.

'Not a sailor, then, Doublett. What do you know about the meat trade?' Jones asked.

44: THE WAITING GAME

Superintendent Jones felt that he had done all he could to keep Scrap safe. The gigantic Mr Sampson Meteyard had welcomed young Charley Dickens — Dickens was still the boy whose godfather had been a friend of Sampson's — and Superintendent Jones, who had collected Henry Meteyard from Lincoln's Inn. Henry Meteyard knew all the alleys and byways of Limehouse, and he was a handy man with his fists, too, having been brought up there. The story was told, Scrap and Doublett ensconced in one of the outhouses, Doublett provided with a bloody apron and a cleaver, Scrap relieved of his top hat but allowed his coat and a cap and a bloody apron beneath — a butcher's boy; Henry Meteyard back in his old bedroom; and Dickens, a visiting parson from the country in the attic room, prayer book and spectacles tucked in his pocket and the parsonical hat on a hook behind the door. Mug in his kennel in the yard, guarding the back door. Superintendent Jones with John Gaunt at John's mother's house in Narrow Street; Rogers sleeping at the windmill by Kidney Stairs; Constable Stemp making his own eccentric arrangements nearby — an upturned boat, Rogers guessed, and Inspector Bold's men out and about.

Jaggard's name was known by the docklands police forces, and the names Martin Todd, or William Todd, had been noted. Jaggard might well go under another name. He might use his real name or steal Pell's Christian name. Not likely to use Titus or Tiddy, or Cragg. He might be anyone, Jones reflected, but his description was circulated, too. He wouldn't get passage to America unless by stealth. It was all that could be done, Jones had told Dickens. They had to accept that he might get away.

Henry Meteyard was impossible to disguise. The neighbours were used to seeing his tall figure about the streets. No one paid much attention to his old schoolfriend, a bespectacled clergyman from his country parish in his shovel hat and long coat — not very talkative, but then he wasn't in his pulpit, and he was a finicky sort, it seemed, a handkerchief at his nose, and a tendency to shrink back when Mr Meteyard was accosted by a neighbour. Mug, the dog, seemed to like him, however, though whether the parson liked the dog, it was hard to tell. He patted the large head rather nervously as Mug leaned affectionately against him while they waited for young Mr Meteyard to finish his chat. That young Constable Gaunt was seen at the shop now and again, but that wasn't unusual.

The parson and the butcher's son walked through the teeming streets down to Kidney Stairs sometimes and chatted to the fish wife who lived there and their lodger. No one knew who he was, nor were they interested. River folk had enough to do to make their own livings without worrying what other folk were doing. People passed through Limehouse all the time, up and down the river, to and from the docks, on and off the ships and the steamers.

And the streets were thick with people, strangers, travellers, ticket of leave men, pedlars, and potboys from pubs, messenger boys, milkmaids, captains and shipmates, hustlers, housewives, voices from every nation, tattooed faces, bruised faces, hard faces, sly ones, merry ones, all about their own business. Carts and horses, dogs, pigs, chickens. Shops, the slopsellers, the sellers of oilskins and pea coats, parrots, canvas trousers, sailors' hats, nets, needles for them, hams, hammocks, rum, ropes and anchors, opium, onions, ivory — anything anybody wanted. And could pay for or filch. No one paid attention to the labouring man who seemed to live on an old boat, nor to the ragged boy in a cut-down coat who talked to him sometimes.

It was in the Grapes public house in Narrow Street that the barrister and his companion fell into conversation with a tall, grey-eyed man who was passing through. The barrister and the grey-eyed man enjoyed a mug of ale. The parson took a small glass of sherry wine. He took the same when they boarded three Ships, one just above Kidney Stairs; there was a Ship Aground on Limehouse Causeway; two Shipwrights, one Jolly and the other a bit down in the mouth where the parson risked a brandy and warm — it was very cold, colder still in the second White Swan. Or was it the third?

On the third day, the butcher took the parson to meet the Volunteer, but no information was to be had in that insalubrious tavern about a missing boy. The parson went on his own up Church Lane to see the pawnbroker, Mr John Decker, who greeted him in the shop as an old acquaintance, very surprised to see him up from the country. They talked for a good while in Mr Decker's parlour, where there was a grey-eyed man sitting by a cheerful fire. Mr Decker promised to keep his eyes open, and his ears, for a green-eyed gentleman who might want to sell gold or silver or jewels.

The labouring man, who lived on the boat, sometimes went up to the market on Rose Lane and to visit some lodgings in a nearby alley, where on the fourth day a lodger told him about Mr Tipper, who had sold ironmongery.

Queer business, opined the lodger, ol' Tipper gone without a trace. Drown-dead, he thought, ol' Tipper. Wooden leg, see. Lot o' pain an' business want no good. Didn't advise the stranger to take it on. Tipper wunce a coiner down at windmill. Man called Jaggard ran that. Saw 'im not long since up at Eel Pie House — oh, a pub up at Mount Pleasant near the cut.

Wunce a potman there — didn't get on with it. Landlord a tartar. Jaggard? Couldn't rightly recall. Mebbe a week ago. Friendly wiv the lan'lord, that Jaggard. Ol' Tipper want no friend o' Jaggard.

The labouring man took himself off to take a walk along the Limehouse Cut, noting the old factories, the warehouses, and the red-sailed barges. He studied the water for a few moments, nodded and walked on, contemplating the empty fields surrounding Eel Pie House, the towpath a little distance away, the lime kilns and the derelict manufactories nearby, the Common Sewer, and the empty marshes beyond where some lads had been found in a cow byre. He walked back deep in thought, not even glancing at the butcher's boy who was out and about the towpath with the big dog which barked at the passing barges. It was along that path that the butcher's boy encountered a ragged wretch of a boy running very fast. The boy swerved past the barking dog and made off across the fields towards Mount Pleasant and Eel Pie House.

Mr Sampson Meteyard had visitors that night, coming in severally. Constable John Gaunt called in at the shop to warn of thieves about; a grey-eyed man came in through the back yard where the butcher's apprentice and the errand boy had finished their work for the day. Mug, the dog, made no sound — he knew the grey-eyed man from another time when a sea captain had been murdered. The lodger from the windmill came into the shop to buy some chops. He didn't come out again. And, at last, a labouring man came into the yard. Mug barked at him — he looked an ugly customer, but Sampson Meteyard told him to pipe down. Stemp patted his head, at which friendly gesture Mug shook himself and lay down with his paws crossed to dream with gruff barks of an unknown enemy.

45: CRACKBONE

The Limehouse Cut was tidal, which meant that it was unnavigable for several days. At high tide, the water from Bow Creek flowed through Bow Locks and raised the level of the canal. It had been that way since 1770, despite the protests of the bargees. Bad for the bargees' trade, but fortunate, perhaps, for Jaggard's pursuers. Jaggard would not be taking a barge anywhere in the next day or two. Constable Stemp had reported his observations of the canal, and Scrap had reported his sighting of Jacko Cragg racing towards Eel Pie House.

Jaggard was there somewhere. There was nothing for it, but that Superintendent Jones from Bow Street and Inspector Bold of the River Police should pay a visit to the landlord of Eel Pie House.

'Time to flush him out,' Jones had said, and the inspector had agreed. He knew Cracky Crackbone — a name at which Dickens had raised an eloquent eyebrow to Jones — of old. All sorts went on at Eel Pie House, it seemed, a regular den of thieves, coiners, cracksmen, smugglers, old lags, and new ones, and a favourite resort of the river thieves, the scufflemen, the ratcatchers, bum-boat men, even mudlarks with the odd treasure to sell.

'We'll need muscle,' Bold said. 'Crackbone was a boxer once, and though he might tell us that Jaggard is about, he'll warn him. It'll not be a nest of lads we'll be disturbing if we've to go in later.'

A boxer at The Copenhagen, perhaps? Jones wondered. Dickens's web. 'We'll have to warn Crackbone, then — about what we know of Mr Jaggard. Wanted for murder.'

'Something for Mr Crackbone to consider, eh? He'll weigh up the odds — you watch.'

Crackbone sounded solid enough, not likely to speak in riddles, or spout Latin. Superintendent Jones was looking forward to meeting him and rattling those bones.

A fist on the counter that would have cracked open a skull and a pair of shifty brown eyes greeted the two policemen as they entered the bar of Eel Pie House, but the smile, though it did not rise to the eyes, was an attempt at civility. Cracky Crackbone knew Inspector Bold, and he knew by instinct that his companion was a policeman. A big 'un, too, with a face like a hatchet.

'Martin Jaggard,' Inspector Bold began. He and Jones had decided on the direct approach. 'Seen on your premises. Wanted for murder — more than one. And Superintendent Jones from Bow Street wants him.'

Jones saw the familiar calculation in the shifty eyes. Weighing up the odds, indeed. How dispensable was Jaggard? More trouble than he was worth? More police would arrive, and the place would be torn apart. Crackbone's cellars were his private business, especially now with the tide rising and no barges. Jones saw the brief flash in the eyes, as if someone had slid open a dark lantern and closed it again. The eyes, expressionless now, looked from Jones to Bold and over to the door of the pub, where Jones knew that Stemp was standing. The clenched fist opened and the hairy hand relaxed.

It was just as well they had chosen the early morning to come. Crackbone's confederates were nightbirds, but that didn't mean that Crackbone wouldn't be able to muster his troops with a whistle. Jones didn't think he would. The man had decided. Jaggard wasn't worth it.

'Murder, eh? That is bad, Mr Bold, sir. Not hereabouts, I'm guessing, by the presence of Bow Street.'

Oh, he was working it out. No local murder to conceal or to avenge, just a murder elsewhere — someone else's business, not Crackbone's, nor that of his comrades in crime.

'Murders, Mr Crackbone, up in the city. Young woman and her betrothed. Very nasty. And a toff — a lord, in fact. Big noise, friends in high places. All associates to be questioned and taken up if we have to. Orders, Mr Crackbone. The commissioner himself.'

Bold was leading the way as they had planned. Superintendent Jones retained what he hoped was an inscrutable silence. Stemp's silence was more menacing than inscrutable. The handcuffs dangling from his fist chinked in the quiet which followed Bold's even tone. He sounded like a man enquiring about a lost dog, but there was no mistaking the ice in his eye.

'Lime kiln. Just by the cut —' Crackbone jerked his thumb to indicate a north-east direction. 'He's waitin' for a barge. Meant to come tonight. It won't. Neap tide, see. No one I know, Mr Bold. Just what he told me. Came in for a drink.'

'A lad with him?'

'Seen a lad about the lime kiln. Mebbe his, I dunno.'

'Man with a wooden leg — known as Tipper.'

Crackbone was a liar to the bone. 'Nah, never heard of him.'

'I should close up tonight, Mr Crackbone. You'll not want to be entertaining any unwelcome guests.'

They heard the bolts being shot as they walked away along a narrow, overgrown footpath. They had come up from Limehouse by a series of paths, some of which skirted the Common Sewer. The smell was appalling, but no one would have seen them from Eel Pie House nor from the lime kilns.

This different path would take them back to the East India Road.

'Worth the risk?' Bold asked.

'I'd say so. Crackbone knows which way the wind blows. Your canny remark about friends in high places tells him that Jaggard isn't worth it. And Crackbone's nothing to fear from Jaggard. Only him and the boy, I'd guess.'

'Tonight, then.'

'Right, let's go and work it out.'

'I'll use some of my men to go into Crackbone's. No barges for the next few days — there'll be interesting stuff in his cellars.'

'Two birds with one stone.'

'Jaggard'll be relieved that the raid is on the pub. He'll not know some of us are on our way to the lime kilns, and we'll send a party to those old factories that line the canal.'

'I'd take my hat off to you, Mr Bold, if it weren't so damned cold.'

The sky rolled darkly above, pushed on by the wind. No moon or stars, only patches of greying light, and the lime kilns' squat shadows on the horizon, blurred by the driving rain. Henry Meteyard led the way along one of the footpaths, crouching from time to time to open his dark lantern very briefly to get his bearings. Jones was at his side with Dickens and Scrap behind, followed by Stemp.

Inspector Bold, John Gaunt and Sergeant Rogers took another path to reach the warehouses. There were a couple of derelict cottages there, too, where the lime kiln workers had lived. No one worked there now. There was no fire to be kept going all night. No stonebreakers. No barges to bring limestone and coal or to take back the quicklime to the docks for distribution to builders and farmers — or to the theatres. *Limelight*, Dickens thought. Jaggard would not want to be in that tonight.

But there was no light anywhere to be seen as they came closer. The lime kilns were like round towers, almost medieval in the dying light, their archways deep black and fathomless. Tramps sometimes dossed there, Bold had told them, and they had been used by smugglers and other folk interested in hiding themselves or their stolen goods. They could hear the wind whistling through the gaping brickwork. Dickens and Jones took the first kiln; Henry Meteyard, Stemp and Scrap went to the second.

Dickens and Jones waited at the entrance, peering into the dark, cold depths. There was the smell of rat droppings, mould, and damp, and the faint, but still acrid, smell of smoke and lime in the walls, and a stronger smell of smoke from a recent fire. There was no sound except the wind. It was like entering a tunnel. They kept close to the walls and found themselves eventually in an open space. The lime kiln bowl. They could see the restless sky above and feel the rain coming down. Jones lit his lamp.

The ashes of a fire, still faintly warm, a couple of earthenware bottles and some bread. They had gone. Outside Henry Meteyard, Scrap and Stemp were waiting. Nothing in the other kiln. The old factories and warehouses then, looming tall and black above the canal, showing the faint gleam of broken glass in the old windows and on the ground of the narrow alleys that separated them.

Stemp and Scrap took one of the alleys, Meteyard and Dickens another, and Jones went into the middle one. He would be bound to find Bold and Gaunt, who needed to be told about the fire in the empty kiln.

Rotten staircases glimpsed through propped-open doors, roofs open to the sky, rickety wooden steps down to underground storehouses and cellars where rats squeaked and scuttled, rotting barrels and planks of wood, mute engines, rusty old iron, remnants of tile making, blackened walls, an office with a broken desk and mildewed ledgers. Henry and Dickens shone their lamps into black corners and twisting passages, and onto stinking water pooling across cracked floors and flagstones, and up rusted drainpipes, and up an iron ladder leading to a rooftop where a flagpole leaned drunkenly, and a ragged flag blew about in the wind.

'*Raise the flag, raise the flag to jag, jag, jag* —'

Dickens heard the high-pitched voice and the ring of a foot on metal, but he was too late. He felt the rush of wind and heard the crashes simultaneously. A rain of bricks, a cry, and Henry down. His own shoulder burning and his lamp out, and a face above him, looking down. Then gone, and a shape flying like some great black bird. Something screaming. The crack of bone, the thud of a head, and a silence that meant the end of something. And in that brief silence, whispered words in Latin: '*Omnia bona, salute.*' A blessing. A figure in a hood, rising and vanishing into the rain-washed dark.

The silence riven by the sudden roar of a rattle. Running boots beating on stone, and Stemp helping him up. Scrap with a lamp and Henry Meteyard with a bloody face struggling to his feet.

Scrap's horrified face looking down at the thing lying on the ground. The broken bird. Jacko Cragg. The dropped child. Jaggard was his hero; he had copied him, given him his childish loyalty, sung for him to the last. His mouth still open, his head split apart, his bones smashed. His eyes closed.

Dickens felt pity, not anger. A wild beast, but a child in this last sleep, the rain falling on his face. And Jaggard away over the rooftop, careless as a pirate on a tall mast.

'On the roof — Jaggard,' Dickens managed.

'They'll get 'im, Mr Dickens. Time fer us ter get out.'

Superintendent Jones blundering round the corner, glass cracking under his boots, stopping at the sight before him, getting his breath, his eyes checking Scrap and Dickens, leaning for a moment on the wall.

46: THE WEB UNRAVELLED

They did get him on the other side of the canal, where two of Bold's men were waiting to drag him out of the water. He'd jumped in to evade his pursuers, intending to swim across, not knowing that two lay in wait. They'd caught him in a large fishing net and landed him, soaked and spluttering, on the bank. It took an age for John Gaunt to drive a cart all the way from Limehouse to pick him up. Bold's constables smoked a pipe apiece while they waited in the shelter of the pot ash factory. Jaggard was alive, but he wasn't going anywhere — except to the gallows.

A net, of all things, Dickens was thinking as he looked down at the man in the cell. That tangled web woven by Jaggard himself. It had seemed so knotted. All those twisting strands leading them hither and yon: to Belle Isle, to Clerkenwell, the workhouse, Fitzroy Square, Grafton Street mews, every pub in Limehouse, so it seemed, Wapping and those empty marshes, and at last to the lime kilns. Limehouse, where Jaggard had begun and where he had come to his fate. Like Iago, he had made the net that had enmeshed them all. But that net had enmeshed him, too. And from this time forth, like Iago, he would never speak a word — so it seemed.

Martin Jaggard stared back at Superintendent Jones, his green gaze unblinking, perhaps just a hint of condescension in it. He still wore the cabman's greatcoat, from which steam was rising. His hair was plastered to his head, his face was bruised and muddy, his shirt torn and dirty, and yet, he held his head high and his shoulders straight. His handcuffed hands lay loosely on the table before him. Not a sign of a tremor. He was no common man, that was certain.

Superintendent Jones began by asking the prisoner to confirm his name as Martin Todd, illegitimate son of one Louisa Todd, daughter of a wooden leg maker in Wapping, nephew of Mrs Maria Jaggard of The Strand Union Workhouse. There was no response. Otherwise known as Martin Jaggard? The prisoner inclined his head.

Jones outlined the facts of the case against him, beginning with the murder of Sir William Pell, whose valet the prisoner had been. Martin Jaggard had entered the victim's laboratory on the night of the murder. Did the prisoner admit that he had been in the laboratory? Jaggard inclined his head. Jones asked if he were responsible for the murder of Sir William? Jaggard inclined his head. Could the prisoner give any motive for the violent attack on his former master? Just a smile then, a slight shrug of the broad shoulders, as if to ask if it mattered. The green gaze unchanged.

A former footman had been found murdered and a small quantity of gold and other stolen items recovered. Did the prisoner know anything about the dead footman? No response. The footman did not matter, either.

And so it went on — for hours, it seemed to Dickens, who kept his head lowered and wrote everything down in shorthand, including any reaction from the prisoner. The prisoner took no notice of the scribe. *Not a gentleman*, Dickens thought to himself, half inclined to laugh. *Just a clerk*. Every now and then he stole a glance when there was a pause in the proceedings, all the pauses engineered by Superintendent Jones. He gave the prisoner time to answer the charges of complicity in the murders of Darius Henchman and Miss Hormel. The green gaze did not falter, but he acknowledged the charges with a nod and a slight lifting of a corner of those full red lips.

Martin Jaggard's eyes did not change at all. Dickens was surprised that Jones was not mesmerized into a magnetic sleep, so intense was that green gaze. Rogers, standing at the cell door, kept his eyes on the prisoner, and behind Jaggard, Constable Stemp stood — just in case Jaggard might turn violent. Dickens thought he would not. Jaggard knew it was over, but he was not going to explain himself.

Jones reached the night at the lime kilns and the death of the child, Jacko Cragg — pushed, he said, by the prisoner. A witness, Mr Henry Meteyard, barrister of Lincoln's Inn, would testify to that. Jaggard shrugged. The boy mattered no more to him than a dog.

Jones went through the list of witnesses who were prepared to testify against him, beginning with Cora Davies, mother of his own child. Dickens looked up at the pause created by Superintendent Jones. Jaggard stared on. Joey Speed, the superintendent continued, found in possession of forged notes. There was Miss Livvie Slack, Miss Phoebe Miller, Mrs Amelia Wand. It might have been a list of strangers.

Finally, Jones asked if Mr Jaggard wished to consult a lawyer. He was entitled to defend himself against the charges. Perhaps, Sir Titus Jaggard...

The prisoner laughed then, a loud, ringing laugh. Jones had heard it before, in a coining den in St. Giles's.

They left him. Dickens was to transcribe the interview into long-hand so that it could be copied by Sergeant Rogers. There would be an additional sentence which would state that the prisoner, Martin Jaggard, confessed to the murders outlined in the transcript.

'But it's not his name,' Dickens pointed out. 'Is that legal?'

'If I put Todd, he won't sign, and he has to. He is not going to speak, and we don't use the rack nowadays.'

'More's the pity,' Rogers said. 'I'd turn the screws on him.'

'The rack, the block, the axe — nothing to him. He'd go to the stake with a bow to his torturers. He won't speak,' Dickens said.

He did not speak, but he read it all through with the air of a lawyer teasing out the particulars of a tricky case. He took his time. Dickens felt as though they were all on the rack.

Jones gave him pen and ink. He signed the papers as though he were a duke signing a cheque, giving away hundreds that mattered nothing to him. The gentleman, Martin Jaggard, signed away his life.

47: A SNUG LITTLE DINNER

Dickens had given up his mustard plaster. Now it was a large pinch of high dried Welsh snuff mixed in water with a teaspoon of sal volatile. Supposed to do wonders for headache, catarrh, difficulty in breathing. It tasted vile and the vapour made his head spin. No wonder he could not think straight, his head full of fumes and fog and marshes, and a man dissolving into fragments of darkness as if he were made of night and mist.

And was it true? Had he heard that final blessing on the dead child? Had a hooded figure been there and vanished again? He had not said anything about what he had heard. No one had mentioned it, but if Sir Lucius Dry had been there and blessed the child, then Dickens was glad of it.

Fire, water, wind, golden eyes aflame, incantations, blessings, curses, prophecies, moonstone eyes like water, a woman in white, and a song of silver notes, like a voice from a dream, but it had foretold a death by the rope. That would be real enough.

The judge in his black cap, the sentence of death, the hammering outside the prison building, that hideous scarecrow phantom of a gallows, the roaring crowd, a prisoner in his hood, the smile wiped from his face. It would come true, even for Martin Jaggard, who had thought himself above the common herd — which was the way of many a murderer, he reflected. Not true. They were made of flesh and blood and could be killed, too, and made to meet their maker. Then Martin Jaggard might have to speak.

Truth was, indeed, stranger than fiction, Dickens reflected, a thought which was hardly productive in the present circumstances, given that Byron had also observed in his next line "how much novels would gain in the exchange." He looked at his list of characters for *Bleak House*. Their names seemed to blur, the letters switching themselves about to make new words so that he did not know who was real and whom he had invented. Was it Lady Honoria Dedlock whom he had met in Fitzroy Square, or was it Lady Nora Lockhart? Inspector Bold or Inspector Bucket? Jacko Cragg or Jo, the crossing sweeper? Miss Tiddy's dolls or Esther Summerson's doll, which she had buried in the garden? An odd thing for a child to do, but no odder than Miss Tiddy herself. Stranger than fiction, Miss Tiddy Doll, with her silver eyes. Mademoiselle Hormel or Hortense? Patrick Quilp or Daniel — wrong book now.

Dickens felt like a man in a dream, but his head had better be on straight in a minute or two. He was taking Mr Jones, superintendent, for a dinner in the quiet purlieus of Lincoln's Inn so that Sam might recover from another meeting with Mr Mayne. Of course, there would be good tidings to report. Jaggard taken, and enough witnesses to condemn him to hang. Not Mr Tipper, alas, of whom no trace had been found. Drown-dead, perhaps, one of those two thousand souls who vanish every year. Plenty of witnesses to dispatch Phoebe Miller, Livvie Slack, and Amelia Wand to the Old Bailey. A notorious coiner apprehended, and a possible continental trade in forged banknotes nipped in the bud. And the murderer of Sir William Pell surely to be sentenced for that crime — the crime which began it all.

Mr Richard Mayne, commissioner, ought to be satisfied. And not a whisper of the name Charles Dickens to annoy him. Henry Meteyard, barrister of Lincoln's Inn, had witnessed the fall of the child, pushed by Jaggard, and had been injured by falling bricks. Bruised and bloody, but unbowed. It would take more than a Jaggard to finish off Henry Meteyard. Dickens's own shoulder was bruised, but that was nothing. He was lucky his head had not been knocked off.

He heard Sam's voice in the next room, and then Catherine's. He waited, listening to Sam's deep, kind tones asking how she fared and telling her that she looked very well, asking about the children. He heard Catherine responding, telling him that they were all well, and asking about Eleanor and Tom, and the little servant, Posy, telling him how glad she was that Posy had been found, safe and well, and, to Dickens's relief, saying that she knew how glad Elizabeth would be. Elizabeth again. It was safe to go in.

'I have ordered,' Dickens said when they were settled beside a cheerful fire in Mr Stagg's private parlour in The Ship. 'Secret enough for you? I have my wig and dark glasses in my pocket.'

'Very amusing,' Jones retorted. 'This will do me.'

Dickens had wanted to take Jones to the Athenaeum Club for their snug little dinner. The dinner might have been snug, Jones had thought, but the Athenaeum was far too grand with its classical portico, its statue of the goddess Athena, and the marble busts in the hall. Superintendent Jones had been allowed in during the investigation into the suspicious death of a journalist, Pierce Mallory. He had no wish to be explained to the porter by Charles Dickens. In any case, it was far too public. Their dinner would probably be interrupted by passing members. Many of Dickens's friends were members, including Mr John Forster who always looked at Jones with a hint of suspicion, not quite approving of Dickens's involvement in crime. Mr Thackeray and Sir Edward Bulwer-Lytton were members. Jones had met them — both connected to his and

Dickens's investigations. There was Mr Maclise, too, whose name had conjured for Jones that haunting song sung by Miss Tiddy Doll. And worse than any of that had been the thought that he might come face to face with Mr Commissioner Mayne dining with some lord — after all the trouble he had taken to keep Dickens's name out of the case.

No, he had insisted, somewhere quiet, a place where they could talk and eat in peace. Dickens had given in, though he had threatened to wear his magician's wig, given that the superintendent had developed such an unaccountable desire for anonymity. 'Bailiffs in the hall, Samivel? Sheriff's men on the stairs, creditors in the scullery?' Questions upon which Samivel had declined to comment.

Now Dickens outlined the nature of the feast. 'Baked sole, leg of mutton stuffed with oysters, mashed potatoes, greens, and apple pudding — and a nice bottle of claret, and the sole is ready, so Mr Stagg promised. In the meantime, your very good health, Samivel.'

Mr Stagg brought in his crispy soles and a little jug of shrimp sauce, and very delicious it was, thought Jones, as he tucked in. No one came in to disturb them, which was just what he had intended.

'He's still not said anything?' Dickens asked when they had put down their knives and forks.

'Not according to the chaplain, or the lawyer. Of course, he's been questioned in Newgate, but he wouldn't answer. However, those papers will be read out in court as part of the evidence. I'll need him to nod his head when asked if he has signed it voluntarily, but the evidence of the rest should be enough. Phoebe Miller, Livvie Slack and Mrs Wand are all ready to testify that they were terrified of him — all innocent victims, of course. When the jury members see him, they might well believe it.'

'Unless they're mesmerized into acquitting him.'

'Don't even think it. The facts are clear enough. Livvie Slack's diamond ring was part of Pell's collection, by the way. So much for her terror. And they'll be questioned about the forging business. I have Cora Davies and Joey Speed up my sleeve for that. Joey Speed, hoping to impress the judge by his ignorance of the fact that the banknotes he had were forged. But he had them and they are evidence, as are the fragments of paper from the fire and the mangled printing press and plates.'

The mutton and oysters came, which looked as good as Mr Stagg had promised. He brought it with great ceremony on a large platter — it would have served ten men with very good appetites.

'My own recipe, sirs,' Mr Stagg announced. 'Them oysters is fresh as the mornin' — boiled an' mixed with parsley an' some fresh herbs. That's the secret, an' the mutton, gentlemen, braised, but not too long. Fall off the bone, that will. Watercress —' he pointed to the dish of greens — 'with scallions — very light. See that mutton and them oysters is very rich, and the sauce. Now, that's…'

They listened patiently to the cookery lesson and congratulated Mr Stagg on his feast. At last, he departed with an injunction that they should take their time and ring the bell if they wanted anything more.

'Posy?' Dickens asked when they had done some justice to the mutton in its rich brown sauce.

'That's a quandary. I don't want to force her to give evidence. I think there's enough from me, Rogers and Stemp about what happened on the quay, and Ma Cobb about the hotel, the landlady in Quag Lane, and Scrap, of course, and

Elizabeth will be called. Posy might be ready. I don't think anything happened to her, and Eleanor's convinced her that it was Phoebe Miller's fault. She's stopped apologizing. She was planning a Swiss pudding when I left, Mrs Dickens's book open on the kitchen table.'

'That sounds like she's very much better. What about the Henchmen?'

'Inspector Bold will give evidence about Jaggard's coining enterprises in Limehouse and Inspector Fall about the explosion. He's showing the evidence that the production of forged banknotes was the intended use of the factory. Darius Henchman's involvement with Jaggard will come out, and Julius Henchman's suicide. And, in a very satisfactory development, the police in Epsom have a bank clerk in custody, and his brother, employed at the paper mill there — the paper mill that has been manufacturing special papers for the Bank of England for over a century.'

'Epsom, that is an interesting connection.'

'Indeed. The bank clerk's brother worked in the sizing room, where the sized paper is dried off before glazing. He has admitted to stealing paper for his brother who was very keen to name Mr Julius Henchman as the person to whom he sold the paper. I don't know yet if it was actually Julius or Darius.'

'Julius Henchman found out what brother Darius was up to — tempted himself to make some money, given his financial difficulties?'

'Could well be. However, the racket's been uncovered. The prosecution of the two Epsom brothers is a matter for the Epsom police, but the mere mention of the involvement of the Henchman brothers is enough for me now that Jaggard's off the streets and Posy's safe.'

'Amen to that,' Dickens said, raising his glass.

Their apple pudding came. Mr Stagg expatiated on the sweetness of Kentish apples and the richness of the cream from Miss Creevy's dairy just down the way, off Lincoln's Inn Fields. Dickens, who knew Miss Creevy, or possibly her mother, and had purloined her name years back, agreed that her cream was always fresh as the morning, fresher if that were possible, and Mr Stagg, master of the cliché, vanished with the remains of the mutton.

'A night out, Mr Jones, is what is called for.'

Jones noted a sly smile and a mischievous glint in Dickens's eyes. *What now?* 'This is a night out.'

'Ah, but I had an idea — a treat for Posy, for Scrap, for all of them, my own included. The Wizard of the North is appearing at the St. James's Theatre.'

'No magic, if you please, not even from you.'

'Cheekish, Mr Jones. Elephants at Astley's, then — we owe a debt to those beasts. I should like to see the happy couple again. Ah, you've no taste for elephants. That's a pity. *Harlequin's Festival?* That's on, too. Six sprites in a romantic dell. No spirits, I see. No moonlit dells. No romance, my ancient. Ah, well, let me see. *The Road to Ruin* at the Olympic? *Circumstantial Evidence* at the Strand Theatre — very good reviews—'

Jones laughed. 'You're making this up.'

'The newspaper, Mr Jones. All there, as true as the steamship timetables.'

'Don't remind me. Elephants indeed.'

'*Harlequin Charley* at the City of London — opens in a dismal swamp, apparently.'

'Been there.'

'Waxworks, then. Five bloomer costumes on display. Something for the girls. For the boys — Chamber of Horrors still sixpence.'

'I have supp'd full —'

'Droll, Mr Jones, so not *Macbeth*, but these children deserve a show of some kind.'

'Oh, all right, *Harlequin Charley* — for your sake.'

'A hit, a very palpable hit, Samivel. But my preference is for—'

They were never to know what Dickens's preference would be, for the door opened and an apologetic Rogers came in. 'Sorry, sir, sorry, Mr Dickens —'

'What?' Jones asked.

'Suspicious death, sir — Sir Fabian Quarterman.'

'Good God, the judge,' Dickens said. 'I know him. I saw him only—'

'I'd better go. You needn't—'

Dickens looked at Rogers and Jones. Three of them. 'One for all,' he said, 'and all for one.'

HISTORICAL NOTES

Clerkenwell was famous for its jewellery and watchmaking industries, but notorious for its criminality and its dreadful poverty. In 1847, *The Illustrated London News* did not mince its words: 'the dingy, swarming alleys, crowded with sodden-looking women, and hulking unwashed men, clustering around the doors of low-browed public houses ... where thieves drink and smoke. The burglar has his crib in Clerkenwell...' The reporter went on to say that Clerkenwell was 'remarkable for crimes of the darkest kind ... more murders take place in Clerkenwell than in any other part of London...'

He refers to the dilapidated property and the 'foul and ugly rubbish' filling the street and gutters, and to the undersized and undernourished children with 'pale and ghastly faces, forms hideous with premature disease.'

It seemed the right place for Jaggard and his coining confederates. There was plenty of gold and silver to steal and plenty of abandoned children to be used and abused. Inspector Shackell observes to Dickens that Fagin is still about. The reference is, of course to *Oliver Twist*, published in 1837. My novel is set in 1851. In *The Household Narrative of Current Events*, January 1851, the supplement to *Household Words*, there is an article from the newspapers describing 'A Den of Juvenile Thieves' discovered in Islington under a railway arch. The den was furnished and even had a fireplace and a 'cooking apparatus', a veritable Fagin's kitchen. A gang of boys was arrested and sent to prison for three to six weeks. As Dickens knew very well, when they were released, they would just begin their criminal activities somewhere else. In the same year and in *The Household Narrative*, there is the case of two boys, aged 14 and 10, whose heads 'scarcely reached the top of the dock' who had been arrested for stealing a loaf of bread. Their defence was that they were starving. They were sentenced to be whipped in the House of Correction in Clerkenwell. The fourteen-year-old, James Cook, had begun his criminal career at the age of eight. In another case, Thomas Ellis, aged ten, had been convicted eight times as had another boy, twelve-year-old John Collins. After his last offence, he was transported for ten years. All versions of the Jacko Cragg I invented.

There were some infamous gangs of boys who terrorised their neighbourhoods. I based Jaggard's boys on the notorious Golden Lane Gang, one member of which was well-known in Clerkenwell, and came before the magistrate for stealing handkerchiefs, but the gang was a particularly brutal one. They carried 16-inch sticks loaded with lead at the end. In 1851 a man who tried to rescue his son from the gang was beaten up and struck in the mouth with a stick. Residents of Golden Lane were reported as being too frightened to leave their houses and no stranger would pass unmolested. In another case in 1851, they terrorised a shopkeeper by throwing potatoes at his windows and his assistants. The shopkeeper was brutally beaten when he tried to remonstrate with them.

Abandoned girls were particularly in danger of being drawn into prostitution; even girls with homes and parents were lured away from home or even kidnapped and kept prisoner under the power of the brothelkeeper, who had clients who asked for untouched girls — you can see why the Jones's servant girl, Posy, was effectively kidnapped with the help of Phoebe Miller. There were cross-Channel traffickers who took girls to France and Belgium where they, too, were kept captive, and there was traffic from France and Belgium to England. Boys and girls were used by coining gangs as messengers, lookouts, and for their little fingers, which were useful for pouring the molten metal into the moulds — there were several cases of children being badly burnt. In one case I came across, a child died from drinking vitriol (basically sulphuric acid), which was used in the making of bad money.

Coining, known as 'the yellow trade', was rife in London and in the provinces and I found many cases, ranging from small 'family-run' businesses to large-scale operations run by master criminals, including the case of the Paris coiners — a gang run by a ruthless Spaniard, who escaped the police. He recruited his workforce from the gutters and told them that 'henceforward you are my creatures.' If they betrayed him, death would be their fate, probably by having their heads crushed. Seemingly the Spaniard masqueraded as a gentleman and called himself a count. A Belgian man escaped when another Paris gang was broken up. You can see where Jaggard came from, and all the stories of forging foreign currency were found in the newspapers, too. In 1851, a case was brought against an Italian immigrant for the forgery of Austrian banknotes, and in 1845, two men were prosecuted for forging Russian banknotes. The case of the forged Belgian notes, remembered by Superintendent Jones, occurred in 1842.

The forging of banknotes was a much more professional business, demanding more investment and skill, which is why a trained engraver was essential — enter Thoddy Cragg. A printing press was necessary, too. Highly skilled engravers and printers could print a good enough facsimile of a Bank of England note that would be difficult to spot even for an expert. The paper was the problem, but that could be stolen if the gang had a man on the inside. The most famous case occurred in 1861, when paper was stolen from the Laverstoke papermill in Hampshire, where Bank of England paper had been manufactured for years.

There are two articles on banknotes in *Household Words* in September 1850, written by Dickens's sub-editor, Henry Wills, which give the history of the trade. Banknote forgery began in 1797, when the Bank of England circulated one-pound notes instead of golden guineas. At that time, it was easy to make good money, easy to buy goods worth five shillings, offer your dud pound note and walk away with fifteen shillings profit. In 1817 there were 870 prosecutions for banknote forgery. By 1850, forgeries were less numerous, but cases, as we have seen, continued to be prosecuted.

Dickens began writing *Bleak House* in November 1851, when he was settled at last in Tavistock House. In June 1852, *Bell's Weekly Messenger* carried a review of the story so far, praising especially the portrait of Jo, the boy crossing-sweeper:

Mr Dickens invariably shows that few public abuses escape his observation … touching upon the neglected condition of those poor creatures, the ragged boys of London, who know no parents and no home…

Jo is just one boy, but he is an emblem of all the neglected children in London at that time, many of whom were drawn into crime because, like the two small boys in the dock, they were starving. Dickens wrote of 'the darkest ignorance and degradation at our doors.'

The newspapers of the 1850s make grim reading when you are steeped in crime and poverty. And another thing that gave me pause for thought was the number of court appearances by persons named Briggs — some particularly criminal types, I'm sorry to say. However, I did feel a pang for Emilia Briggs, remanded to trial on a charge of stealing potatoes. I'm sure she must have been starving — even though she was drunk at the time.

Ah, though, there is Sir Thomas Briggs, G.C. St. M and G. — Grand Cross of St. Michael and St. George. He'll be my ancestor, surely.

On a lighter note, a comic pantomime entitled *Mr and Mrs Briggs* could be seen at Astley's Royal Amphitheatre. It came on after the two elephants, which appeared in an entertainment called *Bluebeard; or, Female Curiosity*.

A NOTE TO THE READER

Dear Reader,

It was Lord Byron who observed that 'truth is always strange, stranger than fiction.' You only have to browse newspaper archives to realise that. It was where I found my elephants. I wasn't looking for them. I was looking for cases of forgery, but there they were, arrived from India into St. Katharine's Dock on November 24th, 1851: … *a brace of gigantic young elephants, a male and female, purchased in India. They will be put into training immediately and make their debut as soon as they will be accomplished in the novel roles they are to sustain.*

They were destined for Astley's circus, which was situated in Lambeth on the south side of the River Thames and famed for its equestrian performances. Shakespeare's *Othello* was performed on horseback, it seems — an idea I can't quite get my head round. There were 'zoological spectacles' as well, featuring leopards and lions and tigers, even zebras. In 1853, Mr William Cooke's elephants were advertised to appear in an entertainment entitled *The Magic Gong* — my elephants, I wonder? Dickens wrote about Astley's in *Sketches by Boz* and *The Old Curiosity Shop*. He was all for entertaining the working people, whose lives were generally poor and pretty miserable. Dickens didn't comment on the treatment of the animals at Astley's, but he did protest against the practice of feeding live animals to the seventeen-foot-long boa constrictor at Regent's Park Zoo. The practice did not end until nearly twenty years later. However, there is evidence of the devotion of some keepers to their exotic charges. Jumbo, the elephant, arrived in 1865 in a very poor condition. His keeper, Matthew Scott, looked after him with constant and loving care. Alice also arrived in 1865 and was walked from the dock all the way to the zoo, accompanied by several hundred dirty, ragged urchins.

Aside from the natural revulsion I felt as a modern reader at the idea of performing elephants and elephants enduring such long sea voyages — as much as five months — as a writer I couldn't help being tempted to ask how I might squeeze — perhaps not the right word — them into the story. What part might they play in *The Jaggard Case*? An important one, as you have witnessed, in the capture of Livvie Slack. In October 1850, an elephant did escape onto the quay at St Katharine's Dock and went on the rampage — good for him, I say. He was eventually caught and tethered and went on his way to Regent's Park Zoo, where he lived a blameless life.

What I had not realised until I continued my browsing into elephants was that there were so many elephants about in Victorian London. I thought I had discovered something amazing, but there were elephants all over the place, in the Regent's Park Zoo, in menageries, on stage, in travelling circuses, even a 'Wonderful Performing Elephant' to be seen at the Adelaide Gallery. This was a huge automaton, I was glad to discover.

The first elephant ever to be seen in England came in 1254, to Henry III, who had a menagerie at the Tower of London. It was a present from his son-in-law, King Louis IX of France. A cage, measuring forty feet by twenty, was built to house it. It was not alone. The king kept lions, leopards, lynxes, camels, even a polar bear which, secured by a stout rope, was taken down to the river to fish for its own supper.

In the eighteenth century, the Tower menagerie opened to the public, who could pay three halfpence to see the lions — a popular spectacle was the feeding of a cat or dog to the hungry felines. There was at least one elephant and a selection of grizzly bears.

In the early nineteenth century a man called Edward Cross had a private menagerie at Exeter Change where the animals were kept in dreadful conditions. There were also travelling menageries, such as the one owned by George Wombwell. An 1850 article in the *Household Narrative of Current Events*, the supplement to *Household Words*, reports the death of one Ellen Bright, niece of George Wombwell, who was attacked and killed by a tiger which had clearly been offended by her tapping it with her whip when she was in the cage.

On 27 April 1828, the Regent's Park Zoo opened to visitors who were admitted only with a member of the Zoological Society. Elephants could be seen in a special paddock. In 1828 there was a picture in the *Mirror* of the Indian elephant in his bath! Jack came in 1831, bought from a Captain Smith for £420. He was very popular, and a stall sold cakes and buns, especially for his consumption. Jack lasted almost twenty years despite his unsuitable diet and died on 6 June 1847. Dickens's friend, the artist, George Landseer, brother of the more famous Edwin — he of the lions in Trafalgar Square — made an illustration of Jack for *The Illustrated London News*. Another elephant, Betsey, and her infant, Butcher — who turned out to be a girl — were brought from Calcutta with another elephant intended for Jamrach's.

Johann Christian Carl Jamrach was the most celebrated animal dealer in London — his shop was on the Ratcliffe Highway just opposite the London Docks into which, of course, the animals came, just as my two elephants came on the day Dickens and Jones are pursuing Mrs Wand.

It was Jamrach who first imported the budgerigar into England. The artist, Dante Gabriel Rossetti, bought his wombat from Mr Jamrach. Rossetti was devoted to the creature, which slept in the bowl of a hanging lamp. You could buy anything from Jamrach. The most famous story about him was that he rescued a child from the jaws of a runaway tiger.

William Herring of Quickset Row, who appears in this novel, was well known to Dickens and he really did keep a menagerie with peacocks, wild cats, and other exotic beasts — not on the scale of Mr Jamrach, however. It was from Mr Herring that Dickens acquired his pet raven, and Herring stuffed it for him when it died.

Grip, Dickens's pet raven, died in 1841. Apparently, it could speak, and its last words were 'Halloa old girl'. Though Dickens wrote about Grip in his letters, praising its eccentric talents, it was not popular with Dickens's children, whose ankles it very often pecked. Dickens gave the name 'Grip' to Barnaby Rudge's pet raven in the novel of that name.

An unwelcome pet was the eagle given to Dickens by his friend, the painter, Robert McIan — a token of esteem, it seems. At least it wasn't an elephant. However, Dickens wasn't too keen on his new pet and passed it on to Edwin Landseer, who kept a variety of animals at his home in St John's Wood — not lions. The model for the Trafalgar Square lions was a dead one from the Regent's Park Zoo. Landseer popularised Newfoundland dogs in his paintings and Dickens kept two at his home in Gad's Hill, Kent, called Bumble and Don. He had a St. Bernard called Linda, and his daughter, Mamie, had a little Pomeranian called Mrs Bouncer, and there was a deaf kitten at Gad's Hill which became known as 'the master's cat' and followed Dickens everywhere like a dog.

Dickens was an animal lover and animals feature in many of his books, and although he did not protest against the treatment of animals in menageries and on the stage, he did support a lady called Mary Tealby, who was the first person to open a refuge for lost dogs. Dickens wrote about the refuge in his periodical, *All the Year Round* — after this, donations flooded in. The refuge eventually became Battersea Dogs' Home.

I hope that you enjoyed reading my novel and I thank you for taking the time to do so. Reviews are very important to writers, so it would be great if you could spare the time to post a review on **Amazon** and **Goodreads**. Readers can connect with me online, on **Facebook (JCBriggsBooks)**, **Twitter (@JeanCBriggs)**, and you can find out more about the books and Charles Dickens via my website: **jcbriggsbooks.com** where you will find Mr Dickens's A–Z of Murder — all cases of murder to which I found a Dickens connection.

Thank you!

Jean Briggs

Sapere Books is an exciting new publisher of brilliant fiction and popular history.

To find out more about our latest releases and our monthly bargain books visit our website: **saperebooks.com**

Printed in Great Britain
by Amazon

19800836R00200